# THE ART OF
# DIPLOMA-BEE

# THE ART OF
# DIPLOMA-BEE

Icalos

**Podium**

*To all the drones and workers who gave their lives ensuring
the survival of new beehives.*

Cover design by Leah Kochevar

ISBN: 978-1-0394-7875-6

Published in 2025 by Podium Publishing
www.podiumentertainment.com

Podium

# THE ART OF DIPLOMA-BEE

# CHAPTER ONE

# HEAVY BEE-CISIONS

**B**elissar spoke with the queens a bit about his newest goal and what they could do to achieve it. So far, they had built a solid foundation of a tower that would one day be filled with happy bees. The karnuq had become his sworn defenders, now living in and fighting for his tower. That had proven fortunate when they were unexpectedly attacked by a turtle-shade that had been invulnerable to the numerous light attacks by his bees. Chief Rohsuak had burned the shade to a crisp with her powerful Blessing of Fire.

But Chief Rohsuak was old, and throwing around magic that powerful had drained her. Besides, the Hunger had already displayed the ability to adapt to their defenses. Belissar knew that he couldn't just rely on Chief Rohsuak or the karnuq to defend him now. If he wanted to build a tower full of happy bees, he needed a bee army powerful enough to defend their home. Fortunately, Chief Rohsuak's feat had drawn the attention of the God of Fire, who was now offering to become a secondary patron for his tower, if Belissar could raise a suitably rare fire-type bee. A quest endorsed by his original patron, the God of Bees.

The apiary queens were already well on their way to accomplishing this, though they were running into some snags. The transition from a normal monster beehive to a burning monster beehive was proving more complicated than with the medicinal or maddening hives, as every burning worker evolved and every bit of burning honey stored increased the temperature of the entire hive, making it increasingly uncomfortable for the normal workers and the queen. If the hive grew too hot, any part built of regular wax would melt, and even the wooden frames were beginning to scorch from the heat. It took a lot of a given type of honey to evolve a queen, and the hives were reaching the limits of their heat tolerance before they had gathered the sufficient quantity.

Belissar had some ideas on how to fix that. He had already built underground beehives consisting mainly of dirt, and now he had access to stone and metal as well. If he could build a new beehouse out of those materials next to the hive in question, the queen could move all her burning workers over to the new, fire-resistant hive. This would allow her remaining workers to remain safe until they too had evolved and could handle the heat.

Belissar would probably need the karnuq's help for that. He hadn't done much stonework, unless stacking rocks to make basic ovens and firepits counted. He wasn't sure the karnuq would have either, but at the very least they could help him lift the stones.

Once they had settled on their plan, Belissar moved on to the next order of business: the rewards from the turtle-shade purification. He had received two random rewards for defeating the shade, and he was feeling hopeful about them. There was a possibility, after all, that he could acquire a Fire attribute monster bee right away. And even if not, it was clear that he needed to continue strengthening the bee army and the tower's defenses.

*Please select a reward:*
*- Uncommon Monster Choice (At least one uncommon or better option)*
*- Rare Room Feature Choice (At least one rare or better option)*
*- Uncommon Room Choice (At least one uncommon or better option)*

Belissar smiled at the sight of the rare room feature and nearly chose it immediately before stopping himself. Getting a rare room feature after a full nine common options would be incredibly gratifying. But, given the latest purification, Belissar did not want to make this decision impulsively. It was at least worth considering if a new monster or room might be more important . . . not to mention that he was supposed to prioritize fulfilling the God of Fire's mission. So, he tried to see if he could open the next reward choice before deciding on this one.

*Please select a reward:*
*- Uncommon Room Choice (At least one uncommon or better option)*
*- +100 max mana*
*- Uncommon Monster Choice (At least one uncommon or better option)*

Belissar turned to his bees. "So, for the first reward, we can get a new monster, a new feature, or a new room, and then for the second, either a new room, more mana, or a new monster. What does everyone think?"

The bees were quiet this time as well. The Second First of the First slowly danced.

"Bees . . . not strong enough. Need to be stronger. Need bigger attacks."

Some of the bees danced their agreement, and then they all fell still. Belissar frowned at that. Even Niobee wasn't saying much and her antennas were drooping. He felt his chest tighten.

The bees gave their all for him and wanted nothing more from him than his praise. He saw how happy they were with anything he gave them, even a roughly built beehouse made out of unprocessed logs that the old beekeeper, Mrs. Imkomos, would have never approved of. He thought of the First of the Fifth's dances anytime he gave her praise.

To see them as they were now made him sad. And angry.

"Everyone, please look at me."

All the bees complied. Belissar glanced around at each and every one of them. Niobee, his best friend. The Second First of the First, who had risked her children's lives and even her own to protect the tower. The First of the Fifth, who spared no effort working to make as much honey for him as she could. Beero, the wounded soldier bee, watching from the memorial, lightning crackling in place of the missing wings she had lost in battle.

Not a single one of them had any reason to be ashamed.

"You all are doing really well. Honestly, I had no idea how to run a tower at all. I never fought a shade before this. If there's anyone to blame for our losses, it's me. But we made it, and that is thanks to you. It is thanks to all of your hard work and sacrifice that we have come this far, and there's no one I'd rather have protecting my tower. What I'm trying to say is . . . I'm proud of you all. Keep up the good work."

Belissar had never really had to comfort anyone before. So, he just said what he honestly felt. These bees had given their all and accomplished so much, and he had no doubt that they would do so again. So, he would not let them blame themselves for his own failures. It was he who was in charge of the tower, who chose the options. It was he who should have expected the Hunger would adapt.

The bees stood still for a moment before breaking out into a flurry of buzzing and dancing. Mostly along the lines of "No! King is best king!" and other such disagreements with his assertion that anything could be his fault. He shook his head. They truly thought too highly of him.

"Okay, okay. I'm just saying, you're all doing well, so please don't feel bad. I'm very happy with you all. And we're all going to work together to get stronger. You and me . . . and, uh, I guess the karnuq too."

The bees still didn't seem satisfied but at least began to agree with that. Belissar exhaled his breath and tried to keep a smile. The bees, at least, weren't looking all down anymore, so Belissar felt he could move on.

"Okay, so, in line with that, I'm thinking a new room feature and a new monster. The room feature will either be a defense that can surprise a shade or maybe something that you and the karnuq can use in the future. The monster will hopefully make our army stronger. Does that sound good?"

Niobee, of course, led the bees in their response.

"Okay! Whatever King chooses! King is best king!"

Belissar chuckled as he made his choices.

*Please select a room feature:*
*- Beehive Bomb (Rarity: Uncommon, Type: Bee, Trap)*
*- Gravilion Flower (Rarity: Rare, Type: Gravity, Nature, Trap)*
*- Treasure Chest (Rarity: Common, Type: Resource)*

Well, if the decision was up to him, then of course he was taking the rare room feature. He could get either an uncommon room or uncommon monster with the next choice anyway. Still, he figured he should read about each option.

### Beehive Bomb

**Type:**  Bee, Trap

**Mana Upkeep:**  5 (3 with Blessing of Bees)

*A beehive that explodes into a swarm of bees on contact. The bee swarm will pursue all targets in the area until the mana comprising them expires.*
*If bee monsters are available, different bee types may be chosen for an increase in upkeep.*

Belissar rubbed his chin. He had mixed feelings about this one. From the sound of it, it didn't create real bees per se, but rather made bees out of mana that only existed for the duration of the trap. That would actually be great, as it would give him a way to attack with bees in their normal swarming manner without worrying about the casualties. And the part about being able to choose different bee types based on what his tower already had was especially promising. A beehive full of maddening or sedative bees could have great potential.

But on the other hand, while this provided Belissar a new way to utilize bees and prevent casualties, it did not, in fact, offer a truly new option. He already had plentiful bees to swarm a shade with, so long as he could resolve himself to the casualties they would take in the process. The problem he was trying to solve now was what to do when that method didn't work. This option would not solve that problem, and it would not have particularly done anything to the latest shade they faced. Perhaps the next one might?

### *Gravilion Flower*

|  |  |
|---|---|
| **Type:** | *Gravity, Nature, Trap* |
| **Mana Upkeep:** | *10 per node, 5 to enable in compatible rooms* |

*A unique dandelion strain attuned to the force of gravity. Utilizes gravitational fields to launch its seeds at high velocity. When gravilion flowers are gathered in numbers, gravity may behave erratically nearby, causing random increases or decreases in effective weight.*

Belissar tilted his head. Gravity? What was gravity? Apparently, it was some sort of type or attribute, but it wasn't one Belissar had ever heard of.

"Hey, Niobee, do you or any of the queens know what gravity is?"

Niobee flew around to each of the queens before slowly flying back and dancing unsteadily.

"Sorry, don't."

Belissar shook his head. "Don't worry about it, neither do I."

Well, the description said something about increases and decreases in weight so . . . it apparently made things heavier or lighter? Belissar thought about it for a couple more minutes before shrugging. Yeah, he didn't really know what he was looking at here. But it was a flower that counted as a trap and was also considered rare, so if nothing else it would hopefully be useful to the bees. Belissar didn't know if gravilion honey would have any particular effect or result in any special bee types, though. It was somewhat of a risky choice in that regard.

### *Treasure Chest*

|  |  |
|---|---|
| **Type:** | *Resource* |
| **Mana Upkeep:** | *Depends on possible contents* |

*A box meant to hold rewards. Can be set to generate resources or products available in the dungeon at regular intervals. Mana cost will depend on resource generated and interval of generation chosen. May also be used as general storage.*

Again, Belissar tilted his head. It . . . was a box. He could select different materials for the box, but generally it appeared as a wooden one. And it . . . would generate resources? But then, how was that different than the resource nodes or the beehives?

Belissar didn't really understand what this option was for. He guessed more resource generation was nice, but it said resources available in the dungeon . . . so, resources he already had available in his tower? He guessed it was for challengers or something, since he couldn't see how this would help during a purification.

So, he could go with expendable beehives, a rare flower that he didn't understand, or a box that, unless he was missing something, didn't do anything that resource nodes and beehives couldn't. He had planned to check the next option before deciding, but in this case the choice seemed pretty straightforward to him.

"How about some new flowers?"

"Okay!"

Niobee was the only one to respond directly, but Belissar chuckled as he saw the First of the Fifth and the other apiary queens shuffling about excitedly.

*Gravilion Flower selected.*

Well, that was one choice down. Now for the second . . .

# SOLEMN BEE-BRIEFING

**B**elissar went ahead and made his next choice, selecting the monster option. Three monster types appeared for him to choose from.

*Please select a monster:*
*- Monster Bee Burster (Rarity: Uncommon, Type: Bee)*
*- Monster Bee Lancer (Rarity: Uncommon, Type: Bee)*
*- Monster Digger Bee (Rarity: Common, Type: Bee, Ground)*

Belissar glared at the choices for a bit. Of course *now* the choice offered monster digger bees again. Long after he'd wanted dirt tunnels and scouts for the Underway. After so long that he had acquired Ground mana flowers thanks to Noigakkuq and evolved his own digging bees. Heck, even the previously offered mason bees might have been a better choice at this point, given his new stone-working needs. He didn't know if mason bees could actually work with stone, but he imagined they had a better shot of it than digger bees.

And that wasn't even the only repeat option! Monster bee bursters had also made their return. But Belissar was no more inclined to choose them than he had been the first time. His tower may have needed more power, but Belissar still wasn't going to blow up his own bees unless he was certain the tower would fall without him doing so.

That left one new choice, monster bee lancers. Belissar read out the description for good measure.

### *Monster Bee Lancer*

**Vitality:** Minor
**Strength:** Small
**Speed:** Average+

| | |
|---:|:---|
| **Magic:** | *Minimal* |
| **Defense:** | *Minor* |
| **Resistance:** | *Minimal* |
| **Special:** | *Minimal* |
| **Notable Skills:** | *Poison Thrust, Flying Charge, Death Blow, Brood Offspring* |
| **Evolves From:** | *Monster Bee Soldier* |

*A monster bee soldier evolution. This bee focuses its growth into a large and powerful stinger that can impale foes as well as poison them. It is optimized for high-speed dives to take maximum advantage of its weapon, though note that the stinger is unwieldy up close and the lancer lacks agility relative to its top speed.*

*In addition to evolving from existing monster bee soldiers, some monster bee soldiers may spawn as monster bee lancers, though this requires more resources from the hive.*

Belissar hummed and nodded. Like the monster bee blader, the monster bee lancer was about the size of a small dog, though the lancer was shorter, thinner, and longer than the blader. It was sleek, smooth, and carried a massive stinger that ended in a sharp point.

Well, sometimes the choice was very easy. It was the lancer, the bee that was born to die, or the bee that he already had a substitute for. But just in case, he turned to the queens before making the decision.

"What does everyone think?"

The Second First of the First was fidgeting, along with the rest of the flower meadow queens. Belissar stared at her until she slowly began to dance. Belissar chuckled as she attempted to keep her dance at an even pace.

". . . New soldier?"

Belissar nodded and glanced at the First of the Fifth.

"Whatever King chooses! Already have digging bees, though."

Belissar looked around, but the Fourth of the Seventh and the other queens all just said, "Whatever King chooses!" So, Belissar shrugged and confirmed his choice.

*Monster Bee Lancer now available! Monster Bee Soldiers may now evolve into Monster Bee Lancers!*

As this one was an evolution option, Belissar declined to make a spawner for them. He'd rather the flower meadow queens add them to the army at their own pace, though he'd consider it if there was another emergency purification before then.

Instead, he went ahead and added two gravilion nodes to the tower. One he added to the apiary, so that the queens there could test out its nectar for any special properties. The other he added to the flower meadow, near the entrance. It was listed as a trap, after all, so Belissar also wanted to see what it would add to their defenses.

With the options finished, Belissar decided to get to work on the two gods' missions and left to ask the karnuq if they knew anything about masonry . . .

The queens and the Conduit remained after the King had left. Silence hung over them like a curtain of dark clouds that would keep a hive from foraging. Most of the bees kept glancing at the Firstborn, but she remained still save for the twitching of her antennas.

The First of the Fifth could guess what she was thinking. The Firstborn's one goal, her one duty in the hive of hives, was to defeat invaders and keep the bees safe. She had failed at that today, and it had taken the intervention of one of the former outsiders to bring the invader down. So, how could she speak confidently now? How could she tell the others what to do if her decisions up until now had not prepared them for the fight?

Once upon a time, the First of the Fifth would have been ecstatic that her great rival had failed where she had succeeded, since it had been her honey that helped the powerful karnuq deal the fatal blow. But now . . . now she knew that the King would not be pleased with such things. Additionally, she had experienced her own such failures in the past, failures that were completely of her own making.

So, the First of the Fifth decided to speak.

"Need honey, right? Will provide."

The Firstborn stopped twitching and turned to face her. The First of the Fifth decided to press on. "Please show hive. Need to know how much you need for current soldiers. Will give enough for new evolutions too."

The Firstborn stared at her for a moment before stumbling and then starting to dance.

"Right. Thanks, First of Fifth is lifesaver. Come, will show you."

"Oh! Want to see too!"

The Firstborn then led the First of the Fifth to the bee barracks, with the Fourth of the Seventh happily following along. The rest of the queens, unsure of what else to do, followed suit.

The First of the Fifth had to stop herself from pausing when she flew inside the bee barracks. She had been aware that the flower meadow queens had formed some sort of joint hive just like her daughter had with the Fourth of the Seventh, but to see it with her own eyes was another matter. There were no divisions within the bee barracks, just endless rows of trays with countless workers flying in and out. If she hadn't checked the mana of the workers, she would not have been able to tell where one hive ended and the next began. Even then, the mana of different hives jumbled together and had begun to blend, making the boundaries blurry. She even noted workers from one hive clearly carrying honey to a different hive's section.

She paused again when she saw a particularly large bee crawling out toward them.

"A queen? Why wasn't at meeting with King?"

The Firstborn answered. "Is my daughter. Was growing, just finished."

The First of the Fifth fell still once again. The Firstborn's daughter, huh? It had been long since the First of the Fifth raised a daughter of her own, so that was no surprise.

What *was* a surprise was that the Firstborn's daughter was clearly in the middle of the Firstborn's hive section. The First of the Fifth hadn't noticed with all the different mana jumbling together, but on closer inspection she now realized the Firstborn's section included her daughter's workers as well as her own.

That gave the First of the Fifth a lot to think about. She had several new flowers and mushrooms she needed to test. She needed to make regular deliveries of honey to the flower meadow, even more now so that they could evolve the new bee type the King had granted them. And she wanted to investigate exactly what the dangerous karnuq had been doing with honey and if it had any implications for her own production. All of that required more and more workers and more and more attention. So, perhaps it was time to consider scaling up her operations in ways she had not yet considered. Ways the Firstborn, the Fourth of the Seventh, and the First of the Fifth's own daughter had already implemented.

That would all have to wait, however, as the First of the Fifth turned attention to the task at hand. First of all . . . the Firstborn's honey production line was *atrocious*. Workers were flying in all willy-nilly and dropping off the nectar at the first free cells they could find. Trays held nectar from all different sources together, requiring the workers to go through them one by one to ensure each had sufficient mana density. Those cells then would dry at different rates, leading to wildly inconsistent quality and viscosity as the workers processed them as if they were all the same.

She had known the Firstborn wasn't as efficient at honey production as herself, but she hadn't expected . . . *this*. She slowly turned to face the Firstborn.

". . . Have some suggestions on honey production. Want to know?"

The Firstborn, who apparently saw *nothing* wrong here, replied happily.

"Ah, yes. Would help a lot!"

The First of the Fifth gathered herself.

And then she launched into a rapid dance, beating her wings as fast and hard as they would go as she pointed out every single mistake she had seen in the mere minute since she had arrived. She didn't recall all the details of her dance, but by the end of it the Firstborn was lying flat on the ground with her antennas drooping, while the other flower meadow queens were trying to avoid her notice.

And so, the hive of hives began to tighten its cooperation.

# CHAPTER TWO

# THE BEAR-EST MASON-BEE

**B**elissar made his way to the karnuq and Metsaitti came out to meet him.

"Hello, Sacred Den Master. I apologize, but Chief Rohsuak is currently resting. I could take you to her, if you wish."

Belissar shook his head. "No, I would rather not bother her right now. I just wanted to ask if you have any masons. I'm, uh, hoping to build a stone beehouse."

Metsaitti crossed his arms and rubbed his chin before shaking his head. "I am sorry, Sacred Den Master, but we have not built much out of stone in recent memory. We do know how to dig and mine, however, so we could assist you with gathering the materials at the very least."

Belissar furrowed his brow before slowly nodding. "Ah, yeah, that would help. I, um, need to figure out what I'm going to build first, though."

Metsaitti gave him a small smile. "I'm sure you'll figure it out. That home you built for them at the entrance was impressive enough."

Belissar rubbed the back of his head. "Oh, um, thanks? Um, could I come visit your dirt tunnels and maybe get some help with the stone node? I at least want to see what the stone looks like."

Metsaitti saluted by striking his chest with his fist. "Of course, Sacred Den Master. I'll see to it at once."

A short bit later, Belissar had traveled to the second-floor dirt tunnels with a couple of the karnuq and was standing before the stone node he had placed in one of the dirt tunnels' walls. It took the form of a rough wall of stone breaking up the dirt, with a few spots slightly glowing. One of the karnuq stepped forward and placed his hand on the stone, flaring his mana. Cracks began to appear in the stone, forming a rectangle around the glowing area.

Then the stone began to pull itself out of the wall. The karnuq jumped back nimbly as a rectangular block moved out of the wall and dropped onto the floor. The block was the size of Belissar. All of them stared at it with wide eyes.

"Um, do you know how to make these . . . smaller?"

Metsaitti slowly nodded his head. "Muuraqi here can use that same technique to break it up. He doesn't have the most mana, though, so it will take time."

Belissar rubbed his chin. "If I give him mana honey, will that help?"

Metsaitti's eyes widened further but he nodded. "That's most generous of you, Sacred Den Master, but yes, it would speed up the process. As you've seen, however, there are risks to using more mana than your body normally handles, so there will be a limit."

Belissar stared at the block for a second. "Um, by the way, was that some sort of Ground mana?"

Metsaitti turned to Muuraqi who nodded. "Yes, Sacred Den Master, sir. I learned a bit from my father, before he passed."

Belissar frowned when Muuraqi mentioned losing a parent, but he tried to stay focused. Fortunately, he came up with an idea. "In that case, I might be able to help as well . . ."

Belissar checked on the digging queen, but her hive was still transitioning over to digging bees. She had some digging workers already available, but Belissar did not want to split her efforts until her new hive was fully established.

"Later, though. For now, could you cut it about this big?" Belissar motioned the dimensions he wanted.

Muuraqi saluted and got to work as Metsaitti asked Belissar, "Would you like us to help you move it as well?"

Belissar nodded. "Yes, that would help."

Muuraqi and the rest of the karnuq worked together. Muuraqi used Ground mana to create some cracks in the stone outlining the size Belissar wanted. The other karnuq who had accompanied them then began to break apart the stone with more conventional tools, such as pickaxes, hammers, and chisels. With their strength, the task was completed relatively quickly. The karnuq then lifted the stone and the group set off.

Belissar guided them to the apiary, right next to the hive of the Third of the Sixth, the queen with the most burning workers. Belissar then created a cavern in the third-floor dirt tunnels below, which opened right up into the apiary, forming a large hole in the ground with a gentle slope on one side for the karnuq to walk down. Then, as he had done with the nests for the bumblebees and the digging queen, Belissar created an alcove in one of the walls. He asked the karnuq to carry the stone down into the cavern and place it over the entrance of the alcove.

He figured that since neither he nor the karnuq had much experience with stonework, he'd keep things simple. A hive in the ground should be relatively resistant to fire, and then all they'd need was the stone for the entrance. Although, Belissar *did* want to try and make some frames for the honeycomb. Which he probably should have installed . . . *before* installing the big stone door. His face scrunched up and he glanced away.

"Um, I'm sorry but . . . could you set the door to the side for now? I remembered there's a bit more work to be done."

Fortunately, the karnuq didn't mind. Belissar hesitated to ask them for the next pieces, since they had already done so much for him, but he had no choice. He went ahead and added a basic stone node right there so at least the karnuq wouldn't have to travel all the way back to the second floor. This time, Muuraqi made the rectangle much narrower when gathering the stone, resulting in a long, thin block that was nearly a plate. He then attempted to crack out a frame-sized section, and then to chisel out the center to leave a hollow, rectangular frame.

It wasn't exactly pretty, but it worked. It was noticeably heavy compared to his usual trays, however. Still, Belissar and the karnuq got it standing upright within the alcove. Although Belissar dreaded the thought of having to gather and haul one of them every day, he didn't have any other fireproof material to work with, so they carried on until the alcove was full of frames. At that point, they placed the stone door back and the karnuq managed to drill an entrance hole for the bees. Belissar adjusted the dirt walls around the door until the fit was perfect.

He then tried to apply a beehive feature.

*Variation unlocked. Belissar's Beehouse and Beehives*
*may now use stone as a material.*

Belissar exhaled his breath as the tower's mana began to flow through the dirt and the stone. He then turned to the karnuq with a smile.

"It worked! Thank you all for your help."

Muuraqi glanced around a bit before saluting. "I-It's our honor, Sacred Den Master."

Belissar frowned a bit at that. The villagers had always told him he should be honored to help them whenever they forced him to do work . . . and gave him little or nothing in return.

"I should give you something. Would mana honey do, or is there something else you want?"

Most of the bear people's eyes widened and they began to mumble, but Metsaitti stepped in with a smile. "That would be great, Sacred Den Master. Thank you for your generosity."

Belissar shook his head. "It's not really generosity when you just did a bunch of work for me, and the bees."

With that, he gathered some mana honeycomb trays from his stock and distributed them to the karnuq present. He also gave Metsaitti a medicinal mana honeycomb tray for Chief Rohsuak. Once they were off, Belissar walked over to the Third of the Sixth's hive. The queen had been watching the construction out-side her home with great interest. Belissar smiled at her.

"How do you like it? I figured we should make something fireproof for you now, so that you can have your burning bees work there while you and the rest of your workers stay here, until you all can evolve?"

The Third of the Sixth immediately began to fly around Belissar, performing an aerial dance as fast as she could.

"Amazing! Incredible! King is best king!"

Belissar could only laugh at that. "Okay, let me move the flowers over, too."

He took the flame radish node and moved it as far down into the cavern ramp as he could while remaining in the apiary. Not only would this make it easier for the burning bees to forage, but it would also keep the hot flowers separated from the rest of the apiary's plants. After seeing what Chief Rohsuak's attack did to the flower meadow, Belissar had decided there was no such thing as too many fire safety precautions. This would also give him a good place for a Fire mana flower node once the Third of the Sixth evolved.

"There you go! Let me know if there's anything else you need, or any other way we can help you evolve."

The Third of the Sixth just continued her celebration dance while Belissar chuckled, even as her burning workers began to explore the new hive and started to add their fireproof wax to the stone frames. It seemed now that nothing would stop her from evolving soon.

# GO BEE-YOND! MAKE THE
# IMPOSSIBLE POSSIBLE!

After completing the new beehouse, Belissar was just admiring the bees working for a bit when suddenly a notification made him jump.

*A challenger has been fully blessed.*
*Gained 20 DP.*

He rushed his tower sight down to the second floor. There, he found Muuraqi kneeling before the Shrine of Bees, as wide-eyed as he was. And just like that, a third karnuq had been blessed. Belissar smiled.

At this point, he was extremely happy with his choice to trust the karnuq. They had significantly expanded his plant and mushroom options by sharing their resources. They had helped him build a fireproof beehouse out of stone he would have struggled to gather, much less process and transport. And, certainly not least of all, Chief Rohsuak had handled a purification that had given his bee army some serious trouble. He was starting to think it wasn't so bad having some people around after all.

Putting that aside, however, Belissar did need to consider his defenses, and what he could do to improve them. After double-checking what he had, he moved the new gravilion flower patch to just in front of a pit trap by the flower meadow entrance. The description said the flower could randomly make things heavier, so he figured that would make it harder for a shade to jump across a pit or climb out of it. Or it would make the shade lighter and help it soar across the trap, but Belissar *hoped* it would be the helpful option.

Beyond that, Belissar wasn't sure what else to do. He couldn't imagine the options he had at present working against another turtle-shade. Some thorny roses didn't seem like they would bother a shade that could resist full-speed dive stings by the soldier bees. Though there was no guarantee the Hunger would try another turtle-shade.

There was one option, though, that could work. A side effect of Chief Rohsuak setting the flower meadow on fire was confirmation that the fire breaks he'd made actually worked. So, didn't that mean they could intentionally set the flower meadow on fire without putting the bee barracks at risk? That'd certainly be one option to take down a shade . . . assuming the next shade was still vulnerable to fire. Maybe he should also ask the karnuq their opinions. Metsaitti and Chief Rohsuak had apparently visited other towers, so they might have some suggestions.

Beyond that, he decided to hold off on the planned expansion purification. The turtle-shade made him a bit wary of taking on another unexpected challenge, and besides, he had just acquired some new options that would take time to develop. He at least wanted to give the bees a chance to raise some lancers first. Plus, there were the missions from the gods that might give him something too.

Above all, Belissar was worried. The Hunger could apparently take it upon itself to attack him when it wanted to. Additionally, during every single expansion or emergency purification thus far, the Hunger had always tried something new, something that would specifically bypass one of his defenses. That . . . made it seem like the Hunger was paying attention to him. And if it was paying attention to what he and his bees were doing inside the tower, then surely it had noticed his tower purifying a larger and larger area, right?

He didn't know the answer. He wasn't sure he wanted to.

But, speaking of his tower purifying a larger area, he realized he should also be paying better attention to the tower's exterior. And, fortunately enough, it seemed some of his queens were about to make a move on that soon. Yet another reason to hold off on more expansions just a bit longer . . .

The Fourth of the Seventh flew back to her hive with uncharacteristically few deviations in her flight path, with the First of the Fifth's First Daughter following closely behind. Her communer came out to meet them at the entrance of the hive.

"Queen okay? Feeling upset?"

The Fourth of the Seventh picked up a bit of speed at that. "Fine! Happy you asked!" Her dance slowed a bit. "It's just, King is worried. Bee army couldn't stop invader. Needed help from karnuq."

The communer's antennas drooped. "Right, saw through scout. But what can we do if flower meadow queens can't handle? Don't have many soldiers . . ."

The Fourth of the Seventh placed her legs firmly on the ground as she danced. "Doesn't matter! We do all we can! We're hive of hives, so if can't fight, we help!"

The First of the Fifth's First Daughter stepped forward at that. "That's right, Fourth of Seventh's stems helped queen mother deliver honey."

The communer rose to her feet and began a salute dance. "Queen . . . queen is right. Okay, we work harder then. New queens hatching, so lots of work to do."

The Fourth of the Seventh perked up and rushed into the hive. "Oh! Want to meet!"

The communer was about to apologize to the First of the Fifth's First Daughter only to find the second queen had also rushed into the hive. The communer began flying too, so as not to be left behind.

The First of the Fifth's First Daughter kept her eyes fixed on the cells as the brood tenders pulled off the wax caps and helped the young queens inside climb out. The First Daughter then stepped forward to brush her own daughter's antennas.

"Welcome, daughter."

Her daughter, the First of the Third Generation of the First of the Fifth's line, shook her body, beat her wings, and then began a salute dance.

"Go now, but once your mating flight is finished, come back, okay?"

Her daughter's antennas twitched about at random in response.

"Look, this hive is bigger than one colony. We are part of a hive of hives, and you'll be too. We'll all build one big hive together. I'll help you."

Her daughter gave a rapid salute and then set off. The First of the Fifth's First Daughter then repeated this speech for each of her daughters before sending them off. She greeted her drones as well, though she didn't tell them to come back. Drones never survived the depleting of their mana, after all.

A short while later, a whole squad of queens returned . . . with mana signatures now a blend of her own and the Fourth of the Seventh's. She couldn't help but start a happy dance at that before calming herself, for she had something to take care of.

Not the queens, though. Workers were already directing the new queens to vacant sections of the hive she and the Fourth of the Seventh's communer had already prepared ahead of time. Her daughters would find plenty of space and honey there, where they could raise their initial brood without needing to forage for their own nectar. The First Daughter had been gifted honey by her queen mother, so she saw no reason not to do the same for her own offspring. Especially when these queens belonged to the Fourth of the Seventh as well as to herself.

But no, the queens were all well taken care of. The First Daughter had another task. She found the Fourth of the Seventh's communer. The communer gave her a salute, and then they both moved to find the Fourth of the Seventh.

Who happened to be with the new queens anyway, telling them stories about the King, as it were. The First Daughter let her finish before approaching her.

"Hi! Need me?"

"Yes, have an offer for you," the First Daughter confirmed. She took a moment and adjusted her stance before continuing her dance. "Does Fourth of Seventh want to go scout?"

The Fourth of the Seventh, for once, did not move.

". . . What?"

"Now that our hive has more queens, will have plenty of workers. Should be fine now if Fourth of Seventh doesn't lay eggs every day. So, if Fourth of Seventh wants to scout, can now. I'll take care of our daughters and hive."

The Fourth of the Seventh trembled. "That's . . . but . . ."

She turned and glanced at her communer, who danced a confirmation. "First of Fifth's First Daughter and I discussed, won't be a problem! Want queen to do what queen wants. Besides, King asked to go scout, set up mini-hives outside for scouts to rest at. Like queen said, need to help however we can. Queen should help scout. Just take soldiers with, okay?"

The Fourth of the Seventh's trembling grew until she suddenly burst into flight, zipping around the two of them.

"SERIOUS? CAN? AMAZING! INCREDIBLE! COMMUNER IS BEST COMMUNER! FIRST OF FIFTH'S FIRST DAUGHTER IS BEST JOINT QUEEN!"

Neither the First Daughter nor the communer could resist joining the Fourth of the Seventh in her happy dance. The three then finalized some additional details. They laid some more soldier eggs, as the existing soldiers were needed to weave stems and help the apiary transport honey trays. The scouts would begin identifying ideal sites for mini-hives in the meantime, and the Fourth of the Seventh would help the new queens get up and running as well.

But, once all that was taken care of . . . the Fourth of the Seventh's wildest dreams would come true. Or rather, she would head off on an adventure she never dared dream would be possible at all. She would be the first queen ever to see beyond the King's domain with her own eyes.

And it was all thanks to her two favorite bees. They really were the best.

# CHAPTER THREE

# BEE-HOLD ROCK AND STONE!

**B**elissar had a thought. If stone was unlocked for building his beehouses . . . then would he be able to change existing beehouses into stone? He could already turn mundane beehouses into tower features, and likewise could turn regular tower beehives into beehouses, so it seemed like it would be possible. He focused in on one of the apiary beehouses, hoping some sort of tower message might appear.

And indeed, the normal description menu appeared, with an option for upgrades. Belissar went ahead and focused on that, and a new menu appeared.

*Belissar's Beehouse Upgrades:*
*- Expand to Bee Apartment (Cost: 100 DP or 25 if materials provided)*
*- Expand to Bee Barracks (Cost: 100 DP or 25 if materials provided)*
*- Change material to stone (Cost: 50 DP or 12 if materials provided)*
*- Boost honeycomb production (Cost: 25 DP)*
*- Boost growth for inhabitants (Cost: 25 DP)*

Belissar's eyes widened. He had expected the material option, but he had not expected the other four. He could not only change a beehouse into stone, but he could apparently expand the beehouses into apartments or barracks, or boost their effects, though all at the cost of DP. Not much DP compared to the DP shop options, but back when he'd upgraded regular beehives into beehouses each upgrade and each expenditure of DP only affected one hive. So it made sense that it cost less DP, as he'd be upgrading a single feature instead of saving up for new features, rooms, or monsters that could aid his tower as a whole. And, well, his recent experience with buying feature choices had taught him that a lot of DP could suddenly become very little once he started spending it freely.

He held off on the urge to immediately upgrade the beehouse he was looking at and tried to think about it. If he upgraded each and every beehouse that would be . . . a lot. He knew better than to try and figure out those numbers, so he just left it at *a lot*. And, as much as he wanted the best beehouses for his bees, spending all his DP on the beehouse buffs was probably a bad idea. More bees and more honey were both helpful, but he did need to keep expanding his tower's options. New bee types and new features were probably more helpful in that regard, and generally helped his bees as well.

Perhaps if he consolidated the beehouses into bee apartments it might be worth it. But, well, he didn't want to force the bees to live together if they didn't want to. They'd listen to him if he asked, but that was precisely why he wasn't going to ask. He'd bring it up if they suggested something along those lines themselves, though.

In any case, he set aside those ideas and focused on his original one. So, he could upgrade beehouses to stone. He wondered if that'd apply to other features.

*Bee Barracks Upgrades:*
*- Swap to Bee Apartment (Cost: 25 DP)*
*- Change material to stone (Cost: 200 DP or 50 if materials provided)*
*- Boost growth for inhabitants (Cost: 50 DP)*
*- Boost coordination for inhabitants (Cost: 50 DP)*

And it turned out that he could, though the cost increased. That made sense, as the bee barracks was noticeably larger than the beehouses. But still, multiple hundreds of DP was getting up there, so it would certainly be worth gathering the materials by hand.

Which meant Belissar would have to coordinate with the karnuq once more. He decided to give them a break today and ask them tomorrow. He certainly wasn't tired of interacting with them or anything.

The rest of the day passed without issue, as Belissar gave his bees a break from the usual purification. The next day, he made his way to the karnuq once more. Chief Rohsuak had fortunately started to recover, though she still seemed quite fatigued. She insisted she was fine, though, so neither Belissar nor the other karnuq said anything. Belissar thus requested the karnuq deliver some stone to the bee barracks on a daily basis in exchange for some mana honeycomb.

It turned out that Muuraqi had received a Blessing of the Mason, so the process would now go even faster than before. It would still take a few days though, as the bee barracks was large and the karnuq wanted to begin some stone constructions for themselves as well. It turned out Muuraqi had been a bit inspired by Belissar's own works. Given that his design consisted of putting a block of stone in front of a hole in the ground, Belissar wasn't sure how to feel about that.

The problem came when it was time for that day's purification. Belissar frowned and hummed to himself. Niobee flew before him.

"King okay?"

He rubbed his chin. "I'm just wondering if we should even do a purification tonight. Every time we've faced a new shade in an expansion, that kind of shade started showing up in the daily purifications, though smaller and weaker. So, I'm a bit worried about what might happen if another turtle appears. Chief Rohsuak won't be able to help us today if we can't handle it . . ."

Niobee didn't respond right away, so Belissar continued pondering. He turned his gaze to find Niobee drooping a bit.

"Sorry, bees will work harder . . ."

His face softened and he held out his hand for her to land on. "You're doing great. In fact, I have an idea. I think we can just set the field on fire if another turtle shows up. Maybe we have the apiary soldiers drop their flame radishes right on the flowers, and then I can make some mana honey to light it . . ."

Niobee slowly began to dance. "Okay . . . should tell apiary soldiers?"

Belissar smiled and nodded. "Yes, thank you Niobee. Keep up the good work."

Niobee took off with a bit more pep in her wings. Belissar let out a light sigh. On the one hand, he hated to see his bees feeling down about anything. On the other hand, that was no reason to expose them to a danger they couldn't handle. He'd just have to hope the plan would work if they got a turtle tonight.

Once Niobee had relayed the possible plan to the apiary's soldiers, Belissar went ahead and triggered another minor+ purification.

It turned out they got one of the fast cats, so all his worries and plans were for naught. But, well, at least they had an idea if they ever *did* get one of those shades . . . and maybe they'd come up with something new in the meantime. And so, a handful of days passed.

The Third of the Sixth crawled over to a corner of her first hive. She still could scarcely believe how far she had come. Once, she had been the queen born a second too late to receive even one of the King's magical palaces. Now she had two, one of which was a brand-new design made especially for her. One made of immovable rock that no predator could break.

All she had to do now was fulfill her end of the bargain. This palace had been built specifically with the expectation that she and her hive would evolve soon. The First of the Fifth had granted her exclusive access to the flame radish flower patch, including the new mana flower that had sprouted among them, and the King himself had moved that patch next to her hive. All eyes in the apiary were on her, including the King's.

And that's why her current pace was unacceptable. It turned out that her evolution was more complicated than the other queens. With medicinal or maddening honey, all a queen had to do was obtain a sufficient quantity of honey with high enough mana density to fuel her evolution, and a stable enough hive to survive a couple of days without her. But this honey, this honey was different. Its hot temperature required the King himself to design an entirely new hive for her, and its temperature grew along with its mana density. Therefore, the Third of the Sixth had discovered that burning honey with high enough mana density to fuel her evolution . . . was too hot for her to even consume, much less submerge herself in.

But she would not accept failure. The King had seen fit to bless her with one magical palace, and now a second. The First of the Fifth had pledged her support, that arrogant queen even offering her own honey as a gift to help support her hive while she evolved. The Conduit stopped by daily to check on her.

No, she would not fail. So, she began to drink the burning honey, as much as she could stomach without seriously harming herself. It was a slow and painful process, one that brought her egg-laying to a halt as she consumed perhaps a bit more than was healthy for her. But each and every day the pain was a bit muted and she could drink a bit more. She could even sense her mana starting to change, and the air of her original hive had begun to feel chilly. So, she pressed on.

And now, today, she was going to attempt to drink the honey of the Fire mana flower once again. The air grew hot even as she approached the single bright-red cell. Her wings beat subconsciously as her antennas folded back and away from the heat. It took all of her willpower to extend her proboscis even as it burned, a feeling that only grew worse as she finally made contact with the honey. Her proboscis screamed inside and out as fire raged up and into her body.

The pain was nearly unbearable. But only nearly. She . . . could stomach the honey. And while her proboscis was in serious pain . . . it was not so bad that she couldn't endure it. And that meant that it was time.

Wisdom and instinct told her to wait. If she attempted the evolution now, it would be risky and dangerous, not to mention painful. There was a chance she would fail, with serious repercussions.

But she would not make the King wait a single day longer. She gave the order for a cell to be prepared in the new hive for her evolution. She would pass through the flames. And she would emerge from it stronger than ever, if she proved worthy of the boons bestowed upon her.

She gathered herself, even as the honey raged through her stomach, and began to beat her wings. She left her original hive, the magical palace that she had longed for all her life, and flew to her destiny.

# EXPLORATION BEE-GINS!

But the Third of the Sixth was not the only one about to fly to her destiny. The joint hive of the orchard was a flurry of activity. A large group of bees gathered at the front of the hive, including several newly born soldiers, a new communer, a full contingent of workers, and all of the scouts who normally would have spread out beyond the tower. And, of course, the two queens and the original communer. The communer was scrambling around the ground, moving as fast as her legs and wings would carry her as she kept brushing different bees with her antennas.

"Okay, have soldiers?"

The Fourth of the Seventh followed her.

"Yes!"

"Workers to build mini-hive?"

"Yes!"

"Have honey for trip?"

The Fourth of the Seventh crawled over to a piece of honeycomb, which was being tied by many smaller ropes to the worker bees.

"Yes!"

"Know where going to build? Which way to fly?"

"Yes!"

"Not going to get distracted until mini-hive built, right?"

The Fourth of the Seventh flew over to her first communer and brushed her antennas. "Communer, is going to be alright. Not leaving forever, will be back quick! Communer can watch the entire way!"

The communer's antennas and wings drooped, but she paused and allowed her queen to continue brushing her. "Sure? Queen promises?"

The Fourth of the Seventh used her antennas to turn the communer around so that she was facing the bees preparing to depart. "Promise! And won't be alone!

Soldiers will protect, workers will take care, communer will keep track. And if anything happens, will come right back! Believe in sisters!"

The communer drooped a bit more before picking herself up. "Okay, go ahead. Stay safe. And . . . enjoy scouting, Queen."

The Fourth of the Seventh brushed her communer once more before turning to the First of the Fifth's First Daughter and all of the newborn queens standing behind her. They all had the same expression, and the First of the Fifth's First Daughter danced for them all.

"Fourth of Seventh . . . coming back, right?"

The Fourth of the Seventh brushed her antennas as well. "Yes, promise! Will come back lots!"

The First of the Fifth's First Daughter began a happy dance. "Okay! Then go ahead!"

"Okay!"

A moment later, the Fourth of the Seventh gave the command. "Let's go!"

The air filled with buzzing as her force took off. They flew through the entrance to the flower meadow, not even pausing to greet the flower meadow queens as they flew on. They were on a mission for the King and no bee would wish to delay them. They flew through the bee barracks' entrance hall and then to the special entrance the King had made especially for his bees. It was a tight squeeze for the Fourth of the Seventh, but she managed to make it through, emerging into a dark cavern illuminated only by the soft glow of the Queen of All Bees' shrine. She used the glowing shrine as a beacon to guide her to the gate separating the King's realm from the Beyond. She could feel the mana of the King's realm flowing through the gate, surging out to fight an eternal battle against the invader all around them.

For the first time in her life, she was about to leave the protection of the King's realm, where his mana surrounded her and bound her to every other thing that existed within. She would be facing the Beyond, a place of unknown and peril, where the mana of the world ignored its inhabitants . . . at best. For a single moment, the Fourth of the Seventh hesitated. She longed to see all that her scouts had reported to her . . . but was that really worth braving the Beyond? Was it really worth leaving the riches and the comfort the King had built for them?

But ultimately, she would not know the answer until she experienced it for herself, and she did not wish to send her workers on a task she was unwilling to face herself. So, with one final spin of her antennas, she pushed forward and through the gate.

She paused midair as the true sun beat down on her for the first time. She trembled a bit as the mana of the Beyond crashed against her body. There was no warm, gentle suffusion as with the King's mana, but a chilly wind that battered her body without passing through. But with that current came a counter. The

King's mana passed through her once more, a small river of it flowing out from the tower and to her, buffeting her against the cold and callous mana all around her. With that support, she was able to shake off the discomforting feeling and take in her surroundings.

There were no neat and orderly divisions of rooms here, no entranceways to pass through. A field of flowers stretched right out into a forest of trees, like a flower meadow surrounded by orchards, only with their trees far more densely packed. The Fourth of the Seventh's mind raced at the idea of the rooms just . . . bleeding into one another, mixing together with no barrier.

And then, she turned around and glanced at her home for the first time. She had wondered why the King called it a tower, and now she knew. Her home was a mighty pillar, a tree towering into the sky but made of stone and wax instead of wood. A glowing light nearly as bright as the sun adorned its roof, spreading its light and mana out into the Beyond. Upon the walls was a golden banner of a diligent worker gathering nectar from a flower, which the Fourth of the Seventh instinctively recognized as the symbol of the Queen of All Bees. Truly, the King was great to have built such a thing.

But her workers were starting to tug at her, so she shook herself and turned in the direction the scouts indicated. Soon she would have plenty of time to observe and explore the world around her. But first and foremost, she needed to prepare a new hive, a place where her scouts could rest and replenish themselves. And now that she had experienced the cold of the Beyond herself, she was all the more determined to grant her loyal workers as much of the comfort of home as she could. So she set forth, following after the scouts as the soldiers took up a formation around her.

They flew through the forest, trees so tightly packed that their leaves blotted out the sun, creating dim and dark places even in the middle of the day. The Fourth of the Seventh watched as the world shimmered and faded all around her as she passed through shaded areas. It was fascinating, but this was only the beginning. Soon, they arrived at their destination, and the Fourth of the Seventh beheld something entirely new. Structures made of stone, stones she knew had not been scattered randomly. They had been placed here with purpose, hinting at a grander structure that may have once towered over the land. It was even vaguely reminiscent of the King's constructions, only far less grand and in a state of decay. She wondered who built it and what sort of hive it might have housed.

Now it would house hers. This was the place where the Firstborn's scouts had discovered mana flowers in the past. As such, it would make an ideal location for a new hive. The concentration of mana was denser here than anywhere else the scouts had evaluated thus far. That would make the hive more comfortable for the monster bees, and it would assist them with the production of mana honey. If they were lucky, maybe there'd even be more mana flowers around.

The structure itself provided an ideal location. The scouts led the Fourth of the Seventh to a sheltered alcove on top of one of the structures where the rocks blocked the wind on three sides. The Fourth of the Seventh landed in the alcove and paced about it, examining every inch before turning to her workers. She began to dance.

"Looks great! Let's get to work!"

Her workers saluted and construction of the mini-hive began, the first step in the Fourth of the Seventh's scouting of the Beyond.

Somewhere else far, far away, Ruckanos stood imperiously at the edge of his camp as the scouts returned. They had set up for the night in a small forest clearing, hidden from the tower in the area by the trees.

"Well?"

The scouts shook their heads. "No settlements near the tower, sir."

Ruckanos sighed. "Well, let's forage what we can, then."

A wyvern could fly far and fast; in the wild, the species was known to spend nearly all of its time in the air. But even they required food and rest eventually, so Ruckanos had been forced to put down whenever they found a purified area. Ideally, they would find a settlement of relatively civilized folk who they could . . . *persuade* to offer supplies. Unfortunately, they'd had no such luck yet. Records of past Grand Subjugations indicated that beyond the boundaries of the Conclave, the vast majority of towers were small, their purified zones unoccupied by civilized people or even subhumans.

And were he a normal Grand Subjugation participant, this would have been a great find. A small tower like this would be relatively easy to intimidate . . . or conquer. But Ruckanos was no normal participant. He had been chosen by the gods for this mission, and he would not waste time on any tower but the one he was seeking. The gods demanded thus.

Additionally, his force was quite small even as far as the initial scouting wave was concerned. If they wanted to have the strength to deal with the target tower, they could not afford any casualties en route. So, he would ignore this minor tower for now, and content himself with the bounty of its territory. Assuming there was any bounty to find. An isolated tower like this was not guaranteed to have any edible flora or fauna dwelling in its territory at all.

Just then, he heard a buzzing noise. A bee flew past his face, landing on a flower a short distance from his feet. He scowled and pulled back the mana he had subconsciously stirred up. For some reason, despite the long distance isolating each purified territory, every single one they had landed in had bees. In the past, he would have blown away any such creature that dared approach him, especially the ones armed with stingers. However, this was to be a long journey, and preserving their strength was critical. Ruckanos could not permit himself any unnecessary expenditure of any resource, including his own mana. So, he just kept scowling and backed away from the creature.

If they at least had the decency to offer up their honey, he might have forgiven them. But, for some reason, his scouts had failed to find a single beehive in any of the purified territories despite the constant presence of the workers. Ruckanos shook his head and cleared those thoughts. It was a minor annoyance in the grand scheme of things. Such paltry creatures paled in comparison to a mission from the gods, so he'd treat them as the gods did.

Later that night, one of Ruckanos's entourage walked over to his wyvern. He glanced around before opening the pack and slowly removing some of his provisions. After a bit, he found something he had not packed at all. A small beehive, covered in wax. A big bee poked her head out of the hive's entrance hole, the queen herself, if he wasn't mistaken.

The man smiled. "Hello, little bee. We're leaving tomorrow, so don't send out your workers, okay?"

The queen buzzed her wings. The man didn't know if she could actually understand him, but he'd figured these weren't normal bees when they didn't swarm him after he first discovered them. He took his water pouch and dripped a small pool on top of the hive. The queen and a couple of the workers came out to drink from it. The man watched them for a bit.

"Sure you don't want to stay here? Lots of flowers here, you know?"

But the bees ignored him, finished drinking, and then climbed back into their hive. The man sighed.

"No again, huh? I don't think you want to go where we're headed, little bee. None of us are coming back, you know? You don't deserve to share our fate. I hoped you would make it but . . . I guess you can't understand me after all. Ah well, as long as you're happy for now, I guess. That would make one of us on this trip . . ."

The man slowly repacked his provisions before turning in for the night. They had a long trip ahead of them and no end in sight that the man wanted to consider.

# CHAPTER FOUR

# BEE-TING YOUR LIMITS!

**B**elissar awoke to a new day. He walked over to the farmhouse's table and began a breakfast of honeycomb and a cave-potato cake the karnuq had given him. Meanwhile, Niobee brought in a number of worker bees, the ones he had shared his thoughts with. They each reported to him on whatever topic he had asked them to remember, and he sent his tower sight around as was relevant.

"Fourth of Seventh preparing to build mini-hive for scouts."

Belissar nodded and turned his attention to the orchard, where the Fourth of the Seventh was gathering a group of soldiers and workers. He frowned just a little when he saw her leave with them. A queen leaving the tower seemed a bit dangerous to him, but he trusted the bees to know what they were doing. Ultimately a hive's workers were even more protective of their queens than he was, so he knew they would keep her safe.

"All wounded soldiers can use lightning sting now, practicing together."

Over the past few days, Belissar, Niobee, and Beero had finished imparting lightning to all the wounded soldiers. From then on, Beero had begun disseminating her magic to them. Belissar briefly glanced over at the memorial . . . then froze and turned his full attention there. He had expected to see a bunch of soldier bees all practicing their magic one by one.

Instead, all the wounded soldiers were now gathered in the field off to the side of the memorial and had assembled into a circle. Beero was leading them in a dance, each of them forming the lightning honeycomb pattern of their magic. But then, Beero had them begin moving together in a circle, and moving their lightning honeycombs as well. Some lightning trailed behind from each of the honeycomb patterns . . . and then started to link together, until a hexagon of lightning formed in the air above the soldiers.

Beero then changed the course of the dance. One hexagon became two, and then three, and so on and so forth until a larger honeycomb pattern formed from the lightning trails of the smaller ones. The pattern locked into place and then flashed.

A huge stinger of lightning appeared and shot from the pattern into the sky, traveling much farther than the individual bee's versions had . . . or than even Belissar's could. Belissar's jaw dropped.

That was an attack that could actually threaten a shade, and at a distance far enough that the wounded soldiers' lack of mobility might not matter. It wasn't anywhere near what Chief Rohsuak had displayed just yet, but it was a powerful, magical attack his bees had not yet had access to. It was exactly the sort of thing the tower needed to expand its defenses.

"King, King okay?"

Belissar felt Niobee land on his back and tap a dance on him. He brought his attention back to the farmhouse, where the worker bees had ceased their report and were watching him as he zoned out. He flushed a bit and nodded.

"Ah, yeah, sorry. Beero and the wounded soldiers just did something incredible, so I got distracted. They figured out how to cast magic all together, and it was much more impressive than before. I think they might be able to participate in a fight now, if we can keep them safe."

Niobee began a celebratory dance. "Glad! Soldiers can fight again, help hive of hives!"

The other worker bees began to join in the celebratory dance and Belissar smiled. He went and picked up an extra tray of honeycomb.

"How about we go congratulate them?"

"Okay!"

A short while later, Belissar and Niobee arrived at the first-floor flower meadow. Beero and the wounded soldiers were just about to try again when they saw him approach and stopped to salute. Belissar placed the honeycomb tray on the ground before them and smiled.

"I saw what you did, excellent work. It's exactly what we need right now. I wanted to congratulate you and give you a little something in celebration."

The wounded soldiers all froze. Beero even collapsed on the ground. And then, a moment later, she scrambled to her feet and began to dance as fast as her legs would carry her. The rest of the wounded soldiers followed suit. Belissar chuckled. The bees really liked praise, didn't they? He would have to make sure to praise them all more often.

After the celebration, Niobee brought over the Firstborn so Beero could demonstrate the new attack to her. Belissar watched and rubbed his chin. It had a longer range than a sprayer's attack, but not by all that much in the grand scheme of things. A wolf-shade would probably be able to cross the distance after a single attack. A bird-shade or cat-shade might not let them even finish their dance.

And that was a problem, because for all their magical lightning powers, the wounded soldiers were still grounded. They couldn't fly, and bees were noticeably slower on the ground, so they would not be able to escape a shade if it attacked them. They would get one shot, at most, against all but the turtle-shades. Belissar wasn't sure if one of those lightning stingers would be enough to defeat a shade outright . . . and if it wasn't, they would lose some or maybe all of the wounded soldiers. So, the question was: How could they safely take advantage of this new attack?

Fortunately, Belissar happened to have an easy answer. He brought up the wooden platform feature he had gained from building the orchard's bee apartment. A transparent wooden platform supported by a couple of wooden legs appeared. He found he could adjust the height and width to some degree, though the higher he made the platform the less wide it could be. He went ahead and made it as wide as the wounded soldiers' joint dance had been, and then as high as it could go otherwise, resulting in a tower about three stories tall. He went ahead and confirmed it and then turned to the bees.

"Sorry to interrupt, but I have something to show you all. Ah, I can carry you, Beero."

The Firstborn saluted and Belissar held out his arm so that Beero could crawl up onto his shoulder. He walked across the flower meadow toward the entrance. There, standing right behind the first firebreak, was the new platform.

"What do you think, Beero? I figured if you and the others climb up there, you should be able to attack safely."

Beero stared at it for a moment before breaking out into a rapid, incoherent dance. Belissar got the sense that she was very much happy, however, so he chuckled. He then turned to the Firstborn with a frown.

"The thing is . . . I'm not sure how well this platform will hold up if a shade attacks it, so they might need to evacuate. Would your soldiers be able to carry Beero and the others away if they needed to?"

The Firstborn saluted. Niobee then began to dance. "King! Orchard bees can help! Make more stems to help carry!"

Belissar's eyes widened as he nodded. "Ah, that's a good idea. If we weave slings of some sort, that should make it easier. Thanks for reminding me, Niobee!"

The King then carried all of the wounded soldiers to the platform so they could each take a look and practice their dance together. After that, he and the Conduit left to arrange things with the orchard queens. The Firstborn had gone to inform the rest of the flower meadow queens of the new developments. Soon, they would begin training to carry the wounded soldiers.

Beero stood completely still at the top of the wooden platform, feeling the breeze brush past her antennas and her remaining pair of wings as she looked out over the flower meadow. She had not seen it from this height since the day she had been wounded. But now, thanks to the King, she could. She glanced around and saw all of her fellow soldiers standing still as well, likely sharing in her thoughts.

She and her comrades had done it. They had found a way to rejoin the fight and participate in the battle once again. No longer would they be the soldiers who just had to be fed and kept safe. No longer, when she gazed upon the memorial and the numbers that represented the fallen sisters who had left her behind, would she wonder if she should have joined them.

No, now, once again, they would defend their queens, their sisters, the King, and the hive of hives. They would repay the King and the other bees for all the resources and efforts they had expended to save their lives. They would all become true soldiers again, no longer defined by their injuries but by their will to defeat the invaders, same as their unwounded sisters.

Beero slowly began a dance, one she had never performed before and that did not match any in her instincts. It was reminiscent of the dance the Conduit led them in whenever the King brought fallen bees to the memorial, but with elements of a celebratory dance mixed in. Something that matched her present feelings. One by one, the other wounded soldiers began to join her in it, until all of them danced as one. They were not sisters originally, as they had come from different queens and different hives, but now they were united in experience and purpose. They were linked by a bond beyond brood, comrades now who had overcome the impossible together.

For they had lost much, but now, finally, they were going to take some of it back. And they would stop at nothing to defend and repay the King who had given them the chance to do so.

# CHAPTER FIVE

# THE WISE BEE-CISION?

**B**elissar once again stood by the bee barracks as the daily purification commenced. Beero and the others wanted to take part, but Belissar had asked them to hold off for today. He wanted the orchard bees to weave some slings and the soldier bee army to get some practice moving the wounded bees around before he exposed them to danger, so the lightning attack's debut would have to wait.

Fortunately, today's purification was another bird-shade, which struggled in the new dirt tunnels. It kept crashing into the walls and the roof, and eventually just began walking until it finally found the end. At that point, it got hit by a sticky honey trap, then the soldier bee army set upon it, and that was that.

Belissar was pleased to find that the dirt tunnels caused the bird-shades as much trouble as he had hoped.

After the victory celebration, Belissar gathered the queens once again, with Chief Rohsuak and Beero attending too. Well, Beero had always been present, since those meetings were held at the memorial, but they were specifically including her now as the representative of the wounded soldiers, since as a soldier she hadn't felt confident dancing among the queens.

And Belissar had something to discuss with them all.

*DP: 3235*

He once again had enough DP for another choice from the DP shop. His initial instinct was to grab a new monster and expand the soldier bee army's options even further. On the other hand, today's purification reminded him that rooms could also present a defense in and of themselves, as a bird-shade that could terrorize the open air of the flower meadow proved all but helpless in the constricted dirt tunnels. And thus far, most of his room choices had prioritized providing resources for his bees, so perhaps there were great potential defenses he hadn't tapped yet. Additionally, new room types could also provide new flower types and therefore new bee types. A fire-related room, for example, could go along well with the incoming fire queen . . . and maybe the God of Fire himself.

However, all his room slots were currently occupied at the moment, so he'd have to either save up to purchase a room slot, conduct an expansion purification, or else remove an existing room before he could add any more. So, a new monster bee type would probably provide the greater immediate benefit, while a new room would be a choice for the future.

In any case, he asked the bees and Chief Rohsuak for their opinions before sharing his own thoughts. The bees had the usual recommendation of "Whatever King chooses!" but after Belissar prompted them, they eventually stated their preference for more flowers and more bees. The Firstborn was particularly concerned about the strength of the soldier bee army following the turtle-shade, while the First of the Fifth was a bit reserved this time, agreeing with the Firstborn. Beero just saluted as the queens spoke. Chief Rohsuak, for her part, nodded along.

"We seem to have plenty of resources now, Sacred Den Master Belissar, and we are still putting the new ones you've recently made to use. I think now would be a good time to boost your tower's strength."

Belissar nodded at that and made his choice. As much as a new room appealed to him, it would make more sense to wait for an expansion purification. So, he selected the monster option.

*Extra monster choice purchased. One monster choice now available.*
*Please select a monster:\**
*- Monster Bee Captain (Rarity: Uncommon, Type: Bee)*
*- Monster Stingless Bee Queen (Rarity: Rare, Type: Bee)*
*- Monster Bee Gardener (Rarity: Uncommon, Type: Bee, Nature)*

*(\*One or more choices upgraded due to Blessing of Bees)*

The first choice was a repeat, the monster bee captain. Boosting the coordination and effectiveness of the soldier bee army certainly wouldn't hurt. At the same time, though, with communers already boosting communication and allowing queens to direct their workers and soldiers remotely, the captains didn't seem as necessary to Belissar. He imagined they still had to help somehow, but it perhaps wouldn't be a particularly dramatic improvement. He clicked on the next option.

### *Monster Stingless Bee Queen*
**Vitality:**  *Minimal*
**Strength:**  *Minimal*
**Speed:**  *Average*

*Magic:*   *Minimal*

*Defense:*   *Minimal*

*Resistance:*   *Minimal*

*Special:*   *Above Average*

*Notable Skills:*   *Tackle, Wax Coating, Brood Mother, Command Offspring*

*A stingless bee that has accumulated enough mana to become something more. Mostly similar to her mundane cousins, but more aggressive. Lacking a stinger, these bees defend themselves through a combination of physical assaults and coating enemies in wax and propolis. This one is a queen, and capable of building a hive of monster bees.*

Belissar tilted his head at that. Stingless bees? There were stingless bees? Bees without stingers would be convenient for a mundane beekeeper, but how would they defend themselves in the wild? The description said something about tackling and coating in wax and propolis, and maybe that'd work against other insects, but what would they do about something bigger like a bear? Or, in this case, a shade? The description gave Belissar more questions than answers.

Well, he had to imagine their defensive methods had *some* effect on the shades. The gods wouldn't give him a helpless option, right? Maybe coating a turtle-shade in wax could stop it somehow? He didn't see how they could do that to anything moving faster, though.

Still, this one was also a queen, and so it was worth considering. If these stingless bees did prove effective against shades, having entire hives of them would certainly help. Though, they'd also be competing for resources with the existing monster bee queens and the bumblebee queens, and Belissar was currently out of room slots. Maybe they'd be a good option to put near the karnuq on the second floor? Though, if they had no stings, the karnuq might end up taking advantage of them. Belissar didn't think they would, but . . .

Well, there was still one more option to check out, in any case.

### *Monster Bee Gardener*

*Vitality:*   *Minimal*

*Strength:*   *Minimal*

*Speed:*   *Average*

*Magic:*   *Minimal+*

*Defense:*   *Minimal*

*Resistance:*   *Minimal*

*Special:*   *Minimal+*

**Notable Skills:**   Poison Sting, Sacrificial Strike, Tend
                      Plants, Enhanced Pollination, Brood
                      Offspring
**Evolves From:**   Monster Bee Worker

A monster bee worker that has come to specialize in foraging. Most bees assist plants
as a side effect, but these bees take it further. Monster bee gardeners directly boost
the health and growth of plants they visit, including plant features and plant
monsters, by exchanging mana and identifying the plant's needs. They also increase
the rate and impact of pollination between different plants. In exchange for
all this, they also gather more nectar per visit, and the nectar they gather
has higher mana density, boosting their hive's honey production.
In addition to evolving from existing monster bee workers, some monster
bee workers may spawn as gardeners, though this requires more
resources from the hive.

Belissar rubbed his chin and nodded as he read the description. So, a worker
bee evolution that specialized in working with plants? While that wouldn't help
directly combat shades, he could very much see the appeal. More efficient foragers meant more honey, which meant more bees based on the same number of workers and flowers. The apiary queens would produce even more honey, while the
flower meadow queens could support more soldiers off their current worker base.
However, what really stuck out to Belissar were the parts about boosting plant
growth and pollination. Most of his specialized queens—like the medicinal queen,
the maddening queen, and the soon-to-be burning queen that would likely fulfill
a mission from a god when she evolved—had all evolved as the result of plants
that cross-pollinated with mana flowers. So, a bee that would enhance that process would mean even more new types of flowers, and new types of bees along
with them. His entire tower would benefit from that.

This was the first evolution he'd seen that was directly related to foraging from
flowers, the main job of bees to begin with. Currently, the only worker evolution
was the communer, which had an entirely new job. Acquiring an evolution that
would make the workers even better at their original purpose might be a good
idea, one that every hive he had would benefit from.

"Well, what does everyone think?"

Belissar made a show of asking everyone but glanced specifically at the First
of the Fifth. After all, as the queen in charge of the apiary, she was the one most
concerned with honey, and she had also been the one to take the lead on
cross-pollination.

She was apparently trying not to say anything, but she was also trembling and
her legs kept trying to take steps. Belissar smiled, as he believed he could

reasonably guess what she was thinking. She withered under his gaze until finally she started to dance.

"New workers would boost production."

She chose her steps carefully but continued to tremble a bit. Belissar chuckled before glancing around. The Firstborn also seemed reluctant to dance, so Belissar looked at her until she, too, started to move.

"Captains might help with army. But more honey needed too."

He glanced at the other orchard queen, the First of the Fifth's First Daughter, since the Fourth of the Seventh was still working on her outpost hive.

"Captains might also help run hive? More honey, more flowers always helpful."

That . . . surprised Belissar, as he had expected her to agree with the First of the Fifth. Finally, he glanced at Beero, who was standing completely still and refusing to move, and then at Chief Rohsuak. She smiled and shook her head.

"I am sorry, but I am not familiar with any of those. You know your bees best, so please do as you see fit."

Belissar nodded and then thought to himself. It did not take him much longer to decide.

*Monster Bee Gardener now available. Monster Worker Bees may now evolve into Monster Bee Gardeners.*

Captains would help the current bees work better, but they did not provide new options in and of themselves. Stingless bees were interesting and, as brood mothers, perhaps could offer an entirely new line of bees . . . but they were a risk, since Belissar didn't know exactly how effective they might be. And they would compete with existing hives for resources until he could make more rooms. Gardeners, on the other hand? Gardeners would make every existing hive better and could also unlock new bee types through cross-pollination. Of the three choices, they seemed the most helpful for his tower as a whole.

Once he announced the choice, the First of the Fifth finally broke into a rapid happy dance.

"Amazing! Incredible! King is best king!"

Belissar couldn't help but smile and laugh at that.

# CHAPTER SIX

# FIRES BEE-KINDLED

The bee awoke in a world of complete darkness and cold. At first, she wondered if she had made it. Last she remembered, she had been surrounded by blazing heat, so hot her chitin had burned. But now, it was cool, so cool she nearly shivered.

But the shivering simply told her that her body was still alive and capable of moving, so move she did. She found a wall blocking her way and started to pick at it. As she did, mandibles pierced through from the other side and the light began to stream in. Her loyal children removed the cap over her cell and she was free to leave.

And so, the Third of the Sixth emerged from her cell, her formerly yellow color now including reds and oranges. She shivered, the previously hot temperature of her new hive now feeling all too cold even as her mana attempted to heat up her surroundings. But the cold didn't stop her from breaking out into a happy dance.

She had done it. She had survived. She had evolved. She had fulfilled the King's and the hive of hives' request. She had become a burning monster bee queen.

She flared her mana as she danced, and a red glow appeared around her body for a second. The burning workers tending this new hive drew closer and flared their mana as well.

Now it felt pleasantly warm.

Belissar was just getting started for the day when a much-awaited message appeared.

*Mission: Spawn or evolve one Fire attribute monster of rare*
*or better rarity completed!*
*Reward: One fire-type room feature choice*
*The God of Fire offers a minor blessing.*
*A non-patron god, the God of Fire, offers his blessing! The God of Fire*
*will be added to the shrine in some rooms. Accept?*

Belissar smiled and bowed his head.

"Yes, and thank you."

The moment he spoke the words, a wave of mana surged through the tower and his body. This time, the mana was blazing hot, and the world took on a red tinge for a short moment. Then it left as suddenly as it came, leaving Belissar feeling a bit cold.

*Minor Blessing of Fire applied.*
*Effects:*
*- Fire-related options now appear slightly more frequently.*
*- Some special fire-related options are unlocked and may now appear.*
*- Fire monster upgrades and evolutions are now slightly cheaper and easier to unlock.*
*- Fire and fire-type attacks deal slightly more damage.*

Additionally, Belissar could feel one of the shrines change. He turned his sight to the second-floor flower meadow, where the karnuq lived. The shrine there still centered on the God of Bees' statue, but now also included a small brazier to its side, adorned with a red banner with a yellow-orange flame drawn on it. The flickering flames illuminated the statue of the God of Bees, the shifting lights almost making it seem as if the bees carved all over her were actually moving.

The blessing itself was a bit muted compared to the Blessing of Bees, but it had specified that it was a minor blessing. Belissar was content with that, however, because the minor blessing also didn't include any restrictions for non-fire monsters or features. He had been slightly worried about that, but figured the God of Bees wouldn't have led him astray when accepting the quest.

And speaking of his original patron . . .

*Mission: Earn the blessing of a secondary patron completed!*
*Reward: One cross-perk choice*

Belissar blinked at the reward message. The glowing message was split in two. The first half was the golden yellow he knew and loved, while the other half was bright red. And judging from the words themselves, he guessed that meant that the God of Bees and the God of Fire had collaborated on this.

And so, Belissar knew what to do. First, he got up, picked up a tray of mana honeycomb, and walked over to the Third of the Sixth's hive. He found her just leaving her original beehouse, and she began happily saluting once she saw him. He gave her a wide grin.

"Great work, Third of the Sixth, and congratulations on your evolution. Here, I wanted to give you something to celebrate with."

She broke out into a happy dance and began glowing red here and there as Belissar placed the tray by her hive. He also proceeded with his other gift for the new queen, creating a full Fire mana flower node by her new beehouse to go along with the flame radish node he had moved. Notably, the flame radish node couldn't be placed in the dirt tunnels itself, but the Fire mana flowers could, so he placed this one right outside of her hive. The flowers were still extra expensive, but a couple of days of purifications had expanded his mana enough to afford it. They were worth the expense, now that he had a queen who could make full use of them.

The Third of the Sixth began to fly even faster, dropping all choreographed dances to just zip around him in a circle like the bumblebee queens. Belissar chuckled.

"I'm glad you like it, please enjoy. Now, um, if you don't mind, do you happen to have enough of the burning honey that I could take some?"

The Third of the Sixth stopped her zipping just long enough to perform a salute dance before resuming. Belissar chuckled as he climbed down toward her new hive. Sweat began to drip down his brow as the temperature rose substantially . . . but just when it was about to cross the line from uncomfortable to painful it suddenly stopped. Belissar tilted his head. He was somehow aware that the temperature was still rising even though his body didn't feel any hotter. But he shrugged and figured it was just a tower thing before pressing on.

He got to the new beehive, which had a glowing slot in the stone block that covered the entrance. Belissar tapped it and, as he hoped, a tray of honeycomb slid right out. He was very glad for the magic of the beehouse features, as moving the entire stone door to retrieve honey might have been . . . difficult.

Instead, he could pick the tray right up. A very thin layer of stone lined the bright red honeycomb. It was hot to the touch but not painfully so, and just slightly heavier than the normal trays. Belissar could only thank the tower mana and the gods for that.

After picking up the tray, Belissar made his way down to the second floor's flower meadow and found Chief Rohsuak already at the new shrine, bowing to the brazier and the God of Fire's banner. She smiled as she saw him approach.

"You've had recent dealings with my patron, I assume?"

Belissar nodded.

"After you defeated that turtle-shade, he gave me a mission. It was just completed today, thanks to the bees."

Chief Rohsuak smiled, a flicker of flames appearing to dance within her eyes.

"In that case, I must thank you and them. It has been a long time since I've been to a shrine of the God of Fire. It was . . . surprising."

She held up her hand and a flame appeared, rolling across her fingers. She chuckled.

"There might even be an ember or two left for the Blazing Berserker after all."

She then backed away so Belissar could come before the shrine. He took two trays of honey—the burning mana honey tray and a regular mana honey one, since he only had one of the burning trays—and split each in half. He put one half of each into the wax chest and bowed to the God of Bees' statue.

"Thank you again, for everything."

Then he turned to the God of Fire's banner . . . and frowned a bit. There was no chest, so Belissar wondered how he could offer anything to the God of Fire. Maybe everything went through the God of Bees' chest?

Chief Rohsuak cleared her throat.

"Forgive me if I'm interrupting but . . . are you perhaps wondering how to make an offering to the God of Fire?"

Belissar nodded. "Ah, yes."

She chuckled slightly. "I did too, my first time around." She pointed to the brazier. "He likes to do everything through fire, you see."

Belissar's eyes widened as he nodded again and then dropped the two trays into the brazier.

"Thank you for your blessing. I'll, um, do my best with it?"

The fire surged up for a moment, bathing Belissar in a wave of heat. Then it died down, and both the trays had vanished. The God of Bees' statue briefly shone with light as the brazier's fire grew once again. Belissar stood still for a moment before bowing his head.

When he was finished, he turned to find Chief Rohsuak waiting for him. She saluted to him as he approached.

"Sacred Den Master Belissar . . . I was serious, you know? You have no idea how much this means to me. I never thought I would ever find another shrine for the God of Fire. So, if there's anything I can do to thank you, or the bees responsible for this, please, let me know."

Belissar was about to tell her it was alright, as the God of Fire had already rewarded them for this, when he saw her eyes. They were glistening, and moisture had started to build even as Chief Rohsuak made the brightest smile he had ever seen on her. So instead, he paused and rubbed his chin for a moment before nodding.

"Ah . . . so, one of my queens recently evolved with Fire mana. Maybe you could speak with her, and see if there's anything you can teach her about it?"

Chief Rohsuak's smile grew even wider, and she nodded several times.

"It would be my honor and pleasure, Sacred Den Master."

# CHAPTER SEVEN

# BURNING BEE-CISIONS

After thanking the gods, Belissar asked Chief Rohsuak to accompany him and for Niobee to gather the queens. He didn't like to interrupt them during the day, but he felt it was worth doing so in the present moment. After all, they had rewards from not one, but *two* gods to decide on.

Soon, all the relevant parties were gathered at the second floor's shrine. Belissar felt that location appropriate since the God of Fire's brazier was there, and they were deciding on his rewards. As the bees arrived and gathered around him, he stepped forward, smiling at the Third of the Sixth.

"Hi everyone, thanks for coming and sorry to interrupt your work. But, thanks to the Third of the Sixth evolving today, we fulfilled missions from two gods, and now have two choices to make."

The Third of the Sixth fidgeted about, trying not to break out into a happy dance while Belissar was still talking. The other bees turned to face her but likewise waited for Belissar to continue.

"Okay, so, we have a room feature choice from the God of Fire, and then a cross-perk from both the God of Bees and the God of Fire."

Chief Rohsuak's eyes lit up at the mention of the God of Fire, while the bees began buzzing and pacing about at the news. Belissar brought up the choices and began to read them out.

*Select Room Feature:*
*- Fire Spout (Rarity: Common, Type: Fire, Trap)*
*- Metallurgical Furnace (Rarity: Common, Type: Fire, Crafting)*
*- Mini-Volcano (Rarity: Rare, Type: Fire, Ground, Trap)*

He launched right into the descriptions of the three features.

### Fire Spout

**Type:**  Fire, Trap

**Mana Upkeep:**  5

*A nozzle that will spray fire in a straight line when triggered. Providing flammable materials may change effects and behavior.*

### Metallurgical Furnace

**Type:**  Fire, Crafting

**Mana Upkeep:**  5

*A furnace intended for processing metal. May require additional fuel or mana to process certain materials.*

### Mini-Volcano

**Type:**  Fire, Ground, Trap

**Mana Upkeep:**  50

*A small volcano just peeking out of the ground. Will launch burning rocks in the direction of invaders. May also emit ash clouds and slowly flowing lava.*

Belissar couldn't help but whistle at that last one. He had heard tales of volcanos before but had never seen one himself, fortunately. It certainly sounded impressive. He turned to Chief Rohsuak.

"Um, have you ever seen a volcano?"

Chief Rohsuak nodded, staring off into the air with a nostalgic smile on her face. "In a sacred den of fire. Imagine a mountain pouring smoke into the sky, with rivers of liquid fire running down its slopes. Shooting stars soar from its peak before colliding into the ground, and the entire thing can explode into a wall of superheated smoke that reaches from ground to sky."

Belissar gulped. He wasn't sure why Chief Rohsuak was smiling about that memory, but he could certainly see how it might help his tower's defense. However, the feature's cost was as impressive as its supposed effects. That amount of mana could pay for a lot of flowers or bee spawners. The other issue was that, as of now, Belissar had no good place to put it, unless it would fit in the dirt tunnels. Besides the tunnels, all of his other rooms happened to be flammable, and he wasn't sure his little firebreaks would be enough to deal with rivers of liquid fire or burning rocks flying through the sky, even if the volcano was a small one. And would something intended to launch rocks into the sky even work in the dirt tunnels? He wasn't sure. If it didn't, then this would be a purchase for the future, when he could get more rooms. Either a new, less flammable room, or maybe just another room slot so he could put an empty flower meadow with nothing in it that he didn't want burned to the ground on the regular. That last idea . . . actually had merit in general, though.

Additionally, there were two more options. Fire spouts were far less dramatic than mini-volcanos but also far more muted in their effects. Belissar could see an easy use if he put them at the bottom of his pit traps, or used them in combination with the sticky honey traps. The bees wouldn't have to risk dropping flame radish slivers any longer, in that case. And those spouts could be especially effective in the tight corridors of the dirt tunnels, assuming they worked there. If so . . . maybe Belissar wouldn't have to trap shades in pit traps at all before setting them ablaze.

Still, that was spending a choice, and a reward from the God of Fire himself, on a capability he could somewhat match already. Though, the part about adding fuel for different effects had some promise. Maybe it would be like the sticky honey traps, and he could make fires with different effects? And if honey or wax worked as the fuel, then he could get started on that right away.

The other option was a non-combat feature. A furnace to process metal had obvious uses for the karnuq, given that they had metal tools and presumably knew some blacksmithing. And Belissar had just gone and made a bunch of metal ore nodes for them, so a furnace would be exceptionally useful right away. But he did wonder if it was worth using an entire feature on. If the karnuq knew blacksmithing, then surely they knew how to build a furnace themselves, right? He had even unlocked some features for things he had built himself. So, he turned to Chief Rohsuak.

"Um, do you know how to make a furnace?"

Chief Rohsuak thought for a moment before slowly nodding. "Much of our knowledge has been lost, but we should be able to put together something useable. Likely not as well-made as one created by a sacred den, but well enough for basic use. Furnaces would certainly be appreciated, but you do not need to consider it necessary."

Belissar nodded and turned to the bees, but they didn't have much to add this time. The Third of the Sixth looked excited at all of the options offered, while the other bees seemed a bit uncomfortable, given the way they were shifting around. He guessed bees in general didn't love fire, with one exception among his queens, so it looked like it'd be up to him to decide.

He mostly ruled out the furnace, since the karnuq could handle that themselves. With Muuraqi's blessing for stone-working, it shouldn't be all that hard, right? Well, Belissar didn't know what went into building a furnace, but he'd take Chief Rohsuak's word for it. That left the impressive but expensive choice or the weaker but more immediately useful choice. He turned to Chief Rohsuak once more.

"Um, you know fire and the God of Fire, it seems, so . . . any opinion?"

Chief Rohsuak rubbed her chin and hummed a bit before once again slowly nodding. "A word of caution. Volcanos are powerful but they are uncontrollable. Do not build one half-heartedly, and do not deceive yourself that you can contain it. If you are going to make one, you must commit to it and understand that its power is beyond your control. It will bring great devastation, certainly to your enemies, but to yourself as well if you are not careful. Treat it with the respect it deserves."

Well, that nearly settled the decision for Belissar, as he had no confidence in his ability to respect or control a volcano at all, given Chief Rohsuak's description of it. However, he held off from deciding right away, for he wanted to read the next choice first.

*Select a cross-perk (Bee/Fire):*
*- Honeyed Fuel*
*- Fire-Resistant Bees*
*- Buzzing Embers*

There were no rarities this time, and each perk was colored half in golden yellow and half in bright red. Belissar began reading out their descriptions.

*Honeyed Fuel*
*- Flammable honeys and beeswaxes have increased potency as fuel sources.*
*- Fires started with honey or beeswax deal more damage.*
*- Fires started with honey or beeswax with special effects inherit those effects with greater efficiency.*

That perk would obviously play into one of Belissar's main tactics, making the pit traps and sticky honey traps more powerful. If he was reading both the descriptions right, it might also work with fire spouts, should he choose them. And the part about the fires inheriting special effects from the honey . . . well, maddening fire certainly sounded harmful.

*Fire-Resistant Bees*
*- All bees gain increased resistance to fire and heat.*
*- All bees gain increased resistance to smoke and ash.*

This one was simpler and more straightforward in its effects, but by no means less desirable. Making his bees more resilient was always a priority for Belissar, since he didn't want to see a single one hurt if he could help it. Making them more resilient to fire and smoke would help if he was going to use more fire in his defenses. Sure, the burning bees seemed like they were already fire-resistant, but this could mean the difference between one hive fighting the enemy alone and all of them fighting together when there was fire around.

For example, if he chose the mini-volcano and set up a room specifically for it, this perk might enable all of his bees to enter and fight in that room as well.

*Buzzing Embers*
*- Embers and sparks from flames move and swarm around nearby enemies.*
*- All fire attacks may spawn additional embers and sparks*
*if they do not inherently do so.*

That was a curious one that had Belissar tilting his head. It sounded like it would . . . make embers come to life and attack? It said "swarm around," so maybe it would make embers act like bees? That was a curious idea, though Belissar had trouble visualizing what it would actually look like. He ultimately decided to just consider it something that would make any fire stronger.

So, honey and beeswax that made fire stronger, bees that were more resilient to fire, or stronger fires in general? Along with a choice between flame spouts that might be able to be fueled by honey and wax, or a dangerous and expensive mini-volcano? What, exactly, should he choose?

# CHAPTER EIGHT

# BEE BOLD!

**B**elissar first turned the question to the bees, as usual. The First of the Fifth was the first to speak.

"Burning honey . . . like King's fire chasms? King's fire best fire!"

Belissar chuckled. Well, he *was* slightly proud, even to this day, of beating a shade of the Hunger with a hole in the ground and a makeshift fire, so he'd admit he enjoyed hearing his bees praise him for it.

The Second First of the First was still hesitating but managed to convey her opinion.

"Bees need be stronger."

Belissar could always agree with that. He turned to Chief Rohsuak next.

"All of the options have merit, Sacred Den Master. Fire resistance is a must for anyone who doesn't want to be burned by their own blaze. It also sounds as if you've already made use of honey and wax as a fuel source, and reinforcing your existing efforts will make them all the more potent. As for the embers . . . the more ways you have to reinforce your fire, the stronger it will become."

Belissar stared at her for a moment. At this point, he figured that Chief Rohsuak was intentionally holding back her true thoughts, given the vague answers she gave nearly every time. Mrs. Imkomos used to do the same thing when she was teaching him beekeeping, saying she wanted him to learn for himself. He guessed Chief Rohsuak was trying to help him learn something, but he'd much prefer she gave a straight answer. Their lives were at stake here, and there was no way he was more qualified to make a fire-related decision than the Blazing Berserker!

But she just silently smiled at him, so he had to give up and think for himself, once again. The First of the Fifth was right in that honeyed fuel would build upon his existing defenses. If he added fire spouts on top of that, he could even skip the pits and apply the honey-fueled fire plan directly. It would strengthen a proven plan he had pulled off countless times before.

And that was why he hesitated. The First of the Fifth's praise reminded him that this was something he had done before, since the very beginning even. But the Hunger had just demonstrated that it would adapt to his defenses over time, so wasn't it risky to continue relying on the same plan? If he spent all his choices on the honey-fire trap combo, wouldn't he end up in trouble if they encountered a shade that could survive it? The cat-shades, for example, had already run past his sticky honey traps. Wouldn't they run past a fire spout too? And even if not, if they didn't get hit by the honey first, then honeyed fuel wouldn't help, right?

Well, Chief Rohsuak had also said that the more he committed to one specialization, the more options he'd get to overcome its weaknesses, so maybe it was the other way around. But that seemed like he'd end up in a race with the Hunger, trying to adapt his one plan to the Hunger faster than the Hunger could adapt to him. Belissar was not certain he'd be able to stay ahead. As much as he hated thinking about them, it was true that the tower lords were better prepared to become, well, tower lords. Maybe if he had been raised as one, he'd feel confident. But he had not.

But what, then, should he do? Fire-resistant bees as the Second First of the First wanted was a good option, but it didn't do as much for the fire spout–sticky honey trap combo as honeyed fuel would. If they ran into a shade that could survive the traps and that didn't use fire of its own, wouldn't both choices end up useless then? Maybe it was better to just go all in on the traps . . .

At that moment, Belissar's gaze passed over the Third of the Sixth. The new burning queen, the one who had fulfilled the mission and unlocked these choices in the first place. He thought of the efforts they had made before she could evolve. How it had required new flowers and an entirely new beehouse design. An idea began to grow in his mind.

"I think . . . I might have a risky idea."

The Third of the Sixth began her reply dance with no hesitation. "King's choice best choice! Will do whatever King needs, even if dangerous!"

The Second First of the First and the First of the Fifth both began dances affirming this, followed by all the other queens. The four bumblebee queens didn't dance, but they did extend their stingers and buzz their wings.

He glanced at Chief Rohsuak and she nodded at him. "Boldness and caution both have their place. All I say is that you should commit to whatever you choose."

Niobee landed on his shoulder and directly tapped her dance on him. "Bees will do whatever King thinks best. Bees ready."

Belissar nodded. He then took a deep breath and made his decision. He hoped he wouldn't regret it.

*Mini-Volcano is now available.*
*Fire Resistant Bees selected.*

He'd decided that he wanted to do something completely different this time. Sprayers had made even multiple wolf-shades simple to defeat. Dirt tunnels had contained the bird-shades and slowed down the cat-shades long enough for his bees to respond. Chief Rohsuak and her fire had wiped out a turtle-shade immune to all his previous defenses. Throwing something entirely new at the Hunger felt like a good move to him.

Besides, this choice was a reward from the God of Fire, from the mission that had also granted his blessing. It felt wasteful to simply do more of the same when he had the opportunity to open up a dramatic alternative. Fire spouts were common, so maybe he'd see them again now that he had a minor Blessing of Fire, and common room features could even show up as a daily purification reward, after all!

But what ultimately tipped the balance for Belissar was the Third of the Sixth herself. She had evolved into an entirely new kind of bee, one that did not necessarily fit anywhere within the tower at present. She couldn't operate underground in the dirt tunnels, and Belissar had to keep her hive and the flowers she needed separate from the rest of the apiary due to the fire hazard. But what if he made a room entirely committed to fire? What if he added a mini-volcano with its ash and lava and flaming rocks, then filled the room with flame radishes and Fire mana flowers? He could build a room that was absolutely hostile to most of his bees but absolutely perfect for the queen who made this all possible. Especially if he sought out new room types with either his next expansion purification or DP shop purchase, maybe he could even get a fire-related room that would work for them all. This would also fit into his plans regarding the specialization of his bees that he had spoken to the First of the Fifth about previously.

So yes, while the fire spouts and honeyed fuel combo was the safer option that reinforced his existing defenses, Belissar decided that with the reward from a god's blessing, he would take the risk to create entirely new areas for his tower, with new defenses and new bees. And with that decided, fire-resistant bees made the most sense to him. Not only would it make the bees more resilient in general, but it might also enable them to operate in the planned new room if they needed to. He would ideally like to keep as much of his tower open to as many of his bees as possible.

He told as much to his bees, surprised to find his own voice rising as the idea took shape both in his mind and his words. The bees watched his every motion and word . . . and then the Third of the Sixth burst out into a happy dance.

"Sounds amazing! Incredible! King is best king!"

The other queens soon began to join her in the praise dance. Chief Rohsuak smiled and nodded. "A bold decision. I enjoy those. And I can tell you that the God of Fire does as well. He will be pleased with such a move."

Belissar smiled back and then turned to the First of the Fifth, lowering his head. "Sorry we aren't going with the one you wanted. Maybe we can see if different honeys and waxes can work with fire even without the perk?"

He thought for a moment, remembering an instance when honey had caught fire. "Maybe Juosiutik might be able to help?"

Chief Rohsuak stifled a laugh. "Maybe she might."

The First of the Fifth burst out into a frantic dance. "No! King not sorry! King is best king, King's choice best choice! King sees more than bees, makes choices bees can't make! King is best king! Not sorry!"

Belissar held his hands up. "Okay, okay, I'm sorry . . . um . . . for being sorry? Or, um . . ."

Belissar took a moment to clear his throat. He thought for a second and then reached out his hand. The First of the Fifth froze. Belissar then pointed at his hand until slowly, gingerly, the First of the Fifth flew over and landed on it. He then smiled at her.

"I just want you to know that even if I make a different choice, I like hearing your opinion."

The First of the Fifth again went completely still, as rigid as a rock. Belissar got a bit worried about her until Niobee intervened, and then the First of the Fifth burst out into a happy dance.

Belissar once again hoped he'd made the right decision, and that he'd be able to live up to the bees' expectations of him.

# URGENT BEES-NESS

A man stepped into the sacred den and was immediately assaulted by a rise in temperature so sudden it felt like being hit by a solid wall. A stone causeway stretched across the center of a stone-walled room with two rivers of lava flowing to either side. The man tried not to grimace as noxious fumes rose from the rivers and assaulted his nose, his powerful sense of smell a severe detriment at that moment.

The man had unfortunately dressed for the occasion in a suit of chainmail. The metal began to heat up almost immediately, only his thin tunic underneath saving him from vicious burns. Even still, any contact between his limbs and the armor would definitely leave a mark. But the multiple layers also caused him to cook within his own clothing. He was already sweating something fierce and had to fight the urge to let out his tongue and begin panting. The fur on his arms and legs did not help matters, and his bushy tail was already drooping. Not for the first time, his wolf-like features had come back to haunt him.

But the sooner he moved, the sooner he could leave, so he pressed onward. He walked past the gigantic bonfire crackling before the banner of the God of Fire, taking a moment to bow at the Shrine of Fire before continuing onward. He turned to the left and stopped before a double door that was flanked on either side by other wolfkin like himself. These, however, were not clad in chainmail but in obsidian plate armor and visored helmets with triangular protrusions for their ears. And, despite being far more heavily clad than himself, they did not give any sign that the heat bothered them. For many reasons, he was envious of those who had been blessed by the God of Fire.

He gave his name and then one of the guards stepped inside. A moment later, they returned.

"Wait here."

He held back a frown. Waiting next to a divine bonfire and two rivers of lava was not exactly easy for someone without the God of Fire's blessing. But that was the point, he knew. One arrived for an audience with the Inferno Empress at her convenience, not their own.

Only after he was completely drenched in sweat did a torch next to the gate light up. One of the guards nodded and opened the door.

"Enter."

The man gulped and made his way inside. He now walked into a throne room made of pure obsidian, lit by two large trenches of fire that stretched down either side of the center path. Wisps of flame danced in and out of the rivulets, twirling tongues of fire into all sorts of shapes and patterns. Golden suits of armor lined the room holding weapons with bright red blades.

And at the end of the room was an empty throne made of obsidian and gold. At its base lay a black, three-headed dog that was larger than the man was tall, curled up and napping. It stirred slightly as he approached, one of the heads watching him with one of its eyes. It began a low growl as he reached the end of the fire trenches, still a ways away from the throne.

A moment later, smoke billowed into the room and coalesced around the throne. Two bright red eyes appeared in the midst of the dark cloud before the smoke began to disperse, though a thin layer of it still hung around. Finally, he saw the form of the empress herself. She had long, thin ears poking out of the obsidian helmet that covered the top half of her face. Black, leathery wings wrapped around her, obscuring most of her body from view as she leaned back against her chair.

The man spread out his arms, fully exposing his torso toward the throne before kneeling down on one knee.

"All hail the Inferno Empress!"

She glanced at him, red orbs occasionally glimmering in her helmet as her eyes reflected the flickering flames to his sides. She opened her mouth and spoke with a low, raspy voice.

"I have need of my servants."

The man remained kneeling. "But of course, my empress. Speak and your command will be done."

She made no movement, though the smoke surrounding her slowed for a moment. "You are to fetch me some . . . bees."

The man couldn't help but look up and tilt his head.

"Bees, Your Majesty?"

The orbs in her helmet flashed to life and the smoke picked up. The man quickly bowed his head once again.

"Of course, Your Majesty! It shall be done immediately!"

The Empress nodded her head. "It had better. Do not forget the fate of the last clan that displeased me."

The man held back a gulp. What few of that clan had survived had subsequently been exiled from the lands of the empress, doomed to roam the

Underway until the Hunger caught and consumed them. There were very few worse fates.

"That is all. Do not return until you are successful. I shall expect you soon."

With that, she rose to her feet and finally unwrapped her wings, extending them wide. The smoke condensed and wrapped around her, obscuring her from his view for but a moment. And in that moment, she vanished entirely.

The man rose to his feet and left the sacred den as fast as was permissible within the empress's halls. Whatever his mission, he could not afford to delay.

A man with a young appearance sat at a wooden table set up outdoors, giving him a full view of the tree-lined streets. He was dressed in flashy red, yellow, and orange clothing, causing him to stand out from his surroundings. Everywhere, flowered vines wrapped around buildings of white and golden wood. The man sipped his tea, his pointed ears drooping a bit. It was a bit bland for his taste. But, well, few among his people appreciated spices the way he did. The God of Fire's blessing could have unexpected side effects.

Across from him sat a woman of the same age, sipping her tea with a smile. She wore a simple green gardener's dress with a brown apron and had flowers tied into her hair. The man grinned.

"So, I take it we have an agreement?"

The woman smiled and nodded. "Of course. I am curious, however . . ."

The man made a wry smile. "Why bees?"

The woman nodded. "I have not known you to be interested in anything that was not flammable . . ." She paused, and then glared at him. "Urubran, you do not plan on setting them on fire, do you?"

Urubran raised his hands and shook his head. "No, of course not. It's a mission from the God of Fire. Apparently, I am to earn the blessing of the God of Bees."

The moment he said the name, the woman jolted and her back straightened.

". . . There's . . . a God of Bees?"

Urubran gave a small smirk. "Apparently so."

The woman immediately slammed her hands on the table and leaned forward, but Urubran stopped her by raising his hand.

"Calm down, Tarwantrad, I'm going to tell you."

Urubran chuckled as Tarwantrad didn't back down in the slightest, staring at him intently.

"Apparently, I must raise a number of bee monsters of at least rare rarity, though to my understanding most bee queen variants are rare to begin with? Then, I must build homes for them. Moreover, the mission will not be considered complete until the bees are sufficiently happy. So . . . could I request your assistance with that?"

Tarwantrad nodded her head. "Indeed, I would not allow you to make them unhappy in the first place, so I planned to deliver them to you personally.

The gods know how long it took to teach you how to take care of the simplest plant."

Urubran was about to retort about her nearly starving the first Fire monster he gave her but Tarwantrad had already looked away from him, rubbing her chin and muttering to herself.

"I was certain they were happy and I certainly have the variety. Maybe it's specifically the build homes for them part? Interesting, I had always let them take care of themselves, for I believed they knew best how to build their hives, but is that not the case? Should I have been building homes for them all along? Or perhaps it was awareness? I didn't know there was a God of Bees before, after all. If only I could hear from them myself . . ."

Just then, Tarwantrad froze. "Ah . . ."

Urubran grinned. "Got it too, huh? I was honestly wondering why the mission came to me instead of you. Must have something to do with the gods themselves . . ."

Urubran stopped, and then sighed. Tarwantrad was completely ignoring him. Again. He sipped his tea instead and shrugged. He couldn't say he hadn't expected this. The news that there was a God of Bees would have shocked her no matter how he delivered it.

Tarwantrad suddenly snapped out of her daze and began nodding with all her might. "Yes! Of course! Right away!"

She immediately rose from her feet and grabbed Urubran, yanking him up and causing him to spill his tea. "Come, Urubran! We have work we need to do *right now!*"

"Hey, wait a minute, Tarwantrad! Let go of me! I know you're excited, but I can't just up and leave my dungeon unattended! And look, we haven't even paid for the tea yet!"

Tarwantrad tossed a bunch of coins onto the table before dragging Urubran off, heedless of his other complaints.

# HUMANITY'S DUTY

On a bright and sunny day, a colossal tower pierced up into the heavens. Massive red banners coated in flames hung from its walls, interspersed with windows and gates of all shapes and sizes from which all manner of flying creatures took off and landed. On the ground below, a vast city was arranged in a neat grid around wide paved roads to one side of the tower, while empty plains stretched into the distance on the other side. The buildings were uniform and built of stone, miniature fortresses with little adornment save the banners of a red dragon upon a black field.

The sound of hammer upon metal rang out across the city as smoke belched into the sky. Thousands of blacksmiths worked their craft, forging countless swords and spears and suits of armor. Bakers kept their ovens working around the clock as they churned out mountains of bread and hardtack to fill the endless warehouses, weavers sewed together uniforms, bandages, and banners until their hands trembled, and brewers continuously emptied and filled their barrels with as much grog as they could brew. Clerks ran through their offices carrying stacks of paper taller than themselves as they worked into the night to keep track of it all.

Countless soldiers gathered in the fields beyond the city, sparring, exercising, and marching in formations. Dragons and wyverns and griffins and giant birds and all manner of other flying creatures flew in neat triangles, guided by the riders on their backs as they flew over the beast cavalry charging below.

And in the center of the field, a man stood facing three dragon riders. He was a head taller than even the tallest soldier, adorned in a sturdy but worn suit of red-painted metal armor. He held a red glaive in his hands as flames wrapped around him. One dragon flew straight at him, another flew overhead, and to his rear the third unleashed a green cloud of acidic mist.

The man ignored the mist as the fire that wrapped around him flared and pushed it away. He jumped up over the dragon approaching and landed on its head, knocking its rider off with a swing of his glaive. Then he jumped off the dragon's head and propelled himself upward with a blast of fire from his feet. He caught the tail of the dragon flying overhead and pulled it down, swinging the dragon and rider both down toward the third pair. The group collided and collapsed to the ground in a tangled mess before the man landed back on the first dragon, driving it into the ground.

He then landed back on the ground and shook his head as the riders groaned and picked themselves up. He was about to quiz them on their efforts when a courier came running across the field.

"Priority message for High Councilor Rippotis!"

Rippotis shook his head. "*General* Rippotis. Let me guess, it's from High Councilor Heigiosa?"

The courier's eyes widened while General Rippotis shook his head. "She always sends a message around this time. Well, hand it over."

He took the message and read it, still shaking his head. The three dragon riders, now back on their feet, walked up to him.

"What does it say, sir?"

He shrugged. "What it says every time. That she strongly recommends I don't personally participate in the Grand Subjugation this time."

The dragon riders frowned. "What will you do, sir?" one asked.

General Rippotis let out a light chuckle. "What I do every time. Thank her for her concern, and then perform my duty."

The general took out the reply he had written when the Grand Subjugation was first announced. "Here, deliver this to High Councilor Heigiosa."

The courier saluted and departed. General Rippotis took a deep breath. The expected message from Heigiosa was the last thing he had been waiting for; it was now time to begin. The other tower lords were still preparing for the Grand Subjugation, but not the general. He started preparing for each Grand Subjugation the moment the previous one ended. He gathered and trained his forces, stocked his supplies, and even sent out his scouting parties beyond their borders at regular intervals. He already had his forces organized and prepared to march, his targets laid out, and his operations planned in full.

Because he knew, more than anyone, that humanity was at war. A war for its very survival, one that never faded. After all, he had been there. He was there at the beginning, when arrogance and greed brought down a calamity that ended the world as they knew it and drove humanity to the brink of extinction. He was there in the desperate struggle for survival before the intervention of the gods, when the mightiest powers and the most impregnable fortresses in the world fell before a foe no one could stop. He was there when his army had to abandon countless cities and eventually their entire nation just so that a few could live. He was there when a band of refugees fled for their lives for years without end against the relentless onslaught of the Hunger.

That was why he would not be called Tower Lord or High Councilor, but General. So long as the Hunger endured, General Rippotis would never be at peace. He would fight to defend humanity to either his dying breath, or until the threat was extinguished. Heigiosa knew this too, though she wished for him to rely on the power of the gods. For General Rippotis, though, that was not possible. His own role in the disaster, and humanity's role as a whole, demanded that he lead the charge in pushing it back.

Besides, there was also the issue of the beastkin. Their role as the instrument of disaster and tyranny could not be forgotten, but in General Rippotis's opinion the rhetoric had gotten entirely out of hand. It was not like they'd had a choice in their own creation. Still, humanity *had* to be united in the face of a truly existential threat, so he would not allow the issue to break them apart. That meant, though, that the best way to ensure the survival of the beastkin was for him to personally subjugate as many independent towers as he could before the other tower lords arrived, especially those who had been raised on the rhetoric without the knowledge of where it came from.

Well, his soldiers were as disciplined and well-trained as he could make them. He trusted them to follow his orders and his policies, but as a member of the High Council he still felt a responsibility to personally rein in the excesses wherever possible. Heigiosa knew this too, and so she would always fear for his safety, but never go so far as to order him to stay behind. Part of him wished he could ease her concerns, thus why he always waited for her message before departing, but they both knew that he had to go. Every decision that had led them here demanded that he did.

At least, until today. General Rippotis was just about to give the order to launch the subjugation when he paused and furrowed his brow. The dragon riders exchanged glances at the delay, then stared at him in worry. One of them eventually spoke.

"General? Is something the matter?"

General Rippotis turned his gaze to her. "Change of plans. Lieutenant General Krimistis, you are now in charge of the operation until I arrive to take command. Move out immediately and proceed as planned."

Lieutenant General Krimistis's frown grew deeper. "General? If I may speak freely . . ."

"Granted."

"What exactly will you be doing?"

General Rippotis decided to entertain her question, since this was utterly abnormal for him.

"I've received a mission from the gods, which takes priority. I will join the subjugation once my task is complete. But we cannot delay our duty, so you all must see to it that the operation launches on schedule. Am I clear?"

The three dragon riders, his lieutenant generals, all saluted and spoke as one. "Yes, sir!"

General Rippotis turned and departed, walking toward the tower under his command while the lieutenant generals began barking orders. Soon, horns began to blow throughout the city and the field while fireballs shot into the sky from the top of the tower, detonating into planned patterns. His army burst into frantic motion as they organized into their marching formations and set off.

As for General Rippotis, though, he let out a sigh. He guessed Heigiosa would get her wish for the first time since, well, ever. Humanity's debt to the gods, as well as his own, outstripped even his duty to his troops. He would not delay a mission from the gods for anything save the imminent destruction of humanity itself.

Though, one thing caused him to tilt his head.

"Why bees?"

Bees played an important role in agriculture, to be sure, and could present a fearsome threat to the odd predator, but they did not feature much in Rippotis's tower. Ultimately, General Rippotis used the tower more as a training ground. What monsters he used in the field were only those his soldiers had captured and tamed, mostly relegated to serve as mounts or beasts of burden. He firmly believed that humanity needed to take the leading role in the fight against the Hunger, to ensure that they had a personal stake in the war for their own survival. He also believed the towers should be used to support them but not supplant human effort in any endeavor. A swarm of bees was more of a direct combat option than he preferred to use, and he only relied on wild bees for their agricultural contributions. Maybe he could eventually raise a bee monster that could be used as a mount? But he would have to go further than that if he wanted bees to have enough of a presence in his tower to justify the blessing of a god. A god he had not known had existed until today, though that was no excuse not to treat her with the reverence and respect she deserved.

However, the more General Rippotis thought about it, the more he began to nod. After all, bees were tireless workers and perfectly brave soldiers. They worked selflessly for one another and the good of all. And when they were faced with threats infinitely larger than any singular bee, they banded together to fight back at the cost of their very lives . . . and in doing so could overcome a threat no individual bee could ever hope to.

In that, they used the exact strategy that humanity now did. So, perhaps there was a place for bees in his army. Perhaps they could not only support his troops, but also act as an example for them to strive for. He bowed his head and thanked the gods for their guidance. It seemed that even after all this time, there was still much for him to learn.

He would learn and do anything he needed to if it would ensure humanity's survival. And so, General Rippotis, one of the Three Elders of the High Council, Commander of the Dragon Banner Army, Survivor of the Great Calamity, left his army on the eve of a Grand Subjugation campaign to raise and build houses for bees.

# CHAPTER NINE

# THE BEE-ROES' RETURN

With a new plan set out, Belissar decided that his next move would be an expansion purification. He needed either an extra floor or room slot for the planned mini-volcano room, and more options might provide either a fire-type room or additional fire-type features to add to the room. Additionally, Chief Rohsuak had let him know she had received additional blessings from the God of Fire and had grown stronger than she was during the emergency purification. She claimed she was not back in her prime, but launching another fire attack like she had wouldn't be an issue, particularly if Belissar fed her more mana honeycomb.

That went a long way toward reassuring Belissar, but he decided to wait for two more conditions. First, he wanted to give the flower meadow queens a chance to raise some lancers. Next, he wanted to test Beero and the wounded lightning soldiers' attacks and ensure they could be evacuated safely afterward. He figured that those two new attacks, along with the reassurance that Chief Rohsuak could assist them again, should be enough to handle another expansion purification.

Additionally, now that the apiary queens were delivering honey to the flower meadow, the number of maddening soldiers and sprayers was rising. The digging queen's hive was just about stable, so she'd be able to start contributing some honey as well. He might start seeing some sort of digging soldier soon, which would allow the soldier bee army to attack within the dirt tunnels. The bumblebees continued growing their hives as well. The third-floor flower meadow was now filled with bumblebees happily at work . . . and the bumblebee queens had now started to grow larger.

The First of the Fifth's hive was hard at work cross-pollinating. Maybe he'd see a mana flower variant of the sleepy chamomile soon? The hive was working on other plants too, though since they hadn't resulted in new bee types, Belissar wasn't sure if a more magical variant would either. He'd just have to wait and see.

Still, all of that would take time, so upon consulting with the bees and Chief Rohsuak, he decided lancers and a successful lightning attack would be sufficient to proceed. Anything else that occurred in that time would be a bonus.

And it might not be that long at all. The orchard hive had already finished prototypes of woven slings, and the soldier bee army was now practicing moving the wounded soldiers around. Belissar still wouldn't risk it against a faster shade, but if they got some sort of turtle variant they could test out the attack as soon as today.

And indeed, when he triggered the daily purification . . . the moment came. This time, a small turtle-shade appeared, about the height of his thighs instead of his head. Belissar considered the soldier bees' training from earlier today and hesitantly gave his permission. Today, they would see how Beero and company's lightning would fare.

Beero's antennas twitched as the wind blew past her, causing her remaining pair of wings to flutter. The soldiers holding her up released some calming pheromones and mana, which made her antennas droop a bit.

She had mixed feelings as she swayed about in the air, held only by woven stems that wobbled about. On the one leg, having her sisters carry her was not the most comfortable of situations. It was a stark reminder of her current helplessness, of all that she had lost and could no longer do. And the fact that she had to take two of her sisters out of the fight, tasked with carrying her about like a piece of pollen, was . . . less than ideal. She would have never proposed something like this, but she didn't have to. The King had ordered it himself, so neither she nor her sisters could do anything but obey.

And both her queen and her sisters reassured her that she had not detracted from the army's ranks. Since the majority of the soldier bee army held back from the fight in the reserve force, having two carry her about did not actually take them from the fight. Additionally, she now could do something that her sisters could not. It was only natural that they would do what they could, and she would do what she could.

But not all her feelings were negative. Today, she felt the wind blow past her and saw the ground shrink before her once more. She was once again soaring through the air alongside her sisters, something she never thought she'd ever get to experience again.

Some part of her could not help but be happy, to the extent that she wished to dance. But she pushed it down, as her sisters had not been pleased the first time she wiggled about and nearly caused them to drop her. So, she stayed as still as she could while her sisters carried her along.

All too soon they arrived at their destination, and her sisters lowered the stems upon the wooden platform the King had built. Beero crawled off and danced her gratitude. Her sisters twitched their antennas in reply and hovered back, still holding the stems so they could swoop in and pick her up at a moment's notice. More soldiers carried the other wounded bees, Beero's new comrades, and dropped them off beside her. Without any delay, they all scrambled into their positions, ready to stir up their mana at a moment's notice.

For today was the day. The King had informed them the enemy was coming, one that was suitable for them specifically. Indeed, if tales of the latest battle were true, they might be the only bees able to take it on.

Beero knew that was the true reason her queen and her sisters had been so eager to accommodate her. The soldier bee army had failed to stop the latest enemy. So, if Beero and her comrades' newest attack could, then the soldier bee army would spare no effort to assist them. They would stop at nothing to fulfill their duty to the King and the hive of hives. And neither would Beero.

And so, she waited, ready to once again fulfill the duty she had been born to do.

And she waited . . .

And waited . . .

And waited . . .

Until she heard the King speaking out to them all.

"Um, sorry everyone, but . . . it looks like it fell into the first pit trap. It's stuck in the dirt tunnels right now."

Beero . . . didn't know how to react.

Eventually, the King spoke with them. Beero indicated her continued desire to test her attack, and the King agreed. And so, after a bit of rearrangement, Beero was once again being carried by her sisters through the air. They slowly hovered through dark, cramped tunnels while the King himself lit the way with one of his fire sticks. Her two sisters barely had enough room to spread out and hold her up, and the whole group was moving at a crawl. It was not the most pleasant trip Beero had been on.

But finally, they arrived. The enemy was trying to crawl out of the pit, but the effects of the maddening honey were causing it to slip. It had fallen back on its shell, with its spikes driving into the ground and preventing it from flipping itself over. It was utterly helpless, and the King could destroy it in an instant with his fire stick.

"Okay, here it is. Um, Beero, will you be able to direct the attack down into the hole, even if you can't see it?"

She saluted at the King's request. She and the others had practiced sending the lightning sting in different directions, so it wouldn't be a problem.

"Okay, in that case, go ahead. I don't think it can get out, but just watch out in case it uses its breath or something."

Beero crawled forward and peeked down into the hole, memorizing the enemy's position. She and the others gathered up; the tunnel was barely wide enough for their dance, but it would do. On her signal, they began.

The tunnel lit up as lightning crackled over their heads. The shade seemed to notice and began to growl, but Beero and the others ignored it. They danced the dance they had practiced countless times in the recent days without a single leg out of place, each of them performing their part to perfection. Their mana, which should have clashed as they were all from different hives, joined together thanks to the common element of the lightning, while the mana of the King's realm itself wrapped around and bound them all. Beero even noticed the mana of the Conduit and caught a glimpse of her dancing as well. She'd thank her, but later, for now was the time to focus.

The others completed their dance, and then Beero danced to set the final direction. A sphere of lightning moved forward and over the pit . . .

Then a stinger of lightning formed and thrust downward. There was a crack of thunder and the shade roared. Light and smoke began billowing out of the pit as the honey caught fire as well. Beero wanted to step forward and see what they had done, but the King shook his head . . . and then smiled.

"You got it, Beero."

Beero went still even as the black mist of the enemy began to mix with the smoke, indicating its defeat. A moment later, she began to dance, and the others joined her.

It hadn't been the battle they had expected. It was a helpless enemy the King or her uninjured sisters could have dealt with alone. But still . . . she had rejoined the fight and brought victory to the hive of hives. She and her comrades had done that which they had thought would be impossible.

They could once again call themselves soldiers of the hive of hives, and of the King.

# HOW TO BEE HELPFUL?

The Firstborn, and indeed all of the flower meadow queens, began their meeting standing completely still, not a single one starting any dances. They had much to think about recently and had come up with few solutions to their concerns. What could they even say when an enemy repulsed every force in their army, invalidated every tactic and strategy they had prepared, and rendered all of their efforts for naught? When even the King's mighty chasms and honey sprayers could not turn the tide? When the hive of hives had no choice but to rely upon an outsider of questionable trustworthiness?

Well, the karnuq's aid in the battle had shifted the Firstborn's opinion of the outsiders, but that was beside the point. The point was that lately the Firstborn did not feel the flower meadow queens were contributing sufficiently to the hive of hives. They had abandoned everything, including competent honey-making, the very backbone of bee-hood, to build the greatest army bee-kind had ever seen. But for all their efforts, their army could not yet match the power of a single karnuq. And worse still, in doing so they had created an unsustainable situation within their hives. The flower meadow queens now required the First of the Fifth's intervention to continue growing. They had become a drain upon the hive of hives' resources.

That in itself was not necessarily a problem. Even within a hive, soldiers, queens, and drones spent resources while workers gathered them. There was a role to play for bees that did not gather honey, and so in a hive of hives an entire hive that spent more resources than it produced might still have a place. But that was if, and only if, they provided value to the hive of hives that justified the resources. The Firstborn could no longer state this was the case.

There were some new developments. The King had granted them access to a new kind of bee and the wounded soldier, one so honored as to receive a name from the King himself, an honor previously reserved only for the Conduit, had come up with a new sort of attack that could bypass the new shade's defenses. Yet the new lancers would require additional resources to raise, which at the moment meant receiving yet more honey from the apiary queens. And Beero's efforts belonged to her and the other wounded bees alone. The Firstborn and the flower meadow hives had played no part in it besides sharing some of their honey to sustain the wounded. They would be investigating whether the rest of their army could utilize such attacks, but they could not call that their own initiative. They were still receiving from others.

So, the Firstborn was not satisfied with the situation. She slowly began to dance.

"Think . . . I have idea. Want to hear?"

She could no longer confidently step forward. While the flower meadow queens worked together, the Firstborn had been the one to lead them thus far. But with recent developments, she could not continue to do so on her own initiative. So, she waited for the others to dance.

But one by one, the other queens all indicated that she should continue. She wasn't sure if they still believed in her, or if simply no one felt confident taking charge in her place, but either way, she chose to dance.

"Other queens have soldiers, soldiers that work. First of Fifth's soldiers help carry honey. Fourth of Seventh and First of Fifth's First Daughter's soldiers weave stems. Think our soldiers can work too."

The First of the Fourth began to dance. "But . . . if soldiers work, then can't train. Army will be weaker?"

The Firstborn danced her agreement but continued on. "Yes, but not all soldiers fight every day. Can take a few from reserve force, maybe rotate each day so all still can train."

The First of the Second danced slowly. "Could work but . . . how soldiers work? What do? Can't gather nectar. Could help dry? Firstborn has other idea?"

The Firstborn did, in fact.

"Already did before. Helped King build new hives. Should have soldiers build. Dig new chasms, build new hives."

The First of the Fourth buzzed her wings. "But . . . new hives won't help army? Will still make weaker?"

The Firstborn again confirmed. "Yes. Won't make army stronger, won't help army. But . . . will let army help hive of hives. Can send to build new hives for new queens, help apiary expand. Can help karnuq too, since karnuq helped fight. We only take from hive of hives and still can't defend alone. Now can give as well as defend."

The flower meadow queens all fell still. Then, one by one, they slowly began to dance.

"Could . . . work?"

"Would help King, like before."

"Soldiers said want to help again, if could."

"Could use to talk to other hives too."

Eventually, the Firstborn danced once more. "So, all agree?"

And this time, all the flower meadow queens danced a salute.

"Okay, let's let Conduit know and decide on soldiers. Should have one from each hive so all queens can see through communers."

The next day, as Belissar gathered with the bees for his breakfast reports, Niobee started with a dance of her own.

"King! Flower meadow queens have request!"

Belissar nodded. "Oh? What is it?"

"Want to send soldier bees to help build things! King has job?"

Belissar tilted his head. "Oh, hm, I wasn't building anything today but . . . do you know why they're asking?"

"Want to help! Want to do more work and help other hives!"

Niobee hesitated only a moment before continuing.

". . . Karnuq too."

Belissar's eyes widened a bit, but then he slowly nodded. He was a bit worried about the flower meadow queens. They had seemed subdued ever since the emergency purification. He had hoped the lancers might excite them, but they still remained subdued, unfortunately. He guessed this was what they wanted to do to make up for that?

Belissar wasn't sure how else to help them, so he decided to let them do what they wanted.

"I see . . ."

He thought for a moment before starting to ponder aloud.

"Well, the karnuq are still building their homes, so they could use the help. I don't know if the soldier bees are able to lift stones, but if they are, we're still gathering stuff to upgrade the barracks that they could help transport. Hm . . . maybe we could check with the apiary or orchard queens to see if any of them want to expand or raise new queens? If so, we could either build new beehouses or expand some to apartments. Whatever the queens want to do."

"Okay! Will let them know and will ask other queens!"

Belissar smiled and nodded. "Thanks, Niobee. I'll stop by the flower meadow myself to thank them."

Belissar soon made his way over and found the flower meadow queens assembling a group of soldiers apart from the overall army. He walked over to them, causing them all to stop and break out into salute dances.

"I heard you wanted to help with construction? Thanks, you girls really helped last time. How about today you help the karnuq, and then we can figure out if there's more to do? I'm sure they'd appreciate it."

The bees all froze before breaking out into rapid salute dances. Belissar chuckled and smiled at them.

"And . . . you all are doing great. The tower would not exist today without you, and I'm always grateful to you all for defending it . . ."

Belissar paused there. He was about to claim responsibility for the mistakes and failures . . . but the last time he did that it only caused the bees to vehemently object. He wanted to encourage them this time, so instead he stopped and thought about what would make them the most happy to hear.

". . . So, keep up the good work!"

Well, he couldn't think of much, so he just went with that. The flower meadow bees all froze solid once more. Belissar tried to think of something else to say, but before he could, they burst out into a buzzing swarm of rapid salute dances. He smiled a bit, whispering to himself.

"Well, I guess that will do for now. I'm sorry, I'll try my best for you too . . ."

The karnuq then got a surprise visit from the sacred den master and his bees. Chief Rohsuak tilted her head.

"The bees . . . want to help with building?"

Belissar nodded. "Yes, together they should be able to lift a large plank. They're, um, especially helpful for roofs and stuff high up."

Chief Rohsuak shook her head. "Are you certain? Help is always appreciated, but we manage the construction on our own, and we have our tents to hold us over until then. I would not want to take anything away from the tower's defenses."

But Belissar looked her in the eyes with a serious expression. "Please, the bees want to help with this."

Chief Rohsuak paused at the look and then slowly nodded. "Well, if you're certain, then we appreciate it." She turned to the group of soldier bees hovering around Belissar. "Thank you, we'd love your help."

The bees all danced a salute. Soon thereafter, the karnuq watched with wide eyes as soldier bees worked together to lift up entire planks of wood and fly them into place.

And so, the soldier bee army's construction squads were formed and began their work.

# CHAPTER TEN

# CON-BEE-NIENT COINCIDENCE

The First of the Fifth hovered before the apiary's Shrine of Bees with all the other queens hovering before her. They were, of course, not all too excited to be summoned from their hives . . . but their wings were not buzzing and their stingers were not subconsciously extending like they did in previous group meetings. It seemed they were growing more curious than suspicious with each meeting she held. The First of the Fifth didn't blame them for being suspicious. Previously, she had done everything in her power to suppress her rivals. Still, they needed to work together for the sake of the King and the hive of hives, so she was pleased that they were starting to lower their guard. Especially since today, she would be requesting their help.

"Want to raise new queens. Any queens ready to raise too? Can exchange drones this time. If need more honey, can give."

The First of the Fifth had countless tasks at this point. She needed to test and cross-pollinate new flowers. She needed to look into the dangerous karnuq's manipulation of fully processed honey. She needed to ensure that the new, slower queens continued growing at an acceptable pace. She needed to arrange the delivery of honey from the apiary to the flower meadow, even more so now that there was a new, significantly larger soldier type to raise. She needed to continue supplying honey to the King's honey traps. And, of course, to do all of this she needed to not only maintain but expand her honey production, all without sacrificing the quality that the King deserved.

So, she decided the first task to address would be her latest plan to raise new queens, not to send out and claim new territory, but to reinforce her own hive as her daughter, the Fourth of the Seventh, and the flower meadow queens had all done. Scaling up her operations would allow her to then tackle each of her tasks with more resources and attention than she could if she attempted to do so now.

At the same time, though, she was not going to demand that the apiary queens provide her with drones like she had before. All of them were donating honey to the flower meadow, so all of them could benefit from scaling up their operations. It would therefore benefit the entire hive of hives if all the apiary queens raised new daughters. And if the First of the Fifth had to give up some of her own honey to get them all ready, then she would.

The other queens watched her for a moment before the Second of the Sixth slowly began to dance.

". . . Have enough honey to raise queens and drones. Can't expand deliveries to flower meadow at same time, though."

The other queens looked at the Second of the Sixth for a moment, and then slowly began to report their hives' statuses as well. The queens that were still baseline monster bees generally had sufficient honey to raise more queens. The queens that had evolved into more specialized types were a bit short of reserves due to the honey spent evolving all of their workers and, in the case of the digging and burning queens, moving their hives into new beehouses. Still, the situation was such that the First of the Fifth should be able to cover them . . . though, as the Second of the Sixth stated, they wouldn't be able to expand their deliveries to the flower meadow at the same time. She'd have to ask the Conduit about that, as doing so could delay them from raising lancers. For perhaps the first time, the First of the Fifth found herself short of honey, compounding the need to scale up their operations.

Coincidentally, the Conduit arrived just then. The First of the Fifth happily saluted to her. At least they'd be able to ask her right away, while they were all still gathered.

"Hi! Apiary queens want to expand? King wants to build new hives, expand old ones!"

The First of the Fifth froze at the Conduit's words and began to tremble.

"King . . . wants us to expand?"

"Yes!"

The First of the Fifth's mind went blank. She had come up with the same idea as the King? The King was now going to build them new palaces for exactly the purpose she had gathered the queens? The King was . . . *asking* them about it, indicating he planned to collaborate with them on the new palaces as he had for the flower meadow queens?

The good fortune . . . was just too much.

Belissar stayed a bit to help the soldier bees and karnuq work together. It didn't take long before the bees were helping the karnuq build a house's roof. Belissar nodded and then took his leave. The flower meadow queens were, after all, not the only bees he planned to speak with today.

He stopped by to check in on the bumblebees, who were doing great. Bumblebee workers now filled the field and gathered from the flowers, each happily spinning around him when he approached. The queens themselves were growing rapidly. Each was now almost the size of a monster bee soldier already.

That caused Belissar to rub his chin. He wondered if the bumblebee queens would be able to raise soldiers, or any of the other special bee types the monster bee queens could. How about sprayers, communers, lancers, or gardeners? He supposed he would find out soon, as the bumblebee queens were nearing the size the monster bee queens had hit before they started raising their soldiers.

After that, he made his way to the apiary, where Niobee had just finished speaking with the queens there. The First of the Fifth was lying flat on the ground with her legs splayed out, so Niobee flew up to him instead.

"King! Apiary bees wanted to expand, want new queens to live with them! So, can make hives bigger?"

Belissar smiled and nodded.

"Of course, sounds perfect. We'll start upgrading them into bee apartments, then."

Niobee then slowed down a bit.

"Though . . . they said can't give more honey to flower meadow than doing now. Won't be able to help raise lancers."

"Ah . . ."

Belissar paused and rubbed his chin for a moment. That was something to consider, then. But he had to make his choice quickly as he saw the apiary queens begin to stir, since he knew they'd prioritize his plans over their own.

"Um, they'd also need to evolve gardeners for themselves, too, right? I think we should expand first, focus on getting their hives going."

"Okay!"

Well, slower lancers meant a slower expansion purification . . . or fewer options should another emergency purification come about. But Belissar hoped that Beero's new lightning attack would cover them for the latter, so he was willing to wait on the former. If the apiary queens expanded, that would mean more honey for the gardeners and lancers, as well as anything new they got from the next expansion. But, well, Belissar didn't think of all that until after making the decision. The truth was he'd rather the bees focus on what they wanted to do than drop everything for his own plans.

And indeed, the apiary queens would have plenty of their own work to do in the future. Because Belissar had received reports from the bees, and even a message from the tower, that there were several new cross-pollinated flowers now.

A new sleepy chamomile flower had bloomed that slowly pulsed with a faint glow. A light mist condensed around the latest cloudberry and sweetvetch flowers. But there was one in particular that drew Belissar's attention. One whose changes were so great that the tower itself now acknowledged them.

*New plant detected. Slime Flower is now available.*

A new mana flower had sprouted up among the gelatinous heather. Faintly glowing nectar seemed to ooze out of its center, almost a jelly rather than a liquid, and even its stems and leaves appeared moist. Belissar walked over to observe it more closely.

### Slime Flower

**Type:** Slime, Nature, Trap, Spawner

**Mana Upkeep:** 20 per node (40 due to Blessing of Bees),
10 (20 due to Blessing of Bees) to enable
in compatible rooms

*A flower that concentrates its mana into thickening its sap, which will spill out and engulf any creature that damages it. This effect extends partially to its nectar as well, which, if left to pool in sufficient quantities, may eventually condense into a slime core. The slime will carry the flower's seeds along with it as it begins to move, spreading the seeds around while also hunting nearby pests, further protecting the flower.*

Belissar couldn't help but stare at the description. A flower . . that spawned slimes? In fact . . . a flower that was itself a monster spawner.

Just . . . what? How had this happened? How was this possible? Belissar just stared in stunned silence for a good minute before shrugging. He was in a Tower of the Gods, raising bees that could understand human speech, grow as large as dogs, spray venom, and use magic. Why exactly wouldn't a slime-spawning flower be possible? He couldn't answer that, so he decided not to worry about it.

Besides, said flower was extremely expensive. Apparently, since it counted as a monster spawner and was not bee-related, the Blessing of Bees was working against it. Yet Belissar checked his mana and it hadn't changed since yesterday. Apparently, having bred the flower via cross-pollination didn't count and so it wasn't costing him. Any additional ones would, however.

He decided he would take it. It was a bit unfortunate that it was in the apiary instead of the flower meadow, though he could move the whole gelatinous heather node it grew out of if he wanted to. He was also slightly concerned about the description. Would the sap, nectar, or slimes try to hurt the bees? The bees wouldn't try to eat the flower, so he didn't think so. And would the slimes listen to him like the bees did? Would they be considered part of the tower at all, given they were spawning from a flower that he hadn't specifically spawned? Well, the new queens raised by the spawned queens were, so hopefully that would be the case here too. Belissar would have to keep a close eye on things to make sure, though.

Because as long as the slimes did get along with the rest of the tower's residents . . . then he had just gotten a new monster spawner for free. Cross-pollination was proving to be a better and better perk with each new flower that grew. If Belissar needed any convincing that the apiary queens deserved to expand, then this would have done it.

Not that Belissar would ever need convincing that his bees deserved nice things.

# A QUESTIONABLE BEE-CISION

The Fourth of the Seventh rotated about in place, glancing all around her. A wall of wax now covered the one exposed entrance of their little alcove, protecting the interior from the elements. Cracks and gaps in the existing rock walls had been patched with wax and propolis for a tight seal all around, while workers continued to line the walls with more. Some honeycomb had been built and workers were currently beating their wings to dry the nectar even as the foragers brought more.

It was a humble hive, especially when compared to the palaces of the King, but it was a functioning one. The scouts would now have a warm and dry place to rest and plentiful honey to drink, which meant they would not have to return all the way to their hive in the orchard each day. They would be able to fly farther than ever before and search the area for new flowers—and more. So, the Fourth of the Seventh's first task was now complete.

The Fourth of the Seventh needed to decide on her next move. Part of her wanted to rush out into the Beyond now that the mini-hive was established, but the greater part of her . . . wished to return now. The Beyond was filled with all sorts of things she had never seen and proved every bit as exciting as she had dreamed. And yet, she missed the workers she had left behind, especially her communer. She missed the First of the Fifth's First Daughter, who was always happy and cheerful whenever the Fourth of the Seventh saw her. Sure, she could keep tabs on her workers through the communer's daily reports, but the Fourth of the Seventh wanted to see them herself, to dance with them and brush their antennas.

Her own instincts were pulling on her as well, for it had been a while since she had last laid an egg. She may have wanted to see the world as a worker would, but that did not mean she disliked her own job, and it had been far too long since she had done it. But . . . she did not want to lay her eggs here. As much as she wanted to see the Beyond, she preferred that her children grow in the warm embrace of the King's realm.

And so, she danced to a newly-raised communer she brought to the mini-hive.

"Okay, going back now. Tell others?"

The newly-raised communer danced a salute dance and relayed her orders. The Fourth of the Seventh almost immediately felt mana flow toward her, sent by her first communer back home.

*"Really?! Queen coming home already?!"*

She danced happily as she replied. "Yes! Mini-hive set up, want to check on hive!"

The first communer didn't respond, but she could perceive a mixed sense of shock and happiness coming in through the mana. She decided she would head back even faster. So, she gathered up her escort of soldiers and workers, and they set off to return to the King's realm.

She could not help but shiver and shake about as she passed through the huge entrance and felt the full embrace of the King's mana once again. As much as she wanted to see the world beyond, this was the place where she belonged.

She flew up through the special entrance to the bee barracks, barely dancing a greeting to the flower meadow bees in the area before zipping into the orchard. She was about to turn and head for the grove when something caught her eye.

There, on the ground, was a single bee. Their antennas were drooping, and their wings were moving slowly and not providing any lift. They were slowly crawling onto a flower that had fallen from one of the nearby trees, sticking out their proboscis to try and drink whatever scraps of nectar might be left within.

The Fourth of the Seventh immediately dove down toward the bee and flew around.

"Worker okay?! Hurt?! Need help?!"

The bee stumbled a bit as they tried to respond.

"Q-Queen . . ."

One of her workers buzzed their wings and flew in front of her.

"Queen, is not worker. Is drone."

The Fourth of the Seventh stopped her dance, her antennas twitching.

"Drone? But new queens already mated. How alive?"

The drone was still stumbling but managed to pull off a dance.

"W-When got outside . . . all queens left. C-Couldn't find any . . ."

The Fourth of the Seventh paused. Ah, that was right, when she was laying queens and drones with the First of the Fifth's First Daughter she had realized at one point that she had miscounted, and laid an extra drone egg just in case. The extra drone must have hatched too late for the wave of queens.

"Okay, then come back to hive with us! Can wait for next time!"

The workers and soldiers all turned to face their queen. One of the workers slowly danced in the air.

"Is drone, Queen. Can't work, can't fight, can't help. Will be useless for long time . . ."

But the Fourth of the Seventh held her ground.

"Is okay! Not good for normal hive, but we hive of hives! All bees help all bees! Even drone!"

The drone himself stumbled at that.

"Q-Queen . . . is true. C-Can't help, couldn't mate. Don't need to . . ."

But the Fourth of the Seventh landed by the drone and brushed his antennas with hers.

"Is okay! Let me help now, you help later! Find new way to help!"

The Fourth of the Seventh was not ignorant. She knew, like all bees, that drones were destined to die, and she had no issue sending them out for that purpose. At the same time, though, she had watched the King save wounded soldiers who couldn't fight anymore. She had received access to flowers from the First of the Fifth when her hive was small and humble. And even now, the First of the Fifth's First Daughter was watching over her hive on her behalf. So, if she saw a bee before her who needed help, she would not refuse it. Even if they were a drone doomed to die.

The drone shrank down, lying on the ground.

". . . Can't fly. Should leave here."

The Fourth of the Seventh responded by crouching down in front of the drone, exchanging pheromones instead of dancing.

"Is okay! Climb on, will carry!"

The workers and soldiers began buzzing their wings while the drone shrank down even further. But the Fourth of the Seventh didn't move, so eventually, the drone slowly climbed on, nearly slipping and falling as he struggled to hold his grip. But, eventually, he was settled on her back, and the Fourth of the Seventh took off once again.

"Okay, let's go home everyone!"

The workers and soldiers glanced at the drone and then at their queen, but they said nothing more and followed as the Fourth of the Seventh took off. To be fair, this was not the craziest idea their queen had ever had.

The First of the Fifth's First Daughter and the Fourth of the Seventh's first communer were waiting for her by the entrance, and the three proceeded to crawl all over one another in happy dances. Only after all three had calmed down did the communer look at the bee on the Fourth of the Seventh's back.

"Queen? Why carrying drone?"

"Saw on way here! Drone was born too late for mating, was starving. So brought back to help! Will help all bees, like King!"

The First of the Fifth's First Daughter's antennas twitched again.

"Is drone but . . . is also Fourth of Seventh's drone so . . . will take care! Will make sure is okay!"

The communer, for her part, stood completely still for a moment. The other workers all turned to her, uncertain how to respond. Eventually, the communer began to dance.

"I . . . see. Well, queen is queen. Come, will have brood tender take a look and feed. Then will find . . . something for drone to do."

"Okay!"

The communer climbed onto the Fourth of the Seventh's back to observe the drone and check for injuries as the Fourth of the Seventh carried them inside, and all the other workers went back to their jobs. The drone, who could hardly move at this point, could only emit some weak pheromones.

"Sorry . . ."

But the communer just brushed his antennas.

"Queen has decided. And has had stranger ideas before that worked. So, get better and then find way for drone to help, okay?"

". . . Okay."

The drone shrank down at the gazes of all the workers around them, but since both queens and the communer were there the workers figured it was handled and moved on. The drone was brought to the brood tenders, who determined that he was simply malnourished and running low on mana. He was led to a cell of mana honey and made to drink, which slowly pulled him back from the brink.

And so, for the first time within the tower, a drone survived past his first flight and returned to the hive of his birth.

# THE LAST OF BEES

The next day, Belissar spoke with the First of the Fifth and the apiary queens about upgrading their beehouses into bee apartments. While they decided the general structure of the new bee apartment was fine, the First of the Fifth pointed out numerous small optimizations that would assist with better honey production. Multiple entrances so that foragers coming and going wouldn't get in each other's way, isolated trays for honey types that could impact their surroundings, like burning mana honey, slight rearrangements for better airflow, and other such improvements. Belissar took all of this into account and, once the structure had been fully planned out, began the construction work.

He actually had the DP to just upgrade the beehouses outright, but he decided to build them manually. Since they had wood trees in the orchard, and the flower meadow queens wanted to help with construction anyway, there was no point in spending extra DP just to cut down on resources and effort. Besides, he also enjoyed having a personal hand in the bees' abode. It made them happy, and given all they were doing for him, that was the least he could do.

There was the question of the hives for the digging and burning queens, seeing as those were dug into the ground instead of being wooden structures, but the digging queen herself provided the solution. Her workers, as per their name, were quite good at digging, so they could easily expand the subterranean hives. Belissar would just need to provide them with additional frames and maybe an extra entrance or two, and they could handle the rest. The queen offered to do so for the Third of the Sixth's hive as well, but both Belissar and the Third of the Sixth decided to wait. After all, he had plans for the future regarding her abode, so they both agreed to wait until Belissar could build his envisioned volcano room before making major expansions to her hive.

And so, Belissar set off on his task for the coming days or weeks until his tower would be ready for the next expansion.

There was one queen, however, who was not ready for either the expansion or the move to bee apartments. The Fourth Queen of the Eighth Spawner's First Dynasty, the first of her line, had the dubious distinction of being the last queen spawned in the apiary. She had even been the lastborn in all of the King's realm until the King had raised the bumblebee queens.

But that had been little comfort for her. The bumblebee queens were an entirely different species from the rest of them . . . and even now, they had begun to grow at a rapid pace. They were already larger than her and showed no signs of slowing down. They, unlike her, appeared to possess a unique advantage.

Which left her, once again, as the least remarkable of the King's queens. Born last, the slowest to grow, the slowest to expand her hive. The queen who lived farthest from the King in the apiary, born too late to even participate when the prime territory was claimed. The queen who had been least likely to receive a magical palace. The queen who, even after receiving a magical palace, still lagged behind the others.

And that was a problem, for she was about to be left behind once again. The First of the Fifth's superiority went without saying, an existence beyond anything she could ever hope to achieve. The Fourth of the Seventh had set out and claimed an entire room to her name. The Second of the Sixth and others had now set themselves apart by evolving on the honey of special flowers, and they had received entire patches of flowers to themselves from the King as a result. The Third of the Sixth was going to receive an entire room like the Fourth of the Seventh.

New flowers had grown and were now available, but the Fourth of the Eighth would never reach them. The First of the Fifth assigned them in order of productivity, granting them to the queens who donated most during the daily honey deliveries to the flower meadow. The Fourth of the Eighth and her children worked as hard as they could, but so did all the others, and so her contributions always fell short of theirs. She would be the last to gain exclusive access to a special flower, if ever.

And now the King was expanding their hives, which would lead to an explosion of growth. The First of the Fifth and the other highly successful queens would form huge joint hives with their children, doubling in size and productivity nearly overnight. The queens of more middling success had gathered together and come up with a plan to respond: Like the Fourth of the Seventh and the First of the Fifth's First Daughter, they would join their hives together, which would allow them to compete.

None of them had invited the Fourth of the Eighth to participate, of course.

For her, the expansion would just be herself and however many queens she could raise. Which wasn't many. She needed donations from the First of the Fifth to even participate in the expansion in the first place—which, of course, would likely cause the First of the Fifth to write her off completely when it came to acquiring special plants. So, she would have nothing to set herself apart, and her hive just didn't have the bee-power to keep up with either the powerful single queens or the newly forming joint hives.

Well, if that happened it happened. She was grateful that she was even allowed to participate in the expansion, so she couldn't particularly complain if she wasn't in a position to take advantage of it. And, as the lastborn, she was more than used to her own circumstances. At first, she had completely accepted her place in the world.

That had changed, though. The Fourth of the Seventh had once been a queen in the very same position as herself. All it had taken was one set of flowers from the First of the Fifth to completely change the trajectory of her hive. And now, the Fourth of the Seventh was held in as high esteem as the Firstborn and the First of the Fifth, one of the great queens who ruled over the others. The Third of the Sixth was now set to do so as well, after having spent so long as one of the queens without palaces like herself. So now . . . now the Fourth of the Eighth couldn't help but imagine what could be. Couldn't help but wonder if there was any way she might be able to change her fate. Any way she might be able to set herself apart from the others and become more than just the lastborn.

The obvious way to do so was with the special flowers, but she couldn't think of any way to gain access to them. She needed the flowers to set herself apart, but she needed to set herself apart for the First of the Fifth to grant her the flowers. If only there was some way she could acquire special honey without the flowers . . .

She froze. Because . . . she now remembered that there *was* a way. The King, mighty and miraculous as he was, could create honey out of nothing but mana. He required no flowers and no nectar to do so. And while acquiring honey from *the King himself* was not something she could even imagine, he was not the only one who could do this. He was not the only one who had learned such a secret.

Before she knew it, the Fourth of the Eighth was beating her wings and rising into the air. Her idea was a long shot and required her to make an incredibly insolent request. And yet . . . it was a chance to change the course of her hive. Maybe her only chance. So, before she knew it, she was flying toward the exit of the apiary.

Beero was about to start another training session with the other wounded soldiers when one of them began dancing, signaling that someone was approaching. Beero turned around and her antennas began to twitch. One of the queens was flying toward her, and not one she recognized from the flower meadow.

"Hello, am Fourth of Eighth from apiary."

"Hello, am Beero. How can help?"

The Fourth of the Eighth slowly landed on the ground with her antennas twitching. Her wings buzzed a bit and she fidgeted in place, but eventually, she began to dance.

". . . Have . . . request."

"Okay, what request?"

The Fourth of the Eighth paused, and then began to dance rapidly with her wings beating.

"Beero can make magic honey, right? And can make tiny-lightnings? Can make honey with tiny-lightnings? If so, can get some? Know it's bad to ask for, but could really, *really* use. Just a little bit, just enough for a worker. Will give honey in exchange, as much as can. Will help however can."

The queen was dancing so rapidly Beero barely managed to catch what she was saying. But once she processed what was going on, Beero froze.

That . . . was right, wasn't it? She could make honey now. She had been so focused on trying to get back into the fight that she had forgotten about that. Hadn't she already seen some of her sisters evolve into maddening soldiers by drinking special honey? That . . . probably would have been a better way to give her comrades lightning than zapping them and hoping they'd endure.

But what was done was done, and they had all endured as well as she had, so Beero put that aside and considered the Fourth of the Eighth's request. She needed only a moment to decide.

"Yes, can make honey with tiny-lightnings. Will give as much as can make."

There was no question at all. Beero had been supported by her own hive when there was nothing she could do. Even before she was injured, she had relied on the workers for her meals, and afterward she had been fed vast amounts of honey when she could neither work nor protect the hive of hives. So, now that she could do *both*, and a member of the hive of hives was asking for her help, she would never even consider turning them down. Indeed, it would be her honor to now provide honey for the workers as they had always done for her.

The Fourth of the Eighth suddenly stopped her dance and stared at her.

"Wait . . . what? Really? Really will give?!"

Beero danced a salute.

"Of course! All bees help hive of hives, however can!"

So today, instead of practicing their lightning sting, Beero led the wounded soldiers in the honey-creating spell. And the Fourth of the Eighth began to hope that maybe, just maybe, she might become more than the lastborn after all.

# CHAPTER ELEVEN

# UN-BEE-LIEVABLE DEVELOPMENTS

And so, several days passed. Belissar was currently checking in on the bumblebee meadow, as he had taken to calling it. Bumblebee workers buzzed and circled around him as he walked through the meadow. Belissar responded by creating some magic honey in his hand for them to take a sip of, smiling as he walked. Soon, he arrived by the nests, and the queens crawled out to greet him.

Belissar felt a breeze blow into his face as large wings beat in the air, shadows passing over him as large shapes circled overhead. A moment later, huge balls of fuzz gently landed on his back and shoulders. He cupped his hand, filled it with honey again, and lifted it up so the bumblebee queens could get a sip as well. The queens had grown dramatically over the past week and were now the largest bees in the dungeon. They weren't yet as large as the incoming lancers would be . . . but they were still growing.

So far, only the bumblebee queens had grown to that extent. The workers were a bit larger than normal bumblebees, but ultimately still bee-sized. However . . . Belissar had noticed that recently the bumblebees had started to build some larger wax cups. He couldn't wait to see what they planned to do with them.

But, most importantly, the bumblebees were happy and growing well, and that was enough for Belissar. He laughed a bit as the queens crawled over him and he gently scratched their backs.

Belissar did not spend the entire week just checking on the bumblebee queens, however. The apiary had been transformed. Previously, around fifteen beehouses had been scattered around the area behind the farmhouse. Now the apiary looked like a small village, with ten structures even larger than the farmhouse now arranged around the flower patches and the hole leading to the third-floor dirt tunnels where the digging and burning bees each had their own underground hive.

Belissar and the soldier bees had worked hard, and all of the apiary beehouses were now upgraded to bee apartments. The soldier bees grew increasingly efficient at lifting and arranging the wood, to the point that Belissar had to ask the karnuq to help with the woodworking in order to keep pace. Fortunately, since they had been offering Belissar a portion of any wood they cut for themselves, he had plenty of raw materials, so the work really took off.

As for the digging queen, her workers had managed to expand their home at the same time. She had even raised a few digging soldiers with thick, tough mandibles well-suited to larger-scale excavation. Belissar had simply needed to fill in the space with some frames and add a few more doors to some new entrances to make her home eligible for upgrading as well.

Of course, the other apiary queens were not idle, either. One day during the week, the First of the Fifth called him over. Hovering beside her was another queen whose hairs had turned a dull white color.

"This is First of Eighth, managed to evolve."

Belissar smiled and held out his hand. The First of the Eighth hesitated but eventually flew over and landed on his palm. He took a closer look . . .

### Sedating Monster Bee Queen

| | | | |
|---|---|---|---|
| *Vitality:* | *Minimal* | *Defense:* | *Minimal* |
| *Strength:* | *Minimal* | *Resistance:* | *Minimal* |
| *Speed:* | *Average* | *Special:* | *Minor* |
| *Magic:* | *Minimal* | | *Sedating Poison Sting* |
| | | *Notable Skills:* | *Brood Mother* |
| | | | *Command Offspring* |

*A monster bee raised on honey with soporific compounds.*
*It now produces the compounds present in the honey in its own venom glands.*
*Its stings, in addition to the normal bee venom effects, may cause numbness,*
*drowsiness, and in very high dosages, unconsciousness.*
*This one is a queen and lays sedating variant offspring by default.*

He grinned at her.

"Guess you evolved from the sleepy chamomile?"

The First of the Eighth happily danced a confirmation. Belissar reached down and brushed her back.

"Great work, that will really help! And thanks to you for helping her and showing me, First of the Fifth!"

Belissar chuckled as both queens burst out into happy dances at his gratitude.

The First of the Eighth evolving was not the only way the apiary had grown, either. While Belissar and the soldier bees expanded their homes, the apiary queens had been laying new queens and drones, which had just hatched today.

Belissar frowned a bit as he saw the drones fall to the ground after completing their tasks. He thought of taking them to the memorial . . . only to watch their bodies fade into sparks of mana as their power was spent. But then he noticed the sparks were not moving at random, but rather drifting toward the nearest Shrine of Bees. He turned his tower sight to the memorial in the flower meadow and found new numbers written upon a new pillar. He took a deep breath and nodded.

After that night's daily purification, Belissar walked over to the memorial.

"Let's thank the drones who gave their lives today."

Niobee paused, and then began a slow, unsteady dance.

"King wants to honor . . . drones? But . . . drones don't fight. Don't help . . ."

Belissar chuckled and held out his hand for Niobee to land on.

"No . . . but they have an important job to do, you know? The new queens couldn't build hives without them, and they perish in the process. That, I think, deserves some recognition."

Niobee spun around rapidly.

"Really?! Drones important?! Help queens?! How?!"

She turned to the queens. The Firstborn, the First of the Fifth, and the other queens danced their confirmation.

"Spawner queens fine, but new queens have to mate with drones before raising workers."

Niobee continued rapidly dancing around in circles.

"Useless drones . . . not useless? Drones . . . important, even though don't work? Queens need drones to raise workers?!"

Belissar chuckled and nodded, then pointed to the new pillar.

"Yep, the God of Bees says so too."

Niobee spun around a few more times and then came to a stop, lowering herself to lie on Belissar's hand for a moment before dancing slowly.

". . . Okay. Then . . . honor . . . drones?"

Belissar smiled as he answered.

"We'll honor all bees."

Belissar and a hesitant Niobee then led the bees in one of their memorials for the bees who had given their lives for the hive of hives, though not in any battle. And, unbeknownst to Belissar, a certain bee dragged along by the Fourth of the Seventh was present as well, his eyes fixed upon Belissar, the memorial, and the dance of honor.

The rest of the tower continued working as well. The new queens raised by the Fourth of the Seventh and the First of the Fifth's First Daughter had grown and begun to raise workers of their own. Worker bees now spread out beyond the grove where they lived, visiting the rows of apple trees and exchanging pollen between those trees and the mana flowers in the grove.

The Fourth of the Seventh had begun the scouting missions in earnest now that the mini-hive was established. Niobee now included bees from her hive in the morning reports to Belissar, so he was receiving daily reports from the scouts. So far, they mostly just told him about finding more trees and flowers, but Belissar preferred that to finding anything dramatic . . . and potentially dangerous. Additionally, the scouts had begun to identify different flowers and trees that Belissar didn't have in the tower. The Fourth of the Seventh and her escort soldiers were gathering seeds and samples to carry back each time she returned to her hive. It would still be a while before Belissar could spawn a pine tree, but he'd eventually be able to increase the diversity of the tower's flora.

And, of course, the karnuq were not idle either. Chief Rohsuak's new blessings improved the amount of mana she could use each day, increasing how much wood she could dry. This, combined with Muuraqi's growing ability to manipulate stone, boosted the karnuq's construction efforts, and they had a small village going by now. Additionally, they had started on metalworking. At the moment, it mostly consisted of cold-working copper into simple tools, but they had also started constructing a stone furnace for some more sophisticated techniques. Their next expedition to the Underway would be largely for scouting and hunting, but the karnuq also planned to try and pick up some clay they had passed previously. If Belissar could absorb and create clay, pottery would be in the works as well.

But ultimately, the greatest growth came not from any of them, but from the flower meadow.

The Firstborn, and indeed all the flower meadow queens, gathered together now before a new tray, a brand-new addition to the bee barracks. The flower meadow queens had requested the material and then had their soldiers assemble the tray themselves, not wanting to distract the King from his work on the apiary queens' homes. And, as more and more of their soldiers participated in the construction work elsewhere, they found they had the bee-power to make something simple like this themselves.

The tray was the same shape as any other built by the King, but with one very key difference: it was far larger. Not only did it frame a larger area, but the frames themselves were also noticeably thicker. When filled with wax, it became more of a box than a tray, expanding out in all three dimensions as the combs were built far deeper than normal.

It took great efforts to build and even greater efforts to fill, but the flower meadow hives had seen it done. They had even made the radical decision to cease laying soldier eggs altogether. The queens had concluded that, at the moment, the soldier bee army was large enough. They had enough to completely encircle an invader while keeping several additional encirclements' worth of soldiers in the reserve force. More soldiers would not make them much stronger . . . and they needed the honey.

They instead focused on reorganizing and expanding their workers. The First of the Fifth's feedback had been *incredibly* enlightening. The Firstborn knew honey-making wasn't her forte, but she hadn't realized just how far behind she had fallen on account of her negligence. Their production initially dipped a bit, as they had much to reorganize, but once they had implemented the First of the Fifth's feedback they saw their honey output *soar*. The flower meadow queens then all agreed to expand their worker numbers to a level that would keep the workers from scrambling and becoming disorganized in the future.

And since they weren't raising more soldiers, they took all that additional honey and stockpiled it. The apiary hadn't cut its donations either, so combined with their own increases in production the flower meadow's combs were soon overflowing with honey.

And that brought them to today. Each of the queens had taken the oldest, strongest, and most experienced of her soldiers and encased them in cells far too large for any existing bee, packed with the richest mana honey available in the bee barracks. The soldiers had slept away in their sealed-up cells for several days now, but the Firstborn sensed that the time was near.

The sheer amount of work had taken her mind off of her failure, but now that things were winding down it weighed on her once more. Their army had failed more than once against the intruders. Would that continue in the future? Would they always remain one step behind the invaders threatening the hive of hives? Was it impossible for them to defend the King?

The Firstborn didn't know. Her record wasn't the greatest, so she could not claim confidence in facing whatever lay ahead. But all she knew was that, even if it were impossible, even if she would fail, she would not stop trying. Beero, a soldier from her own hive, had gone from a cripple unfit for battle to a warrior who could bring lightning itself down upon their foes. The Firstborn would do no less. She would spare no effort to overcome their present weakness.

And the first of those efforts would show themselves today.

The wax covering one of the cells began to bulge. Workers and even soldier bees moved to tear open the huge cap covering an equally huge cell. A moment later, a bee even larger than the Firstborn began to crawl out. The flower meadow queens stood in silence, eyes poring over the new bee even as the workers cleaned off the last remnants of honey sticking to her body. This . . . this was a larger bee than any of them had ever seen, as large as the smallest invaders even. Her chitin was sleek, her wings long and firm, but it was her abdomen that drew the Firstborn's attention. Her stinger was not retracted and hidden like the rest of theirs. No, it couldn't have been hidden even had the bee tried. The stinger was built into the back of the abdomen across its entire width, extending out in a long and sleek cone ending in a sharp tip. That tip alone was as long as an entire soldier bee.

The Firstborn would not content herself with believing that this was enough. But she did allow herself to hope that it was a strong step in the right direction.

Especially as the other cells in the massive tray began to bulge out as well.

# CHAPTER TWELVE

# BEE-GIN THE EXPANSION

**B**elissar watched as eight lancer bees climbed high into the sky. They then angled themselves so that their stingers were facing down and began beating their wings in the other direction. They fell from the sky like arrows from a bow, plunging down as fast as they could. In but a moment, they struck and plunged their stingers deep into the ground.

Belissar crossed his arms and grunted. This was what he'd been waiting for, and indeed the lancers seemed quite powerful. They were far larger than any other bee, even the bumblebee queens. They were even as large or larger than the mini-shades that the karnuq challengers had faced previously. He guessed the lancers could match any shade he'd seen before . . . most likely. They might have trouble hitting a cat or bird-shade depending on how fast it was moving. But anything they did hit would likely not survive, or at least not emerge unscathed.

And yet, he couldn't rid himself of that last, lingering anxiety. Every expansion purification shade was a shade he had never seen before, so who knew what this next one would do? Would it be another shade that could defeat everything he could throw at it?

But he shook his head and forced himself to uncross his arms. The fact was, he didn't know . . . and couldn't know. His bees and his tower had reached the point he had wanted, so there was nothing for it but to trust in them now. He turned to Niobee and the Firstborn and nodded.

"Well done. I wasn't expecting you to evolve these until later, so, um, nice work. We'll go ahead and fight an expansion purification, then. Let's tell everyone to prepare. Now . . . do your best."

Belissar was about to warn the Firstborn that this would be a shade they had never seen before and to be careful, but he decided against it. The flower meadow queens were the experts at this point and had seen more than enough new shades to know that would be the case. So, he decided to just trust them to know what to do.

The Firstborn danced a solemn salute dance and flew off to the bee barracks, while Niobee flew off to inform the orchard and apiary bees. Belissar himself went to speak with the karnuq and let them know of the plan as well.

He hoped they wouldn't need Chief Rohsuak's help this time, but he was going to make sure they were ready for anything.

Later on in the day, everyone finished their preparations. The soldier bee army was arranged in front of the first-floor flower meadow's entrance, while Beero and her wounded lightning bees stood on top of their platform. Chief Rohsuak and the karnuq were waiting by the bee barracks, with Chief Rohsuak standing next to a couple of mana honeycomb trays delivered by the apiary queens. The Second of the Sixth, the medicinal queen, had brought most of her hive and was waiting on standby with medicinal honey.

Belissar had even removed the bees' secret tunnel that linked the bee barracks to the tower exit in the first-floor dirt tunnels. He didn't think a shade would find it, and the bees *should* be able to handle anything small enough to fit in it, but he didn't want to leave anything to chance. Anything he could do to ensure the bees' safety, he did.

He considered deploying the new digging soldiers to the dirt tunnels but decided against it. There were only a handful of them at the moment, and he somewhat doubted this purification could be handled by a single squad of soldier bees. Likewise, the burning, sedative, and bumblebee queens were still limited to workers at the moment, so they wouldn't be participating except in emergencies. The slime flower had also not spawned any slimes yet. Belissar was curious about that, but now was not the time to think on it.

For the time had come to launch the purification.

"Everyone ready?"

The bees and karnuq alike all saluted in their fashion. Belissar took a deep breath.

*Attempt expansion purification? Estimated purification strength: Small+.*

"Okay, here we go."

He confirmed, and the tower's mana lit up and the doors swung open as the tower's might poured out to confront the Hunger once more.

*Expansion purification attempt commencing.*

Without missing a beat, the Hunger crawled up the tower's mana to the gateway. Even though he was expecting it this time, Belissar still couldn't help but shiver. The Hunger wasted no time in coalescing. This shade was low to the ground, shorter than the turtle-shade had been, though wide enough around to match the wolf-shades despite its short legs. It had a smooth head with blazing orbs for eyes and a toothless set of jaws. It wiggled its body as it crawled on smooth, squat legs. Belissar, to his surprise, recognized the shape of the creature immediately. It was a salamander, no different than any other save for its enormous size relative to those Belissar knew. It didn't have any spikes or wings or extra fangs and claws. It didn't have any extra pairs of limbs or even an extra set of eyes.

But that did not mean it was normal. The mist of the Hunger surrounding it swirled and flowed with far greater speed than with the other shades. It flickered and lashed in ephemeral tongues. It appeared like . . . fire. As if black flames wrapped every inch of the shade's body. It even made the appropriate crackling noise.

Belissar gulped. If he was seeing what he thought he was seeing, Chief Rohsuak might not be able to help this time.

*Expansion purification begun. Remaining hostiles: 1*

The shade let out a roar and then began scrambling across the ground. Black flames were left in its trail, appearing to scorch the very dirt as the Hunger spread where the flames burned. Belissar held his breath as the shade approached the first pit trap. If they were lucky, maybe it would fall in . . . though he might not be able to set this shade on fire even if it did.

But he wouldn't have the chance to find out. Upon stepping into the pit, the shade just placed its feet on the walls . . . and stuck right to them. It thus crawled along the walls over the pit without slowing down. It seemed they would have to fight after all.

Belissar began to confer with Chief Rohsuak, Metsaitti, and the bees as the shade made its way through the dirt tunnels. It was faster than the turtle-shade, but slower than all the rest that had come before it, so they had plenty of time. Chief Rohsuak stated she had burned fire-type creatures in the past, so it wasn't guaranteed it would be immune to her . . . but that had been in her prime, and it had always taken a lot out of her even back then. Her latest blessing from the God of Fire aside, she couldn't state with confidence that she'd be able to deal with this shade. So, it might be up to his bees to handle it.

Belissar wasn't sure if they could. He didn't know how powerful those flames were in general; the first-floor dirt tunnels didn't have much flammable material, so they had no baseline. At least, not until the shade passed by one of the wall-mounted sticky honey traps. The shade was not moving fast enough to escape the flow of honey and so was caught dead-on.

The honey caught fire and began to burn before it even touched the shade. Some of the honey managed to splatter on its body, causing it to growl, but was quickly burned away. The shade was only slowed for a moment, and showed no signs of intoxication from the loaded maddening honey as it continued through the dirt tunnels.

Belissar was not encouraged by this turn of events.

Eventually, the shade made its way to the final stretch. As it neared the exit to the tunnels, a squad of sprayers took up positions and launched their attack across the entire tunnel. Once again, even their venom started to burn in the air as it approached the shade. And since they sprayed less and thinner fluid than the sticky honey traps, none of it managed to hit the shade proper.

And then the shade responded by unleashing an attack of its own. It opened its mouth and a cone of black flames filled the tunnel. The sprayers were forced to flee at maximum speed as the fire burst from the tunnel, setting the flower meadow beyond ablaze. A black brush fire started up and was soon spreading across the first quarter of the flower meadow, leaving corrupted ground in its wake.

The flower meadow queens were gathered together. Since each queen could order her soldiers through her communers now, they all worked together to command the soldier bee army during battle, with one queen appointed to make overall decisions. The commanding queen ordered the withdrawal, the other queens all danced their commands, and then the sprayers in the army pulled back, all in sync and without delay. The soldier bees moved forward in their place.

Soon, the shade stepped out into the flower meadow itself, wading into the burning flowers without pause. A squad of soldier bees attempted an attack run and managed to push through the smoke, their new fire resistance proving invaluable. But it was fire resistance, not immunity, so once the bees approached the shade its own flames began to assault them. The soldier bees did not immediately burn or catch fire but pulled back as they realized the danger was still too great.

The flower meadow queen in charge for today, the First of the Fourth, turned toward Belissar and began to dance.

"Soldiers can't reach without taking losses. Want to send lancers but might get hurt. Can?"

Belissar frowned as he watched the shade crawl through the burning flower meadow. So, the soldiers couldn't approach and the sprayers' attack couldn't make it through the flames. They could still try Beero's lightning bees. But that was risky as well, since the shade could breathe fire at a distance. If the wooden platform caught fire, Beero and the others would not have much time to even flee, much less pull off their lightning dance.

"Do you think the lancers will survive?"

The First of the Fourth didn't hesitate.

"Should, bigger and faster than soldiers. Should hit enemy before hurt too bad."

Belissar took a deep breath. The lancers might not die, but they'd certainly be hurt diving right into fire like that. It would probably be safer to see if Beero and the others could hit the shade with lightning first.

Or . . . would it? Belissar considered the fire breath attack, how far and how quickly it had moved. If the shade sent it directly toward the top of the wooden platform, could Beero and the others really finish their dance before then? If not, would the soldier bees even be able to evacuate them before the fire hit?

Either way, it seemed his bees were going to have to brave the flames if they wanted to take this shade down.

# CHAPTER THIRTEEN

# REJECT FEAR, EMBRACE BRAVER-BEE

**B**elissar furrowed his brow, trying to think as quickly as he could while the shade continued its advance. He ended up sighing and shaking his head. At the end of the day, it was just too risky. Why would he allow the lancers to jump into a literal fire, or the wounded and immobile lightning bees to face a fire breath attack, when he had another option? He opened his eyes and turned to ask Chief Rohsuak to intervene.

Until he caught sight of the bees.

The First of the Fourth was dipping, her wings beating slower and slower the longer Belissar remained silent. She was about to land on the ground at this point. The other bees were faltering as well, all of them either hovering as motionless as they could or else slowly dropping from the air. Even Niobee was uncharacteristically still, with only a slight sway to her hovering. Belissar frowned.

He recalled the past few weeks. He recalled how subdued the Firstborn and the flower meadow queens had been after the emergency purification. He recalled how hard Beero and the others had worked just to take part in the fighting once again.

He now thought of how they all would feel and act should Chief Rohsuak handle this purification as well. The bees who had made it their main mission to defend the tower from intruders, who had devoted all of their efforts to strengthening their army . . . held back from the fight without even deploying the newest bees.

He held his tongue and rubbed his chin once again. What was the right move here? Should he protect his bees no matter how it made them feel, or should he let them face unnecessary danger and harm so that they could feel useful? He closed his eyes and grunted to himself.

Well, the truth was he already knew the answer. He had been through this argument with himself before. He already knew what the bees wanted. He

already knew what the God of Bees wanted. He already knew what he was supposed to do. What the master and defender of a tower had to do. He just didn't
want to do it.

Belissar opened his eyes and turned to his bees, looking over the First of the
Fourth. Her drooping paused at his attention. He took a deep breath.

". . . Do it. Send in the lancers. Second of the Sixth, get your medicinal workers ready, we'll probably need them soon. Niobee, ask Beero if they can prepare
their spell ahead of time. If so, have them get started."

The First of the Fourth immediately shot up into the air, her wings once again
beating fast as she quickly saluted and began relaying commands. The Second of
the Sixth did likewise and then began arranging her workers. Niobee was already
dancing with a communer. Belissar slowly exhaled his breath.

At the end of the day, the only reason not to use the lancers was his own desire
to avoid seeing bees hurt. Chief Rohsuak may have gotten a new blessing, but she
also hadn't gotten any younger, and it would strain her if she had to keep handling purifications on his behalf. Besides, there was no guarantee her fire would
even work this time, and no guarantee the shade wouldn't attack her with its breath
attack while she was preparing her spell. Additionally, it was important to find
out exactly how strong the lancers were, and to allow the soldier bee army to continue fighting and growing.

And well . . . would he depress the bees for his own desire? Would he prioritize his own wants over the wants of both the bees and their god? Was it truly
kinder to hold them back from the battle they desperately wanted to fight?

Was he truly worried for the bees' sake, or was it that he just didn't want to
lose anything more himself? So, he gave the order. He had told himself he trusted
in his bees, so that is what he would do.

Behind him, Chief Rohsuak made a sad smile and whispered to herself, "Well
done, Sacred Den Master. Not everyone can bear the burden of leadership."

The bees soon responded to Belissar's command. The Second of the Sixth led
her medicinal workers closer to the battlefield, while the orchard hive's soldiers
carried trays of medicinal honey for them. Beero and the lightning bees began
their dance, holding a comb of lightning above their heads as they paused on the
final step.

The lancers, meanwhile, flew high into the sky, with the soldier bees clearing
the area so they could get an unobstructed view. They looked down with their
large eyes to observe their target's location, size, speed, and direction, as well as
how quickly it could turn. They swayed about in the air, testing how it moved
against their wings and chitin and checking for wind. With all calculations concluded, the bees turned so that their abdomens faced down and their wings and
heads were up and far away. They then began to dance to one another and arranged
themselves into a cross formation centered on the target: one bee in the center,

aiming directly at the target's core, two bees in front and behind, and two bees to either side, all aiming at an angle.

And then, as one, they stopped beating their wings. Their wing joints twisted to reverse the wings' angles, and then they swung them in the other direction. The five lancers plunged from the sky, beating their wings in reverse to increase their speed further. The air blew past them like gusts of wind and the view from their main eyes became a blur of golden light from the sun, the blue from the sky, and yellow and black streaks as they rushed past their smaller sisters, until special plates of chitin extended out to protect the big eyes. A small protrusion extended on the back of each of their heads, holding two smaller eyes just above the rest of their body. These eyes focused in on the shade, allowing the lancers to adjust their aim. Their legs mostly pressed tight against their bodies, but sometimes shifted and extended out, causing them to change angle as needed.

Down, down they dove as the smoke from the fires rose into their path. They ignored it, their antennas already safely tucked into special grooves on their faces to protect them mid-dive. Smoke burned through their tracheas, but their speed was such that it left as quickly as it came, and they had all taken a deep breath before the dive began in any case. They did lose sight of the target, but mana helped them stabilize their paths, ensuring that they would not drift off course so long as the target didn't either.

A moment later, they passed out of the smoke. The target had shifted slightly to the right, so all the lancers spread out their legs to tilt in that direction. Another moment later, they felt heat flicker against their chitin as they passed the first tongues of fire, but warm mana rose within them to counteract it.

And then, they struck.

The lancer to the left could not change her course quickly enough and fell short of the shade. The lancer to the right over adjusted to avoid colliding with the center bee, and so overshot the target. Both of these plunged into the ground. But the three bees on the center line all struck true. Their stingers plunged deep . . . and then out the other side of the shade. One in the center of its torso, one where the tail connected to the main body, and one right on its neck.

The shade didn't have time to even let out a sound as it crashed into the ground from the impact.

The lancers had no time to even verify the effect of their attack, however, for fire burned all around them. And this close to the center of the blaze, neither their thick chitin nor the warm mana within them proved a sufficient defense. The two side lancers pulled out of the ground fairly easily and took off quickly, with only minor singes and ash on their chitin.

The three center lancers found it more difficult. Black flames surged around them from the shade, engulfing them and lashing at their bodies. The warm mana concentrated on their wings and faces, leaving the rest of their body dependent solely on their chitin. They scrambled to take off again, but the shade dispersed underneath them, giving them nothing solid to push off of. They slowly rose into the air as the flames assaulted them, leaving parts of their chitin black and smoking. Every inch of their bodies burned.

But they pressed on, beating their wings as quickly as they could. Slowly, ever so slowly, they rose, but bit by bit they gained speed. And then, all of a sudden, they broke out of the flames and back into the smoke-filled air. Their bodies now burned from the lack of oxygen as their pre-dive breaths began to run out, but they had passed out of the fire.

They had made it.

And if the black fires dying down were any indication . . . they had *won*.

CHAPTER FOURTEEN

# DEFINITELY RANDOM BEE-WARDS

**B**elissar gulped as the lancers began their dive. He held his breath as they passed into the smoke, and then into the fire. He couldn't bring himself to watch them burn through his tower sight, so he just froze, not even breathing as they disappeared into the inferno and as a surge of black flames shot into the sky.

And then . . . the black flames began to die down. Two lancers pulled out of the fire from either side. Belissar still held his breath as he waited for the rest.

And then, finally, Belissar caught a glimpse of the other three. Burned and smoking, but still flying. He finally exhaled his breath and nearly fell to the ground, placing his hand on the wall of the bee barracks to steady himself.

"They made it."

And then, a moment later, he felt the tower's mana surging.

*Expansion successful.*
*Reward: Floor limit increased to 4. Receive one perk choice*
*and two random reward choices.*

He allowed himself a small smile.

"In fact . . . we won."

The bees began celebration dances, zipping through the air. The First of the Fourth began whizzing around him in a "King is best king!" dance. Chief Rohsuak and Metsaitti both smiled.

But Belissar's attention turned away from them all to focus on the lancers. They were flagging and dropping out of the air. The nearest soldier bees moved in and began pushing and pulling at them, helping to prop them up until they were clear of the flames below. The moment they cleared the first firebreak, they all but crashed into the ground. Belissar took off running in their direction, monitoring the situation with his tower sight until he could arrive.

The Second of the Sixth's workers immediately swarmed over the lancers, flaring their mana and giving the lancers their healing stings. Belissar could tell from the lancers' mana that they weren't in immediate danger of dying, but they were not in good condition either. Their chitin was burned, their wings were singed, and smoke still leaked out of their bodies. His heart began to pound as the scene came within sight of his eyes. Medicinal workers continued to rotate in and out as their mana and medicinal stings depleted, while the Fourth of the Seventh's soldiers placed trays of medicinal honey in front of the lancers to drink. The three most heavily injured barely had the strength to suck up the honey.

When Belissar finally arrived, they tried to salute, but he immediately shook his head.

"Don't get up. Rest and let the medicinal bees do their thing."

He then forced himself to smile.

"And . . . great work. You won."

The lancers beat their wings and tried to stir, but the medicinal workers all buzzed at them so they stopped. Belissar couldn't help but chuckle at that. He then made some honey in his hand, pouring as much mana into it as he could, and gave each of the lancers a drink. He didn't know if it would heal them like the medicinal honey would, but it helped restore their mana reserves and made them happy, and he wanted to do whatever he could. They deserved no less from him.

Belissar held a grand victory celebration as soon as the lancers were safe to move. The lancers were at the center of it all, each with a tray of the First of the Fifth's finest honey spread out before them at Belissar's request. Eventually, though, the Second of the Sixth noted that they needed to rest and heal, and the celebrations came to a close. Belissar once again thanked the God of Bees and now the God of Fire for their help. Thanks to the fire resistance from their cross-perk, he did not need to hold a memorial today.

Afterward, the queens and Chief Rohsuak all gathered once again. It was now time to determine the fruits of their victory. Belissar first checked the two reward choices.

*Please select a reward:*
*- Uncommon Room Choice (At least one uncommon or better option)*
*- Uncommon Monster Choice (At least one uncommon or better option)*
*- Common Perk Choice*

*Please select a reward:*
*- Uncommon Perk Choice (At least one uncommon or better option)*
*- Uncommon Room Choice (At least one uncommon or better option)*
*- +150 max mana*

Belissar turned to the bees and Chief Rohsuak.

"So, what does everyone think?"

The bees immediately replied with "Whatever King chooses!" while Chief Rohsuak chuckled.

"I think you already have a plan, don't you?"

Belissar stared at her, then sighed and nodded. Well, since she had him figured out already and the bees didn't have a preference for the choices, he might as well go with his own desires. He now had another floor with three more rooms to work with. So, he very much wanted to build a fire room for the mini-volcano and the Third of the Sixth. However, he had noticed by now that he didn't always get the choices he wanted when he wanted them. So, his plan this time was to pick one room choice . . . and if he didn't get anything suitable for a fire room, to possibly pick a second. And even in the worst-case scenario, where he didn't get what he wanted, he'd at least have two new rooms to fill up the new floor with. His DP was nearly at three thousand, so he'd then be able to buy a new monster or a couple of new room features on that front. Well, if he had the option of a rare monster or room feature he might have gone with that, but he did not, so that was a moot point.

With no objections, he went ahead and enacted his plan.

*Uncommon Room Choice selected.*
*Please select a room:*
**- Lava Field (Rarity: Uncommon, Type: Fire, Field)**
*- Hedge Maze (Rarity: Common, Type: Nature, Labyrinth)*
*- Fungal Tunnels (Rarity: Uncommon, Type: Ground, Fungi, Labyrinth, Resource)*

Belissar couldn't help but crack a smile as he read the first option, highlighted in bright red. He guessed the God of Fire approved of his current plans. Still, he at least read out the descriptions of the options.

### Lava Field

| | |
|---|---|
| **Type:** | Fire, Field |
| **Innate Features:** | Lava Flows |
| **Mana Upkeep:** | 20 |

*An open area where lava flows both on and beneath the surface. Newly formed rock creates a bumpy and shifting surface, which can be hazardous given the lava flowing about . . . or bursting out from a seemingly solid crust.*

"Lava is . . . what's in volcanoes, right?"

Chief Rohsuak nodded. "It's actually a type of liquid stone, so hot even rock has melted into a river of liquid fire."

Belissar couldn't help but glance at the Third of the Sixth, who was fidgeting and dancing about. So . . . a room that was practically a volcano already, filled with rivers of liquid fire? Belissar didn't know much about volcanoes, but he couldn't have imagined a better room for his current purposes.

"So, um, anyone want to hear about the others? Fungal tunnels? They're, um, tunnels . . . with fungi. Mushrooms and stuff . . ."

Chief Rohsuak just gave him an amused smile. The digging queen actually looked a little interested in the fungal tunnels, but, well, at this point the bees also knew what he was going to choose. The Third of the Sixth was struggling not to break out into a happy dance. And Belissar wasn't going to disappoint her.

*Lava Field is now available.*

And that meant that Belissar didn't need to use the second choice for a room either. He could pick from another perk, another room, or an extra hundred and fifty mana. Which . . . he needed to stop and think about, since he had been somewhat anticipating not getting what he wanted from the first choice, and so hadn't expected to consider anything but another room with this one.

Perks . . . could be anything. It could unlock powerful new options like cross-pollination had. It could be something that empowered his entire tower, like fire-resistant bees had. Or, on the other hand, it could be just a small buff to one type of bee, like the various monster bee worker, queen, and soldier buffs he had acquired from daily purifications. It was hard for him to say, and he already had a perk choice waiting, so did he really need two? Perks did have a notable advantage: most of them didn't take any work to implement. He wouldn't have to spend any mana or build anything new like with rooms, room features, and monster spawners. The perks just sort of . . . did whatever they did. He was going to focus his mana and attention on setting up the new lava field, so something he didn't have to think about might be nice.

Or he could go with his original idea and get another room. He did have three room slots to use and only one new room so far to fill them with. A new room could mean new flowers, which would also mean new bees. There was also the fact that the Hunger had just sent a fire shade, so adding something else besides a lava field might be a good idea. Belissar didn't want to spend everything on the new fire room only to face more shades that were already immune to it.

Or he could grab more mana. More mana never hurt, and he was going to have to spend a lot on the new room. Though, the daily purifications largely had that covered.

As he rubbed his chin, part of him wished the lava fields had come in the second choice . . .

# CHAPTER FIFTEEN

# BEE PERKED UP!

And so, Belissar decided . . . to check out the waiting perk choice first. Maybe whatever he got there might sway his decision.

*Please select a perk:*
*- Piercing Stingers (Rarity: Uncommon)*
*- Gardener Planting (Rarity: Rare)*
*- Hardened Wax (Rarity: Common)*

Belissar's eyes widened. A rare perk? Most of the perks he had seen were limited to common or uncommon, so this was unexpected. Still, he wanted to consider his choice carefully, so he put aside the desire to select the rare one immediately and read out the perks in order.

*Piercing Stingers: All stingers gain increased penetration.*

Well, he wasn't sure what he had expected, but that description still seemed a bit . . . brief. He supposed, though, that little more needed to be said. He had learned firsthand with the turtle-shade that his bees had trouble fighting anything their stingers couldn't pierce. This perk would directly address that issue. It needed nothing else to appeal to him.

The flower meadow queens need no encouragement either. They began fidgeting and vibrating as Belissar read out the perk. Belissar didn't need to ask why. They'd felt bad after the soldiers proved unable to pierce the turtle-shade's defenses. This perk would help prevent that from ever recurring, making the soldier bee army stronger and more capable of handling new threats in the future. It was certainly something to consider.

But, well . . . it was the next perk he had his eyes on.

*Gardener Planting: Gardeners not only pollinate plants but also carry*
*and plant their seeds. This boosts seed growth of plants pollinated*
*by gardeners and boosts rate of cross pollination of plants*
*pollinated by gardeners.*

Belissar rubbed his chin. On the one hand, for a rare perk to only affect one type of bee, the gardeners, seemed a bit limited in Belissar's eyes. And it wouldn't even make them any stronger for fighting shades. That made sense, since gardeners were a worker evolution not meant for combat, but it still stood out to Belissar given his recent concerns regarding purifications.

But at the same time, it was a rare perk! Rare! Belissar figured there had to be *some* reason this one wasn't common or uncommon. Besides, the apiary queens seemed interested in it as well. So, Belissar took his time and thought about what he had read.

Then he froze and his eyes went wide. If he chose this perk, gardeners would help plants make more seeds and more cross-pollinated seeds, and then carry and plant them. What came to Belissar's mind was the recent slime flower. The slime flower that was a non-bee monster spawner. He was unlikely to find non-bee spawners like that in the reward choices, and even now that he had access to one, the Blessing of Bees made it quite expensive. However, he had received it without spending a choice at all, and paid no mana upkeep for the one he already had. And that was because it *had grown on its own.* And that meant that . . . plants could grow—and had grown—without Belissar spawning them directly, either as a resource node, trap, or general room feature.

So, for example, what if the gardeners helped the slime flower make seeds . . . and then carried and planted them elsewhere in his tower? Could he get more slime flowers, and therefore monster spawners, without expending any mana whatsoever? What about mana flowers and their Ground and Fire versions? Could he put slime flowers in the flower meadow to reinforce the defense? What about the gravilion flowers or the thorny roses? Could he get free traps spread across the bee barracks and beyond? If he got new flowers, could he place just a single node and then let the gardeners spread them all across his tower so that every hive could access them without him spending vast amounts of mana? If he made new rooms and had this perk, maybe he wouldn't have to add as many flower nodes to them, if any.

When he thought of it that way . . . this perk seemed powerful indeed. The growth of his bees was tied to the quantity and variety of flowers he could offer them. An option to expand that quantity and variety with no further investment of the tower's resources could not be overlooked.

It was still true, however, that this perk would not directly increase the strength of the bee army. Additionally, it would take time to take effect, much like cross-pollination had. This perk was an investment for the future that would leave the present up to Belissar and the bees and defenders he already had.

There was one final option.

*Hardened Wax: Monsters and room features may produce*
*harder and denser wax.*

Belissar . . . didn't want to discount this one out of hand. Harder wax meant stronger hives, right? That could certainly prove useful. This perk was not a bad one. But, well, he couldn't help but feel it was not as impressive as the other two offered here. If a shade was attacking the walls of a hive, then something had already gone horribly wrong, so Belissar would prefer to avoid the need for harder wax in the first place.

So, should he strengthen the stingers to address the growing defenses of the latest shades? Or should he enable monster bee gardeners to spread flowers beyond their nodes? Belissar felt he should not consider the choices apart from each other. He had already chosen a new room, the lava field, for his first choice. Then, on top of the current perk choice, he had a second choice to make, which could provide a second new room, a second new perk, or more mana. Additionally, his current DP income would soon enable him to purchase a new monster, a new room, or several new room features as soon as tomorrow. So, what would be the best choice not only out of these options but considering all the others?

When he took into account the new lava field, only one of the available perks directly affected it. A new room would very much appreciate new flowers, which Gardener Planting would provide without using up any further mana. And a new room could mean new flowers to spread and cross-pollinate, so Gardener Planting would enable the new lava field to benefit the rest of the tower as well. On the other hand, the other two perks helped the bees but didn't interact much with the new room.

Next he had to consider the last choice, where he could pick from another set of rooms, another set of perks, or just take more mana. More mana helped, of course, but he could get more from daily purification so it felt like a waste. He instead tried to imagine whether a new room or new perk would fit best with lava fields and any of the available perks, not to mention the possibility of a DP store purchase later. Well, a new room wouldn't exactly interact much with the lava fields, though a second perk choice might. Not to mention, perk choices were far more expensive in the DP store than rooms . . .

That ended up settling it for Belissar. If perks were harder to come by and he was undecided what to do otherwise, he might as well pick up another perk now.

He could get new rooms from the DP shop and more mana from the daily purifications. And in that case, he might as well see what other choices he would have
before he decided on the first perk.

*Uncommon Perk Choice selected.*
*Please select a perk:*
*- Enhanced Toxins (Rarity: Common)*
*- Alluring Honey (Rarity: Uncommon)*
*- Bee-Type Strength Boost (Minor) (Rarity: Uncommon)*

Well, no rare choices this time. The first was a repeat, a general buff to toxins.
It may have been common and humble, but Belissar realized he shouldn't dismiss
it out of hand. After all, he had a lot of toxins now. Most of his bees, from workers
and queens to soldiers and lancers, had stingers. The sprayers attacked solely
through toxins as well. And then there were the various poisonous plants and
mushrooms he had, and the poisonous honey that resulted. Could enhanced toxins boost a sticky honey trap equipped with maddening honey, for example? Even
though the perk itself was not that impressive, it would impact most of his tower's
defenses on account of the abundance of toxins, and that made it worth
considering.

*Alluring Honey: Honey may give an enticing scent that makes it*
*more appealing, especially to corrupted entities. Impact on*
*non-corrupted entities depends on the type of honey used*
*and the nature of the entity in question.*

Belissar found that one curious until he read the line about corrupted entities. So, if he was reading this correctly, this made the shades want his honey? At
first, he wondered why he would want that . . . until he realized that would mean
he could use honey as bait for traps against shades. Or perhaps he could use it to
draw shades in different directions? Thus far, all the shades had moved straight
toward the exit of any given room, save in the dirt tunnels, where the twisting
maze made it unclear which way was forward. That was ultimately why he'd cut
down on some of the pit traps in the flower meadow, since the shades just didn't
venture off to the sides.

But what if he could entice the shades to go that way? That alone could allow
him to buy additional time during purifications. It would also make his traps more
reliable to boot, taking some of the pressure off the soldier bee army.

*Bee-Type Strength Boost (Minor)*
*- All bee-type monsters receive a minor boost to strength.*

Belissar was about to gloss over this one . . . until he realized that it was not one of the average boost perks he saw in the daily purifications. No, this one specified that it applied not to a specific bee, but to all bee-type monsters. So, all of his monsters, at least until the slime flower did its thing. A boost to all of his bees at the same time? Now *that* was worth considering.

Belissar nodded his head as his plan coalesced.

"So, I'm thinking of choosing gardener planting for more flowers, and then one of the other perks to strengthen our defenses. Um, does anyone have any other ideas? And do you like any of the next three perks in particular?"

Of course, the bees did not have any other ideas on the first perk, since he had stated his own opinion the only answer he got was "Whatever King chooses!" Chief Rohsuak shook her head as well. Belissar still wished she'd just tell him what she thought outright, but she apparently had no intention of defying his decision here, so he'd just go with what he thought best. As for the second perk choice, Belissar held back his own evaluation and asked the bees for their thoughts. The flower meadow queens were split between enhanced toxins and the bee-type strength boost. The First of the Fifth flew a bit unsteadily.

"Honey . . . more appealing? Make enemies want? Why want that?"

Belissar nodded at her.

"If it draws a shade's attention, we can use it to lure it into traps."

The First of the Fifth picked up speed, dancing to indicate her understanding . . . and following with a "King best king!" dance. She did not, however, indicate any specific preference for the perk after understanding it.

Belissar rubbed his chin once more, taking his bees' preferences into account. Alluring honey would work well with his traps. He hadn't been able to rely on the traps for a while now . . . but perhaps alluring honey would change that? Especially if the gardeners started to spread some of the trap plants around. On the other hand, either of the other two perks would strengthen his bees directly. As powerful as traps might be, the outcome of tougher purifications generally came down to his bees, especially since the Hunger would ultimately adapt to the traps over time. And then, finally, enhanced toxins could improve both bees and traps, though it was a common perk.

Belissar glanced once more at his bees, then made his choice.

*Gardener Planting selected.*
*Bee-Type Strength Boost (Minor) selected.*
*All bee-type monsters receive a minor boost to strength!*

The bees had been concerned and subdued due to the turtle-shade. They had been worried about their inability to fight. So, Belissar wanted to both make them stronger and cheer them up. He was going to reward them for their efforts and reassure them that he believed in them. And he felt that boosting all of their strength was the best way to do that.

The bees all began to stir as the tower's mana flowed through them, the flower meadow queens in particular. Belissar looked directly at them and smiled.

"I'm counting on you."

The flower meadow queens joined together in a salute dance, followed by all the rest.

# BEE-FOCUS YOUR EFFORTS!

**D**own in the Underway, just past the rot cap field in a dark tunnel, two pairs of eyes lit up in the shadows, barely reflecting the faintest hints of light. A soft voice drifted on the air, a faint whisper that would not be heard over the rustling of the stink bugs in the field beyond.

"Are you certain this is the place?"

"Positive."

"And you're *certain* you saw people here? Not just another cave bear, right?"

There was a low growl. "You think I would mistake an entire hunting band? That I'd just make that up? They were here. That's a fact. Look, the stink bug numbers still haven't recovered."

The first voice gained volume, letting a sigh pierce the quiet. "So? A cave bear could've done that too. And it's been *days* and we haven't seen any sign of anything but stink bugs here."

The second voice hissed, "And we won't if you keep yapping! Quiet down before we're discovered—"

But both voices were cut off at that moment. Neither could miss the surge of mana flowing past them, causing both pairs of eyes to tremble for a bit. The second voice spoke first.

"T-That was . . . ?"

The first voice replied, tone now fully serious and with no hint of their earlier annoyance. "There's no mistaking it. That's a purification wave. And that means there's a sacred den in the area now. Let's go, we need to report this right away."

The Firstborn slowly crawled through her trays, her daughter following along. The younger queen brushed her mother's antennas with a slow dance.

"Queen Mother, okay?"

The Firstborn, though moving slowly, responded immediately.

"Yes, just . . . lots to think about."

Indeed, she had much to consider, for despite everything, the King still trusted them. Still counted on them. She could feel the mana of the realm surging through her body, strengthening her muscles. And they had managed to win a significant victory without the aid of the karnuq.

Yet, she could not simply rejoice. She knew from the past that a victory here did not mean a victory tomorrow. Their work had only begun; their army needed to continue growing. And, most of all, she thought that the King had not trusted them but had *chosen* to trust them. She'd seen the moment of hesitation before he deployed the lancers, the creases on his face that signaled deep thought. She believed that he'd had other plans in mind but changed them in order to let the bees have a chance.

The Firstborn did not know what to think of that. Should she be happy and grateful that the King considered them so, and still planned to rely on them as he could? That they were strong enough to win the victory he needed? Or should she be regretful that the King had been forced to reconsider his plans because of them? That they were too weak to be his first thought?

Well, such questions, no matter how she answered them, would not improve her hive, so she continued crawling, arriving at the worker cells. She turned to face her daughter, who was still watching her with concern.

"I think . . . should be patient. Army still too weak but . . . King trusts to grow. Wants to grow. So should do what can now and trust King to help."

Yes, that was her conclusion. She knew from the failure with the bird-shade that the King was not going to abandon or replace them. That was not his way. She knew from the new strength she now felt in her legs that the King planned to continue growing them. In fact . . . she may have been looking at this wrong from the start. It had been the King who had given them soldiers, sprayers, and lancers in the first place. The army was, therefore, not something they built *for* the King, but something they built *with* the King. It was as much his efforts as theirs, if not more.

In that regard, she would be patient and would not rush to try and grow the army beyond its present limits. She knew that in time the King would provide them with new options himself. What the army needed to do was make the most of what the King gave them, and ensure they were prepared when new options came. They needed to trust in the King's design. They needed to consider themselves as a part of the greater hive of hives.

Her daughter danced a salute.

"Okay, what can do now? More lancers? More soldiers?"

But the Firstborn danced the negative.

"Not this time."

And then Firstborn began to lay some new worker eggs . . . and then gathered together her oldest and most experienced foragers, who crawled into glowing cells packed with honey. Her daughter saluted and followed suit with her own workers.

The Firstborn had originally planned to raise more lancers but had changed her mind. The mana of the realm did more than strengthen her muscles. It also carried knowledge that one of the latest bee types had been improved. A bee type that she had thought intended for the apiary queens, a worker evolution focused on foraging rather than fighting. Something that would help the bee barracks as well but would require them to cease raising soldiers while their limited foragers took the time to evolve. So, the flower meadow queens had not gotten around to laying eggs for that new bee type yet.

But now the Firstborn had decided to adjust her priorities. The honey to evolve a single lancer could not only evolve several gardeners; the remainder could also serve as a stockpile that would cover the hive while its most productive foragers rested in their cells. Taking this step now would improve their honey production, not only allowing them to afford more lancers and other soldier types, but also to have the extra honey necessary if and when the King provided them with new options. While the hive of hives would support one another, it was not good to rely solely on the apiary whenever they needed more honey.

Additionally, this new bee not only improved foraging but would also improve the health of the flowers themselves . . . and would now work to spread the flowers as well. New mana flowers were obviously useful to improve honey production, but that was not the Firstborn's only thought. If she considered herself as part of the greater hive of hives, the soldier bee army as just one part of the King's design, then she should consider her surroundings as well, and the King's other efforts to defend the hive of hives. In that manner, the great chasms and fire sticks, the underground tunnels that bought time, and the honey sprayers could all be considered part of the army.

And then there were the plants. On the palisade outside of the bee barracks grew vines covered in sharp thorns. Farther on in the flower meadow was a flower her foragers didn't like to gather from. They said it disrupted their flight and was difficult to approach. One moment, it would randomly make them heavier, forcing them to fly with all their might not to crash into the ground. The next, it would make them even lighter than usual, causing them to fly above and beyond their targets. It was therefore not very popular among the flower meadow's foragers, despite its high mana density.

But what if those effects applied to the enemy as well? What if the new bees spread those two types of flowers across the meadow? In that regard, there might be more ways for the flower meadow army to fight, ways they could start fighting right now, before the enemy ever arrived.

And what if they combined those efforts with the soldiers they sent to help the King? Could they one day build a wall of their own, maybe one extending across the entire length of the flower meadow? And then, perhaps, spread the thorny roses across the entire thing, so that no enemy could advance along the ground without tearing down tree-trunk-like stakes while thorns ripped into them? With countless of those other flowers to randomly make everything heavier or lighter, disrupting the flight of any enemy trying to pass over the barrier? All the while sprayers could attack safely from behind and above the walls, while lancers adjusted their aim with leisure? If the wall held the enemy back well enough, maybe Beero and her squad could get involved too.

Well, those ideas were distant and vague, but they informed the Firstborn of an important point. There was more the flower meadow could do to prepare for the next battle than just practicing dives.

It was for these reasons the Firstborn made the call to raise gardeners instead of more lancers. The King would expand the army's options when he felt they needed more soldiers, and they would have a lancer squad ready once the wounded had recovered. So, the Firstborn felt their goal in the immediate future should be to prepare, and to join themselves ever more with the hive of hives. Not just with their fellow flower meadow queens, but with those of the orchard and the apiary. With the King's flowers and traps and constructions. Maybe even with the karnuq as well, for the Firstborn had noted their willingness to defend the King's realm.

And everything within the realm, be it bee, flower, or even the land itself, would fight for the King.

# BEE-FICIENT SPECIALIZATION

The First of the Fifth stood in her home. Her new, spacious home that she was certain was larger than any constructed by any bee in the Beyond. Her new home with rows upon rows of trays, more than her hive could ever fill, which were precisely placed to allow ideal airflow that could be adjusted on a per-tray basis for different processing needs. Her home with numerous entrances that the King had made on *her* suggestion, allowing her to precisely organize the flow of her workers so that not a single moment would be lost to confusion or traffic jams.

Before she knew it, she had started another happy dance. But she caught herself and stopped. While the new palace certainly deserved the celebration, she had another task at present. She was currently standing before her children, a line of newly born queens watching her with just a hint of confusion over her sudden outburst. She gathered herself with the slightest twitch of her antennas before dancing.

"All daughters should focus on workers for now. Will provide honey to do so. Will assign brood tenders to help. Will also assign tasks, and workers. Queens should listen to workers and get used to tasks so can do once own workers ready. Understand?"

"Yes, Queen Mother!"

Once she was satisfied with their response, she turned to one of the queens.

"Second Daughter, build in sector one. Job is to arrange honey delivery to other hives. Need to grow and raise soldiers for this."

The new queen saluted, and then the First of the Fifth's workers led her to her assigned trays. The First of the Fifth turned to the next.

"Third Daughter, build in sector five. Job is to investigate new honey processing methods. Will need to watch dangerous karnuq. Work with scouts, they will explain."

Her third daughter danced an unsteady salute, apparently confused about the order. The First of the Fifth would follow up and explain in more detail. She would also need to determine if her daughters could connect to her scouts via communers, or if they would need scouts and communers of their own. In truth, the First of the Fifth was unsure about handing this task off. She knew about the possibility of processing already finished honey, but she had not made any progress on the details, so the only instruction she could give was to watch the dangerous karnuq for clues. However, there were, at present, just too many draws on the First of the Fifth's attention, and this task would require a great deal of time and focus. It would require extensively monitoring the dangerous karnuq for clues, and then likely many failed attempts to map out new production methods from those observations. It simply required more attention and time than the First of the Fifth was willing to spend on it, though the possibilities were too great to drop the idea entirely. So, she would have one of her daughters take up the mantle, and trust that her offspring would be up to the task.

Just like the next two.

"Fourth Daughter and Fifth Daughter, job is honey production for other hives. Goal is quantity, though expect thorough processing. Workers will teach methods."

The two queens saluted. They had the most straightforward and natural task, but it was by no means an easy one. There was ever greater demand for the First of the Fifth's honey these days. That the flower meadow needed her help went without saying. The First of the Fifth shuddered when she thought of the Firstborn's honey-making "process," if it could be called such a thing. The bumblebee queens too, who seemed infuriatingly happy to just let their workers build their haphazard wax cups anywhere they pleased, without any attention to organization or hive flow. This decreased their already paltry honey production, as they barely seemed to produce any surplus in the first place. At this point, the First of the Fifth had largely resigned herself to providing for both those groups in perpetuity.

Even the apiary hives needed her help. Not all the queens had the reserves to raise new queens and drones, so the First of the Fifth's stockpiles had taken a dip ensuring they all could participate. She would also need to monitor the apiary hives in the near future to confirm that all the new queens could grow without threatening their mothers' honey balance.

Meanwhile, the digging and burning queens had just finished evolving their hives and were still working their operations back up to full capacity. The new sedative queen was just starting the process of converting her workers to her own type, so her operations would take a dip as well. And the medicinal Second of the Sixth was still donating notable quantities of her own honey for the sake of the lancer bees' recovery. Not to mention the karnuq, who apparently needed the First of the Fifth's honey to fight. She had to ensure she had a sufficient stockpile of adequately mana-rich honey in case of another sudden attack that required the karnuq's power.

And, of course, the First of the Fifth would allow none of this to cut into her donations to the King himself. The very best honey she could produce would always go to his table. That was one thing she refused to give up on, even knowing that the King himself would probably want that honey distributed among the bees.

So, her hive needed to produce more honey, and fast. Her fourth and fifth daughters had the most straightforward tasks, but they would be pushed the hardest to achieve the goals set forth. The First of the Fifth had learned her lesson after her first daughter, however, and she would closely monitor them to ensure healthy brood growth. And since they would remain in her new palace, they shouldn't be under any threat of hive collapse.

And with that, all her daughters were now ready to begin their work. It would take them some time to get up and running, but once they did, the demands on the First of the Fifth's attention would lessen. It was not easy monitoring and supporting all the other hives like she was, but with the help of her daughters it should be possible. And, likewise, it should be possible to make progress on her next plans.

The First of the Fifth was finally ready to evolve some gardeners. It was a travesty that she hadn't been able to do so for this long. They would, after all, support one of her main duties, the task that she insisted on keeping for herself.

Cross-pollination and testing new nectar types was the first direct collaboration between herself and the King. Additionally, he had directly asked her to help coordinate the specialization of the hives. So, in that regard, her most important tasks were to keep track of the hive of hives and the status of all the hives within it, to raise and identify new flower types, and then to allocate flowers suitable for specialization to the queens ready to convert their hives. Now that gardeners could directly assist the spread of flowers, she could start raising more flower patches to ensure all queens had sufficient resources, taking some of the burden of that duty off the King. Raising gardeners was now her top priority, and she arranged for as many workers as she could to evolve without excessively interrupting production.

Once that was completed, she turned to her other priority task: testing the new honey types. She had two trays that were nearly empty save for a small group of cells in the corner of each. She shuddered a bit when she approached one as she suddenly dropped to the floor one moment, and then felt like she was floating away the next, despite her wings remaining still. Her foragers hadn't enjoyed collecting the nectar of this flower, but they had pressed on and collected a sample. The inefficiency of gathering nearly had her call off the effort . . . but the sheer mana density of the flower in question was too tempting.

The processing had been difficult as well. The nectar had constantly shifted its own viscosity, density, and even volume. Her workers struggled to measure its water content and determine how to fan it for the drying stage. The First of the Fifth had to directly intervene to determine the process, and even then, she'd had to resort to watching the mana rather than the physical honey itself. She was, therefore, not at all confident in the quality and consistency of this batch and would not be serving any of it to even another hive, much less the King.

But they *had* managed to make some . . . gravity honey. She believed that was what the King had named this type of flower, so that was what she would call it.

She would taste it herself, to analyze it and determine what to do with it. As she expected, each cell of gravity honey varied wildly in quality and consistency. She would have been ashamed of such an effort had she not known the difficulties involved in getting it to even this state. The gravity honey itself did not taste all that different from the usual dandelion honey, but as during its processing, the honey continued to vary its consistency within her proboscis and her stomach. One moment it was a dense, almost solid, sticky mass that nearly got stuck in place. The next it was a thin and runny liquid she might have mistaken for raw nectar that had been diluted by rain. She . . . didn't think she enjoyed the experience.

And the gravity honey had other effects besides the consistency. The same weight-shifting effect of the flower applied to the honey as well. With the honey inside of her stomach, one moment she would feel so heavy she wanted to lie on the ground. The next she felt she would float away if she didn't latch on to the honeycomb.

And this . . . was why she decided to lay an egg in the cell with the densest mana concentration.

These gravity flowers and the honey made from their nectar were clearly not normal, and their mana was excessively active even after being stabilized into mana honey. It was to the point that, like the burning honey from the flame radishes, she didn't want to gather too much of it lest it impact the rest of her hive. And that, in turn, made it a prime candidate for brood specialization. There was little doubt in her mind that this honey would certainly affect a bee growing within it. The only question was, would the egg and larva survive to adulthood under those conditions? And what sort of bee might result? Maybe, if it was like the burning honey, a worker raised on the honey might prove more suitable to producing more?

Well, she didn't envy the queen that tried to evolve on such a honey type. Her task was complete, however, so she crawled to the next tray. That is, after the gravity honey finally decided to stop making her feel so heavy.

The next honey was . . . curious. The nectar started extremely viscous, nearly at a honey-like level before any processing at all. It was also highly mana-dense, on par with a mana flower, or perhaps even denser. She couldn't say exactly because of a curious effect of the nectar and the honey made from it. This honey, despite being so mana-dense already, acted like a mana sponge and absorbed as much mana as was pushed into it. Normally, the First of the Fifth had her workers fill up any nectar with as much mana as it could take, but this nectar did not seem to have a reasonable limit. She might try to find it later, but for this first batch she ended up telling her workers to move on to the drying stage before that point. Additionally, as more cells filled up, the honey seemed to . . . gravitate toward itself. It was like it was trying to link up and then condense down even further.

This was strange behavior, not least of which because honey wasn't supposed to have a behavior. This honey was active in a way no other had been. The burning honey had simply raised the temperature around it, but that was just a side effect of the mana within it. Even the gravity honey, for all of its constant changes, was still just honey. She could follow the flow of its mana and see the effects that resulted. This honey . . . was different. Its mana flowed in unexpected ways, without a clear reason for doing so. There was something different to its movements, something the other honeys lacked.

So, of course, she laid an egg in the center cell, where the honey was trying to concentrate. Between the honey's unique behavior and its ability to absorb an unheard-of quantity of mana, she couldn't wait to see if a bee could be raised on it . . . and what might result. Even now, she watched as the honey tried to condense itself and found an egg in the way. And then, the egg began to absorb the honey, and the honey began flowing *faster*, its mana condensing and merging with the egg's.

Satisfied, the First of the Fifth assigned brood tenders to watch the two eggs, then left to check on her daughters and further explain their tasks. A bee's work was never done.

# CHAPTER SIXTEEN

# FIER-BEE EXPERIMENTS!

The next day, Belissar made a quick stop to the slime flower, since it had been on his mind. He rubbed his chin as he looked it over. Try as he might, he couldn't find any slimes either nearby or throughout his tower.

"Does it need more time? Or . . ."

He noticed a worker bee land on the flower, and then he pulled up the slime flower's description once more.

### Slime Flower

**Type:** Slime, Nature, Trap, Spawner

**Mana Upkeep:** 20 per node (40 due to Blessing of Bees), 10 (20 due to Blessing of Bees) to enable in compatible rooms

*A flower that concentrates its mana into thickening its sap, which will spill out and engulf any creature that damages it. This effect extends partially to its nectar as well, which, if left to pool in sufficient quantities, may eventually condense into a slime core. The slime will carry the flower's seeds along with it as it begins to move, spreading the seeds around while also hunting nearby pests, further protecting the flower.*

He confirmed that the description mentioned slimes spawning . . . if the flower's nectar was left to pool in sufficient quantities. So, if the bees were consistently gathering that nectar, maybe slimes would never spawn?

Belissar briefly considered whether he should ask the bees to hold off and test the theory before shaking his head. At the end of the day, the bees were the priority. If they wanted to gather this flower's nectar in quantities that prevented slimes from spawning, then that was what they would do. Belissar was curious about the slimes and how the flower worked, but not so curious that he'd interrupt the bees' work to find out.

With that out of the way for now, he turned to his goal for the day: building the fire room. He walked over to the Third of the Sixth's hive. The queen flew up and out of the hole where her hive was before he even arrived, zipping around him. Belissar chuckled.

"Ready to make your new home?"

Her happy dance increased in intensity, creating little sparks of flame all around him as her temperature spiked. Belissar smiled and then led the dancing queen to the core room. He wanted the Third of the Sixth's input on the new room and recalled that the core could show the image of a new room before he placed it.

Belissar blinked a few times as he stepped into the core room. He hadn't been there since realizing his tower sight could do the same thing as the core, so he hadn't noticed that there had been some changes. First of all, the room had grown dramatically in size, now four times larger than it originally had been. The core was still held up by a statue of a bee, but both the core and the statue had grown. The core used to be about the size of his head and the statue about the height of his chest. Now, the core was twice the size and the statue reached up to his neck, holding the core at eye level. One of the bee statue's legs now also held a lit candle.

The walls had seen the most dramatic change. They were still made of honeycomb dripping honey, but the honeycomb was no longer a single color. Different colored cells now joined together to form images all along the walls, displaying the different types of bees he had in his tower. He even saw some images of the karnuq, including one covered in flames, one mixing a large pot, and one crouching and holding a large stinger.

Belissar took a moment to observe it all before he shrugged. He guessed the core room reflected the current tower? That made sense. In any case, he had a job to do. He turned to Niobee.

"Can you let the other queens know the tower's about to change like we discussed last night?"

"Okay!"

Before adding the new room, Belissar would need to rearrange some of the other rooms. He figured he'd put the new fire room on the first floor, between the dirt tunnels and the flower meadow. He'd put the new floor as the second floor of the tower so the orchard could go there and still stay connected to the flower meadow. The current second floor holding the karnuq would become the third floor, while the current third floor with the apiary and bumblebees would become the fourth floor, remaining next to the core room.

The view of the tower's room and floors as a whole appeared within the core. Belissar moved about the existing rooms as planned, then placed the new room.

The view zoomed in on the new room, displaying what it would look like to him and the Third of the Sixth.

A field of black rock stretched out before them, broken up by bright red rivers. A small hill pushed up in the center and lava flowed out of it into the rivers. Lava oozed and solidified into new rock along the backs of the river, while elsewhere seemingly solid rock cracked open so that lava could pour out. The air across the entire room shimmered from the heat. The field was not entirely flat, either. There were dips and small ridges and outcroppings. Some of these outcroppings had alcoves. The room's borders were marked by particularly tall cliffs.

Belissar tested what he could adjust, finding he could move the lava hill at the center, change the course of the rivers, and move some of the outcroppings, ridges, and alcoves. He nodded and turned to the Third of the Sixth as he pointed at the image.

"Okay, so I think we put the entrance and exit to the room on either side of the right wall, so that the shades will move through there, and then we put an alcove for your hive on the opposite side. How does that sound?"

The Third of the Sixth responded with a nearly unintelligible "King best king!" dance. Belissar shook his head with a smile as he set up a large ridge near the left wall, creating a narrow valley along the edge of the room. He then built a large alcove into the ridge at the bottom of the valley, with its opening facing the left wall, away from the rest of the room.

"Okay, okay. Um, do you have any suggestions? How would you like your hive's alcove to look?"

In this case, the Third of the Sixth mostly just continued praising him. She did mention, as part of her praise, how the rivers looked nice and warm and how that made him the best, so Belissar went ahead and moved one of the rivers to the valley so it would pass in front of the alcove's entrance.

From there, he tried to adjust the room as best he knew for defense. He made as big a river of lava as he could, stretching across the room from left to right, and made as many such lava rivers as he could. He moved the ground up and down with as many ridges and outcroppings in the way as possible. He placed the parts where lava just oozed out of rocks right along the path that formed in the space between the rivers.

And then, he reached out to Niobee.

"Is everyone ready for the changes?"

"Ready!"

Once she replied, he confirmed and placed the room. The core began to glow and the tower's mana surged as it applied his changes. The image within the core seemed to grow more solid, and he could almost feel the heat of the room.

And now that the room was placed came the final touch.

*Compatible feature detected. Swap Lava Source to Mini-Volcano?*

Belissar went ahead and confirmed, turning the hill at the center of the room into a mini-volcano. The hill began to rumble and smoke and ash began to belch out of its center as the flow of lava grew a bit more rapid.

Belissar waited for the volcano to launch its boulders. He wanted to see if the ridge and alcove would hold up to the volcano before he moved the Third of the Sixth's hive there, to ensure that the bees would be safe. Otherwise, he'd just have to place them in an adjacent room. However, the volcano didn't seem to want to erupt just yet. Belissar frowned and brought up the description.

### Mini-Volcano
**Type:** *Fire, Ground, Trap*
**Mana Upkeep:** *50*
*A small volcano just peeking out of the ground. Will launch burning rocks in the direction of invaders. May also emit ash clouds and slowly flowing lava.*

Belissar frowned. So . . . it would launch in the direction of invaders? And not just randomly everywhere? That was convenient in general, but it could be a problem for the current test. Would he have to wait until a purification? And then lead a shade to the alcove?

As he focused in, a new message arrived.

*Launch boulders for a one-time cost of 10 mana?*

"Ah, that's convenient . . . or is it?"

At first, that seemed an immediate solution to Belissar's worries . . . until he saw the mana cost. Paying mana for one test didn't seem like a good idea. Although the message did say it was a one-time cost. Would he get the mana back then?

Unfortunately, no new messages appeared in response to Belissar's questions, so he'd either have to test it himself or just wait for a purification. He decided that ten mana, less than a minor+ purification reward, was an acceptable price to find out what the volcano would do. So, he went ahead and confirmed.

*Mana: 11(21)/765*

A large circle made of red light appeared on the ground in the lava field, and Belissar found he could move it. Was this where the boulders were going to land? Belissar hoped so. He moved the circle to center on the alcove and thought about boulders launching.

"Um, here?"

The volcano erupted. Even safe in the core room, Belissar couldn't help but stumble back as a blast of smoke and light shot from the mini-volcano, shaking the lava field. Rocks the size of Belissar's torso covered in bright flames shot into the sky, with long tails of smoke trailing behind them. They arced through the air, flames burning brightly as they started descending to the ground.

They hit the ridge with a crash, shattering and spreading flames and puddles of lava across the black and rocky ground.

The ridge held with no particular damage. A few scattered pebbles and rocks fell over the edge and in front of the alcove but did not enter the alcove proper. A hive built inside would be safe.

Belissar stared at it for a bit before he started to grin. It seemed this plan was coming together after all.

# CHAPTER SEVENTEEN

# A BEE-UTIFUL HOME?

Juosiutik yawned and stepped out of her house, then stretched her arms out and rolled her shoulders. For the first time in a while, she didn't immediately zip to her pot, but instead looked up at the sun. She took a deep breath and smiled.

"Welcome back."

Juosiutik whipped around and found Chief Rohsuak smiling at her. She flushed.

"Oh, um, sorry. Um, how long has it . . ."

Chief Rohsuak just chuckled and Juosiutik's flush grew deeper. She . . . may have gotten a bit focused on exploring her new abilities. She wasn't actually sure how long she had been working, as she hadn't paid attention to anything else, including the passing of time. Or even . . .

She jumped a bit and her eyes widened.

"Wait . . . the sacred den master! He, um, hasn't been waiting all this time for more lessons, has he?"

Chief Rohsuak chuckled again and shook her head.

"He has had projects of his own. Speaking of which, you may wish to explore the settlement a bit."

Chief Rohsuak waved her arm. Juosiutik glanced around and her eyes went even wider.

"Wait, since when did we start building things out of stone?"

Chief Rohsuak smiled.

"Much has happened. You should speak to Muuraqi before you begin any new experiments. You might benefit from a fireproof structure."

Juosiutik hung her head.

"I'm sorry. I just got so excited—"

But Chief Rohsuak cut her off by patting her shoulder, making a knowing smile.

"Everyone's that way with their first blessing, it's fine. I would have interrupted if we truly needed you. Just tell me this: Was your time productive?"

Juosiutik made a small, sheepish smile. "Well . . . yes. Very." Her eyes gained a bit of light. "I've been testing all the different recipes with magic honey and it works with *all* of them! Not only that, but it makes all of them more effective, and I can even substitute it for a few ingredients we don't have anymore. Plus, they taste much better, so maybe the hunters will finally stop complaining."

Chief Rohsuak chuckled.

"Good, glad to hear you've made some progress. Now, may I assume you've made usable amounts of everything you've worked on?"

Juosiutik nodded and Chief Rohsuak patted her shoulder once again.

"Good. Now that you're ready, we'll have need of you. Let's discuss supplies with Metsaitti later, shall we? And maybe you can show the sacred den master what you can do as well."

Chief Rohsuak chuckled to herself as Juosiutik hung her head. In truth, this was only the beginning of the rampages she expected from Juosiutik. And if the young karnuq got this way just using her blessing on old recipes, how would she be when she saw the other materials the sacred den master had available? Chief Rohsuak wasn't entirely sure about the details of the cross-pollination the sacred den master had mentioned during her meetings with him and the bee queens, but if she had to guess, she'd say Juosiutik's world would soon expand dramatically.

She . . . should probably have Muuraqi prioritize a stone house for Juosiutik.

Belissar double-checked his mana again.

*Mana: 12(21)/765*

He let out a light sigh. It took a few minutes, but the mana had started going back up, so it seemed launching the mini-volcano attack had not been a permanent expenditure. It was also quite good to know he could trigger it manually if he needed to.

He paused, and then checked one of the sticky honey traps.

*Activate sticky honey trap for a one-time cost of 1 mana?*

It seemed he could activate those as well, though they only aimed in one direction, so he couldn't adjust the aim. He wasn't sure why he'd want to trigger those ones manually, though, given that they only ever got one chance to hit a shade anyways. Still, it was good to know for future traps.

He then had a thought and tried focusing on the slime flower . . . but no messages appeared. Maybe it didn't work with spawners? He tried focusing on one of the monster bee queen spawners with the thought of activating it.

*Max spawns active.*

Well, it turned out he couldn't activate the spawners past their limit . . . and all his current spawners had hit their limit a while ago. But a message had at least appeared, so maybe it would work with new spawners?

That also confirmed that the activation ability specifically didn't work with the slime flower. Maybe it was because he got it for free and didn't spend any mana on it to begin with? Well, if he ever made a slime flower through the tower's abilities, he'd check that. If he remembered.

He decided to stop being distracted and get on with his day. He and the Third of the Sixth left the core room and moved back to her hive. The Third of the Sixth then evacuated most of her workers and brood, just leaving one worker and one egg inside, as Belissar wanted to test what would happen to them if he moved the hive while the bees were inside of it. He didn't expect an issue, since he had upgraded beehives into other features with them inside without any problem, but he wasn't going to chance a whole hive on it without confirmation.

He moved the hive around to the other side of its hole. The hive glowed, vanished, and reappeared where he indicated. The worker then flew out and confirmed that she was alright, and the egg was as well.

Satisfied, Belissar had the Third of the Sixth move her bees back inside, and then moved the whole hive to the alcove in the lava field. He then moved the flame radish and Fire mana flower nodes there as well.

*Mana: 35(41)/765*

He nodded. As expected, the lava field was a far better environment for those flowers. They were not only no longer costing him extra mana, but they also had an additional discount due to the more suitable environment.

*Available Resource Plants for Lava Field:*
*- Flame Radish (Mana Upkeep: 10 per node, 5 due to suitable environment)*
*- Mana Flower (Mana Upkeep: 5 per node)*
*- Fire Mana Flower (10 per node, 5 due to suitable environment)*
*- Ground Mana Flower (10 per node)*

He double-checked the resource plant menu for the lava fields but didn't find anything new. Maybe because he already had flame radishes?

Besides, he couldn't imagine any of his other flowers growing here, so that made sense. The only surprise was that Ground mana flowers were available here too . . . and didn't even cost any extra, though they didn't get the suitability bonus from the dirt tunnels. He wondered why. Maybe it was all of the rocks? Hadn't Chief Rohsuak said something about lava being liquid rock?

Belissar shrugged and then made his way through the tower, passing through the new staircase between the orchard and the flower meadow. Since the tower just sort of skipped stairs, it was more like a small room than a staircase, but it still added a small amount of distance between the orchard and the tower exit . . . which would only grow if he added more rooms for defense later. He wondered if there'd be a good way to let the orchard bees exit the tower quickly, since they were the ones scouting outside.

In any case, he continued on his way and soon stood outside of the door to the lava field. He was vaguely aware that the tower would keep him safe from his own features—he could walk over pit traps without issue, after all—but he still needed a moment before stepping into the new room. Every other room up to this point had been fairly normal, and nothing he hadn't encountered in his life beforehand. This one was not.

So, he paced a bit, took one final deep breath, and then stepped inside. He was immediately hit by a blast of hot air as the temperature rose dramatically. His ears were assaulted by crackling, hissing, and roaring noises, something he hadn't noticed from the core's quiet view of the room. His nose was likewise assaulted by noxious fumes that smelled like rotten eggs. He immediately covered his nose . . . but the moment he thought that, the smell faded. He could still detect it, but it didn't completely overwhelm his nose like before. The heat faded as well, to the point that he could tell it wasn't comfortable but it wasn't causing him active discomfort.

He once again thanked tower magic and the gods as he climbed through the lava fields. The rocky floor was not a smooth surface but covered in small ripples and curves and sometimes jagged edges. He had to be careful not to lose his balance, particularly when he jumped over the lava rivers. While he trusted the tower not to kill him, he did not particularly want to touch the hissing, crackling, and glowing red rivers.

Eventually, though, he made his way to the left edge of the room and climbed down the ridge he had set up. He made his way to the alcove, where he found the Third of the Sixth's hive buzzing and swarming over their new surroundings. The red burning bees were flying over the surface of the lava river, apparently not at all bothered by the heat that made the air shimmer. They were also swarming over the Fire mana flowers, which were glowing brighter than

Belissar had ever seen them. The Third of the Sixth rushed out and began zipping around him once more.

Apparently, he didn't even need to ask. He chuckled instead.

"Guess you like it?"

A swarm of burning bees dancing "King best king!" at maximum speed was his answer.

# CHAPTER EIGHTEEN

# READY FOR A BEE-MATCH?

For most of the rest of the day, Belissar watched the Third of the Sixth's hive acclimate to their new home, checking if there was anything he might adjust to help them. The burning bees were flying faster than ever before, the air shimmering around their wings, and drinking deeply from the glowing Fire mana flowers.

Eventually, though, it was time for the next daily purification. Belissar thought about giving the bees a break, but the soldier bee army started forming up at the regular time without any prompting, along with the karnuq contingent. Only the lancers had been involved in the last fight, so the rest of the bee army was still ready to go. In fact, the two lancers who had lighter wounds had recovered enough to join the formation. Belissar nodded his head and brought up the purification message. In the spirit of trusting his bees more, he would acknowledge their willingness to fight. Besides, they had long proved capable of handling minor+ purifications without any—

> *Please select a purification strength:*
> *- Minor (Cooldown: 12 hours)*
> *- Minor+ (Cooldown: 16 hours)*
> *- Small (Cooldown: 24 hours)*

Belissar's mind came to a halt. Right, he had forgotten since it didn't happen last time, but the first expansion purification had unlocked larger daily purifications. Apparently, this last one had as well. Belissar could now choose small purifications for the daily fights, while the cooldown on the other two minor purification strengths had dropped. He could even do two minor purifications a day if he so chose.

Which meant he now had a choice to make. Have his bees face a small purification, which up to this point had been the big expansion fights, or stick with what they knew? Previously he would have just gone with the minor+ to be safe, but since he was trying to put aside his own fears and trust the bees, he felt he should at least consider the big one.

Small purifications. So far, that had been the bird-shade and the two cat-shades. He wasn't sure about the turtle-shade—since that had been an emergency purification, he hadn't chosen a specific strength for it—but he figured to be safe he'd include that as well. The good news was that no new shades had appeared in the daily purifications so far. He wasn't entirely sure if that was because they were daily purifications or because they had been minor and minor+, though, but if it was the former case then he could at least count on seeing something he had seen before.

The bird- and cat-shades were fine. The bees had proven capable of taking them on without issue, though they would have to take on either a bigger bird-shade or two cat-shades this time. The dirt tunnels would help with that as well. The question was, would the bees be able to take on a turtle-shade? Chief Rohsuak could help out again, but even with her new blessing Belissar didn't want to exhaust her on a daily purification.

But, well, they had the lava field now, so the tower had significant fire defenses of its own. And they had two of the lancers up. Belissar wasn't sure how they'd match up against the turtle-shade, but since a full-speed dive from a soldier had nearly pierced the turtle's tail, he imagined a lancer should be capable of much more. They also had Beero and her wounded soldier squad, so the bee army had magic of its own this time.

Slowly, he nodded his head, and then he made his way to the flower meadow. The queen in charge for the day flew to meet him, along with Chief Rohsuak and Metsaitti. Once he had greeted them all, he turned to the queen.

"Hello, looks like you're ready for the daily purification?"

The queen saluted to confirm.

"Then . . . is the army ready to face a stronger one? Like, a big bird-shade, two cat-shades, or a turtle-shade?"

The queen paused, and then quickly began to salute.

"Bees ready. Will stop all enemies and protect hive of hives."

Belissar slowly nodded and turned to the karnuq.

"How about you? Um, would you be ready to help if we needed it again?"

Chief Rohsuak smiled and nodded.

"Of course, Sacred Den Master. We are ready to defend our home anytime."

Belissar took a deep breath.

"Okay, then that's what we'll do."

The queen and the karnuq both saluted once more. Belissar made one last change before triggering the purification. He took the lava field from its current position, between the first-floor dirt tunnels and the flower meadow, and moved it behind the flower meadow. He couldn't help it. The Third of the Sixth had just set up her hive there today. And while most shades had made a beeline straight for the room's exit, he didn't want to risk the Third of the Sixth on them changing strategy, at least not until her hive was better prepared to fight. If a turtle-shade showed up that needed fire to deal with, he'd move the lava field back. Otherwise, he'd let the proven defenses do their thing.

With that, he triggered the purification and the Hunger began to coalesce. Soon, a screech from a massive beak pierced the air of the dirt tunnels. The bird-shade had returned once more. Belissar couldn't help but gulp. He knew his bees had figured out how to deal with bird-shades . . . but all of the ones they'd handled easily had been smaller. They were now facing the full-size, full-power bird-shade for the first time since the expansion purification when it had first appeared.

But his tower had brought one down before, so he trusted his bees to bring it down again. He just hoped there wouldn't be as many casualties this time.

The bird-shade fully emerged and let out another screech. It extended and beat its wings, kicking up gusts of dirt as it launched into the air . . . and promptly landed. The entrance room of the dirt tunnels was wide enough for it to use its wings, but apparently the first tunnel was not. It could just about spread its wings, but it would have had very little room to flap them or maneuver about, so it landed, folded its wings, and began walking. Belissar blinked . . . and even giggled a bit. The bird-shade, so terrifying when soaring through the skies, was far less intimidating while hobbling on the ground. In fact, it had gone from one of the fastest shades to one of the slowest, slower than all but the turtle-shade.

So, while it could still use its wings to hop and glide over the pit traps, it had no means of evading the first wall-mounted sticky honey trap. The shade screeched and unleashed its black lightning attack, but there was nothing to zap, and it was left drenched in thick maddening honey. The shade's pace slowed to an absolute crawl as the honey weighed it down, and it stuck to the ground every time it lowered its feet. As time went on, the shade started to sway as the toxins began to take effect.

And then it encountered the next pit trap.

It leapt and extended its wings out once again, only to plummet into the trap as its drenched and stuck wings couldn't provide sufficient lift. Whereupon it was sprayed yet again by a sticky honey trap, this one inside the pit.

Belissar could only stare and blink repeatedly at this turn of events. He had chosen the dirt tunnels largely for the effect it would have on the bird-shade, but he hadn't expected this. Even the smaller bird-shades from the minor+ purifications had done better than this!

But, well, he could only be happy that no bees would be hurt today. He grabbed a torch, used a bit of flame radish and mana honey to light it, and then made his way into the dirt tunnels, escorted by soldier bees and karnuq alike.

They came to the pit in question to find black lightning surging up from it on occasion. Belissar frowned before remembering he was holding a torch in his hand already. It had been so long since they had swapped over to bee-carried flame radish slivers that it had slipped his mind that he could just toss the torch into the pit from a safe distance.

Which is exactly what he did.

*All hostiles defeated. Purification successful.*

And in the end, the bird-shade that had once soared past his defenses was purified without a fuss. Belissar couldn't help but flush a bit at how much he had worried about it . . . and at the sight of the soldier bees swaying in the air, facing no fight at all after he told them there'd be a tough one.

In the end though, a victory was a victory, and a victory without sacrifice was the best of all. Belissar and the apiary queens still brought out the honey for a celebration. And then, once it was over, it was time for Belissar to consider the rewards.

*Small Purification completed!*
*Please select a reward:*
*- +100 DP*
*- +20 Max Mana*
*- Bee-type Vitality Boost (Minor)*

Belissar had to pause for a moment. The higher DP and max mana offers were to be expected. But . . . a bee-type perk? One that matched the uncommon one he had just received from the expansion purification choices? Well, he supposed this purification had been the same difficulty level as an earlier expansion purification, but it was still a surprise.

He did have a brief thought to his dwindling available mana, especially as he was ready for another DP shop purchase, but at the end of the day, a vitality boost to all of his bees was too good to pass up.

*Bee-type Vitality Boost (Minor) selected.*
*All Bee-type monsters receive a minor boost to vitality!*

It seemed his tower would have many opportunities to grow very soon.

# CHAPTER NINETEEN

# A NEW ROUND OF NEW-BEES

The Fourth of the Eighth stood in front of a cell in her hive. The cell was crackling with tiny-lightnings that occasionally crossed the wax cover and zapped any bee that got too close. It was not particularly popular among her workers, but the Fourth of the Eighth couldn't take her eyes off it.

The honey made by the soldiers was . . . strange. It looked like honey, acted like honey, and tasted like honey. By all accounts, it was honey. And yet, there was something ephemeral about it, quite literally. On her first attempts to store it, she found that the honey evaporated away if left alone for too long. Mana compromised far more of its structure than mana honey made by the normal process, and so would unravel over time.

It was a problem, as the lightning honey needed to last long enough for an egg to hatch and a larva to morph into a full adult worker. The Fourth of the Eighth had to conduct numerous experiments to get it to work. Adding more mana to the honey extended its lifespan, but with diminishing returns, as adding too much would only accelerate its decomposition. Mixing it with regular honey just diluted them both until the lightning honey faded away. Eventually, she had her workers consume it outright and reprocess it. This managed to produce a stable honey with some amount of tiny-lightnings, but in far lower quantities than the original lightning honey. It was also unpleasant for her workers, many of whom continued to twitch and tremble even after finishing the process.

But it *had* succeeded, and, with time and effort, they had managed to accumulate enough to fill a worker cell. The very cell she now watched with every moment she had to spare. Had it been enough? Had they provided enough honey for a worker to grow? Had they maintained enough of the lightning to change the worker? Would the egg and the larva survive growing in such honey? Would any of these efforts have any payoff?

She did not know. She couldn't, until the brood growing with this cell finally stirred . . . or failed to. It had already spent longer under its cap than a normal worker, causing the Fourth of the Eighth to pace around. She knew from speaking with some of the other queens that bees raised on special honeys took longer to grow, but she could not help but worry. Just when would this worker—

She paused. She thought she saw the cap shift a bit. But she fluttered her wings and then groomed her antennas. She had been deceived before, and every previous time it had simply been a trick of the light, the shadow of a passing worker. The Fourth of the Eighth was determined not to get her hopes up.

Until she saw it again.

Her eyes instantly locked to the spot in question. There, she saw cracks form in the wax cover as it bulged out slightly.

She nearly leapt to tear open the cap herself, but her workers beat her to the punch. They ignored the tiny-lightnings jumping to their hairs as they chewed open the cap, freeing the bee within.

And then, out crawled a new, healthy, fully-formed worker. A worker whose yellow hairs seemed a bit brighter, whose wings shimmered with dancing yellow lights, and who had tiny-lightnings jumping between her antennas.

The Fourth of the Eighth slowly crawled to the new worker, who began a salute dance. The Fourth of the Eighth brushed the worker with her antennas, getting a tiny zap from the lightning in the process, pulling her from her shock.

This . . . was a new worker. A special worker, raised on special honey. *Her* special worker, a member of her own hive.

They had done it.

A moment later, she broke out into a happy dance of her own.

The First of the Fifth watched her communers give their report dances. So, the Fourth of the Eighth had apparently raised a new kind of worker with help from the wounded soldiers? With honey that came not from any extant flower in the King's realm but with the lightning that Beero and her comrades commanded?

That was impressive. Even the First of the Fifth had not considered such a method, and might not have attempted it even if she had. The lack of supporting flowers would hamper scaling up a hive based on such honey. But now that the Fourth of the Eighth had successfully raised a new type of worker who presumably would be able to produce new types of honey with normal mana flower nectar . . . it might just be possible.

She would have to reconsider her evaluation of the Fourth of the Eighth. The First of the Fifth had considered giving the lastborn a bit of assistance to bring her up to par with the others, but now that she had gone and created a new type of bee all on her own, the First of the Fifth would accelerate those plans. A new type of bee needed as much support as possible to spread quickly.

More immediately, there would now be another new bee type to present to the King today, in addition to the two standing before her now. The First of the Fifth instructed the communers to send word to the Fourth of the Eighth, inviting her to join the First of the Fifth in greeting the King.

Belissar made his way over to the First of the Fifth's hive, hearing there were new bee types to see. The First of the Fifth was waiting for him there, along with another queen. After happily greeting him, she danced toward the other queen.

"This is Fourth of the Eighth, also has new bee to show."

The other queen flew unsteadily as she greeted him. Belissar gave her a smile. "Great work, I can't wait to see the new one."

The Fourth of the Eighth nearly dropped from the air, causing Belissar to reach his hand out. She landed on his hand . . . then quickly buzzed her wings and took off as quickly as she could. Belissar just shook his head and chuckled.

"It's alright."

He held out his other hand to the First of the Fifth. She nearly dropped out of the air too but managed to catch herself. Then she slowly and gingerly hovered forward until she came to rest in his hand. His smile grew.

"Let's see the new bees then?"

The First of the Fifth saluted, then turned to face her bees and danced for them to come forward. The first was a worker bee with purple hair. Beyond that, she seemed normal at first glance. At least, until Belissar focused on her more closely.

### *Gravity Monster Bee Worker*

|  |  |
|---|---|
| ***Vitality:*** | *Minimal* |
| ***Strength:*** | *Minimal* |
| ***Speed:*** | *Average* |
| ***Magic:*** | *Minimal+* |
| ***Defense:*** | *Minimal+* |
| ***Resistance:*** | *Minimal+* |
| ***Special:*** | *Minor* |
| ***Notable Skills:*** | *Poison Sting, Minor Gravity Manipulation, Sacrificial Strike, Brood Offspring* |

*A monster bee worker raised on honey infused with Gravity attribute mana.*
*Can generate small gravitational fields, which it generally uses to carry*
*more nectar and pollen, as well as to modify its own honey and wax.*

Belissar tilted his head. He vaguely knew from the gravilion flower that gravity had something to do with making things lighter and heavier, but that was still the extent of his knowledge. Therefore, he didn't really know what this bee could do, and the description didn't really help him figure it out. Something about carrying more nectar and pollen . . . so maybe the bee would make the nectar and pollen it carried lighter?

Well, he'd keep an eye on it and watch it in action. Maybe that would shed some light on what gravity actually was. But either way, it was a new bee, which alone was enough to make Belissar happy.

So, it was great that there were two more! The next worker bee was light blue and black, and glowing slightly, with smooth and solid-looking chitin that oozed drops of liquid. She was carrying a small ball of honey with her front two legs.

### Slime Bee Worker

|  |  |
|---:|:---|
| **Vitality:** | *Minimal* |
| **Strength:** | *Minimal* |
| **Speed:** | *Average* |
| **Magic:** | *Minor* |
| **Defense:** | *Minimal* |
| **Resistance:** | *Minimal* |
| **Special:** | *Minor+* |
| **Notable Skills:** | *Poison Sting, Slime Core, Sacrificial Strike, Brood Offspring* |

*A monster bee that acts as a slime core. Will surround itself in a type of slime-honey*
*to act as a slime body. Even if the slime body is destroyed, the slime bee can survive*
*and reform if its bee core escapes. This one is a worker, using its slime body*
*to help gather nectar and pollen, and to harden into wax.*

Belissar's eyes widened slightly. So that was where all the slime flower nectar had gone . . . and boy had it paid off. Now, instead of slimes formed by the flower, he had a bee that could make a slime around itself! Well, Belissar didn't really know enough about slimes to know what the difference was, but he figured he'd like a bee slime better. And it was nice to know that his tower would still have slimes of a sort, even if the bees' gathering prevented the slime flower from ever accumulating enough nectar to generate its own. He was very much curious to see the slime bee in action.

Finally, the Fourth of the Eighth managed to eke out a dance and the final worker came forward. The First of the Fifth danced as well.

"This one raised by Fourth of the Eighth."

The Fourth of the Eighth quickly began tapping out a dance.

"W-With help! F-From soldiers!"

And looking at this next bee, Belissar had a guess as to which soldiers had helped.

### *Shocking Monster Bee Worker*

|  |  |
|--:|:--|
| *Vitality:* | *Minimal* |
| *Strength:* | *Minimal* |
| *Speed:* | *Average* |
| *Magic:* | *Minimal+* |
| *Defense:* | *Minimal* |
| *Resistance:* | *Minimal+* |
| *Special:* | *Minor* |
| *Notable Skills:* | *Shocking Poison Sting, Lightning Resistance, Sacrificial Strike, Brood Offspring* |

*A monster bee worker raised on honey infused with Lightning attribute mana. Lightning infuses both its body and its venom, boosting its ability to gather pollen and to defend itself. Stings will cause minor electric shocks.*

"So, I'm guessing Beero and her friends helped you with this one?"

"Y-Yes!"

Belissar nodded and smiled.

"Great work, you both. I'm excited to see how they work."

Belissar chuckled as the two queens and their three workers took off and began zipping "King best king!" dances. Then he rubbed his chin.

The gravity and slime bees were somewhat expected, as that was Belissar's hope with the special flowers in the first place. The shocking bee was not, for there were, as of yet, no lightning flowers in the tower. And yet, here the bee was, which must have evolved from honey created by Beero and the others through magic. Which caused Belissar to realize something big.

He didn't need to wait for new flowers to raise new bees. If he had a way to create special honey types without a flower, they could then raise new bees. He looked down at his hand and formed a honeycomb pattern out of his mana.

All he had to do, then, was figure out how to make new types of honey . . .

# BEE-ING USEFUL

After checking on the new bees in the apiary, Belissar made his way to the bumblebee meadow, both to see how things were going and because he just liked watching the bumblebees zip around him. He approached to find the workers as usual, leisurely making their way from flower to flower. Each one he approached stopped foraging to fly a few circles around him before resuming their work.

Still, he didn't want to disrupt them too much, so he quickly made his way to the nests to greet the queens and then move on with his day. As he did, though, he heard a loud thrumming noise. Less like the buzz of normal bees, and more like tree leaves rustling in heavy winds. He looked up to find a large shadow blocking out the sun, and then four heavy shapes landed before him with a thud. His eyes widened.

Several massive bumblebees now stood on the ground before him. They were different sizes, but even the smallest was as large as a lancer, while the largest was even bigger than a wolf. They had their stingers extended, each as large as a dagger . . . at the smallest.

The queens flew out of their nests shortly after. Belissar turned to them in a daze.

"Are these . . . bumblebee soldiers?"

The oldest queen flew one circle around him to confirm.

"Wow. They're big."

The queen flew one more circle around him before releasing some mana-laden pheromones to convey additional information. Belissar's eyes went even wider.

"They're . . . not done growing? Even the big one?"

The queen flew one more circle around him. Belissar could only nod blankly for a bit, then started to grin.

"These are really going to help, I think. Great work, everyone."

After that, he was treated to four queens zipping circles around him repeatedly. The four soldiers spread out their wings, beating the air with heavy thuds as they slowly took off. They then flew around him in circles as well, kicking up gusts of wind around him in the process.

Belissar continued to grin. The largest bees he had ever seen . . . and they weren't even done growing yet. At this rate, his bees might be able to face the next shade on even footing. It seemed that monster bumblebees had been an excellent choice after all.

Things, however, were not going as well for the Fourth of the Seventh's drone. The drone had done his best to be useful for his kind and merciful queen mother, and the first communer and the other queen of the hive had done their best to support him, but it hadn't worked out so far.

The first communer and the other queen had tried to teach him how to forage, noting his larger eyes and better senses. However, it turned out he lacked a honey stomach to begin with, so while he could drink nectar, he couldn't store it or pass it along. That also meant that he couldn't help to process the nectar into honey either.

Scouting was the next option . . . but it turned out his senses were tuned to one thing only. He could find and identify other bees easily enough, but he had no instincts for flowers or hive locations. They would be teaching him from scratch for that task.

Next, they thought about having him help dry honey and infuse it with mana . . . but this did not work out either. He did not have the instincts to analyze the honey's current state, so he could not adjust his drying on his own. He could do it by watching the other bees, but he was less efficient at it than them. And, unfortunately, his mana was not regenerating like the worker bees' did, so they considered it too dangerous for him to infuse honey with it. He would end up having to drink more honey to compensate, so it would defeat the purpose.

The brood tenders flat-out refused to have a bee without the appropriate instincts handle the brood. Even guard duty wasn't viable, due to his lack of a stinger.

It turned out that he was built for a single task only. And since that task was currently unnecessary, there wasn't much he was especially suited for. Even the first communer and the other queen were a bit at a loss of what else to do with him, so they just had him fanning the hive to help regulate overall temperatures. A task that was largely unnecessary in the perfectly stable and comfortable climate of the King's realm.

He still conducted that task with all the effort he could muster, but he could not help but wish he could do more. He had failed at his one task, the task his brothers had nobly given their lives to achieve. Whereas they had sacrificed for the good of hive of hives, an effort acknowledged by even the King himself, he had done no such thing and yet continued to drain his mother's resources. He had even offered to leave again—now that they had taught him to forage, he could at least survive on his own—but the other queen and the first communer would have none of it. His kind and gracious mother had saved his life, and so they would not allow him to struggle alone.

So, if he wanted to stop being a burden and pay back the hive of hives for even a little of the honey they had spent on him, he had to find *something* to do. But what, exactly? What could he achieve without instincts or a honey stomach or a stinger or regenerating mana? His sisters could do anything he could and much better. Was he doomed to just wait around for the next wave of queens?

He didn't know, and so he kept his eyes open and his antennas swaying. He at least had better senses than his sisters, so maybe he'd catch something they wouldn't. Though, without the instincts to actually identify anything other than a queen, he wasn't sure what exactly to look for. All he could really see were his sisters hard at work, and the swirling patterns of their mana throughout the hive.

He couldn't bear to watch his sisters do all that he couldn't, so he kept his focus on the mana instead. The mana of the hive was no still, homogenous pool, but a whirling river flowing in cycles. Each worker within the hive absorbed and released their own mana, pulling the mana of the hive toward them while pushing their own mana into the flow. The new nectar brought in released mana of different sorts that was then processed and homogenized by the workers as they made honey from it. The eggs and the larvae released mana of their own, calling for their tenders whenever a problem arose. And above all the various swirls were the large currents released by the queen herself, the main pathway that carried the mana of all the other bees throughout the hive, with the smaller rivers of the communers breaking off and joining back with the main flow as necessary.

The mana of his home hive was particularly chaotic. The river from his queen mother was weaker than usual, flowing much farther away as she was currently out of the hive. The mana flows of his worker sisters, however, were stronger than normal to compensate, and the first communer was reinforcing the main river in the queen's absence. Their system, therefore, was more like a system of smaller rivers than a single circuit, many smaller cycles joining together into a larger whole.

This, however, was in contrast to the other queen and her kin. The other queen kept up a powerful and orderly flow, with each worker joining and breaking off at specific points. A well-ordered circuit without a bee out of place, where even the eggs and the larvae were strategically placed to help support the flow.

Or at least, those ideas were what the first communer and the queen were each trying to do. The two river systems were colliding as the joint hive mixed and interacted. Sometimes the flows were able to mix together without too much trouble, but in other places they collided and formed whirling rapids that disrupted both. The communers seemed to congregate at those locations, giving instructions through physical dances rather than via mana. One such location was right by the drone, in fact.

His eyes fixed upon the chaotic swirl. There was something about it that drew his attention, something that triggered the few instincts he was born with. Before he knew it, he found himself crawling toward the swirl. His antennas twitched and then stretched out in the direction of the densest mana concentration.

And then, suddenly, a bit of the mana swirl brushed against his antennas . . . and locked onto it. The swirl began to split, mana from the two hives now separating and streaming into his two antennas, one type of mana for each. The drone panicked and crawled back; the last thing he wanted was to take the hive's mana on top of its honey. Unfortunately, he could not stop whatever process had begun as the mana stream only intensified, the swirl unraveling into two separate streams flowing into him.

The chaotic whirl reappeared within his body as the two streams collided within him, with his own mana joining in and twisting around them, condensing them down. And then . . . mana began to flow from his body, surging back out into the hive's flow of mana. A single stream of mana instead of two.

The drone fell flat against the floor, hoping that whatever he did had not disrupted the hive. Unfortunately, those hopes were quickly dashed as he saw the first communer and the other queen rushing toward him. The queen started dancing before she even fully arrived.

"Drone! You did this?!"

The drone wanted to fly away, but he managed to dance out a confirmation. The queen whirled toward the arriving communer.

"Fourth of Seventh's communer, can feel?!"

The first communer stumbled as she slowly danced.

"Yes can feel . . . other queen? Can see other workers . . ."

The other queen, the First of the Fifth's First Daughter, suddenly burst out into a rapid dance.

"Amazing! Incredible! Can feel Fourth of Seventh's hive! No . . . AM part of Fourth of Seventh's hive now!"

The drone froze, uncertain what to make of this turn of events. The First of the Fifth's First Daughter then rushed over to him, practically twisting their antennas together.

"Drone! You did, right? Can do again?!"

"T-Think so?"

She nearly began dragging him as she turned.

"Good! Then do! Help join hives together!"

He managed to glance at the communer, who danced her confirmation as well.

"Already asked queen, she says yes. Good work, drone. Will help a lot."

The drone paused at that, and then did his best to dance a salute as the First of the Fifth's First Daughter dragged him along. It seemed he had found a job to do after all.

# THE FIRST EX-BEE-DITION!

The Fourth of the Seventh paused. She was currently in the mini-hive beyond the King's realm, preparing to set out, but something shifted in the back of her mind. There, in the link to the children back in her main hive, she felt a new presence.

*"Fourth of Seventh?! Can hear?!"*

A huge chunk of mana reached her, twisted into a dance by the communer that sent it. The Fourth of the Seventh's antennas twitched and then she began to dance, the communer beside her converting the dance into mana to send back.

*"First of Fifth's First Daughter?"*

*"Yes! It worked! Joined Fourth of Seventh's hive's mana thanks to drone! All thanks to Fourth of Seventh! Amazing, incredible!"*

The Fourth of the Seventh began a happy dance. She wasn't entirely sure what was going on, but it seemed the First of the Fifth's First Daughter was happy, so that was reason enough to celebrate. And it sounded like the drone she rescued had done something too? She was happy he'd found something to do then!

And when she looked more closely, she found she could now see through the First of the Fifth's First Daughter's eyes, just like with her own workers! She could see her first communer glowing and passing along the First of the Fifth's First Daughter's mana. The drone was there too, taking mana from both hives' workers and twisting it together. The Fourth of the Seventh sent her mana to them all.

*"Amazing! Incredible! Great work!"*

She then turned back to focus on her present surroundings. Her workers and soldiers had formed up outside. One flew in and danced a salute to her, the signal that all was clear. With that, the Fourth of the Seventh crawled out of the mini-hive, started beating her wings, and took off into the air. Today, she was joining the scouting party.

The Fourth of the Seventh had initially planned to rely on her communers to watch the scouts, but with all the efforts her hive and the First of the Fifth's First Daughter had made to let her come here, she and her scouts decided that she would join the sweep in person. The scouts had done a preliminary sweep to ensure the area was safe and then set a perimeter to keep it that way, and now it was time for her to move. Her soldiers took up their formation around her, ready to respond to any threats. Another group of scouts made a smaller perimeter around her in case the outer scouts missed anything, and a group of tenders flew next to the queen to monitor her condition.

As for the queen herself?

She flew about at random, letting herself drift to anything that drew her attention. She found a particularly conspicuous pile of rocks on the ground. Conspicuous because they featured the same angular edges and uniform size of the rocks that she had built the mini-hive in, in a way that vaguely reminded her of the King's own constructions. Also, the rocks were connected right to the fallen structure and extended out flat along the ground, in a line extending off into the forest.

If she had to guess . . . this was a guide to the fallen rock hive. If the creatures who built that hive were like the karnuq, then they wouldn't have had wings or the ability to fly. It was hard to imagine lacking such a fundamental skill. How would they get anywhere? How would they orient themselves within the landscape? How would they spot flowers from a distance? So . . . she guessed that maybe this flat pile of rocks was to help them find their hive even if they couldn't see the landscape from above.

Which, of course, made her wonder where exactly it was headed. Maybe to a major flower patch to forage from? She couldn't wait to find out!

And so, the Fourth of the Seventh led her party along the flat rock pile. They flew at a leisurely pace, drifting on and off the path as they went. She landed on flowers she had never seen before and drank from their nectar directly, making note of their locations for the return trip. Before this trip, she and her soldiers had woven some new stem ropes that grew wider in the middle. Each was a basic sling, like she had seen some of the karnuq use, that would wrap around a soldier bee and hang below its torso. She had seen the karnuq give flowers to the King and that made the King happy, so she figured her scouts could try to bring back anything interesting they found on their way home.

But first, she'd fly as far as she could fly and see all that she could see. Everything, from the air to the dirt to the plants themselves, was of a different quality than those made by the King. None of them had the warmth and abundance of mana that his realm offered, yet all of them were different, even from each other. There was a diversity of different plants here that the Fourth of the Seventh had never seen before, from towering trees with thin needles for leaves, to squat bushes that still towered above flowers, to vines that wrapped around other plants. And she took it all in with her own eyes, felt the cool breeze across her own chitin, smelt the scents of sap and nectar with her own antennas. She'd have burst into a happy dance if she weren't flying forward at the moment.

Soon, the Fourth of the Seventh noticed that the forest was beginning to thin out. A short while later, they arrived at a clearing. The Fourth of the Seventh landed on a tree branch and paused.

At the edge of the clearing, they could see the dark and writhing mass of the intruders, what the King and the karnuq referred to as the Hunger. It appeared they had reached the edge of the Beyond, at least until the King took the fight to the Hunger once more. Her workers and soldiers grew agitated, fidgeting about. One of the scouts landed before her.

"Queen, should turn back. Not safe."

But the Fourth of the Seventh hesitated. For there, in the middle of the clearing between her and the Hunger, was another hive of rock and stone. And this one . . . this one was far larger than the one she'd built her mini-hive in. It was even larger than the King's tower, if she wasn't mistaken. It had a crumbling wall surrounding its exterior, and placed along the edges were not just one but *several* ruined towers like the one she had built her mini-hive in. Behind that were the remains of yet a second wall, with additional towers of its own. And in the center of it all, she could see the remains of an even larger structure peeking up over the walls.

"Want to scout that."

The worker danced the negative.

"Not safe. Too close to enemy. And . . . is just rock? Not important?"

The Fourth of the Seventh paused to think for a moment. The worker was right on most counts. It was most assuredly not safe to move that close to the Hunger. And it was, after all, just a pile of rocks—and if whoever built the rock hive wasn't around anymore, then just an empty one.

And yet, she couldn't take her eyes off of it. She couldn't help but wonder what sort of being had built such a hive. Were they like the karnuq? Maybe like the King, though how a being on par with the King could have lost a hive like this she couldn't fathom. The Fourth of the Seventh made her choice and danced her command . . .

"Can wait. King will push back Hunger eventually."

But the worker was still correct. She was a queen, and her hive was already making great compromises allowing her out this far. She would not risk herself or them by flying into the jaws of the Hunger. One day, the King's power would push the Hunger even farther, and then she'd be able to scout the rock hive to her heart's content. Today, it would be a flight too far.

So, she turned around.

"Let's go back, get flowers for King!"

Thanks to the communer, she could see her workers and soldiers conduct a small relief dance, even though her back was turned. She buzzed her wings. Did they really think she would just fly right into danger like that? She only . . . slightly thought about it!

As she left, the scouts made a note of the rock hive's location. They had previously noted it as a landmark but hadn't considered investigating it in full. After all, the field and forest around it were far more likely to hold ideal foraging spots. But the queen had marked it as a feature of importance. Her scouts, therefore, decided to pay a bit more attention to it, as well as to keep their eyes out for anything like it.

And indeed, while the writhing of the Hunger occupied most of their attention at this distance, one scouted noted a faint hum of mana on the air, something other than the Hunger in the distance . . .

# CHAPTER TWENTY

# THE START OF COLLA-BEE-RATION

**B**elissar spent the next hour practicing his own honey-making spell. He was trying to make different honey types, like medicinal or lightning honey, but it was slow going. The honey kept coming out the same, and he wasn't sure how exactly to vary the pattern to adjust it. He asked Beero what she and the lightning bees had done . . . but their honey-making spell pattern was the same as his. It was just that they already had lightning moving along with their mana, so it got caught in the spell.

So, eventually, Belissar came up with another idea. He realized it had been quite a while since he had spoken to Juosiutik, so he made his way over to the karnuq's settlement. Chief Rohsuak guided him to a stone building in progress. Juosiutik caught sight of them and rushed over.

"Sacred Den Master! Um, sorry I sort of . . . stopped the lessons . . ."

Belissar shook his head.

"It's okay. I, um, sort of forgot too. I have a question though, if you don't mind?"

Juosiutik nodded her head repeatedly.

"Of course! What can I help you with?"

"Great, well, you know how there are different honey types?"

Juosiutik froze solid, blinking repeatedly.

"There are . . . different honey types?"

Belissar tilted his head. Did she not know that?

"Um, yes? Like the medicinal one? Or the maddening one I gave to . . . um, the karnuq that gave me the Ground mana flowers."

Juosiutik's eyes opened even wider.

"Medicinal . . . maddening . . . Ground mana flowers?"

"Um, yes? We've had those for a while, even."

Juosiutik began to tremble. Belissar tilted his head even more. Niobee began to buzz and hovered in between them while Belissar's soldier escorts moved closer. Juosiutik glanced at them, shook her head, and then took a deep breath.

"Sacred Den Master . . . I believe we have a lot to talk about."

Juosiutik led Belissar to her original wooden abode and they both sat down on some simple cushions for a long talk. Belissar was thus diverted from his original intent as he began to explain the different honey types and the new flowers he had raised while Juosiutik had been busy exploring her new powers. Juosiutik's eyes were as wide as they could go and her legs were bouncing the entire time . . . though Niobee and the bees continued to hover around her. She stared out into the distance.

"So . . . the bees can make honey that will take on the special properties of any nectar they consume *and* can help cross-pollinate and breed new types of plants?"

Belissar hummed his agreement.

"Yes, that's correct."

Juosiutik leaned back, placing her hands on the floor behind her as she looked up at the roof.

". . . Bees are amazing."

Belissar smiled at that.

"Yes, they are."

Juosiutik took a deep breath as she leaned forward once more. She crossed her arms and rubbed her chin with one hand.

"Fascinating. I had been focused on using the honey as a binding agent to elevate a potion, but the honey is practically a potion in and of itself. So, what if we went the other way and tried to change the honey itself? I suppose that would depend on the bees. Maybe if we fed them the right ingredients ahead of time, it would change the honey they produce? Could they drink a mixture of ingredients and produce a potion straight away?"

Belissar grinned.

"That's actually what I'm here to ask you about."

Belissar subsequently explained how the bees could not only produce different honeys based on the flowers but could evolve based on the honey they consumed. He gave some examples, and then explained what had happened with the lightning soldiers and later the lightning worker raised on the honey they had produced via magic. Juosiutik's eyes managed to go even wider than Belissar had thought possible.

"The bees . . . can evolve and then produce the compounds right in their bodies?"

Belissar nodded.

"Yes, that's right. So, yeah. I was wondering if you had any ideas for making new honey types that we could use to raise new bees."

Meanwhile, Niobee drooped and landed on the ground, crawling about in an unsteady circle. Eventually, she came to a stop, groomed her antennas, and then took off to fly in front of Belissar.

"King . . . can wait? Need to ask something."

Belissar tilted his head.

"Sure, whatever you need, Niobee."

She danced a quick thanks, then flew out of the building. Belissar waited in silence while Juosiutik began muttering to herself. Just a minute or two later, Niobee flew back, now with a worker in tow.

"This is First of Fifth's worker. First of Fifth's hive interested in new honey types, wants to hear if karnuq knows."

Belissar smiled and chuckled.

"Ah, that's a good idea."

He turned to Juosiutik.

"Would you mind speaking with my bees on this? This is a worker from a queen called the First of the Fifth. She's the expert on honey-making."

Juosiutik stared in silence for a moment, and then burst out nodding repeatedly as quickly as she could.

"Yes! Of course! This . . . this is big. The possibilities here . . ."

She took a deep breath and then turned to the worker.

"Tell me *everything*. Tell me all about your honey and I'll tell you everything I know about potions."

The worker paused for a moment before turning to Belissar.

"Queen asks King if okay?"

Belissar reached down and brushed the worker's back.

"Yes, go ahead."

The worker then turned back to Juosiutik and began dancing.

"Queen says okay."

The worker then began to explain in detail the process by which they made mana honey from various sources, and how that honey could then be used to evolve existing bees. Juosiutik listened in silence, her eyes fixed upon the dancing bee as she nodded along.

"It sounds like . . . the bees are practically making potions within themselves in the first place. This is . . ." She rubbed her chin and hummed for a moment. "What about a mixture? Have you tried drinking nectar from multiple sources before processing it into honey?"

"Queen says have but makes honey quality worse."

Juosiutik started tapping her foot.

"I could see that occurring too. Maybe the ingredients clashed . . . or it could be a matter of timing and processing. Does your queen remember which flowers exactly she mixed and when in the process she mixed them?"

"Remembers. First is . . ."

The bee began dancing in detail while Juosiutik followed along.

"Hm, I see. I'm not as familiar with the flowers for the maddening honey, but sleepy chamomile should go along with the medicinal herbs that grow in the sacred den. Would it be possible to add the sleepy chamomile nectar at this point in the medicinal processing . . ."

And so Juosiutik and the First of the Fifth began talking via communer and worker, with Juosiutik speaking louder and louder and the worker bee dancing ever more quickly. Belissar quickly lost track of their conversation.

"Um, seems like you both have a lot to talk about. I, uh, need to take care of something, so if you don't need me I'll take my leave. Um, let me know if either of you need anything?"

Juosiutik flushed.

"Ah, right! Thank you, Sacred Den Master, for everything. I'm sure we'll be able to make something great!"

The worker bee, on the other hand, saluted and proclaimed, "King best king!"

And with that, Belissar took his leave and left them both to it. With the two experts on the job, he had no doubt they'd come up with something better than anything he could think of, so he decided to address a mixture of his own. He made his way back to the apiary and to his farmhouse within, then opened one of the jars waiting there and took a whiff. He hummed to himself and poured a bit into a wooden mug. He took a drink . . .

His eyes lit up. It was mead. In some ways, it tasted like regular old mead. But in other ways, it was something more. That was perhaps the best way to describe it. Mead . . . but more. The taste was fuller and lingered longer on his tongue. The warmth spread through his body more quickly and felt even more pleasant. Likewise, he could feel mana suffusing through his body, mixing with his own as it spread the sensation of the mead throughout.

He made a huge grin. The recipe and taste may have been basic, but he was certain that this was still the best mead he had ever made. His eyes even began to moisten. The day the tower lord's son arrived at his village, Belissar had thought his mead-making days were over. His recipes would go unfinished and he'd never taste it again. But now, after everything, here he was. A mead-maker once more.

And now made from the best honey he had ever had, from hives that he could talk to. From bees who loved him, and who he loved in turn.

He capped the jar and lifted it, then made his way to the Shrine of Bees. He placed the jar in the wax chest and bowed his head.

"Thank you again, for everything. If it weren't for you . . . I'd never have made mead ever again. I know this one is basic, but I hope you like it."

The Shrine of Bees began to glow bright, so it seemed she did.

# CHAPTER TWENTY-ONE

# DIVINE BEE-SIRES

The First of the Fifth couldn't help but tremble as she danced around. Thanks to the King, she had established direct contact with the dangerous karnuq. And despite the danger of doing so, the rewards promised to be unimaginable. The dangerous one held vast knowledge regarding mixing different plants together. Already a single conversation had produced multiple potential processing methods to attempt. If even one of them succeeded, the First of the Fifth might discover a new honey type . . . and possibly new types of bees as well.

And this success was fortunately timed as the First of the Fifth waited at the entrance of her hive. A group of foragers was just returning . . . and these were no normal foragers.

The bees that arrived were large for workers and far fuzzier than normal, more closely resembling the bumblebees than their sisters. Their antennas were fluffy with almost leaf-like hairs, their pollen baskets were large and deep, and their mandibles were large with sharp edges. Their proboscises could extend to a surprising length when fully unfurled.

These were the newly evolved gardener bees, back from their first foraging trip. The First of the Fifth watched as they unloaded the nectar and pollen they had gathered, each carrying noticeably more than the other workers. The gardeners then walked up to her.

"Ground mana flower too bright. Wants less sun."

"Workers taking too much nectar from slime flower. Needs break."

"Gravilion flower has too much nectar, not enough pollen. Needs more visits."

Each of the gardeners reported on each of the flowers they had visited. They were optimized to gather data from the plants they visited, with their large antennas sensitive to whatever scents the plants released, the mana that wafted off of them, or even the tiny-lightnings that changed whenever a bee landed on them. As a result, they could identify the health of a flower in a deeper way than the average worker. This was information the First of the Fifth now needed if she wanted to take care of the hive of hives as a whole. She turned and danced to a nearby communer.

"Will inform King about Ground mana flower. Tell workers slime flower is gardener only now. Will try to raise more gravity bees for gravilion flower. Good work."

The gardeners saluted and then took off again, returning back to the flowers beyond. With their help, the flowers would grow healthier and more numerous than ever before. And with the dangerous karnuq's help, the First of the Fifth's hive would pioneer new ways to process their nectar. The First of the Fifth couldn't wait to see what would result.

"Too much light? Huh, got it, thanks for letting me know!"

The First of the Fifth danced around happily as Belissar thanked her. He subsequently moved the Ground mana flower nodes. Each of them had been placed in their floor's dirt tunnels, but right underneath the entrance to either the apiary or the flower meadow for maximum sunlight and easy access for the bees. Apparently, the flowers preferred things a bit darker, so Belissar moved them just a bit deeper into their tunnels, just enough to keep them in the shade but still visible for the bees.

It seemed the gardeners were already earning their name. Both the First of the Fifth and the Firstborn had evolved their first sets of gardeners, who were now buzzing around the apiary and flower meadow flowers and determining their states. Belissar couldn't wait to see what else they came up with.

Belissar mostly just watched the gardeners do their thing for the rest of the day. Their pollen crops could carry a massive amount of pollen, making them look like they were carrying two round stones as they flew about. Additionally, each gardener connected its mana with each plant it landed on and passed the knowledge it gained through the communers to the rest of the hive. Already, Belissar noted the rest of the worker bees adjusting their foraging routes as the gardeners determined which flowers were over-gathered from and which flowers were neglected. It seemed the gardeners were not only great at foraging themselves but would improve the gathering efficiency of their entire hives.

Eventually, though, the day passed and the time came for the next purification. Belissar selected another small purification. His eyes widened slightly as he saw the Hunger coalesce.

*Small purification begun. Remaining hostiles: 4*

This time it was back to the good old wolf-shades, but with a twist. Belissar watched as the most shades he had ever seen ran into the dirt tunnels . . . and the lead shade then promptly fell into a pit trap and was doused by a sticky honey trap. As with the first pair of wolf-shades, the others stayed by the pit, even jumping down to help when it was clear the fallen shade couldn't escape on its own. And since the bees weren't attacking in the dirt tunnels, the shades managed to climb out again. Belissar rubbed his chin. He'd have to see about getting some digging soldiers soon. The digging queen was established enough to either raise some herself or donate honey to the flower meadow, so it should be about time.

Belissar was free to think about the future as the wolf-shades only slowly made their way through the dirt tunnels. It was not as bad an environment for them as it had been for the bird-shade, but it still wasn't ideal. The wolf-shades lacked either the speed of the cat-shade or the resilience of the turtle-shade, so they were very much affected by the pit and honey traps placed throughout. While they managed to escape and continue moving forward, the maddening honey took its toll on each of the wolves hit by it.

And so, it took quite a while before the four staggering shades finally arrived at the flower meadow, Belissar having kept the volcano room back again until the Third of the Sixth was more established. The shades . . . were then torn to shreds. Sprayers began bombarding them from above, easily evading their counter-breaths. When the shades spread out to avoid the toxic sprays, the soldiers began their own attack runs and cut each shade off from one another. Meanwhile, the two lancers that were still active set up their dives, targeting the shades hampered by the honey traps. Those shades proved unable to dodge, and the lancers' stingers pierced straight through them and into the ground.

It was not long before all four shades were defeated, without a single bee casualty.

*Small Purification completed!*
*Please select a reward:*
*- +100 DP*
*- +20 Max Mana*
*- Wax Torches*

This time Belissar went with the mana. New features were great, but not if he lacked the mana to make more, and he still had two room slots to fill. And with that, the celebrations began. Belissar thought about bringing out the mead, but the one time he had fed it to bees in the past . . . hadn't gone well. He was still full of regret and guilt for the fate of that worker. So, while he had a feeling his current bees might hold up a bit better, he still wasn't going to risk it. Besides, he didn't have enough for all the karnuq hunters that watched each purification, much less all the bees, so he decided to save it up for now.

And well, he soon learned he had made the right choice.

*New mission received: Offer ten jars of mead to the Shrine of Bees.*

His eyes widened slightly. He guessed the God of Bees had very much appreciated the mead. Would that mean that monster bees could handle it? He could probably speak with the queens to avoid any further incidents.

However, Belissar was quickly pulled out of his thoughts.

*The God of Fire wishes to offer you a quest. Accept?*

Belissar tilted his head. Did the God of Fire still have to ask permission to do that? Even after the blessing? Well, Belissar didn't see a reason to refuse right now.

*New mission received: Make and offer mead from Fire attribute honey.*

Well, it seemed Belissar had his next mead recipe to try. Though, that would be a longer-term project, as he wasn't comfortable taking honey from the Third of the Sixth yet. In any case, it seemed his mead was popular with the gods. That . . . was a bit more than he'd expected from his first attempt to get back into the craft.

But, well, he'd just have to do his best and trust in his bees' honey.

The next day, the karnuq launched another expedition to the Underway. Metsaitti noted that the sacred den's purified zone extended in all directions, so there was a need to see how much of the Underway was within its range. And so, much to their dismay, the karnuq made their way to the rot cap field once again, only to find the stink bugs had replaced their numbers all too quickly. As the karnuq fought their way through noxious clouds and smelly mushrooms, several pairs of eyes lit up in the dark tunnel beyond.

"They're finally back. Get ready, everyone."

A faint shuffling in the dark went unnoticed by the karnuq as they fought their way toward the tunnel.

# CHAPTER TWENTY-TWO

# CONTACT BEE-STABLISHED

Metsaitti approached the end of the rot cap field with a cloth wrapped around his face. Besides him was a digging worker bee, currently dancing on the ground, and Noigakkuq, also wearing a cloth around her face. She was tense and puffing her cheeks slightly, likely upset that he had prevented her from fighting this time. But Metsaitti wanted to scout past the rot cap field today, and for that he needed Noigakkuq's nose. They could not afford for her to be drenched with stink bug scents even if she could handle herself now.

But they had made it through the field, so Noigakkuq could now take a more active role. Metsaitti nodded at her and she pulled down her cloth, sniffing at the air. Her face immediately scrunched up.

"Anything?"

She shook her head and spat out her words.

"Nothing. Just stink, stink, and more . . ."

She suddenly paused and then her eyes narrowed.

"There's stink . . . coming from the tunnel."

Metsaitti narrowed his eyes slightly. That *could* indicate another field of rot cap . . . but then the mushrooms should have extended down into the tunnel. Meanwhile, the digging worker flew back to his shoulder and began to tap out a dance.

"Something there. Seven, King-sized."

Metsaitti held out his hand to Noigakkuq.

"Back up."

Noigakkuq frowned but obeyed as she heard Metsaitti's commanding tone. The other karnuq noticed and began to form up a bit behind Metsaitti, weapons at the ready. Metsaitti kept his eyes fixed on the dark tunnel.

And then, slowly, a shape began to emerge. A humanoid walking on two legs emerged from the darkness, wrapped from head to toe in black clothes that revealed only their eyes and concealed a large bulge on their back. They stepped out of the tunnel just far enough to enter the light of the karnuq's light crystals and began to speak with a growling voice.

"Halt. You intrude upon the land of King Ratuatapi. Identify yourselves and state your intentions."

Metsaitti relaxed slightly, though he remained ready to move at a moment's notice.

"I am Metsaitti, defender of the nearby sacred den."

The figure's eyes narrowed.

"Defender? And you have proof of this?"

Metsaitti thought of the bee clinging to his shoulder but shook his head.

"Not presently, but I can arrange for it."

The figure and Metsaitti made eye contact in silence for a bit before the figure finally spoke again.

"You will return here tomorrow with proof of your claims. King Ratuatapi's envoy shall discuss your encroachment upon our lands . . . should you speak the truth."

The figure then backed up and vanished into the dark of the tunnel. Metsaitti turned and let out a light sigh. Their first diplomatic contact as defenders of the sacred den had gone reasonably well, given that nothing was currently on fire. He wasn't certain the sacred den master was prepared for it, however, so could only hope the extra day he'd just bought would be enough.

Belissar frowned as he stood before the Shrine of Bees in the battle meadow, as he had started to call the first floor's flower meadow in his mind. He was joined by Chief Rohsuak, the ever-present Niobee, and communers from the queens, having gathered them after hearing of the latest event from Metsaitti and the bee accompanying him. The queens had wanted to come in person, but since it was the middle of the day, Belissar insisted they continue with their own work for this meeting.

"So . . . what do we do?"

Chief Rohsuak looked him in the eye.

"That is up to you, Sacred Den Master."

The bees all began to agree with "Whatever King chooses!" dances, causing Belissar to groan. Chief Rohsuak held her gaze.

"It is true, Sacred Den Master. My people and your bees both are sworn to your defense and service. We are both extensions of your will and we shall be viewed that way outside. Even if you tell us to do as we please, all that we do will be presumed as your command by those who do not know you. Therefore, it is important that you express what you want us to do or not to do regarding this King Ratuatapi."

Belissar heaved a sigh.

"Then . . . do I need to go speak with them?"

Chief Rohsuak shook her head.

"You need not do anything, Sacred Den Master, besides what your sacred den requires of you. And to be honest, I would not recommend that course of action. It is unusual for a sacred den master to venture beyond their own domain. It would be an insult if they insisted upon meeting outside your den . . . at least after they have proof that we are sworn to you."

Belissar crossed his arms.

"And what would work as proof for that?"

Chief Rohsuak smiled as she glanced toward the soldier bee army training in the field beyond.

"I believe a handful of your larger bees would do the trick. No one has ever tamed monster bees, to my knowledge."

Belissar rubbed his chin.

"And . . . what do you think these people want from us?"

Chief Rohsuak eyed him for a moment before starting to rub her own chin.

"Hm, it is good they have revealed themselves and spoken directly to us. They would not have done so if their current intentions were hostile. They opened by naming their king and calling us intruders, and did not ask to see the sacred den. That implies to me that they are more concerned with protecting themselves and their current possessions, and wish for us to acknowledge their authority, at least over their own lands. More than that, I cannot say."

Niobee buzzed her wings at that.

"If hurt King, will sting."

The rest of the bees began buzzing as well. Chief Rohsuak chuckled and then nodded.

"Indeed. We, too, shall come to your defense should they have ill intentions toward you." She then looked him in the eye again. "So, Sacred Den Master, how do you wish for us to respond?"

Belissar groaned. He glanced down and took a deep breath.

". . . Honestly, I don't know. I don't know the first thing about talking to people like this, or what I'm supposed to do . . ."

Indeed, this was the first time Belissar had to decide something like this . . . with time to think about it, at least. The karnuq had just sort of arrived, and Belissar had been distracted by the implications of the karnuq being people in the first place. This time, he had the opportunity to think about it, and he realized once again how out of his depth he was. What did he know about negotiating with some king?

Chief Rohsuak's face softened.

"There is no 'supposed to' for you, Sacred Den Master. In my experience, sacred den masters do as they please and then it is the duty of others to follow. You are the one who holds back the Hunger, after all. So, do not worry about what you are supposed to do. Ask yourself, what would you want from these people? Do you wish for friends and allies? To exchange goods with one another? Do you wish for us to conquer them in force, to take their lands and force them to bow to your authority? Do you wish for us to drive them away? Or do you wish to be left alone and interact with them as little as possible? That is a choice as well, and whatever you decide we will all do our best to see fulfilled."

Belissar rubbed his chin once more. What *did* he want? Well, he immediately ruled out conquering in force. He had no wish to burn down anyone else's village, that was for sure. And as he thought about it, he realized he didn't want much at all. He was quite happy with his tower and his bees and the karnuq, and as long as they kept growing strong enough to stop the shades he didn't need or want much of anything else.

Though, at that moment, he glanced at his bees. *He* didn't want much else . . . but his bees could always use more flowers.

Belissar took a deep breath and uncrossed his arms.

"Um, okay. I don't want much of anything from them and, uh, definitely don't want to conquer them or anything like that. But, um, if we can get more flowers and stuff from them, we should try. Oh, um, by trade, or something like that. Other than that . . . let's leave each other alone?"

Chief Rohsuak bowed her head.

"As you wish, Sacred Den Master."

The bees began their salute and "King best king!" dances as well. Belissar grimaced a bit. They were all responding very seriously to his half-hearted and uncertain reply, but what else could he do? If Chief Rohsuak and the queens were all deferring to his lead, then who else could he turn to? He would just have to do his best to ensure that whatever happened was beneficial for his bees, and the karnuq as well now. He supposed that was what it meant to be a king.

Well, soon he'd apparently meet an actual king, so he was about to find out if that was true.

# CHAPTER TWENTY-THREE

# RESPONSI-BEE-LITY

After that, Belissar and Chief Rohsuak discussed further details. Peace and trade was great and all as an overall goal, but it turned out there was a *lot* more to be considered for a discussion like this than Belissar thought.

First of all, there was no guarantee that King Ratuatapi would agree to that sort of relationship. If he refused to trade, would Belissar try to convince him or let him be? If he made demands of his own, would Belissar consider them? If he claimed the Underway beyond the rot cap field, what would Belissar say? What if he claimed land above ground that Belissar's tower had purified? What if King Ratuatapi demanded access to Belissar's tower? What if he wanted to become a sworn defender as well? What if he claimed authority *over* Belissar's tower?

And if none of that occurred and King Ratuatapi agreed to trade . . . then there was a whole new set of questions. What was Belissar willing to trade? What would he never trade, even if asked? What prices would he accept? How often did he want to trade? What would he do if King Ratuatapi attempted to cheat them?

And then, finally, the question arose of what Belissar would do if the talks broke down and things came to blows. If this King Ratuatapi became hostile, how would Belissar respond?

Belissar could listen in and even speak with the karnuq when they went to talks, but Chief Rohsuak pointed out that most of this should be determined ahead of time, as it would leave them at a disadvantage in the talks if they had to stop and discuss everything that occurred. In the case of trade, it would be wise to bring some samples of what they could offer, which therefore needed to be prepared ahead of time. And in the case of talks breaking down and turning violent . . . well, the karnuq wouldn't have the chance to calmly ask Belissar what he wanted them to do.

And, of course, while Chief Rohsuak was willing to offer advice, it was ultimately Belissar who had to answer all of those questions. They managed to cover enough of them to proceed with the negotiations tomorrow, but Belissar found himself utterly exhausted. That had been a lot of decisions to make for someone who'd spent most of his life being told what to do. And even the tower rarely presented more than a few options at a time.

Speaking of which, he had over four thousand DP at the moment. It had slipped his mind, but he was ready to purchase a new monster or room or room feature at any point. Which he would do . . . later. He had *just* finished the long meeting with Chief Rohsuak, after all.

Belissar instead set to work prepping some more mead jars. He had plenty of mana honey; the limiting factor was the number of jars that had come with the apiary farmhouse. He thought about trying to make some barrels, but he wasn't particularly an expert on that. Funnily enough, barrels were one of the few things the village had been willing to give him in both numbers and good quality . . . probably so that he'd have mead for them to take. He could *probably* work something out with wax and propolis, which he'd try later on. For now, he just wanted something to do that was simple and straightforward.

For not only was he exhausted, but he was distracted by his thoughts as well. He could not help but worry about this new development. He had been fortunate so far in that the karnuq had been very friendly, but there was no guarantee that would be the case with these new people. There was every chance that tomorrow could end up in a fight . . . or even a war. Belissar knew very little of war, besides the general war against the Hunger. Even that had been taken care of by the tower lords back when he was a peasant, so war was something distant and unknown. According to tower lord doctrine, humanity had experienced countless wars with itself in the days of the wicked kings but had united after the Hunger appeared. Belissar had no idea if that was true or not, but he did know that he had never experienced war himself.

What would he do if it came to that? If his bees had to start killing people . . . or if people started killing his bees? He knew that if he ever encountered the tower lords he would have to face that scenario, but in recent times he had grown less worried about them, since Chief Rohsuak seemed to indicate they were far, far away. But now, the possibility had suddenly become very real. More real because Chief Rohsuak had asked *him* what *he* would want to do should it happen.

Making decisions that could end the lives of people and bees both. Belissar was once again reminded of how woefully unqualified he was for the job. For the first time in a long time, he even wished he was a tower lord, or that one of them were here. They might have been terrible people, but at least they were prepared to deal with such matters.

He finished his mead work all too quickly, and so he turned to his tower sight, just letting it wander through his tower. He watched as gardener bees flew among the flowers, guiding and directing the other workers to the various flowers. He watched the bumblebees spin about and cover themselves in pollen before flying to the next flower. He watched the First of the Fifth confer with her daughters as her workers crawled and flew in neat lines. He watched as soldier bees lifted wooden planks onto the roof of a stone house as the karnuq finished the walls. He watched Juosiutik talking quickly to a worker bee while she stirred a pot. He watched the First of the Fifth's First Daughter dancing with a drone, of all things, as the joint hive spread across the trees of the orchard. He watched the Second First of the First greet the first squad of bumblebee soldiers as they flew to the battle meadow, the entire soldier bee army pausing for a moment to gaze upon their newest, giant sisters. He watched lancers dive, soldiers fly, and sprayers spray, all while communers flared their mana and a queen danced commands. He watched Beero lead the wounded soldiers in yet another lightning dance. He watched the burning bees happily flying among the ash and flames of the lava field.

He took a deep breath and frowned. No, no he did not wish a tower lord was here. He had a feeling that no tower lord would have built a tower like this. And perhaps they would have made something better . . . but it would not have been the Bee Tower he had grown to love. This was his tower, his bees, and his people.

His heart settled. Because Belissar now knew what he wanted and what he would do. Come what may with these new people, he would protect this tower and all who lived in it.

The next day, another karnuq expedition marched down to the Underway, this time led by Chief Rohsuak herself. She was accompanied by a squad of soldier bees and sprayers, each of them carrying a digging worker bee. Unfortunately, the digging queen had only recently begun delivering honey to the battle meadow queens, so there were no digging soldiers just yet. Chief Rohsuak, however, had pointed out that this could work in their favor, as people living in the Underway might perceive digging soldiers as a threat. They had even ruled out bringing lancers or bumblebee soldiers for that very reason.

The bees hovered close to the karnuq and their light crystals . . . which, upon reflection, Belissar realized he should have asked about. For now, though, it was the only source of light to help the soldier bees fly, though the digging workers riding on their backs would help them if they got separated from the group.

The group made their way to the rot cap field once again, where, thankfully, the stink bug numbers had not recovered from yesterday's sweep. This time, they found people waiting for them in the field proper standing around a stone table flanked by light crystal–tipped poles. Most of the people were dressed like the one the karnuq had met yesterday, completely wrapped in black cloth save for their eyes. However, there was one standing before the table who dressed differently, giving the group and therefore Belissar their first glimpse of who exactly they were meeting. She was a woman wearing a blue dress made of silk. She had pale skin, black eyes, and round ears on the sides of her head that were covered in black fur. Most striking was her hair, which blended into fur that went down her neck and back and under her dress until it emerged again as a large and bushy tail. Most of the fur was black, but the hair on the top of her head was white, splitting into two strips of white down her neck and shoulders, until the white and black blended together on her tail.

Belissar tensed and narrowed his eyes. It was a color pattern he could not forget. More than once he had driven away a skunk trying to feast on his hives . . . and suffered the consequences whenever he did so poorly. As the karnuq approached them, he could only hope that these skunk people did not take after their animal counterparts when it came to bees.

# CHAPTER TWENTY-FOUR

# THE ART OF DIPLOMA-BEE

**H**alt."

Belissar watched from his tower as two of the skunk people stepped between the karnuq and the woman at the table. One appeared unarmed, while the other carried a spear that was made out of some sort of chitin.

"Present proof that you defend a sacred den before you approach."

Some of the karnuq frowned at the aggressive tone, but Chief Rohsuak simply smiled and nodded. Watching from afar, Belissar took that as the signal and sent his command to the soldier bees. The soldier bees gathered into formation and flew as a group, taking up positions around Chief Rohsuak. The skunk people tensed and held up either their empty hands or the weapons they carried. One of the two in front widened their eyes and glanced at their partner, who raised an eyebrow.

"Monster bees?"

Chief Rohsuak held up her hand and, at Belissar's command, one of the soldier bees landed in it. The calm skunk person watched for a moment before turning and bowing his head toward the woman.

"It appears they speak the truth."

The woman nodded.

"Let them through."

The skunk person saluted by striking their chest with their fist, then turned to Chief Rohsuak.

"You may pass."

At that, the two skunk people in the way moved to either side. Chief Rohsuak stepped forward, one of the soldier bees still in hand. The other soldier bees and karnuq hung back, while Metsaitti walked forward until he was around the same distance from the chief as the two skunk guards.

The skunk woman smiled.

"I am Second Queen Berbiya of Clan Ratuatapi. Who do I speak with?"

Chief Rohsuak smiled back.

"I am Chief Rohsuak of the karnuq, disciple of fire and sworn defender of Sacred Den Master Belissar."

She then held up the soldier bee.

"This is one of his defenders, a soldier of his army."

Second Queen Berbiya nodded directly to the bee.

"Welcome, and thank you for sending your representatives, Sacred Den Master. Please, have a seat."

Chief Rohsuak sat on a stool around the stone table along with Second Queen Berbiya, placing the soldier bee on top of the table. Second Queen Berbiya motioned, and skunk people brought three cups and plates. Chief Rohsuak thanked them and took a sip. The soldier bee extended her proboscis and dipped it into the cup . . . before rapidly beginning to lap up the liquid within. Belissar made a note to find out what it was. Second Queen Berbiya sipped from her cup as well, watching silently. When Chief Rohsuak made no move toward the food, the Second Queen placed her cup down and folded her hands on the table in front of her.

"Then, let's get to it. King Ratuatapi and his people have lived in these halls for many a generation, and you are the first visitors we have had in many years. He wishes to know where you came from, and what the sacred den master's intentions for this land are."

Back at home, Belissar's face scrunched up as he crossed his arms. Chief Rohsuak had told him that in diplomacy, every choice of every word could have a specific meaning. Unfortunately, knowing that this queen meant more than what she was saying out loud didn't mean that Belissar could figure it out. Well, Chief Rohsuak had also stated that as a sacred den master he could choose to just ignore all of that and let others adjust to him, but he didn't want to be ignorant forever.

Fortunately, Chief Rohsuak directly shared her opinion this time, and he heard her voice in his head.

*"They are coming out strong, launching directly into the main topic like this. She has attempted to lay claim to authority by mentioning their history in this land and painting us as outsiders."*

*"I see . . ."*

Well, he understood, but he didn't particularly know how to respond to that knowledge. Fortunately, he was not the one speaking.

"Sacred Den Master Belissar has recently begun purifying the Hunger from these lands, and my people have chosen to assist him in this sacred duty. He wishes for little more than mutual respect and, if possible, benefit with those outside his halls."

"I see. And what sort of benefit does the sacred den master envision?"

Chief Rohsuak reached into a pouch and pulled out small carvings of wood, stone, and copper that the karnuq had prepared.

"An exchange of goods, if King Ratuatapi is open to it."

Second Queen Berbiya relaxed her expression slightly.

"That could be arranged. King Ratuatapi would be happy to exchange the bounty of our lands . . . should we achieve the mutual respect you speak of. What does Sacred Den Master Belissar consider respect?"

Chief Rohsuak motioned to the soldier bee still lapping up the drink before her.

"To do no harm to any denizen of his sacred den and to acknowledge the sanctity of the sacred den itself."

Second Queen Berbiya nodded and narrowed her eyes.

"And the lands beyond?"

Chief Rohsuak grinned at her.

"The Sacred Den Master shall patrol and utilize the lands he purifies as he sees fit to defend his sacred den and advance his sacred duty. Regarding King Ratuatapi's land in particular . . . he has no designs and is willing to leave you be, provided you do not present a threat to his den or his mission."

They held eye contact for a second. Second Queen Berbiya gave a small nod.

"Then, allow me to inform you where King Ratuatapi's lands lie."

From then on began an increasingly animated discussion between Chief Rohsuak and the Second Queen that Belissar struggled to follow as they began to discuss the twists and turns of the Underway. After all, borders were not clear lines along flat ground in the deep, where twisting tunnels could loop around, above, and below one another and where mining species could dig new ones at will. Second Queen Berbiya wanted the rot cap field and everything beyond it considered as their land . . . without mentioning the exact limits of those lands. Chief Rohsuak required more defined borders on the sides of their territory, and pointed out that no territory above ground had existed prior to Belissar purifying the area. Second Queen Berbiya countered that demanding King Ratuatapi reveal the full extent of his lands and then denying his people the lands above would threaten their safety. Belissar grew worried as their voices rose. The two women even shouted at each other at one point, causing the soldier bee to stop drinking and buzz her wings. Chief Rohsuak signaled she had it under control, however, so Belissar kept the bees calm . . . although he himself was absolutely not.

Eventually, Second Queen Berbiya frowned openly.

"You ask much of us. I will have to speak with the king on this matter."

Chief Rohsuak gave her a light smirk as she reached into her pouch.

"Very well. But as you speak to your king, keep in mind that we ask for far less than most sacred den masters would demand. And before you go, here, a gift for your king."

Chief Rohsuak pulled out a small package and slowly unwrapped it. Second Queen Berbiya's eyes widened a bit as a small chunk of gently shimmering golden honeycomb began to glisten in the light. She quickly glanced at the soldier bee on the table before controlling her expression. Chief Rohsuak smiled at her.

"There is more honey . . . and more of the bees that made it, depending on which is required."

Second Queen Berbiya stared at her for a moment before nodding to one of her guards, who wrapped up the honeycomb and stored it. She then rose to her feet.

"Then, I will return here two days from now."

Chief Rohsuak nodded.

"We shall as well."

Back in his tower, Belissar let out a sigh. On the bright side, things had not come to blows so far. But on the other hand, the talks had not concluded with an agreement, so he could not relax yet. And now he had to wait another two days before the talks resumed. He groaned at that.

Why did this all have to be so complicated?

Second Queen Berbiya stood before a half-circle of stone thrones, each occupied save for her own just left of the center. It was rare for the whole royal family to gather, but her report today was that important. After all, what occurred next could seal the fate of their people.

On the throne to the right of the center sat the First Queen, her face now wrinkling with age, though she still held herself straight and tall. All the other queens held their tongues until she spoke.

". . . So this sacred den master may have designs on our lands after all?"

Second Queen Berbiya frowned.

"His envoy left it open. She emphasized trade and said he would leave us alone . . . but she also said that he'd do anything necessary for his mission."

On a throne on the edge of the circle, a young queen dressed in armor instead of silk scowled.

"That is unacceptable. They could justify anything they wanted as 'necessary' and invade us at will. If that is their condition, then we cannot trust them. I say we strike now, while the sacred den is still young. We could lose everything if we do not act quickly."

The First Queen did not react but looked to Second Queen Berbiya with a calm expression.

"Pezuya has a point. What do you think, Berbiya? Do you believe we should fight?"

Second Queen Berbiya shook her head.

"I would not recommend it. The sacred den master sent monster bees as large as my hand."

Pezuya scoffed.

"That is to our advantage. They will be lost in the dark and cramped in the tunnels. Easy prey for us."

Second Queen Berbiya shook her head again.

"If they attack us, then yes; they did not look comfortable underground. But that means that the sacred den is up above, doesn't it? Will we be able to defeat a swarm of flying monsters up in the open sky? If we mean to attack, that is what we'll have to do. On the other hand, if they do betray us, we should be able to defend ourselves down below as you have said, correct? Would it not make more sense to stay on the defensive, then?"

Pezuya glared at her.

"For now. But this sacred den will only grow if we do not deal with it, so we may not have a choice later. And we have not shed the blood of generations building our civilization here, out in isolation, just to bow to another sacred den master in the end. I will not stand idly by and just let them do as they please!"

The First Queen shook her head.

"It is not your decision to make, Pezuya."

The First Queen hummed and rubbed her chin before turning to the throne at the center of the room, whose occupant had so far remained silent.

"That is the situation, my lord. What is your will?"

All others fell silent as King Ratuatapi opened his mouth.

# CHAPTER TWENTY-FIVE

# AN UNEXPECTED BEE-CISION

With two days before the next talks, Belissar turned his attention to other endeavors. He had enough DP to purchase another room as he had planned, which could also provide either additional resources to trade or additional defenses if the talks fell through. He planned to make the purchase tonight, as usual right after the purification and celebrations when all the queens would be gathered. So, all that was left was to handle the day's purification, which Belissar didn't expect to be too difficult.

But as the soldier bee army waited and Belissar began the purification, it seemed the Hunger had other ideas in store. Once again, it took the form of a salamander, but this time, Belissar didn't have the full lancer army to combat it. Only two of the lancers were fully healed. Belissar sucked in his breath . . . until he looked at the salamander shade more closely. This one was noticeably smaller, and not completely covered in black flames. In fact, it only had one modest black flame covering the tip of its tail.

He supposed this salamander-shade was a lower-level purification than the original, but he decided to wait and watch it brave the dirt tunnels before he relaxed. The salamander shade crawled its way through, climbing the walls whenever it encountered a pit trap. And then, it reached a wall-mounted sticky honey trap.

The shade was doused by the honey. It spun and spat out a breath of black flames but didn't manage to ignite the spray before it was coated in honey. Small flames danced across its body but failed to burn away the viscous coating.

It was then that Belissar released his breath and relaxed his shoulders. Indeed, the shade was weaker than the larger variant. Most importantly, its flames did not form the same kind of shield and left it vulnerable to the honey traps. And that meant that it would be vulnerable to the bees as well.

The increasingly disoriented shade took a while to get through the dirt tunnels, as it was both weighed down and increasingly intoxicated by the maddening honey stuck to its body. Finally, it arrived out in the battle meadow . . . and was promptly attacked from all sides by sprayers. As Belissar had hoped, its flames were not hot enough nor spread wide enough to burn away all the poison before the toxic sprays struck home. It was not long before the shade was weak enough for the soldier bees to attack as well, at which point its resistance died quickly.

*Small Purification completed!*
*Please select a reward:*
*- +100 DP*
*- +20 Max Mana*
*- Arrow Trap*

The arrow trap was tempting, but tonight Belissar needed the mana. If all went well, he'd soon have a lot to spend it on. A quick celebration later and Belissar gathered with Niobee, the queens, and Chief Rohsuak.

*Extra room choice purchased. One room choice now available.*
*Please select a room:*
*- Farm (Rarity: Common, Type: Resource, Settlement)*
*- Stone Labyrinth (Rarity: Common, Type: Labyrinth, Settlement)*
*- Fairy Grove (Rarity: Rare, Type: Nature, Magic, Field)*

Well, Belissar practically knew what he wanted to pick just from the rarities alone, but he went through the options for good measure. Farm was a repeat and quite straightforward. A simple farmhouse, plus a bunch of fields in which crops would grow. Though, simple and straightforward did not necessarily mean undesirable. So far, Belissar had been limited to his resource plant nodes, which were fairly small in the grand scheme of things. He had no doubt the karnuq might appreciate a larger source of food. And depending on what kind of plants they could cultivate there, a farm might prove quite useful for his bees as well. Rows upon rows of flowering plants could feed many a hive.

Still, he very much wanted to view the other options before settling on a practical, but somewhat mundane one.

### *Stone Labyrinth*

**Type:**   Labyrinth, Settlement
**Innate Features:**   None
**Mana Upkeep:**   5

*A stone structure built as a maze to disorient and trap invaders. Has no innate features, but its tough walls force all but the most powerful of invaders to search its twists and turns for an exit. Numerous rooms within may also be used for habitation.*

Belissar furrowed his brow and rubbed his chin. He couldn't quite remember where, but he had a feeling he had seen this one before. Maybe as one of the earlier choices when he had still been too shocked by becoming a dungeon master to pay close attention? In any case, this choice was perhaps even more straightforward than the farm. A labyrinth like the dirt tunnels, but made of cut stone instead of dirt.

He could pretty much rule this one out. First of all, it didn't provide much that any of his bees would want. No flowers—well, no flowers that Belissar was currently aware of would grow inside a stone structure. Rooms for habitation might help the karnuq, but he'd prefer his bees in beehouses, bee barracks, or bee apartments. So, this room would be purely for defense . . . and didn't really provide anything that the dirt tunnels didn't. He guessed a stone maze might be useful if they faced a shade that could dig through the dirt, but so far they hadn't. That scenario was not currently worth spending a room choice on.

And that left the last option. Belissar took a deep breath and smiled. This was it. A rare room choice! Even the lava field had merely been an uncommon option. So, what exactly would a rare room have to offer?

### Fairy Grove

| | |
|---|---|
| **Type:** | Nature, Magic, Field |
| **Innate Features:** | Fairy circles |
| **Mana Upkeep:** | 40 |

*A fae forest filled with wonders unseen. Fairy circles dot the forest, concentrating mana for mystical and unpredictable effects. Those who do not watch their step may encounter that which they do not expect, for good or for ill, or be led onto paths they did not intend. Plants and animals raised in and around the circles may develop along unexpected lines.*

Belissar rubbed his chin. Fairy circles. That was something that most often appeared in children's stories, where they signified grave danger. And while few people believed in them after growing up, tower lord doctrine specified that all magical phenomena, including fairy circles, were to be reported immediately without any interaction.

That the tower lords would warn their subjects against such things was enough to convince Belissar that fairy circles were probably real and probably full of magic and probably not nearly as deadly as the tower lords implied . . . probably. But, well, that didn't mean Belissar had any idea of what fairy circles actually did. Tower lord-approved children's stories weren't a reliable source of information, but the description of the option was also sparse on detail. If anything, it was very much hammering the point that the circles were unpredictable.

That gave Belissar pause. He had seen enough of Juosiutik's potions explode to know that magic could indeed be dangerous. In fact, most of the magic he had encountered in his tower was generally dangerous and violent, just directed toward shades instead of himself. So, introducing unpredictable magic into his tower seemed . . . risky. But, well, he could walk through a lava field unharmed, so perhaps he could trust the tower to keep this danger aimed at the Hunger.

There was one piece of information he could glean from the description: Plants and animals raised in this room would develop along unexpected lines. And that meant there was a possibility this room would lead to new flowers and new bees. Unpredictable, magical bees did not sound bad to Belissar at all.

After reading the descriptions of the rooms, he turned to those around him. "What do you all think?"

The First of the Fifth was the one to dance first this time.

"Last room . . . new flowers?"

Belissar smiled a bit. He'd thought the First of the Fifth might catch that too.

"I'm not sure, but I think so."

The rest of his bees mostly handed the decision back to him. None of them mentioned the stone labyrinth, for why would they? A few were interested in the farm after he explained what it would be like, but the First of the Fifth seemed more interested in new flowers than the mass flowers a farm might offer. And so, Belissar turned to Chief Rohsuak. He rubbed his chin for a second.

"So . . . um, I'm guessing you've been quiet here because you want me to make choices on my own? I *would* like to hear if there's anything you think I should consider. Especially if you've heard of fairy circles before. I've, um, only heard children's stories, and the description here isn't very detailed."

Chief Rohsuak gave him an amused smile and shook her head.

"You think too much of me, Sacred Den Master. I may have some experience leading my people, but I know little about the inner workings of a sacred den, so do not hold my opinion above your own. You defended this sacred den before we arrived at it, after all."

She then rubbed her chin.

"That said, my people's encounters with fairy circles were fortunately rare, and I've not come across them outside of stories and legends. All that I know is that they are not to be trifled with lightly, and so I ensured that my people did not approach anything that would even hint at such powers. While it is not guaranteed to go badly by any means, we could not afford the risk."

She frowned and her face turned dark.

"The other thing I can say is . . . the power of the fairy circles has apparently not stopped the Hunger's march. So, in that regard, perhaps they are not superior to the power of a sacred den, though magic is often not so simple."

Belissar slowly nodded along. It sounded like the karnuq and the tower lords shared a similar view of the fairy circles. But the thought that whatever power the fairy circles possessed still could not stop the Hunger was a sobering one. A reminder of why the gods themselves had to intervene . . .

And that calmed whatever fears Belissar had in his heart.

*Fairy Grove is now available.*

Whatever threat the unpredictable fairy grove might pose paled in comparison to the threat he knew the Hunger did. And so, Belissar decided to hope that those unpredictable powers would assist him and his bees against whatever dangers the future might hold.

# CHAPTER TWENTY-SIX

# A FAIR-BEE ODD ROOM

The next morning, Belissar set up a fairy grove. First, he considered where to place it. The empty rooms were currently on the second floor, which at the moment only held the orchard, since he had moved the karnuq and apiary floors up a step each, but he could always rearrange the rooms as necessary. There was an argument for placing the fairy grove ahead of the battle meadow so that an invading shade would have to face its unpredictable effects before reaching the bee army. On the other hand, a major reason Belissar had chosen the fairy grove was the promise of new flowers and new bees, in which case it would be better to keep it closer to the apiary and the bees working there.

Hypothetically, he could always set up two fairy groves, as he had the room slots open. However, the fairy grove was the most expensive room he had by far, even more so than the lava field. Belissar was not comfortable spending that much mana to set up two rooms when he still didn't know exactly what they did. And since he didn't know exactly what they did, he decided not to overthink it. He went ahead and placed a fairy grove off to the side of the orchard for now. He'd think about moving it elsewhere once they had figured out how it actually fit into his tower. He also didn't bother adjusting anything about the room, since he didn't know enough to know what, if anything, he should change.

He turned to Niobee.

"I'm placing the new room by the orchard. I'm, um, still not sure about where it's going to go in the end, but there's a chance we'll use it to defend, and we still aren't sure what will happen with it. So . . . maybe we shouldn't set up any hives there for a bit, until we know how the room works."

Belissar then jumped a bit and waved his hands around.

"Ah, the bees are welcome to visit and forage though! They should, in fact!"

Niobee took it in stride with a salute dance.

"Okay! Will tell queens!"

As Niobee began to dance and flare her mana, Belissar finalized placing the room. From the tower sight, it looked just like a forest, but with some circles in the ground here and there formed of darker grass. It . . . didn't seem like all that much from there.

So, Belissar decided to go check it out in person. He walked to the orchard, where a new path had opened in the tree wall along one of the room's sides. A number of worker bees from the orchard hives buzzed around the door, turning to him as he approached. Niobee flew over and danced with them.

"King, Fourth of Seventh's workers want to scout new room! Can?"

Belissar slowly nodded.

"Sure. Just . . . be careful. We aren't sure what this room does yet, and it's supposed to be unpredictable."

The worker bees saluted and then hovered by Belissar. They followed along as he stepped into the room. At first glance, it appeared to be a forest like any other. Mostly broadleaf trees, close enough to form a canopy but spaced out enough that it wasn't difficult to walk through them. The canopy itself covered most of the sky but was sparse enough that light shone down all through the forest, keeping it relatively illuminated. A gentle breeze blew through on occasion, rustling the leaves above. There were bushes and such that occasionally barred Belissar's way, causing him to twist and turn as he moved toward the closest fairy ring.

All in all, it seemed like a peaceful and pleasant place, not at all like he'd expected given the warnings. The only thing of note to Belissar was that the mana here was denser and flowed more actively than in other rooms. Belissar furrowed his brow as he walked. Honestly, with all the stories of fairy circles and the sheer mana cost of the room, he'd been expecting a bit more than a peaceful forest.

"King?"

At least until Niobee danced in front of his face. Belissar tilted his head.

"Yes?"

She flew a bit unsteadily.

"Where going? Not going to see circle?"

Belissar was about to respond when he paused, and then started glancing around. His eyes widened slightly. Without knowing it, he was now deep into the forest, surrounded by trees on all sides. The entrance to the orchard was nowhere in sight. Furthermore, the inconsistent amount of bushes had made him naturally follow a winding path, such that he couldn't be sure he had headed in a straight direction. And indeed, when he checked with his tower sight, he found that he had turned *away* from the closest fairy circle and was now headed deeper into the room.

The mana began to twist and surge. The breeze picked up a bit and the rustling of the leaves grew louder. For a moment, Belissar thought he heard something more than the wind, especially as the wood began to creak and groan. The shimmering light filtering through the canopy above flickered and shadows danced at the edges of his vision, though when he turned his head to look, he found nothing.

He gulped. It felt as if something, or someone, was there. And this was despite the fact that Belissar could use his tower senses to get a full and complete picture of his surroundings that confirmed there was nothing else in the room besides his bees and himself. He rubbed his chin.

"I think . . . there's something more to this room after all. Um, let the workers know to be careful. It might be easy to get lost in here."

"Okay, will."

Well, the bees were flying above the bushes, so at least they wouldn't have gotten turned around by those, but Belissar didn't want to take any chances. He'd have to keep an eye on this room to make sure the bees didn't get lost.

After finding his bearings and taking a deep breath to gather himself, Belissar once again set off toward the closest fairy circle, using his tower sight to stay on course. Eventually, they arrived. Right in between three trees, obscured by bushes on all sides, was a ring of darkened grass about as wide as Belissar was tall. An easy thing to miss if he hadn't been specifically looking for it.

At least, physically speaking. But in terms of mana . . . Belissar's eyes widened at the sight before him. The flows of mana through the forest all coalesced at this point, forming a twisting and chaotic whirlpool within the circle. Mana generally appeared to Belissar as colored light: The most common mana in the air was a light blue, while mana near plants generally took on a green tone. The Ground mana flower colored mana brown, while the lava field and Fire mana flowers were filled with red. Belissar's own mana matched that of his bees: a bright and orderly yellow.

The mana in the fairy circle was a shimmering rainbow, different patches and streams of the mana within it all constantly changing colors independently of one another, creating a dazzling display of light and motion to Belissar's eyes. Occasionally, a stream of the mana would shoot out from the mass, either flowing back into one of the larger rivers of mana in the forest or into something in the surroundings. Most often the ground, but sometimes the bushes and the trees as well.

"Well, I guess that's where all the mana went . . ."

Belissar turned to see how his bees were responding. The workers were hovering and buzzing around the circle, though remaining at a distance from it.

"What do you all think?"

One of the workers flew over to Niobee and danced a bit.

"Says dangerous, but lots of mana. Wants to see if flowers nearby."

Belissar nodded, and then paused and rubbed his chin, for he had a thought.

"Niobee, could you ask a gardener to come here?"

"Okay!"

He had been about to start placing mana flowers and the like, but then thought he should ask a gardener for help. Not only could the gardeners tell him which of the flowers might like it here best, but they could also help spread the flowers themselves. Which might actually be a better option, given the purpose of this room. Belissar had not chosen the room to fill it with mana flowers, but to see if flowers raised here might develop differently. On that count . . . maybe it would be better to plant seeds and let them grow the normal way instead of relying on the resource nodes that magically grew the plants in an instant?

A while later, Niobee guided one of the gardeners to the circle. Belissar turned to her.

"Could you check this place out and tell me which flowers you think would like it here?"

The gardener saluted as quickly as she could and then took off. She flew around the circle, landed on the grass, dug a bit into the dirt, and flew through the air several times. She even flew a bit into the circle at one point, her antennas twitching every which way.

After a bit, she came before Belissar and began dancing her results.

"Any!"

Belissar tilted his head.

"Any? All the flowers would like it here?"

The gardener paused, her dance slowing down a bit.

"Area strange . . . but good. Lots of mana, lots of types. Flowers will drink and grow."

Belissar slowly nodded.

"In that case, could you help me plant some flowers in this room?"

At that, the gardener took up speed once again, saluting as quickly as she could.

"Can!"

Belissar began to smile. He had made rooms on his own. He had made rooms for the bees. But now, with the gardeners' help, he'd make a room *with* the bees. Despite all the questions he still had about this room, he had a feeling it could end up as the best one yet.

# THE DAILY BUZZ

The First of the Fifth's First Daughter drew her attention away from the gardener and scouts she had sent to accompany the King. She then turned to a communer standing next to her, one that was not the Fourth of the Seventh's or her own, but she could feel mana flow through the joint hive, into the communer, and then onward to her. She shook herself a bit. The mana still resonated with her, but it tickled now, not flowing as naturally as it had in the past. Still, it was enough that she could feel the attention of another queen upon her.

"Queen Mother, have news. King built new room as discussed yesterday. Room strange, but gardener says good for flowers. King wants gardeners to help raise many flower types there."

The First of the Fifth's First Daughter was still, well, the First of the Fifth's daughter, and made regular reports to her mother on the state of affairs in her hive as well as the orchard in general. She felt her mother's reply through the communer her mother had assigned to her hive.

"Amazing, incredible, King is best king! Can take care of room with orchard hives?"

She danced her salute.

"Can."

"Good, then do. Let know if need help. If find new flower types, recommend give to one subordinate queen."

The First of the Fifth's First Daughter saluted once more and then felt her mother's attention pull away. She sent word through her mana for her own daughters to gather. And, thanks to the drone, her mana passed through the Fourth of the Seventh's communer as well, and then on to the Fourth of the Seventh's daughters. She started a happy dance, seeing once again that the Fourth of the Seventh's hive could now act as one with her own.

Which meant she was now well positioned to fulfill the Fourth of the Seventh's duties within the hive of hives in her place. The new room was fortunately timed for the orchard queens, as their daughters were just getting up and running. Additionally, some of their daughters had indicated a desire to see more than the grove they had been born in, no doubt due to the stories their mother told them. The First of the Fifth's First Daughter had so far focused on raising them into excellent queens with well-ordered workers, and so could not allow them to venture abroad.

But now? Now there was a brand-new room that was their responsibility. A strange room that was more difficult to traverse than usual, and which had an unpredictable nature. Even the King, in all his wisdom, and the Conduit, with all her experience, did not know what to expect. It would, therefore, make a perfect place for her daughters to send their first scouts, a chance to explore the unknown without leaving the safety of home, all while fulfilling a task assigned them by the King himself. The First of the Fifth's First Daughter could finally let them follow in the Fourth of the Seventh's footsteps.

So, she would gather the queens of the joint hive and the Fourth of the Seventh's communer to discuss and organize the scouts and gardeners required. And, while she waited for her children to gather, she gave another command.

"Scouts, visit flower meadow. Tell about new room and drone. See if any news from them."

The Fourth of the Seventh's workers had once traveled the breadth of the King's realm, from the apiary to the flower meadow, seeking news for their curious queen and exchanging information between the queens in turn. The First of the Fifth's First Daughter took that task upon herself while the Fourth of the Seventh was away. It was a task for which she was well suited, given she could speak directly to her mother via communer. So, all she had to do was send messengers to and from the bee barracks and she could remain in contact with the entire hive of hives, ensuring all were up to date on the latest developments everywhere else. Additionally, she would then gather a great deal of new information to share with the Fourth of the Seventh in person when she finally returned.

And with the latest batch of news, all would learn even more of the Fourth of the Seventh's brilliance. Who knew that drones held the secret to making the hive of hives a physical reality? Who but the Fourth of the Seventh would have preserved a drone long enough to find out?

And so, the First of the Fifth's First Daughter diligently carried out the duties of the joint hive, eager to report her successes to her partner queen.

The Firstborn crawled through the bee barracks, greeting the various queens as she went. The gardeners had hatched, and the Firstborn was waiting to see how they affected honey production before deciding how many and what types of off-spring she would lay next, so in the meantime she was taking stock of the hive. She had certainly been chastised by the First of the Fifth over the state of her hive, so she had resolved to keep a better eye on what was going on at home.

She found workers assembled into groups with gardeners dancing before each one. The gardeners had gone through all the flowers of the flower meadow and verified their state and were now instructing all the workers of the bee barracks on how to maximize both their honey production and the health of the flowers. Notably, the flowers the King had planted by the memorial apparently required foraging. The Firstborn and the other flower meadow queens had held off on for-aging from those, for it somehow felt wrong to do so. Apparently, they had been mistaken, and the flowers very much wanted some visits, so they were now arrang-ing to do so.

The same went for the strange gravilion flower the King had planted, which was both far away and difficult to gather from. But the gardeners discovered it had grown sluggish and quiet due to the lack of foraging, which was unfortunate since it was supposed to contribute to the defense. The flower meadow queens had thus resolved to ensure it too received regular visits.

All this was yet another reminder of all that the Firstborn had neglected. She had missed much due to her fixation on soldier bees and stingers, including much that had direct relevance to her mission. She turned her gaze to the army training in the field. She once again stood in awe of the huge shadows buzzing overhead. A squad of her own soldiers flew to the bumblebees and rubbed their antennas, causing the bumblebee soldiers to descend. The giant soldiers dove to the ground with a crash as they drove their stingers deep. It had taken some time to figure out how to coordinate with the giants who didn't seem to dance, but they were now working it out.

And what a help they would be once they did. The Firstborn was still shocked that the bumblebee queens had raised soldiers larger than her own lancers. And they had done so with help from the First of the Fifth, help that had only been possible due to the First of the Fifth's meticulous focus on honey production.

And that was why the Firstborn was glad to be part of the hive of hives now. Each queen made up for the weaknesses of the others, and all played their parts. The Second of the Sixth worked to heal the wounded lancers the flower meadow queens had raised. The First of the Fifth helped the bumblebee queens raise sol-diers larger than any others, who the flower meadow soldiers were now trying to integrate into the army. The apiary queens continued to donate honey, including a new shipment from the digging queen, so that the flower meadow queens could raise soldiers that would fight in the dirt tunnels. And in turn, the flower meadow soldiers now helped the karnuq lift wood and cloth and ropes to build mighty hives as the King had done for them . . . all the while listening to the karnuq's instructions and taking note of how such things were made.

For the first time in a while, the Firstborn could say she was satisfied. Her hive still had many flaws and was dependent on many others . . . but such was not fatal in the hive of hives. As long as she continued to contribute however she could and raise the army as best she was able, the hive of hives would carry the day.

And speaking of which, she received word that messengers from the orchard had arrived, bearing news. Yet another symbol of the hive of hives, that the orchard hive would spread information to the others rather than keeping it for themselves. She went to greet them personally, and listened intently as they described the newest land the King had built. She had no doubt such a room would elevate the hive of hives in new and unforeseen ways—

"Wait, dance that again."

The Firstborn immediately halted her line of thought and stared intently at the messengers as they repeated the last piece of news.

"Drone that Fourth of Seventh saved found job. Can bind mana of different hives together, let queens command other queens' workers."

The Firstborn spun around and began a frantic dance to her workers.

"Assemble the queens! Need talk!"

This changed *everything*.

# CHAPTER TWENTY-SEVEN

# RESUMING DIPLOMA-BEE

**B**elissar planned to let the gardeners handle planting for the fairy grove, but he at least checked the flower and resource plants lists to see if there was anything new. There wasn't . . . but, curiously, the fairy grove could grow every plant and mushroom he had available. Mushrooms otherwise limited to subterranean environments would work as long he placed them in the shade, Ground and Fire mana flowers could grow without any increase in mana cost, and even the underworld phlox previously limited to the area around the memorial was available. In fact, all of the plants and mushrooms could be grown here for their base cost, save one.

*Manage flower types? Available types:*
*- Mana Flower (Mana Upkeep: 3, 1 due to suitable environment)*

*Available Resource Plants for Fairy Grove:*
*- Mana Flower (Mana Upkeep: 5 per node, 3 due to suitable environment)*

Mana flowers were notably cheaper here. It was the first time he had seen their upkeep change. Between that and the fairy grove's ability to grow every other plant, Belissar was tempted to replace all the foraging rooms of his tower with fairy groves, if not for the unpredictable nature of the room and its own high mana cost.

In any case, Belissar went ahead and enabled mana flowers, since the room seemed so favorable to them, though he held off on resource patches for the time being. Some mana flowers began sprouting immediately by the fairy circle he was watching, attracting the worker bees' attention. Belissar smiled at that and then made his way out of the room, keeping close watch through his tower sight to ensure he was headed the right way.

\* \* \*

The night's purification featured two small bird-shades, which were ironically tougher than their larger counterpart. They both managed to fly through the dirt tunnels without being caught in any of the traps . . . only to find the soldier bee army waiting for them. The soldier bees' training paid off, and they were able to form two encirclements around each of the small birds and bring them down. Belissar ended up selecting a mana reward again today, wanting to ensure he had enough to add features to the fairy grove if needed. And with that, the day came to a close.

Which meant that it was now time for Chief Rohsuak to meet the skunk people once again. Belissar moved the lava field to the side of the battle meadow as he had before so that the karnuq could leave without crossing burning rivers, and then they were off.

The karnuq safely made their way into the Underway and to the rot cap field, where they found the skunk people waiting for them. Second Queen Berbiya stood with a serious expression on her face.

"You're here, good. If you don't mind, let's begin right away."

Chief Rohsuak raised an eyebrow but sat down at the table, along with one of the soldier bees. The soldier bee glanced around, but no beverages were brought out this time. Second Queen Berbiya glanced around at the guards around her before taking a deep breath. Chief Rohsuak broke the silence first.

"Is something the matter? Forgive me, but you seem a bit tense."

Second Queen Berbiya locked eyes on Chief Rohsuak.

"A great deal rests upon the outcome of our talk today, Chief Rohsuak."

Chief Rohsuak nodded.

"Indeed. Then, shall we get started?"

Second Queen Berbiya nodded back, taking another deep breath.

"King Ratuatapi has considered your terms and offers this: He is willing to define and map out the current boundaries of his territory, including a reasonable buffer and room for future expansion. He is willing to concede ownership of the surface to the sacred den master but wishes that no settlements be established above his lands without his approval. He likewise requests that he be prioritized and granted first offer should the sacred den master seek to give away those lands to others. He is willing to open up a friendly trade relationship. But, in turn, he requires that his sovereignty over his lands be respected in full, and that the sacred den master agree not to interfere with or encroach upon them, even should the sacred den master consider it important to either his defense or his mission. He requires a promise in the name of the sacred den master's patron that the sacred den master and his servants will never violate our borders under any circumstances, save by explicit invitation of King Ratuatapi himself or the kings that will succeed him. Is the sacred den master willing to accept these terms?"

Chief Rohsuak folded her hands. Second Queen Berbiya glanced at the soldier bee before holding Chief Rohsuak's gaze and diverting no further.

*"Well, Sacred Den Master Belissar, are you willing to consider this?"*

Back at the tower, Belissar rubbed his chin and frowned.

*"Um, I mean it sounds okay? We get the surface and trade as long as we don't mess with them, right? But . . . something seems weird here, right?"*

Chief Rohsuak showed no change on her face even as she replied.

*"You would have to give up all claim to their current territory, but that is unavoidable if you do not wish to subjugate them. There is risk to allowing someone to do as they please within your sacred den's territory, so we should require some caveats to the border violation clause as well as full reciprocation . . . but I agree that something is not right here. Look closely at the Second Queen."*

Belissar did as Chief Rohsuak suggested. Second Queen Berbiya was keeping her face mostly expressionless and gazing intently at Chief Rohsuak, but as Belissar focused in, he caught a faint quiver to her eyes.

*"She's . . . afraid?"*

*"That's my understanding as well. Moreover, she is not managing to hide it from us. She has also skipped all hospitality and maneuvering to present her king's terms immediately."*

Belissar furrowed his brow.

*"And what does that mean?"*

Chief Rohsuak remained quiet for a moment before replying.

*"The situation may be dangerous, so I will speak plainly. I feel that she has a time limit to get us to agree, and there will be an outcome if she fails that she wants to avoid. And given the terms she's emphasizing . . . they may launch an attack against you if you reject these terms, for fear that you intend to conquer them either now or in the future."*

Belissar rapidly shook his head.

*"I don't! Um, shouldn't we agree then?! And quickly?!"*

Chief Rohsuak didn't reply right away. But then, she slowly began to nod. Second Queen Berbiya held her breath.

*"We will need to negotiate the exact details and reciprocation, but I agree we should at least demonstrate openness to her terms if you wish to avoid a conflict. I must point out that the promise they ask for, though, means that you will never be able to go back on your word, so make certain that this is something you will not change your mind on."*

Belissar took a deep breath, holding his chest to try and still his pounding heart. What was there to think on? Was he going to change his mind in the future, when war was the alternative? He didn't see a reason to refuse, particularly not in this circumstance! But Chief Rohsuak had gone out of her way to caution him, even while she was the one sitting right in front of the skunk people that might attack her, so Belissar tried to calm down and consider it as she said.

He thought over Second Queen Berbiya's words. He wouldn't be able to enter their land without permission. At first, he didn't see why he'd want to . . . until he considered that it would include his bees. So, for example, if they found a flower they liked but that was on the other side of the border, he'd have to ask for permission before his bees could forage from it. And for the no settlements on the surface above . . . maybe that would include beehives? So, no hives there without permission? If he thought about it like that, he guessed there was a downside after all. He didn't like the idea of restricting his bees in the lands that they had fought to purify. And the skunk people would attack them over that? Just over the possibility that Belissar might do something to them, when they knew nothing about him and he had no reason to do so? That thought made Belissar clench his teeth.

But was he going to risk a war over it? Was he going to watch bees die to the skunk people just in case they one day found a flower the skunk people wouldn't let them have? No, he was not. At the end of the day, Belissar wanted them to leave his tower and his bees alone. So, it only made sense that he agreed to do the same.

*"Yes. Do it."*

Chief Rohsuak smiled.

"The sacred den master finds those terms acceptable as a starting point. We'll need to discuss the details further before he swears any oaths but you can consider his response as favorable."

Second Queen Berbiya spun around to look at one of the skunk people, who took off running into the tunnel they came from. She then turned around and let out a huge sigh, allowing her shoulders to droop in the process.

"Thank you, Chief Rohsuak, and Sacred Den Master. I'm immeasurably pleased to hear that."

She then waved and the skunk people brought out drinks like last time. A small corner of Belissar's mouth curled up as he watched the soldier bee immediately scramble over and begin drinking from hers.

Yes, at the end of the day, Belissar just wanted his bees to be happy and safe. So, the last thing he wanted was for them to die in a fight he could avoid. If he could save his bees, then the skunk people could keep whatever land, for all he cared. He had everything he needed right in his tower.

# CHAPTER TWENTY-EIGHT

# SHALL WE DO BEES-NESS?

Second Queen Berbiya calmed down and put on a diplomatic smile once more. It appeared they had averted the outcome she was afraid of, so now the talks could resume at a more leisurely pace. Chief Rohsuak returned her smile.

"King Ratuatapi and his people will reciprocate in kind, correct? The sacred den master's authority shall subsequently apply to all current and future purified territory beyond the borders we decide on, with all the same terms regarding his sovereignty over them and your people's promise to respect them. Any violation of the sacred den master's borders by your people, or by anyone else using your territory, shall release the sacred den master and his servants from all promises on his part."

Back in the tower, Belissar's eyes widened a bit. That . . . was a good point. He definitely didn't want to promise to leave the skunk people alone if they weren't going to do the same. He really should have thought of that. But, well, that's why he was glad Chief Rohsuak had agreed to represent him.

Second Queen Berbiya paused for a moment when Chief Rohsuak started to speak but kept her smile and then nodded.

"Yes, of course."

Chief Rohsuak nodded in turn.

"Then, shall we discuss the details?"

Second Queen Berbiya had one of her people join the conversation with some maps, while Chief Rohsuak invited Metsaitti to join the discussion. Belissar couldn't follow too closely at that point, but he trusted that the karnuq knew what they were doing as people who had traveled the Underway for a long time. Belissar . . . may have found himself watching the soldier bee lap up her beverage rather than paying attention to the conversation. More than once.

In the end, the talks proceeded along. Chief Rohsuak insisted on terms Belissar again hadn't thought of; in this case, having the skunk people escort them through the proposed borders before finalizing the deal, since neither Belissar nor the karnuq knew what was in that area. This would allow them to map out the area and mark out which parts of the surface lay above. The skunk people would also need to point out any potential issues, such as dangerous wildlife that might cross over the border. All this would allow Belissar to better understand what he was agreeing to . . . and would keep the skunk people a little more honest, according to Chief Rohsuak.

From there, the talks turned to trade. Belissar paid a bit more attention here, although Chief Rohsuak took the lead on this, since most of the trade would likely be between the karnuq and the skunk people. Still, this was where Belissar could acquire benefits for his tower and his bees. He was particularly interested in whatever beverage Second Queen Berbiya had offered them.

So, he frowned when the pair started off discussing lumber and minerals. Yes, getting some clay or metals and stuff would be nice and honestly pretty useful for expanding his mead-making, but still! He had specifically requested Chief Rohsuak ask about the drinks! So, he couldn't help but fidget as the talks went on.

". . . Should I remind her?"

He trusted Chief Rohsuak, but she and Second Queen Berbiya had reached a lull in their conversation and she still hadn't mentioned it! Instead, Chief Rohsuak relaxed and began to drink from her cup.

"This seems like a good amount for a first exchange, and we will both need to confirm with our superiors. Why don't we call it there for the day?"

Belissar jumped.

*"C-Chief Rohsuak! What about the drinks?!"*

*"Not to worry, Sacred Den Master. Take a look at the Second Queen over there."*

Belissar did so and realized that Second Queen Berbiya hadn't responded. She glanced over to the soldier bee at the table. She glanced back at Chief Rohsuak, who simply continued drinking in silence. Finally, she spoke.

"About that . . . King Ratuatapi wishes to know more about the honeycomb you gifted us last time, and if more may be available?"

Chief Rohsuak hummed and rubbed her chin.

"I am not certain. The honeycomb came from the sacred den master directly, and so I cannot speak for it. Even we don't often gain access to it."

Second Queen Berbiya nodded.

"I understand. Please let him know we are interested, and that King Ratuatapi is open to a direct trade if there is anything he desires."

Chief Rohsuak then smiled.

"I will let him know. Off the top of my head . . . he seemed curious about this beverage, particularly after he learned his monster bees enjoyed it. May I ask what it is?"

Second Queen Berbiya's face lit up. She motioned and the skunk people brought over a jar.

"This is the honeydew from King Ratuatapi's personal aphid farm, produced by only the finest of our giant aphids. We intended to offer this as a gift for the sacred den master once today's talks concluded successfully. We could arrange for larger quantities if the sacred den master is interested?"

Belissar tilted his head. Giant aphids, huh? As far as he was aware, aphids were just a pest that could infest the crops. But apparently, they made something that the bees liked? Well, that was all Belissar needed to know to want them.

*"See if we can get some of those giant aphids."*

Chief Rohsuak nodded.

"I will ask him. He may be curious about those aphids as well . . . as am I."

The talks wrapped up after that. Unfortunately, Chief Rohsuak did not manage to acquire aphids yet, but Belissar guessed that would have to be for next time? He'd much rather just get it all figured out with one talk. But, well, at least he had one jar of honeydew coming.

It probably wouldn't go very far among his bees, but it was a start. He'd just have to hope that the skunk people would trade with them in the end. It seemed that they also liked his bees' honeycomb, so hopefully they could come to an arrangement.

Belissar then rubbed his chin and hummed a bit. Something Chief Rohsuak had said stayed with him, mainly that not even the karnuq had much access to mana honey. That, of course, had been intentional at first. Belissar hadn't wanted to give up his bees' great efforts to the karnuq easily. He just hadn't trusted them, so he kept close that which he cared about most.

But now? Belissar wasn't sure if he fully trusted the karnuq or not. He hadn't trusted a living person in quite some time. But so far, the karnuq had been helpful and had made good on their word. They had helped his bees by building the stone beehouses he might otherwise have struggled with. They had defeated foes his bees could not. And now they were speaking on his behalf with a new group of people who did not seem nearly as friendly. In retrospect, Belissar had begun relying on them more than he thought. In fact, Chief Rohsuak was the one he turned to whenever he had questions . . .

His chest ached a bit as his interactions with Chief Rohsuak reminded him of the old beekeeper Mrs. Imkomos, but he shook his head and tried not to get distracted. The point was . . . did he still need to be so wary of the karnuq? And should he offer them more opportunities to acquire honey, especially when he was about to offer some to an outsider? He had set up that little pit challenge, but their relationship had changed dramatically since then. Plus, he wasn't particularly proud of that effort in the first place.

As of now, he was offering honey to the karnuq that joined the purifications and to karnuq that helped him out in some way, such as Muuraqi with all the masonry work. But perhaps he should think of new ways to reward the karnuq. Maybe he could make new challenges and have them resume the daily remnant hunts? Or was there some other way to do it?

He turned his tower sight to the karnuq settlement as he pondered. His sight came to rest on Juosiutik's place, where the young karnuq was mixing a potion while speaking to a worker bee buzzing around her. He watched bee and karnuq work together for a bit, communicating about things he only vaguely understood.

Maybe . . . he should start thinking of the karnuq more as part of his tower, rather than as a separate group of people living in it. The bees of the battle meadow had started helping the karnuq with construction without asking anything in return. Juosiutik was sharing her knowledge with the First of the Fifth without any agreements in place at all. Chief Rohsuak hadn't asked him for a reward before heading off into the Underway to meet with the skunk people on his behalf.

Maybe . . . he could trust them after all. Maybe he could let them interact more directly with his bees, as the bees were already starting to initiate. And maybe, just maybe, he could do something with all those honey trays piling up in the apiary farmhouse.

He had a lot to think about as the karnuq expedition made their way back toward the tower.

# COLLA-BEE-RATION GROWS!

Juosiutik walked out to the side of her home. There, in a small fenced area, was a garden. Or rather, a mostly empty patch of dirt with a handful of flowers growing. One of them had barely managed to bloom. She frowned and turned to the pair of worker bees flying around her. Apparently, the First of the Fifth wanted her daughter to work with Juosiutik in the future, so both queens currently had a worker accompanying her.

As far as Juosiutik was concerned, the more the merrier.

"This is quickblossom, a key ingredient in the potion I told you about."

The First of the Fifth's worker buzzed her wings as she danced.

"New flower? Why didn't give to King?"

Juosiutik's face fell.

"I would have, but this is all I have. If I remember correctly, the sacred den master normally needs a few more before he can reproduce them. I'm trying to grow a few myself to make sure he has enough. As you can see, it's been slow going."

Juosiutik motioned to the one flower that had bloomed so far.

"You're welcome to drink from the one here, though. In fact, I'd be grateful if you would."

The worker bees zipped around her.

"Will send one gardener," the First of the Fifth's worker danced. "Third Daughter will send workers to gather."

Juosiutik tilted her head.

"Gardener?"

"New type of worker. Checks plants, finds what they need, helps spread. Will find best way to forage."

Juosiutik froze.

"A bee that . . . can tend to plants? And help spread them?"

"Yes. Need to go now. Talk to Third Daughter if need."

The First of the Fifth's worker stopped dancing, but Juosiutik hardly noticed. Her mind was racing with the information the First of the Fifth had just dropped on her. She glanced over at her sad little garden, and imagined it filled to the brim with quickblossom . . . and new flower variants the bees could supposedly help create. She couldn't help but grin.

"Bees are amazing."

A short while later, a group of bees flew to Juosiutik's garden. Juosiutik stared at the promised gardener with interest as she flew to the quickblossom, rubbing her fluffy antennas all over it while flaring her mana. After a bit, the gardener flew over to where the worker bees and Juosiutik were waiting.

"Not enough mana, hard to grow."

Juosiutik tilted her head.

"Really? The ambient mana in the sacred den should have been higher than where these were gathered . . ."

"Wrong type. Wants . . . tiny-lightnings?"

Juosiutik's eyes widened and she slowly nodded.

"Ah . . . if I remember my . . . mentor said that quickblossom normally blooms after thunderstorms. I'm not sure myself, I never had the chance to see it . . ."

She then frowned.

"So, it won't work, then? I haven't seen a cloud in the sky of the sacred den since arriving here . . ."

But, to her surprise, the gardener bee danced a negative.

"No, is fine. Queen will ask Beero to help."

Juosiutik paused at that.

"Um, Beero?"

"Wounded soldier. Makes lightnings with mana now. Queen will ask Fourth of Eighth to help too."

Juosiutik could only tilt her head at that. There were bees . . . that made lightning? Well, she supposed that these were monster bees created by a sacred den, after all.

"Queen says okay. Beero coming now."

Juosiutik slowly nodded. She guessed she would see these bees soon enough.

A short while later, Juosiutik heard a commotion, with karnuq shouting and scrambling about. She looked over to see what the matter was and her eyes widened.

There, up in the sky, casting a large shadow over the settlement, was the largest bee she had ever seen. A big ball of black-and-yellow fuzz flew over the karnuq, its wings causing a loud beating noise heard across the room. The flowers of the field around them swayed in the breeze created by its wings as it began to descend upon the ground . . . directly toward Juosiutik, in fact. She couldn't help but take a step back when the bee landed right before her. To be fair, now that it was on the ground it hardly came up to her knees, but it was still gigantic for a bee.

"U-Um, hi?"

The bee crawled about in a circle before flattening itself against the ground, and then several more bees crawled off of its back. These were the usual soldier bees, if she considered bees the size of her hand normal now, but with one glaring exception. All of them were missing at least one pair of wings, and all of them had crackling lightning flowing in place of those missing wings. One of them crawled to her and started to dance.

"Hi, am Beero. Heard need lightning?"

It took Juosiutik a second to reply.

"Ah, um, yes. Hi. I'm . . . Juosiutik, nice to meet you? And, uh, yes, the quick-blossoms need some lightning, I think?"

She turned to the gardener who flew over and began dancing with Beero. Beero danced a salute and then led the wounded soldiers to Juosiutik's garden.

"How much lightning?"

"Lots! Normally wants big sky-lightnings!"

Beero danced her salute and then spread the wounded soldiers around one of the quickblossoms, the one that had already bloomed. Juosiutik's eyes went wide as the wounded bees began to dance and their lightning wings crackled. Lightning mana began to form in the air and then link between the bees. They began to move in a circular dance, causing the lightning mana to spin around as well.

Bits of lightning then began to shoot off of the circle, pulled into the quick-blossom. The flower began to grow before Juosiutik's eyes, blooming fully. The other flowers around it also began to grow and their buds started to open.

"They're . . . casting lightning magic? . . . Bees are really amazing."

The Firstborn paced about in a circle, buzzing her wings and cleaning her antennas over and over. To her side, a tight ball of red burning bees buzzed and crawled over each other, trying to keep warm. The Third of the Sixth was presumably somewhere underneath them all, but the Firstborn was paying them no mind. After all, how could she? Her mind was completely occupied with the final guest she was waiting for.

And there he came. The King himself strode toward the flower meadow's shrine, standing tall and brightly illuminated by the pseudo-sun he had made overhead, the Conduit flying by his side. The Firstborn came to a stop for but a second before she launched into salute and apology dances. She had originally wanted to discuss her matter with the Third of the Sixth and the Conduit, but the Conduit had told her to ask the King directly. The Firstborn had objected heavily, but the

Conduit stood firm. Or, rather, the Conduit had just left to go get the King herself, leaving the Firstborn no choice but to wait for him.

"King! Thanks for coming! Sorry for calling, shouldn't have interrupted—"

But the King just raised his hand and spoke with that voice that rumbled through her body.

"It's fine, you didn't interrupt anything. I want you to tell me anything you think of."

The Firstborn completed three "King best king!" dances before she caught herself and proceeded to stop wasting the King's time. The ball of bees stopped climbing over each other and spread out, revealing the Third of the Sixth shivering underneath.

"Yes! Had idea, w-wanted to ask if okay?"

The King smiled at her with all his kindness and grace.

"Of course, I'd love to hear it."

She stopped herself from celebrating and proceeded.

"Spoke with First of Fifth, recommended specializing queens. Can use latest delivery. Means won't use honey for soldiers, some queens will be evolving too, so less new soldiers. If King planning battle, then won't. Also, want to raise burning queen, but would need to move to new room. Wanted to ask if King and Third of Sixth approve, burning queen will follow Third of Sixth if so."

The Firstborn had spoken with the First of the Fifth and heard how the apiary queens had been specializing. She'd also reflected on the Second of the Sixth assisting them with her medicinal hive, and the Third of the Sixth moving into the lava field, which might one day face the shades before the flower meadow. At this point, she felt it would be beneficial for the hive of hives if some of the flower meadow queens started specializing as well. Not only would it diversify the army and reduce the burden on the apiary queens, but there were some honey and bee types that just didn't fit well within a mixed hive. Most notably burning bees like the Third of the Sixth, whose home was too hot for any other kind of bee and who was now feeling chilly in the regular temperatures of the flower meadow. The flower meadow queens had been about to raise some digging soldiers when they realized that depending on Ground mana honey donations from the one digging queen in the apiary would restrict the number of such soldiers they could raise, a major problem when those soldiers would have to fight alone in their intended environment. Most regular bees couldn't fight in the dirt tunnels on account of the dark and tight quarters. As such, it made more sense to use that honey to evolve a queen who could then keep the digging soldiers' numbers up.

Of course, all of this was contingent on the approval of the King and the Third of the Sixth. The Firstborn would not allow her ideas to interfere with the grand designs of the King, of course. And the Third of the Sixth was now the queen of the lava field, so it only made sense to check with her before any other queen moved into her territory. She could only tremble as she awaited the King's judgement. Not only had she called the King from his work to propose this idea, but she was also a queen who had failed at her duties more than once. What merit did her ideas and plans have? How dare she waste the King's time with them? She knew that he, as gracious and kind as he was, often sought their opinions, and that was the only reason she dared to dance at all now. But now, she could not help but feel she had made a grave mistake . . .

But the King just kept smiling at her and nodded.

"That sounds like a great idea. What about you, Third of the Sixth? I can add new beehives so you won't need to share yours."

The Third of the Sixth was already dancing.

"Okay!"

The King nodded at her and turned his smile back to the Firstborn.

"Sounds like it's settled, then. Let me know if you need any help, I also have extra honey if you need it."

The Firstborn danced a refusal with all her might. The King already graciously shared his tribute with them during the victory celebrations. She could not possibly ask him for more.

"Haha, okay. Great work, both of you. I look forward to seeing the queens!"

It took the Firstborn a while to get to it, though, for her mind went blank for quite a while at this turn of affairs.

# CHAPTER TWENTY-NINE

# BEE FRIENDLY!

The bumblebee soldier stood before Juosiutik's house. She began to groom her-self, if only to have something to do. The little queens had asked her to fly here with the little soldiers, and that she had done. Now, the little soldiers asked her to stay here so she could take them home later. So, that's what she did.

The bear-King things were watching her, but she paid them no mind. She could smell the King's mana on them, though fainter than on her sister bees, so she knew they were part of the same hive. She focused on her grooming, brush-ing her hair and antennas with her legs.

But then, one of the bear-King things made a move. It was smaller than the others, though still taller than herself. The bumblebee soldier might have thought it was a worker but there weren't enough bear-King things its size for that to be true, unless the bear-King hive was preparing for a winter hibernation. That was a bit confusing, since the bumblebee soldier hadn't noticed any signs of the sea-sons changing, but she was just a soldier, so winter preparations weren't her job in the first place.

And neither was figuring out what the small bear-King thing was, so she went back to her grooming. At least, until the bear-King thing got closer.

"Um, hi?"

The bumblebee soldier turned toward the bear-King thing, the King's mana telling her this was a greeting. She responded in kind, buzzing her wings and releas-ing friendly pheromones. The bear-King thing tilted its head. The bumblebee soldier wasn't sure what that meant, so she went back to grooming herself.

Then, the small bear-King thing slowly crept forward, reaching out with its upper legs. The bumblebee soldier paused as the bear-King thing touched her hairs.

"It's fuzzy."

The King's mana indicated the small bear-King thing was expressing happiness as it began to help the soldier groom, brushing her hairs. The bear-King thing's upper legs felt warm and pleasant. The bumblebee soldier knew that mutual grooming could help clean spots she had trouble reaching, so she began to groom the bear-King thing as well, rubbing her legs across it. The bear-King thing made a noise that was also translated as happiness.

"It tickles!"

There was some commotion in the other bear-King things, but then most of them began to disperse and return to their work. As did the bumblebee soldier, continuing to groom the small bear-King thing . . . and other bear-King things that began to approach her.

Belissar went over to the karnuq settlement, hoping to ask for Muuraqi's help. The Third of the Sixth could help provide Fire mana honey and fireproof wax for a flower meadow queen to evolve, but all that Fire mana honey would dramatically increase the temperature of its surroundings. Even with the fireproof wax, it would make the bee barracks uncomfortable for the rest of the bees if the honey was stored there. Belissar decided that it would be worthwhile to build a small stone structure where a queen could evolve without impacting the rest of the barracks, and with no risk of starting any fires.

On the way, he saw a bumblebee soldier outside of Juosiutik's house, surrounded by a couple of karnuq children who were petting it. The soldier seemed to enjoy the attention and was petting the children back. Belissar couldn't help but smile . . . and noted that the bumblebees enjoyed pets. That was knowledge he planned to act on as soon as he completed his present tasks.

Chief Rohsuak soon met with him.

"Hello, Sacred Den Master, how can I help you?"

"Hello, I was wondering if Muuraqi was available? I'm trying to build some stonework, a small one."

Chief Rohsuak smiled and nodded her head.

"For you, he is available anytime, Sacred Den Master."

Belissar smiled back.

"Great! Ah, I'll give him some mana honey for the trouble, along with anyone else who comes to help."

Chief Rohsuak's expression wavered for but a moment before she resumed her smile.

"That is most generous of you, Sacred Den Master. I'm sure he'll appreciate it."

Belissar then realized this was a good moment to pitch another idea he had.

"Also . . . you've done a lot for me recently, talking to the skunk people and stuff. I feel like that could have gone badly if you hadn't been there, so, um, thank you."

Chief Rohsuak's smile grew but she shook her head.

"Think nothing of it, Sacred Den Master. Those negotiations heavily concerned us as well. It is only natural we lent you our support."

But this time Belissar shook his head.

"Still, I really appreciate the help. So, I was thinking maybe I could set up a beehouse feature by your house? They produce honey even without any bees somehow, so you'd get a tray each day. Um, if you want it, that is."

"YES!"

Belissar gasped as Chief Rohsuak pounced forward and clasped both his shoulders with her hands . . . only to quickly flinch and jump back as Niobee and the soldier bees began buzzing and moving in. She quickly waved her hands and then cleared her throat.

"Um, sorry for that, I did not mean any harm or disrespect. What I meant was . . . I would be most honored."

Belissar shook his head a bit and then nodded.

"Got it. Um, I should mention that it would just be regular honey, unless some of the bees move in. And, um, since I don't know how it's even making the honey, I don't know exactly how good it will be. I, um, told the bees to give you space on this floor, but . . ."

Belissar glanced over at the bumblebee soldier and the karnuq children.

". . . If you're willing to share the space and the flowers and take care of the bees, I could see if there are any willing to move in?"

Chief Rohsuak stood still for a moment, blinking a couple of times. Then, she made the widest smile Belissar had seen yet.

"We would be honored that you would trust us to that degree, Sacred Den Master. If you and your bees wish to dwell with us, I swear to ensure their comfort and safety."

Belissar was about to reply, but someone else beat him to it.

*New mission received: Teach the karnuq the art of beekeeping.*

His eyes widened. Chief Rohsuak tilted her head.

"Sacred Den Master? Is something the matter?"

Belissar shook his head.

"No . . . just the opposite, in fact. It seems the God of Bees approves of this . . . and wants me to teach you beekeeping."

Now it was Chief Rohsuak's eyes that opened wide. Then, she knelt down and bowed her head.

"We would be most honored."

Belissar rubbed his chin.

"In that case . . . maybe we should do more than just one hive? Um, the God of Bees said she wants the karnuq to learn, so maybe more of your people can help too, then."

Chief Rohsuak nodded.

"This is your area of expertise, Sacred Den Master, both beekeeping and fulfilling the will of the gods. Please, instruct us as you see fit and we will do whatever you say. If you wish, I will gather as many of our people as you need."

At this point, Niobee flew before him.

"King! Bees help too!"

Belissar smiled and held out his hand for Niobee to land on.

"Thanks, Niobee, I know you'll always help."

Belissar then rubbed his chin with his other hand.

"Okay. I think . . . I'd like a bit of time to think about how to do this. You, um, are also talking with the skunk people again tomorrow, right? Um, is there another name for them besides skunk people?"

Chief Rohsuak nodded.

"Yes, we plan to work out the final details. They have not named themselves yet but perhaps they will once the final agreement is in place."

Belissar nodded back.

"Okay, maybe we'll start the day after, then?"

Chief Rohsuak hummed.

"About that . . . Sacred Den Master, I do need to ask you something. You are aware that you and King Ratuatapi will need to confirm the final agreement, right? And since it is supposed to include you promising in the name of the God of Bees . . . you will likely need to invite them into the sacred den to complete the deal in person. Would you agree to this?"

Belissar paused, and then his face fell. So, he would have to speak to them himself after all. He had hoped that Chief Rohsuak might be able to handle everything, but apparently not. He was about to agree . . . but then he had a thought.

"So, they have to come into the tower before agreeing? Could that be dangerous? There's a chance they are planning to attack us, right?"

Chief Rohsuak nodded with a solemn expression.

"Indeed. And since you will be meeting them face-to-face, that would be their best chance to attack as well. It is indeed dangerous."

She then glanced back at the bumblebee soldier and smiled.

"On the other hand, it will be on your territory and your terms. You will have all of us and all your bees at your disposal. We can negotiate limits on who they can bring for that very reason . . . and even the gods would disapprove if they used such an occasion for treachery. It is still not without risk, but so long as we prepare, I believe we can maintain control of the situation."

Belissar frowned, but slowly nodded.

"In that case . . . I'll, um, do what I have to. Just . . . make sure they know I won't forgive them if they hurt the bees."

Chief Rohsuak made a fierce grin as she narrowed her eyes.

"No, we would not."

# CHAPTER THIRTY

# BEE-HOLD THE KING!

A couple of days passed. Belissar and Muuraqi built a small stone chamber for burning queens to evolve in, then Belissar tried to keep himself busy planning for the beekeeping lessons. He did not start on them, though, for he was preoccupied with the ongoing negotiations. He, the karnuq, and the bees had many discussions on what preparations they could make, then spent much time and effort making those preparations. Not only he and Chief Rohsuak, but all the karnuq and the bees had roles to play.

In the meantime, Chief Rohsuak met again with Second Queen Berbiya to hammer out the final details of the deal, tour the proposed borders, and arrange for Belissar and King Ratuatapi to make the final agreement. As Chief Rohsuak predicted, the skunk people requested to visit the sacred den and observe Belissar make his promise before the Shrine of Bees. Chief Rohsuak and the Second Queen then had animated discussions on the details of that visit, particularly how many guards King Ratuatapi would bring along with him.

But eventually, they worked it out. Neither side wanted to waste any time, so they set the date for the day after that talk. That day was now here.

Belissar frowned as he held his arms out.

"Is this really necessary?"

Metsaitti nodded as he placed a heavy fur coat across Belissar's shoulders.

"Even a cave panther can be intimidated by a fearsome appearance. This is a weapon as well, Sacred Den Master."

Belissar could only take the karnuq's word for it as they dressed him up. It turned out they didn't have much clothing in his size, so the karnuq had done a rush job adjusting everything. They had no choice, though, since Belissar's own wardrobe was limited to worn tunics . . . and that was before he had become a sacred den master with only the one on his back.

He now wore a far newer tunic and pants under the fur coat Metsaitti had just put on him. He was adorned with pieces of honeycomb that the workers had built in the shape of bees. On his head, he had a crown of woven mana flowers, still faintly glowing. Metsaitti then handed him a spear that was just a bit too large for him, but Belissar managed to hold it upright. Metsaitti nodded.

"Almost ready. Just need your own touch."

Belissar took a deep breath and then turned to his ever-present companion hovering around him.

"What do you think?"

Niobee danced happily about.

"King is best king!"

Belissar chuckled and then inclined his head toward her. Niobee landed right on his head, while worker bees landed on the mana flower crown. He then straightened himself and took another deep breath.

"Okay, let's go."


A karnuq emerged from the Underway, leading King Ratuatapi's procession. The group consisted of thirty of his finest warriors, no longer dressed for stealth in the Underway but in the finest armor they had available. Metal combined with chitin and dyed silk formed black and red shells over black and white fur, with spears, shields, and swords of similar colors. Second Queen Berbiya walked with Fourth Queen Pezuya at the head of the procession, Berbiya in her silk dress and Pezuya in full battle garb.

And at their center, riding on a giant rhinoceros beetle larger than a cow, was King Ratuatapi himself. He was a young man just shy of two decades, with a handsome face and immaculately groomed fur. He wore a silver crown with a large diamond set in the center and shining armor over a fine silk robe. He was also glancing around, his eyes and mouth wide open as he took in his first-ever view of the surface.

The rest of their entourage did likewise, save for the most disciplined of the guards. Second Queen Berbiya herself could not help a small gasp after her eyes adjusted to the blinding light. The sun shone down on them, illuminating the world in a way no light crystal ever could. All around them were trees, larger than she had ever thought possible, reaching to the sky not by clinging to rock walls but on the strength of their own trunks. The entire world was filled with green and brown.

It was, more than anything, clear proof that a sacred den had been at work. Not a single living person among them had seen the surface with their own eyes, until now. Second Queen Berbiya couldn't help but glance at the queen beside her. Fourth Queen Pezuya's hand tightened around her sword as her eyes opened wide.

"The true power of a sacred den," Second Queen Berbiya said softly.

Fourth Queen Pezuya turned to glance at her, then frowned.

"The power of the gods, not of the man."

Second Queen Berbiya frowned right back.

"A man acknowledged by those same gods."

Fourth Queen Pezuya said nothing in reply. Second Queen Berbiya furrowed her brow. She had not wanted the Fourth Queen to come to what was sure to be a delicate meeting, but what could she do? The Fourth Queen led their clan guard. She could hardly be prevented from escorting their king into the jaws of a sacred den.

The Second Queen's anxious feeling only grew as their karnuq guide led them into a clearing, where they got their first glimpse of the sacred den. King Ratuatapi's eyes went wide once more . . . but not Pezuya's. The Fourth Queen smiled.

"Not so big after all."

Second Queen Berbiya glared at Pezuya before glancing at their guide. But if the karnuq had heard them, he did not give any indication of it. Instead, he led them up to the sacred den and opened the gate. Fourth Queen Pezuya stopped and turned.

"This is it. Are you ready, Your Majesty?"

King Ratuatapi took a deep breath and spoke with all the gravitas he could muster.

"Proceed."

And with that, they stepped inside. Inside, they found a meadow filled to the brim with flowers, a colorful rainbow stretching across the ground. Two columns of karnuq warriors were arranged before them, holding spears at attention. At the end of the two columns was a large throne made of stone, rising right out of the flowers. To the left side of the throne was a statue holding a glowing sphere and a wax chest, likely the shrine of the sacred den's patron, given that its colors and theme matched the yellow banners on the sacred den's exterior. To the right side was Chief Rohsuak, now standing tall. The air shimmered around her, and even from a distance Berbiya could feel the heat emanating off of her. Berbiya's eyes widened a bit. Chief Rohsuak had not displayed that much mana when they had last spoken.

Fourth Queen Pezuya, on the other hand, frowned as she gazed upon the throne, for it was empty.

"What is the meaning of this? Where is the sacred den master?"

Second Queen Berbiya was about to chide her and apologize, but Chief Rohsuak simply smiled.

"He will arrive shortly. May I assume this is King Ratuatapi?"

Second Queen Berbiya stepped forward before the Fourth Queen could say anything.

"Yes and thank you for welcoming us today. May I present King Ratuatapi, head of Clan Ratuatapi, ruler of all sigmaka."

Second Queen Berbiya felt Pezuya glare at her but she kept her eyes forward. Chief Rohsuak's smile grew and she inclined her head toward King Ratuatapi.

"Greetings, King Ratuatapi, and welcome to the sacred den. Allow me to introduce the sacred den master. If you'll wait but a moment . . ."

Chief Rohsuak then burst into flames. Both Second Queen Berbiya and Fourth Queen Pezuya took an involuntary step back at the heat. Before Pezuya could react, Chief Rohsuak lifted her hand up into the sky, a bright ball of light rushing from it into the air. It burst and covered the sky in red flames, causing the newest of the clan guard to crouch down while the more experienced gathered around King Ratuatapi. The king himself was clearly sweating.

But the fire died down as quickly as it appeared. Pezuya grabbed the hilt of her sword.

"What is the meaning of—"

But she was cut off, for then they heard the buzzing. A cloud appeared in the distance, rushing toward them across the sky. As it grew closer, they saw black and yellow stripes cover the air, with occasional other colors such as bluish-green and purple mixed in here and there. Berbiya's eyes widened as she realized what she was looking at.

A swarm of bees, large enough to blot out the sun.

Fourth Queen Pezuya tightened her grip on the hilt of her sword. The sigmaka entourage began to back up, and even Second Queen Berbiya couldn't help a quiet gulp. The cloud continued to fly at them at full speed.

But then, the swarm stopped. It split apart, bees swirling around each other in twisting rivers of black and yellow. Then, they began to form up. The bees began to assemble into squares of perfectly spaced rows, the squares forming a checkerboard across the sky. One of the clan guards spoke with wide eyes.

"Fourth Queen . . . they're organized . . ."

"Steady. Organized or not, they're just bees . . ."

But Fourth Queen Pezuya trailed off even before she finished. The whole formation began to descend toward them until they could start to make out the individual bees. They grew larger . . . and larger . . . and larger still. Second Queen Berbiya gulped as she realized that this swarm was not of worker bees, but of the soldier bees as large as her hand that she had seen during the negotiations. The karnuq, for their part, did not react at all, even as the bees began to hover over and around them. Soon, there was a formation of bees on all sides save their rear, with additional formations arranged at a short distance farther beyond. Each bee hovered in position, not an antenna out of place as entire formations moved in perfect sync with one another.

"Fourth Queen . . . what do we do? This is not what we planned for . . ."

Second Queen Berbiya barely heard the clan guard over the loud buzzing of bees all around, but once she did she quickly spun toward the Fourth Queen. She found Pezuya's face turning pale as the Fourth Queen glanced around at the soldier bee army assembling all around them, as well as to Chief Rohsuak, who was still clad in flames, and the karnuq warriors all around them.

"That's . . ."

Pezuya seemed unable to say more.

Second Queen Berbiya quickly strode over and clasped Pezuya on the shoulder, making the Fourth Queen turn to face her. Berbiya looked right into her eyes.

"It is no matter, for we are here to confirm the agreement and establish peace between us. Isn't that right, King Ratuatapi?"

Berbiya looked back toward their king, who was drenched in sweat and gulping.

"Y-Yes, that's right!"

Pezuya glanced toward their king, then looked back at Berbiya with wide eyes that quivered for a moment. Her face fell and she took a deep breath.

"Yes . . . as the king commands . . ."

And then, in the midst of the formation, she saw him. A man sat on a woven sheet, held in the air from its four corners by the largest bees she had ever seen, big enough to reach her past her knees, maybe even as tall as her waist. The bees lowered the sheet down directly on the throne and the man sat upon it, slowly rising to his feet as the four giant bees landed on the ground around him. On top of his head was a bee about the size of the soldiers all around them, but as the man rose it began to glow as bright as a light crystal.

"Welcome to the Bee Tower. I am its keeper, Belissar, and I welcome you here today."

And so, King Ratuatapi and the sigmaka finally met the sacred den master . . .

# CHAPTER THIRTY-ONE

# SECURING BEE-CEFUL RELATIONS

**B**elissar held in the urge to gulp as he stood before the skunk people, or the sigmaka as they apparently called themselves. It had taken much, *much* practice for the bumblebee soldiers to place him on the throne without him stumbling, but fortunately he had pulled it off here. He still could not help sweating at the many, *many* eyes turned his way. The bees once again saved him, as the workers crawling over his crown lapped up his sweat before it could drip down his face.

Fortunately, the sigmaka appeared as nervous as he felt. King Ratuatapi did not have bees to lap up his sweat as he disembarked from his mount and stepped forward.

"I am King Ratuatapi. Thank you for welcoming us today, Sacred Den Master Belissar. I . . . hope that we may establish peace and prosperity between our peoples."

Belissar blinked as King Ratuatapi nearly stumbled over his words. Belissar didn't know how the sigmaka aged, but if they were anything like humans then King Ratuatapi appeared similar in age to himself, possibly even a few years younger. He had been trying to steel himself to face some sort of wise and experienced ruler . . . though, for all he knew King Ratuatapi could still be far more experienced compared to himself, even if he was younger. Still, the way King Ratuatapi sweated and kept glancing around at the bees at least reassured Belissar he wasn't the only one uncomfortable here.

He used his tower sight to glance at the bees without moving his eyes, as Chief Rohsuak had recommended, and took heart from the soldier bee army hovering around him. He then deployed yet another tactic recommended by Chief Rohsuak: nodding slowly with a light hum while he tried to remember what he was supposed to say.

"Then . . . shall we proceed?"

He just managed to remember to swing an open hand toward the Shrine of Bees . . . and managed to catch himself before his usual "um." He then had to resist the urge to sigh. This was all very exhausting.

King Ratuatapi nodded slowly as well. Second Queen Berbiya and Chief Rohsuak led their respective rulers toward the Shrine of Bees, with the armored sigmaka and karnuq warriors following behind. Belissar and King Ratuatapi walked up to the shrine alone, save for Niobee and the other bees on Belissar's person. Chief Rohsuak had told him something about the order mattering or something, but Belissar just wanted to finish up already, so he went ahead and started.

"I, Belissar, Keeper of the Bee Tower, swear in the name of my patron, the God of Bees, to honor the deal agreed on today. To respect the land, the borders, and the sovereignty of King Ratuatapi, his clan, and his people, and never to violate them without permission, so long as neither King Ratuatapi, his clan, or his people harm my people or violate my borders, nor allow any other to do so from their lands."

Fortunately, Chief Rohsuak could remind him of the exact wording as he spoke it. He had done his best to memorize it on his own, but the exact wording of an oath before the gods was very important, so they'd both agreed not to take any chances. Chief Rohsuak had fought hard for the various conditions within the oath, after all, so it would not do if Belissar forgot them or accidentally left a hole by forgetting a specific word.

As he finished the final word, the Shrine of Bees began to glow, pulsing once with light before falling dim again. Belissar's eyes widened as he felt something settle upon him and constrict around his heart, and it took all his self-control not to begin trembling. It appeared an oath sworn before the shrine of a god was not to be taken lightly. He was once again glad that Chief Rohsuak had helped with this and worked so hard on the exact wording.

King Ratuatapi jumped a bit when the Shrine of Bees glowed, then gulped.

"I, King Ratuatapi, ruler of Clan Ratuatapi and of all sigmaka, swear in the name of my ancestors and on the lives of my people, with the God of Bees as witness, to honor the deal agreed on today. To respect the land, the borders, the servants, and the sovereignty of Sacred Den Master Belissar, and the mission he performs on behalf of the gods, and never to violate them without permission, so long as neither Sacred Den Master Belissar nor his servants harm my people or violate my lands, nor allow any other to do so from their lands."

The Shrine of Bees pulsed once again. King Ratuatapi apparently could not control himself and shivered lightly. Then, both he and Belissar turned to one another and shook hands, nodding at each other silently.

Chief Rohsuak smiled and held up her hand, creating a bright and colorful flame around it.

"Let our peoples know peace!"

The karnuq all slammed the butts of their spears against the ground and cheered. The bees all began to buzz their wings, filling the air with a thunderous roar.

Second Queen Berbiya nodded.

"Let our people know peace!"

She then glared at Fourth Queen Pezuya. The Fourth Queen limply drew her sword and raised it into the air. One by one, the sigmaka guards followed her and lifted up a cheer of their own.

And so, Belissar and King Ratuatapi agreed to peace.

After the oaths, the karnuq brought out a couple of tables to hold a small banquet with all the best food they could prepare, along with some mana honey courtesy of Belissar and the bees. Second Queen Berbiya had arranged for some gifts as well, so the sigmaka made their own contributions. Karnuq and sigmaka then intermingled and sat among each other, while several large bowls of honey and honeydew were set aside for the bees. Belissar and King Ratuatapi sat next to each other at a smaller table. Neither of them said anything as they ate and drank. Chief Rohsuak had said the two leaders were supposed to make a show of being friendly, but Belissar couldn't think of anything to say.

Fortunately, King Ratuatapi broke the silence first.

"So . . . you like bees, huh?"

Belissar jumped a bit but managed to calm himself and nodded.

"Yes. Yes, I do."

He smiled a bit at Niobee, who was lapping up a bowl of honeydew next to Belissar's plate. She stopped for a second to dance happily at the attention before resuming her lapping . . . all the while keeping her eyes on their guest.

King Ratuatapi watched her as well and glanced at the bees still crawling on Belissar's flower crown.

"I'm truly impressed. My ancestors supposedly tried to tame monster bees in the far past, but never managed to do so before we made our way underground. We had to stick with aphids, since even the giant ones are docile."

Belissar turned to face King Ratuatapi.

"Actually, I'd like to hear more about those aphids. The bees love their honeydew . . . oh, and I do as well."

King Ratuatapi smiled.

"I'm glad, I raised the ones that made that jar myself. Well, I say raised, but the aphids mostly do their own thing. We just have to make sure they're healthy and well-fed, and they take care of the rest for us."

Belissar nodded along.

"It's the same for bees, actually. My . . . mentor always said the bees will be bees regardless of whether we're there or not. We just do our best to give them a nice home and help them deal with any problems, and then let them do their thing."

King Ratuatapi grinned.

"Sounds like my mentor as well."

From there, Belissar and King Ratuatapi started discussing the intricacies of beekeeping and giant aphid ranching, to the approving nods of Chief Rohsuak and Second Queen Berbiya. The Second Queen, for her part, turned to the woman beside her. Fourth Queen Pezuya was staring down at her plate and mumbling.

"Isn't this better, Fourth Queen?"

The Fourth Queen lifted her head up just enough to glare at her.

"Better? You call us dooming ourselves to subjugation by a domineering force we cannot contend with *better*?"

Second Queen Berbiya gave her a sharp look.

"Compared to the alternative? Yes, yes I do. Which is why I worked so hard to bring about this outcome, you know, and why the First Queen agreed with me in the end. As long as no one breaks the agreement, there shall be no subjugation, period."

She then made a mischievous smile.

"Besides, you don't seem to hate that honeycomb there. If you are so opposed to our new neighbors, perhaps I should take the evidence of our doom off your plate?"

The Fourth Queen looked away with a huff, but also protectively crouched over her plate. Second Queen Berbiya let out a light giggle before turning her eyes back to her own plate. For the first time since the sacred den had been discovered, she could truly enjoy her meal. Her eyes lit up as she bit into a huge chunk of honeycomb.

And what a meal it was.

# IN DEFENSE OF HER KING

Belissar's eyes widened. The banquet had concluded and the sigmaka had departed for home. He was currently meeting with Chief Rohsuak and the bee queens to discuss what had happened.

"Really? They were going to attack us?!"

Chief Rohsuak nodded, no smile on her face this time.

"I believe Fourth Queen Pezuya planned on it, at the very least, though whether or not the rest of them were in on it I cannot say. Her reaction to the bee army was too extreme, and then there was Second Queen Berbiya's hasty conversation with her. I'm guessing she was hoping to ambush you but thought better of it once she saw the soldier bees."

Belissar frowned.

"They would really do that? Just attack us out of nowhere after all those talks and agreements?"

Chief Rohsuak sighed, letting her shoulders droop.

"In the end, Sacred Den Master, verbal agreements are just that. Unless enforced by power, whether yours or someone else's, they can be broken at will. I must admit that we ourselves have done so in the past, when necessary to survive."

Belissar ground his teeth.

"Then, how can we trust them? What was the point of all this?"

Chief Rohsuak stepped forward and patted his shoulder.

"Creating trust was the point of this. For the sigmaka, they have the reassurance that your patron god will enforce the agreement on your end. And as for them . . ."

Chief Rohsuak grinned with a dangerous glint in her eyes as she waved to the soldier bee army still hovering around.

"Now they know you have the strength to punish them should they deceive you."

Belissar slowly unclenched his jaw, then sighed and let his own shoulders droop. This whole affair had been exhausting, and a clear reminder of how out of his depth he still was. Sure, he knew how to make tower rooms now, but he didn't know a thing about dealing with people even as an equal, much less as a superior. And, had he done it wrong, it could have ended up in disaster. The sigmaka could have attacked, leading to a war and dead bees and karnuq. Or he might have agreed to a very poor deal indeed. He hadn't even thought to ask that the sigmaka reciprocate when they initially demanded he respect their territory. That . . . well, that could have led to the exact kind of relationship he'd had with the village beforehand.

He took a deep breath and looked up.

"Chief Rohsuak . . . can you teach me more? Um, about making deals and talking with leaders and stuff. I . . . think I need to know more before we have any more talks like this . . ."

Chief Rohsuak smiled at him.

"I'd be happy to."

Niobee watched from atop her King's head as the outsiders finally went home. She found she very much enjoyed the position. Her King's hair wrapped around her like the petals of a flower, but his body below provided a warmth no normal flower did, while his mana embraced her from all sides. Additionally, from here, she could keep watch of his blind spots, ensuring that no one could approach her King from above or behind.

But, alas, all things must come to an end, and so she lifted off her King's head. She had other tasks she needed to attend to today. Her King was not like other queens, after all. Niobee was aware her King was a human, and that humans were different from bees. From what she observed, humans were more like solitary bees, with each individual making their own hive. As a result, while her King could raise queens and build hives better than anyone else, he did not lead them the way a monster bee queen would. But that was fine! Niobee's old queen didn't either, after all, since she also had not been a monster bee. In her old hive, the workers just followed their instincts and did whatever work was in front of them. And when they had to make decisions, they all decided as a group.

So, Niobee did something similar. If her King didn't make a decision, then his bees would make it themselves! If there was a task he left unaddressed, then Niobee would take care of it! That way, her King could continue raising queens and building hives, as a good queen did, while she did any other jobs needed, like a good worker did!

She still wasn't certain on the difference between a queen and king and how her King could claim to be a drone while fulfilling all the tasks of a queen in amazing and incredible ways. But figuring that out was not her job, so she focused on what was.

Mainly, deciding what to do about these new outsiders. Niobee didn't like them. They seemed to make her King feel bad, and she had decided that she would sting anyone who made her King feel bad. But her King also didn't want her to sting them, since that would lead to a fight that bees might die in. He was too kind. It was only natural for bees to sting those who got too close to their hive. And it was only natural for bees to die. Niobee had watched thousands of her own sisters perish over the years, though for some reason she herself continued on, until it was just her, her queen, and her King who endured. She felt that her fellow bees would have been happy to die in order to keep away people who made her King feel bad.

But bees dying would also make her King feel bad, so she didn't ask the soldiers to do so. It was a bit of a conundrum. How should she best take care of her King? How should she protect him when talking to people who made him feel bad, if stinging them and losing bees would also make him feel bad? But, well, Niobee then realized the obvious solution. All she had to do was make sure they could sting the outsiders without losing bees!

So, that was what she did. She flew to the core room and began to dance on the core. The mana flowing in and through the core had its own dance to it, twisting and flowing to touch everyone and everything within her King's domain. It was a hive on a grander scale than any other, and Niobee found she was something like a communer for it. The flow of mana passed through her before heading off to . . . somewhere. She didn't know where. But she could watch the mana as it passed and learn from it.

She could see the Firstborn, both angry to find out the outsiders might have attacked the King and yet proud that her army had intimidated them enough to stop. She could see the First of the Fifth as the queen paced relentlessly through her hive, as worried for the King as Niobee was. She could see the Fourth of the Seventh watching the outsiders with interest, her scouts following them as far as they were allowed to go. She could see one of the more heavily wounded lancers buzzing her wings, left behind by the army as she still hadn't healed enough to fly. She could see a newly hatched digging gardener visiting the mushrooms hidden in the depths of the dirt tunnels. She could see the slime bee and gravity bee workers cooperating to gather nectar from the gravilion flower, the gravity worker helping the slime bee extend a tunnel of slime from the flower to the edge of the flower's magic to funnel nectar and pollen to other workers. She could see one of the flower meadow queens curled up in the new stone mini-hive, struggling to adapt as the hot honey all around her burned her body.

Niobee began to dance and the mana of the core began to dance with her. A stream of mana passed into the healing honey the wounded lancer was drinking, increasing its potency. A river swirled into the stone mini-hive and the queen within, helping her connect with the Fire mana all around her. Little tendrils contacted the Firstborn, the First of the Fifth, and the Fourth of the Seventh, reminding them of the King in that moment and renewing their strength. The Firstborn set about to discuss the bumblebee soldiers with the other queens, and how the army might use their strength. The First of the Fifth turned her pacing into action, rushing off to review all of the apiary queens and how she might assist them. The Fourth of the Seventh flew off with renewed vigor, taking her scout party to map out new lands.

Niobee would do anything she could to make sure the hive grew as strong and healthy as possible. Because if the hive and the bees within it grew strong enough, they could then sting whoever they wanted without losing anybody!

And then, she paused. She groomed herself a bit, rubbing her legs over her hairs and her antennas. And then, slowly, Niobee resumed her dance. The mana flowed once more . . . but not to any bees. A light stream of mana adjusted the mana honey the dangerous one was adding to her pot, calming a concerning buildup of mana within it. Mana flowed through the body of the helpful one as he cut a boulder, allowing him to cut yet another without rest. Mana enveloped the karnuq larvae as they ran about, encouraging them to grow strong.

This was the other reason Niobee did not sting the new outsiders. She had watched the karnuq for a while now . . . and so far, they had proven her fears wrong. They had not hurt her King like the other humans had. Instead, they assisted him, working for his hive as they could. Perhaps, she could one day consider them part of the hive. After all, her King, a human, had become the best queen she could ever ask for. So, perhaps these karnuq, too, could become adequate workers.

And if that was the case . . . then perhaps the new outsiders would not need to be stung after all. Niobee didn't fully understand how human hives worked, and these humans were different from either her King's humans or the karnuq. So, perhaps, in time, they would prove themselves as the karnuq had and would stop making her King feel bad.

And if they did not . . . then Niobee would be prepared to protect her King, and never again let anyone treat him the way his old hive had.

## BEE'S BEST FRIEND

Tarwantrad looked away with her arms crossed and her cheeks puffed. Urubran smirked. Tarwantrad glanced at him, saw his smirk, and turned away with another huff. Urubran chuckled and shook his head.

"I'm sorry Tarwantrad . . . or, well, I'm not, but I do understand this is upsetting for you."

She clenched her teeth.

". . . How? *How* did you get the blessing before me?!"

Urubran shrugged and then smiled, his eyes full of mirth. Tarwantrad scowled.

"No, don't you say it . . ."

Urubran said it anyway.

"I built a home for the bees . . ."

Tarwantrad growled.

"Don't you dare say it!"

But Urubran did not show mercy.

". . . and made them happy."

Tarwantrad grabbed her hair, pulled, and screamed, drawing looks from pedestrians and the other café patrons.

"How?! How are your bees happier than mine?! All you did was stack some rocks and dead wood together! I wove together a wonderful grove of their favorite flowers, right into the walls of their home!"

Urubran raised an eyebrow.

"You're the one who told me they actually prefer flowers a bit farther away from their hive, though?"

Tarwantrad clasped her mouth shut to try and hold in her next scream. Urubran chuckled once more and then began to rub his chin. He decided he should probably stop teasing her if he ever wanted her to speak to him again.

"Hm, you know, that's probably it."

Tarwantrad narrowed her eyes.

"What is?"

Urubran looked up at her, now with a serious expression.

"We both know it's unlikely my bees are happier than yours, and we both know it's impossible your bees are unhappy in the first place. So, the key is probably in the homes."

Tarwantrad crossed her arms once again.

"Are you saying your bee home is better than mine?"

Urubran shook his head.

"We both know that you know bees better. The home you made is probably better too. But . . . I built mine myself."

Tarwantrad furrowed her brow.

"What are you . . ."

But her eyes started to widen as she trailed off. Urubran clasped his hands together.

"Let me guess . . . did you use the God of Flowers' blessing to form the home?"

"Ah."

Urubran smiled a bit as Tarwantrad stared off into space with wide eyes.

"That's probably it. It's not about making the best possible home for the bees . . . it's about doing something for the bees that fits the God of Bees. Using your blessing to grow flowers would probably fall more into your patron's domain than that of the God of Bees, if I had to guess?"

Tarwantrad's face fell as she slumped forward. She then whispered in a barely audible voice, "Can you . . . show me what you did? I, um, don't know how to build things."

Urubran's smile grew.

"I'll do you one better."

He held out his hand and a flame grew above it. The flame spread and thinned out until it was more light than heat, and then the light flickering in its center began to shift and swirl, turning into an image displaying a box made out of wood. Tarwantrad looked up and then tilted her head.

"What . . . is this?"

Urubran shrugged.

"Got it from the God of Bees. It's called Belissar's Beehouse."

The Queen of All Bees slowly grew more aware as she tried to move her groggy body. She shook herself and waved her abdomen about to try and boost her breathing. She spread her wings out, attempting to soak up as much sunlight as possible. Bees milled in confusion all around her, with some of the guard bees opening and retracting their mandibles over and over.

She soothed them as soon as she could. She knew that their instincts told them that bees showing signs of sickness or poisoning were to be removed from the hive by all means necessary . . . but that she, as the Queen of All Bees, could not be removed, leaving them at a loss as to how they should respond. She may, in fact, need to communicate to them that not all poisoning was worth a death sentence.

Indeed, this sort of poisoning could even be desirable. This was not the first time the Queen of All Bees had tasted alcohol. The various plant gods who made use of her services had shared with her their wines and ales before, but this was different. This was *mead*, an alcohol made from honey. That was made with the help of bees. That could *only* be made with the help of bees. It was, therefore, an alcohol fully within her domain . . . and so it was one that could affect her deeply. That spread to her innermost being, such that she took on its properties to represent them in full.

Once again, Belissar had proven himself her best dungeon master, even if he wasn't her only one. She had been only vaguely aware of mead, having never been offered it by a follower before.

Now . . . well, now she had *plans*. Plans based on an aspect of her being that was new even to her. She now understood why the various gods kept asking her to take it up . . . and now she planned to deliver.

Yet another thing her best dungeon master would need to be rewarded for. And now, that moniker had begun to take on meaning. She had now been established in other dungeons as well, even if she wasn't their main patron. And, thanks to Belissar's efforts, she could only imagine more dungeon masters would follow suit and seek her blessings.

Indeed, some might seek her out sooner than even she imagined. Just then, one of the flowers in her domain began to grow. New buds split off and bloomed and split off again as the flower grew far beyond its normal size. It emitted a sweet scent as it began to resemble a tree more than a flower with all its branches, each holding a budding flower of its own. And then, the flowers began to change color, shape, and even species.

Soon, they began to assemble themselves into the form of a woman. Flowering trees made up her legs, a huge bell flower became her skirt, and a pitcher flower became her torso. The branches of flowering bushes and creeping ground cover twisted into her arms, a pair of sunflowers bloomed as her eyes, and rose vines grew down from her head as hair.

The God of Flowers had arrived. And a moment later, she leapt at the Queen of All Bees, wrapping her arms around the bee.

"BEE! Why didn't you tell me you have a dungeon now?!"

The Queen of All Bees was going to answer, but the sight and smell of the God of Flowers overwhelmed her, and instead of answering she began drinking sweet nectar from one of the flowers on the God of Flowers' arm. In fact, all the bees in the area began to swarm around the God of Flowers, lapping up sap and rolling around to cover themselves in pollen. This caused even more flowers to bloom and grow on the God of Flowers' body, which continued growing as more and more bees arrived. Soon, flowers with smoking centers drew the attention of burning bees, blood bees swarmed a flower dripping red liquid, and bees with ice for chitin landed on a flower surrounded by frosty mist. The God of Flowers' body grew in size and gigantic flowers began to bloom from her back to hold the weight of equally large bees.

The God of Flowers then spun around, swinging the God of Bees back and forth.

"This is amazing! We have to celebrate! You should have told me, we could have issued joint quests to our followers from the start! But anyway, we'll talk about that later. Let me get . . . wait, are you drunk?!"

A vine extended from the God of Flowers' arm to pick up a jar on the ground.

"This is . . . mead?! Bee, you got mead after all?! Hey, hey, let me have some too! And then I want to see your dungeon! I can't imagine the flowers that will grow with all those bees! And then our power will intertwine and I can bring you to all of mine! This is going to be great!"

Somewhere, deep down, the Queen of All Bees wondered if it was a good idea to let the God of Flowers drink mead. After all, mead was made of honey, which itself was, most of the time, made from the nectar of flowers. So, what would happen if the God of Flowers drank it? But such concerns quickly faded at the sight of all the wonderful flowers blooming in front of her.

Well, it would be fine, wouldn't it? She was set to get more mead later in any case, and the God of Flowers was one of her closest friends, one who always gave her as much authority as she could. The God of Flowers was not one of the most popular gods herself, so she didn't have all that much to spare, but she always prioritized the Queen of All Bees.

Suddenly, though, the taste of the nectar changed, growing a bit less sweet as something else slipped into the nectar.

"And then you can tell me why you let that God of Fire into your dungeon first. So, let me drink some of this mead, okay?"

Ah, that was right. The God of Flowers . . . had some thorns as well.

# CHAPTER THIRTY-TWO

# BELISSAR'S ACADE-BEE

Belissar woke up the next morning to an immediate surprise.

*A non-patron god, the God of Flowers, wishes to offer you a quest, and will grant you a blessing should you succeed. Accept?*

*New mission received: Earn the blessing of a new secondary patron.*

Belissar blinked, then rubbed his eyes, then blinked again. Yes, both messages were still there. It appeared he had attracted the attention of yet another god. And the God of Bees had preempted his question and approved with a mission of her own. So, he had no reason to refuse or delay.

He couldn't help but grin as he accepted the mission. The God of Flowers! If there was any other god he wanted to invite into his tower, that was the one! There was no better partner for bees!

*Offer accepted.*
*New mission received: Spawn or evolve one Flower attribute monster with the help of bees.*

Belissar nodded. That made sense, it was a similar mission to the God of Fire's. Then he paused and tilted his head, rubbing his chin as he furrowed his brow. How, exactly, should he spawn or evolve a Flower attribute monster? For the Fire attribute, he'd had a burning queen already evolving, so he hadn't actually needed to think about it.

But then he smiled. With the help of bees, the mission said. Belissar would have preferred that even if it hadn't been specified. And that also revealed the likely answer. Perhaps cross-pollination between the right sort of flowers would result in a flower that counted as a monster in and of itself? His bees had already cross-pollinated slime flowers, which spawned monsters, so why couldn't they cross-pollinate a flower that was a monster?

Belissar then got up fully, ate a bit of honeycomb, and began reviewing his day with Niobee and the worker bees keeping track of various topics for him. The karnuq had just about gathered enough stone to upgrade the bee barracks, so he'd have to ask the flower meadow queens about that upgrade. Additionally, he now had the DP for another store purchase, another topic to bring up to the queens and Chief Rohsuak after today's purification. And as the reports wrapped up, Belissar brought up a topic of his own.

"Hey Niobee, could you ask the gardeners to gather after tonight's purification as well?"

"Okay!"

Belissar didn't particularly know which, if any, of his flowers might become a monster. But he figured if anyone would know, it would be the gardeners, so he aimed to get their input on the matter. Additionally, he wanted them to spread flowers of all sorts to the fairy grove, which meant gathering flower seeds from all across the tower, so he thought it might help them if they could talk to each other as well.

With that, he set off to start his day. He had to make his rounds to visit the bees and gather some honey, present offerings to the gods, practice his mana, and then start leadership lessons with Chief Rohsuak, as well as his own beekeeping lesson for the karnuq. It was going to be a busy day.


Belissar and Chief Rohsuak sat in her house with Niobee hovering around. Her home was now a completed building with walls of stone and wood furnishings. Muuraqi had been hard at work, and at this point, most of the karnuq now lived in stone houses. Chief Rohsuak gave him a smile as he glanced around.

"We have to thank your bees for their help as well. We could not have built our homes as quickly without them."

Belissar smiled at that, and then they got into it. Chief Rohsuak nodded and hummed a bit.

"I believe you have already learned the most important lesson of being a leader."

Belissar jumped.

"Huh? Really?! I've, um, never led anything before this. At all."

Chief Rohsuak gave him a warm smile.

"In my opinion, the hardest and most important lesson to learn is that it's not about you. A good leader should care for their people above themselves, which means setting aside their own pride, desires, and preferences for the good of the whole. From what I have seen, you already do this."

Belissar couldn't really say anything, so just fidgeted instead. Niobee, ever-present as always, flew around to respond in his place.

"King is best king! Was always best king!"

Chief Rohsuak chuckled and nodded while Belissar fidgeted even more. She then let her smile drop and narrowed her eyes.

"I think for you, Sacred Den Master, the next lesson is to accept conflict."

Belissar frowned at that.

"Accept conflict?"

Chief Rohsuak nodded, keeping her serious expression.

"I was not able to mention it at the time given the urgency of the situation, but the sigmaka were quite demanding of you, and most sacred den masters that I know of would have rejected them out of hand for their tone alone."

Belissar furrowed his brow.

"Even if it led to war?"

Chief Rohsuak nodded.

"Even if it led to war. In this case, it worked out, as they were amenable to an equivalent agreement, so your willingness to accept their terms averted an unnecessary conflict. But that will not always be the case. One day, you will encounter people who would take advantage of your desire for peace and demand terms that are detrimental to your side if you are not willing to fight. And there are some people who will not bother with negotiations in the first place. What will you do in those cases?"

Niobee once again flew between them, buzzing her wings as she extended her stinger.

"If hurt King, Niobee will sting!"

But for once, Niobee didn't make Belissar smile. Instead, his face fell.

"I . . . don't want my bees to get hurt . . ."

Niobee fell still at that. Chief Rohsuak watched in silence. She was about to speak when Belissar continued. He looked to Niobee, reaching out to brush her back.

". . . but I know that's not how they see it. So . . ."

He took a deep breath, closing his eyes for a moment. Then he opened and narrowed them.

"I think . . . if someone wants to take advantage of us, wants to hurt the bees, then we shouldn't let them."

Chief Rohsuak softened her expression just a tad and nodded.

"That's good. Hold to that resolve, Sacred Den Master."

From there, Belissar, Chief Rohsuak, and Niobee began discussing different scenarios, how to approach negotiations, and situations the karnuq had faced when negotiations went wrong. Belissar could not say he enjoyed these conversations. The thought of people fighting and killing his bees made his blood boil and his stomach churn. But it was necessary for him to consider. He doubted the tower lords would be as agreeable should they discover him, and even the sigmaka had nearly betrayed them despite the agreements.

In the end, Belissar would do anything necessary to keep his bees safe.

After that, Belissar, Niobee, and Chief Rohsuak stepped outside of her house and made their way to an open space near the karnuq village. Several other karnuq were waiting for them, including some of the children who had played with the bumblebee soldier the other day. Now was time for a far more pleasant lesson, in Belissar's opinion. Chief Rohsuak joined the rest of the karnuq and nodded at him.

"Whenever you're ready, Sacred Den Master. We are honored to learn from you."

Belissar nodded. It was time to start the beekeeping lessons.

"Um, right. So, first things first, let me show you how I make a beehouse."

Belissar had asked the karnuq to prepare some wood for this lesson. He planned to teach them how to build and manage beehouses before he let any bees move in, and he figured the best way to do that would be to build one with them.

"We found that if you put these frames at the right distance apart, the bees will build straight honeycomb within them. With regular bees, you might need to put some comb in the corner to get them started, or stop them if they start building between the frames, but if you have it at the right distance they should leave that space empty. That way, you can pull the trays right out whenever you need to check the hive or gather honey."

To be fair, that lesson was only relevant for regular bees, since monster bees could be asked nicely to build their combs in any shape desired without any trays at all. They could even figure it out themselves without him asking at all. But the God of Bees' mission said to teach the karnuq beekeeping, not tower keeping, so Belissar figured he should teach them how it would work under normal circumstances as well.

Belissar put together the beehouse, explaining its various parts and what he did with each one, then upgraded the completed beehouse to a room feature. He smiled as one of the trays began glowing immediately.

"And this . . ."

He enjoyed the gasps of the karnuq as he pulled out the magically completed tray.

". . . is what it looks like when it's full."

And so, Belissar began instructing the karnuq in the art of beekeeping.

# CHAPTER THIRTY-THREE

# A CRUSHING VICTOR-BEE!

The time had finally come. Belissar finished up the day's beekeeping lesson by passing out the honey from the empty beehouse feature's daily tray, which was greatly appreciated by his students. After that, he rearranged the first-floor rooms and made his way to the battle meadow to prepare for the day's purification. As usual for the daily purifications, he placed the dirt tunnels first, followed by the battle meadow, and then the lava field.

The Hunger coalesced, and this time, it took the form of a small turtle-shade. Belissar rubbed his chin and quickly nodded his head.

"Change of plans, everyone! I'm moving the lava field in front of the meadow. Third of the Sixth, hang back and keep your hive out of sight. Be prepared to evacuate if the shade heads your way."

With the buzzing of countless salute dances in the background, Belissar quickly made the changes. Since the shade was already in the dirt tunnels, Belissar could only place the lava field between the tunnels and the battle meadow, but he put the entrance to the lava field at the front of the dirt tunnels before even the first pit trap, right along the shade's path. His hope was to test the defensive features of the lava field against a turtle-shade, both to test the room's power against the turtle's robust defenses, and also since the turtle was slow enough that the Third of the Sixth would have time to evacuate her hive if worst came to worst.

Fortunately, the shade acted as he hoped. Once it found the door to the next room, it crawled inside. It slowly made its way across the volcanic rock, growling with a low rumble as the heat raised all around it, but continuing forward without any ill effect.

Then came the moment Belissar had been waiting for. The mini-volcano began to rumble, sending tremors echoing across the room. Then, with an explosion of light and ash, a flaming boulder launched from its mouth into the sky, burning across the air like a shooting star. It plunged toward the ground, flames roaring all around it as it descended down. It landed with a crash, kicking up waves of ash and smoke as flaming debris scattered across the area.

It had also landed in an entirely different section of the room from the shade, which made its way forward without any sort of response.

But Belissar held his breath as yet another boulder launched . . . and then sighed as it struck the entrance to the room, long after the shade had left. Then came another . . . and another . . .

It was the fifth boulder, just before the turtle-shade reached the first lava river in its path, that finally struck true. And, in Belissar's opinion, it had been worth the wait. The shade *vanished* under the cloud of ash and fire, which was still rising as Belissar immediately received the message.

*All hostiles defeated. Purification successful.*

Belissar smiled.

"We won, everyone. The shade got crushed by a mini-volcano boulder."

Belissar chuckled as he watched the bees start their celebration dances, then rubbed his chin. The mini-volcano had proved powerful indeed. Its boulders could crush at least a smaller turtle-shade in a single blow, and anything that survived would find itself on fire and choked by smoke and ash. Yet, the boulders were not at all accurate, or particularly fast. A faster shade might have crossed the room before it was struck, at least if it could get past the lava rivers. Belissar might be able to deal with that by manually activating the volcano . . . but what if the shades specifically dodged the attack? The boulders were not exactly hard to miss as they descended. Belissar felt it might not be wise to rely solely on the volcano.

In the end, it would still come down to his bees. The volcano might not catch a fast shade before it could cross the room, but that would change if there was an army of burning bees blocking its way.

Belissar nodded to himself. The room had done as he'd hoped. The volcano was powerful enough to deal with a shade that might ward off his bees, and his bees could hopefully handle anything nimble enough to dodge the volcano. It would be a powerful addition to their defenses once the lava field bees raised a soldier army of their own.

And with that, it was time to decide on the rewards.

*Small Purification completed!*
*Please select a reward:*
*- +100 DP*
*- +20 Max Mana*
*- Shortcuts*

Belissar blinked, and then focused on that last option.

### Shortcuts

**Type:**   *Utility*

**Mana Upkeep:**   *3*

*A shortcut enables quick travel between floors and rooms. Only usable by those the dungeon master permits. Corrupted entities may not use shortcuts, as contact with corruption will disable the shortcut until purification.*

At first, Belissar tilted his head . . . but his eyes slowly widened as he thought a bit further. Quick travel between floors and rooms. He was guessing that meant the shortcuts could be used to bypass rooms otherwise in the way? Would that let his bees quickly travel between the rooms as necessary? Would that allow the karnuq to bypass the first floor if they wanted to leave the tower, so that Belissar didn't need to move the lava field out of the way each time? That seemed like an amazing feature to have.

And even his worry that a shade might use it was resolved by the feature's own description. Not only could he decide who got to use the shortcut, but the Hunger specifically would not be able to use the shortcuts since they'd be disabled upon contact with a shade. With that, there was no reason to hesitate.

*Shortcuts are now available!*

Belissar wanted to try one out right away, but instead he turned to Niobee.

"Hey Niobee, can you ask a bee to remind me about shortcuts at tonight's meeting?"

"Okay!"

He put it aside for the time being, for now was the time to celebrate another victory with the bees.

Belissar once again gathered with the queens and Chief Rohsuak, along with the gardeners as he had requested.

"So, we have a lot to go through tonight. First . . . um, sorry I made this choice without telling you all, but we have a new feature. They're called shortcuts . . ."

Chief Rohsuak's eyes began shining the moment Belissar said the name. The bees began to buzz their wings and dance about as Belissar read out the description. The Fourth of the Seventh flew right in front of him.

"Can fly right to Beyond from orchard?!"

Belissar rubbed his chin but slowly nodded.

"We'll have to test it, but I think so."

At that point, Chief Rohsuak cleared her throat.

"Actually, I can assist here, Sacred Den Master. I've encountered shortcuts in other sacred dens and they do exactly as you think. You can use them to go straight from the entrance of the sacred den to higher floors, or to move between otherwise disconnected rooms."

All of the queens, led by the Fourth of the Seventh, began dancing at that.

"Amazing, incredible!"

Belissar smiled and nodded.

"I think it will be. We'll start setting some up tomorrow morning, so . . . maybe think about where you'd like to be able to go?"

All the bees saluted at that, while Chief Rohsuak grinned.

"Next . . . we have another three thousand DP to spend. We can get another room for that last open slot, another monster type, or up to three new room features. Oh, um, we've never actually considered these before, but we can also buy extra room slots, more mana, or new perks. Those are more expensive, though, so we'd have to save up. Does anyone have any suggestions?"

Belissar actually had an idea of what he wanted to buy, but he was trying to get the bees to share their opinions with him, so he didn't mention it just yet. They mainly had the usual responses of "more flowers," "more bees," and "whatever King chooses!" Belissar chuckled and turned to Chief Rohsuak. He would certainly like to hear her thoughts, though he knew that she was holding her tongue intentionally, so he didn't expect her to speak up this time.

Surprisingly, though, she did.

"One thing to consider, Sacred Den Master. Now that we are opening trade with the sigmaka, consider that the more types of goods your sacred den can produce, the more we will have to bargain with. They may also wish to send challengers one day, so you may wish to prepare for that, if it is something you want."

Belissar nodded at that. Those were good points. He ideally wanted some of those aphids and he wasn't sure if the sigmaka would part with any, so having more materials to trade could be a good idea. He hadn't considered sigmaka challengers, but he guessed he could always invite them in if he wanted some? That would improve his DP income and help with that ongoing mission to help challengers receive blessings.

On the other hand, he was not sure he wanted to let any sigmaka into his tower just yet, especially armed ones. He had gotten along with King Ratuatapi well enough, and the sigmaka had sworn not to harm his bees or the karnuq, but finding out that the sigmaka might have attacked him made him wary of inviting them back in anytime soon.

Belissar's own preference started to solidify, but he had one more question to ask before he made the final decision. He looked around toward the gardener bees, who were currently hovering a bit farther away behind their respective queens.

"I'd like to ask the gardeners something now: can we cross-pollinate some sort of monster flower?"

# CHAPTER THIRTY-FOUR

# CON-BEE-NIENT IMPROVEMENTS

The gardeners flew forward, the queens hovering back to make room for them. They flew among themselves, milling about and exchanging dances and pheromones for a few minutes. Eventually, one of them slowly flew forward, beginning an unsteady dance.

"Sorry, don't know."

Belissar smiled and shook his head.

"It's alright, I just wanted to check if you did. Is there anything you think we might need for that?"

The gardeners convened once more before the responder returned to answer again.

"Sorry, don't know. Maybe new flowers, or more mana."

Belissar nodded.

"Got it, I'll see what I can do then. You all just keep up the good work and let me know if the flowers need anything."

The gardeners saluted at that, leaving Belissar to rub his chin. At first, he had thought that maybe a new monster choice might give him a chance to fulfill the God of Flowers' mission. He quickly dispelled that notion, though. He hadn't yet seen any monster choices that weren't bees, so the odds were low that he'd get a monster flower. More importantly, the mission specifically said he had to complete it with the help of his bees, so getting a monster flower by a purification reward might not work even if he was offered one.

Still, that didn't mean reward choices couldn't help here. If a monster flower needed a specific environment, he could try to pick an appropriate room. If they needed a specific object, or more plants, then maybe a feature could help. And cross-pollination itself was a perk, so there might be an answer there as well. The problem was that Belissar didn't know what would or wouldn't help in general. He had no idea how to raise a monster flower, or what would be needed to do so.

He figured cross-pollination and the gardeners would be the key, but how exactly he wasn't sure. So, if the gardeners didn't know any specific requirements, they'd just have to try different methods until they learned what worked.

He turned to Chief Rohsuak one more time.

"Do you or any of the karnuq know anything about monster flowers? Juosiutik, maybe?"

Chief Rohsuak thought for a moment.

"I will ask her, but . . . in my memory, our interactions with monster plants were minimal. There were some magical plants in the sacred dens I've visited, though I am not certain if any of them were monster flowers specifically. We also encountered a few monstrous plants on our journey, but, as you may imagine, most of our interactions with them were short and violent. I can tell you which of them were flammable, but not how they grew."

Belissar rubbed his chin and then nodded.

"Okay, could you ask Juosiutik and let me know whatever you do know? I'll hold off on any purchases until then."

Chief Rohsuak nodded. Belissar wanted to make the purchases sooner rather than later but figured that waiting one day wouldn't hurt, particularly for the sake of gathering what information his tower had available. He turned to the gardeners once more.

"Um, as you may have guessed, we have a mission from a god to raise a monster flower. I think for now, just try to cross-pollinate as many new types of flowers as you can and let me know if there are any you think could become a monster flower. Also, let's try to plant as many flowers as we can in the fairy grove. Maybe you could coordinate together to make sure we get them all?"

The gardeners saluted as one. Belissar smiled at them.

"Thank you. That was all I needed you girls for, so you can go home now."

The gardeners saluted and checked with their queens, who sent them home to follow Belissar's command. Belissar then nodded at Chief Rohsuak and all of the queens in turn, save for those who lived in the battle meadow.

"That was all for everyone. We'll meet again tomorrow to decide on the purchases. I do need to talk to the bee barracks queens, but the rest of you can head home for the night."

Belissar turned to the queens in question while Chief Rohsuak and the other bees dispersed. He pointed over to the stack of rocks.

"So, I guess it's a bit late to ask this, but . . . how would you all feel about turning the bee barracks to stone? Would that make things more or less comfortable for you?"

The Second First of the First took the lead and responded immediately.

"Would make barracks stronger?"

Belissar nodded.

"At least, harder to destroy."

The Second First of the First immediately danced the affirmative.

"Whatever King chooses!"

All of the other battle meadow queens followed suit. Belissar made an amused smile. He figured that's how they would respond but wanted to at least ask.

"Got it, are you and your hives ready to upgrade now or should we wait for tomorrow morning?"

"Can now!"

Belissar nodded and focused on the bee barracks.

*Bee Barracks Upgrades:*
*- Swap to Bee Apartment (Cost: 25 DP)*
*- Change material to stone (Cost: 200 DP or 50 if materials provided)*
*- Boost growth for inhabitants (Cost: 50 DP)*
*- Boost coordination for inhabitants (Cost: 50 DP)*

He selected the "change material" option, confirming that he had provided enough stone for the discount. The bee barracks and the stack of stone blocks next to it both began to glow. A moment later the light faded, and the stone pile had vanished entirely.

The bee barracks itself now had stone walls, a stone roof, and a stone floor. Belissar looked inside with his tower sight and found the frames remained wood, though some of the pillars that held them in place had converted to stone as well.

He turned to the queens, intending to ask them what they thought. He found them already dancing in the air.

"Amazing, incredible!"

He smiled at that.

"Glad you like it."

The structure seemed far tougher than before, though Belissar hoped it would never be put to the test.

The next day, Belissar awoke, intending to hear the reports, eat his breakfast, and then make his gathering and tribute rounds as usual. His eyes widened as he stepped out of the bedroom, however, to find the Second First of the First, the First of the Fifth, the Third of the Sixth, and the Fourth of the Seventh all waiting for him. The queens saluted as soon as they saw him, while Niobee danced before him.

"King! Queens came to report for shortcuts! Talked together!"

Belissar smiled.

"Thank you all. Shall we get to it, then?"

"Okay! First of Fifth's First Daughter had idea. Give all rooms and entrance shortcut to orchard, so all bees can go to all rooms or outside! All queens want too!"

Belissar's eyes widened a bit as all the queens danced to confirm Niobee's report.

"Ah . . . that's a good idea!"

The queens, especially the Fourth of the Seventh, danced happily at his response. Belissar went ahead and thought about shortcuts. Once again, his tower sight zoomed out to show the tower as a whole. A transparent door appeared in his sight along the apiary wall, which he could move about. He could move it along the walls or even the ground, the door transforming into a tunnel entrance when he did so. He ended up placing it on the apiary wall closest to the bee apartments for easy access. He then had a variety of options on the door's appearance. He could leave it visible like any other entrance, but there were options to conceal the door from those not permitted to use it or hide it altogether. For now, he chose to conceal it from those not permitted.

A transparent second door then appeared. Belissar could move this one out of the room entirely, which he did. He took it all the way down to the orchard, then placed it on the front wall close to the bees' home trees. The two doors then materialized as Belissar confirmed the placement.

Once he did, another message appeared.

*Shortcut (2F Orchard–4F Apiary) Permissions:*
*- Defenders: All permitted*
*- Challengers: All permitted*
*- Specific individuals allowed: None*
*- Specific individuals denied: None*

As the description had promised, Belissar was able to adjust who could use the shortcut. It could be set to specify monsters or sworn defenders only, or none. Challengers included numerous groupings, such as allowing or blocking animals, or those blessed by a particular god. For now, Belissar blocked all challengers, setting this shortcut to defenders only. For now, he left it on all defenders; while he mainly intended this one for his bees, he trusted the karnuq enough not to block them without reason. They hadn't left their area of the tower without permission, in any case.

"Okay, I set one up. Shall we check it out?"

"Okay!"

Niobee and the queens all followed along as Belissar left the apiary farmhouse and walked past the bee apartments. There, a new door opened up within the tree wall surrounding the room, displaying the orchard. Belissar stepped through and found himself right in the orchard. It was no different than stepping through the other room entrances.

He smiled as the bees flew through and began zipping about.

"This seems pretty useful."

From there, he did as suggested and created one shortcut in almost every room that connected to the orchard, though he didn't add any to the karnuqs' rooms for now. He then created a shortcut right next to the tower's exit that connected to the orchard and finished off by placing all the shortcuts' orchard-side doors right next to each other along one of the orchard's walls. Now, the entire tower, save the karnuq floor, was linked together with the orchard as the hub, vastly decreasing the time it would take the bees to get anywhere they wanted to go. Nowhere in the tower would be inaccessible for them.

And that put a smile on Belissar's face.

# CHAPTER THIRTY-FIVE

# AN INFORMED BEE-CISION?

The First of the Fifth was just hovering in the air, staring as scouts from all the different hives flew in and out of the new door in the apiary. This . . . changed everything. The bumblebee soldiers could now fly right from their nest to the flower meadow. The apiary queens had but to fly to the closest wall to make their honey deliveries. Her foragers could access every flower in every room nearly as easily as the mana flower patch next to her hive.

Her mind buzzed with the implications. Resources could now be pooled and shared between all the King's hives. Specialized honey could be produced anywhere and delivered to anywhere else with no loss of efficiency. Hives far away from the flower meadow could contribute soldiers to the army as easily as the queens that dwelt there. Queens and messengers could meet at will.

She was truly proud of her daughter for this suggestion. And now, as the queen the King had tasked with organizing the others, it was her turn. She would have to see this wonder come to fruition.

She started to fly once more as she began to plan.

After setting up those shortcuts, Belissar made his honey-gathering and tribute rounds, then headed out for the karnuq floor. Chief Rohsuak was waiting to greet him when he arrived. The first thing they did was set up shortcuts for the karnuq as well. He placed two shortcuts in the karnuq's flower meadow, setting up the doors next to the regular room exits. One led directly to the tower's exit so that the karnuq could come and go at will, while the other led to the orchard to connect the karnuq with the rest of the tower . . . and the bees.

After that, Chief Rohsuak, Metsaitti, and Juosiutik all gathered with Belissar in Chief Rohsuak's house to discuss their encounters with monster plants.

"It, um, drinks . . . blood?"

Metsaitti nodded.

"The roots were covered in thorns and wrapped around anything that approached. We saw a bunch of desiccated animal corpses in their grasp. We saw one wolf-mole get caught . . . it wasn't pretty. Ultimately, we took a detour around the area. Never saw what it looked like on the surface."

Belissar ruled that one out.

"Seemed to have acid running through it, extremely corrosive. Any wound would cause it to spray out. There were also these bulges on the roots that would explode with the lightest touch, even sound could set them off. We didn't see any corpses, but I presume the roots would drink up any liquified remains."

Belissar gulped as Chief Rohsuak spoke.

"I . . . see. Um, anything else?"

Chief Rohsuak shrugged.

"They were highly flammable, acid included. We had to wait a while for the fumes to clear up, though. There was some pool of liquid that smelled terrible, but we avoided it, so I can't tell you more."

Belissar guessed he was ruling that one out too.

Juosiutik shook her head.

"There's very little in the records I have about monster plants. I did find this excerpt regarding some swamp flowers, but it's more about preventing monsters than raising them."

Belissar shrugged.

"Well, I guess anything might help? I don't really know what I'm looking for, to be honest."

Juosiutik nodded.

"Says here there are flowers in the bogs that would start attracting slimes if left for too long. This could be avoided by draining nectar from the flowers on a regular basis."

She let out a sigh.

"That's all, though. If there was more about those flowers, those notes were lost. I don't even have a picture of them. If I had to guess, though, I would say the slimes like to drink the nectar?"

Belissar tilted his head.

"Huh, sounds like the slime flowers."

Juosiutik froze.

"Slime . . . flowers?"

Belissar nodded.

"Or flower, since there's only one right now. It, um, apparently spawns the slimes itself, rather than attracting them, so maybe it's different?"

At that point, Juosiutik approached Belissar in such a way that Niobee responded. The conversation quickly derailed to Belissar describing the slime flower in as much detail as he knew.

In the end, none of the karnuq's encounters held any concrete leads for Belissar. He moved on to discussing negotiations and diplomacy with Chief Rohsuak and then instructing the karnuq on beekeeping.

After that came the daily purification. Belissar swapped the lava field back behind the battle meadow and let the soldier bee army handle the purification as usual. The options weren't particularly notable, so he went with mana.

And then, finally, he was back with the queens and Chief Rohsuak, ready to make a purchase. He nodded at everyone.

"I think we should go with room features this time."

With no particular leads on monster flowers from either the gardeners or the karnuq, Belissar was left deciding on his own. Room features were a catchall that could include anything from traps to resources to geographical features, so he figured there'd be a decent chance that something there might help flowers become monsters. A new room was another option, since a new environment could lead to new flowers, but Belissar decided to hold off on that. He was still waiting to see what became of the fairy grove, and there was a chance he might want to add a second fairy grove with the last empty room slot, so he figured he might as well wait for the next expansion before expanding the room options. Additionally, since he didn't actually know what he was looking for, going with the cheaper room features and getting more options might increase the chances of getting something useful.

And if all else failed, and the room features didn't help with monster plants at all . . . well, more resources would give them more products to trade with the sigmaka, while more traps could improve his defenses in general.

The bees, of course, praised him for making that choice as they did for . . . well, practically every choice he made. Chief Rohsuak simply smiled and nodded. And with that, Belissar brought up the DP store.

He could only hope it wouldn't be all commons this time.

*Extra room feature choice purchased. One room feature choice now available.*
*Please select a room feature:*
*- Dirt Trails (Rarity: Common, Type: Utility, Decoration)*
*- Beeswax Candles (Rarity: Common, Type: Bee, Fire, Decoration)*
*- Boulder (Rarity: Common, Type: Ground, Decoration)*

Belissar glared at the message in silence for a moment. All commons, and two he had seen before. But, well, glaring at it wasn't going to change the choices, as far as he knew, so he heaved a sigh and then started reading them out.

### Dirt Trails

**Type:**   *Utility, Decoration*
**Mana Upkeep:**   *0*
*A trail of packed dirt. Slightly boosts speed of ground movement.*

Belissar shrugged at that. It still didn't help any of his flying bees. He guessed it was a little more useful than the last time he had seen it, now that he had the karnuq, but he had also just installed a bunch of shortcuts, so faster movement wasn't really a concern for him right now.

### Beeswax Candles

**Type:**   *Bee, Fire, Decoration*
**Mana Upkeep:**   *1 (0 if wax is regularly provided)*
*A beeswax candle that provides light, and a bit of heat. Effects may vary if special wax types are provided.*

Beeswax candles were the same as before. Again, maybe they would help light the way in the dirt tunnels, but he could also make candles himself if he really wanted to. There *was* that line about special effects, though, so maybe it was worth taking as a feature.

And then, finally . . .

### Boulder

**Type:**   *Ground, Decoration*
**Mana Upkeep:**   *0*
*A big rock. Can hold certain features that require rocky or Ground attribute terrain.*

. . . It was a rock. A big rock, sure, but just a rock. Maybe it would have been useful if he didn't have basic resource minerals to provide useful stone, but otherwise . . . it was a rock. Maybe he could put it on a hill and roll it down on a shade? If he could make hills steep enough, that was, as the flower meadows only allowed gentle slopes.

Belissar rubbed his chin. Come to think of it, he *was* able to make vertical entrances to dirt tunnel rooms. They could hypothetically drop rocks down those. Or down a pit trap as an alternative to fire. Now that he thought about it, big rocks might be surprisingly useful.

But the question was, did it justify using up a feature choice? Hypothetically, Muuraqi could cut big rocks for him from the mineral nodes, so he didn't necessarily need the feature to implement those ideas. In fact, which of these three choices was worth taking?

Belissar shrugged.

*Beeswax Candles are now available!*

When in doubt, Belissar chose bees. The line about special waxes, in particular, drew his attention. Perhaps his bees could do something with those? He would, however, ask the karnuq about the dropping rocks plan at some point.

Belissar glared at the DP shop before making the next purchase. He might not have known what he actually needed right now, but he sure would like to get something other than a repeat common option.

# CHAPTER THIRTY-SIX

# THE BEST BEE-CISION

**B**elissar held his breath as he confirmed a second purchase.

*Extra room feature choice purchased. One room feature choice*
*now available.*
*Please select a room feature:*
*- Spike Trap (Rarity: Common, Type: Trap)*
*- Firebomb (Rarity: Uncommon, Type: Fire, Trap)*
*- Random Resource Mineral (Rarity: Common, Type: Resource, Variable)*

Belissar exhaled, letting the tension flow from his body. Finally, the DP shop had given him a room feature that wasn't a common! He had been starting to wonder if the DP shop just couldn't give him anything better, so it was nice to confirm that wasn't the case. He had just been extremely unlucky!

Somehow, that didn't make Belissar feel better, so he stopped that line of thought and began reading out the choices.

### *Spike Trap*

**Type:** *Trap*
**Mana Upkeep:** *1*
*A spike held within a surface under tension. Springs out*
*to impale the target when triggered.*

Well, this one was quite simple. But that didn't mean it wouldn't be useful, for this one was a direct way to attack shades. Most of his traps either didn't directly harm shades, like the sticky honey traps or the gravilion flowers he still didn't understand the use of, or else were passive, like the pit traps and thorned roses. Using a spike trap instead of a sticky honey trap would turn a given trap from debilitating to deadly . . . assuming the spike was fast enough to hit a shade and strong enough to pierce it.

On the other hand, it was a one-mana common option, so Belissar guessed it wouldn't be all that impressive. At least, probably not compared to the next option.

### Firebomb

**Type:**   Fire, Trap

**Mana Upkeep:**   5 (3 if fuel provided)

*A container filled with flammable material (oil by default). Explodes and ignites on contact, covering the area with burning fuel. Fuel may be provided to reduce the upkeep and may change the trap's behavior depending on the type used.*

Belissar nodded. Well, that was certainly an option. Indeed, it took his original plan of coating shades with honey and kindling and then setting them on fire to the next level, wrapping it all up in an explosive container that could be placed anywhere and would ignite itself. So, not only could this make his pit traps deadlier, but he could forgo the need for the pit traps in the first place.

The only downside was that the indiscriminate explosion meant the bees would need to keep their distance from any such traps, or the flames that resulted. They did have some fire resistance, though, especially the burning bees, so even that might not be a major issue. Worst came to worst, he could just place the bombs in the lava field.

It was worth considering, at the very least.

### Random Resource Mineral

**Type:**   Resource, Variable

**Mana Upkeep:**   Variable

*Unlocks a random resource mineral type for use in matching features and rooms.*

Belissar rubbed his chin. The description sounded like it would give him another option for basic resource mineral nodes? That was certainly helpful . . . though he might have preferred a resource plant, as so far his bees hadn't interacted with the mineral nodes save the salt one. It would help the karnuq, though, and could provide another resource to trade with the sigmaka.

As usual, he turned to the others and asked them what they thought. Most of the bees had little opinion on this set of options, though the Third of the Sixth was curious about the firebombs and the digging queen showed some interest in the minerals. Belissar made a note of that before glancing at Chief Rohsuak. To his surprise, he found her looking thoughtful instead of her usual "you decide" smile.

"I think . . . it would be possible for us to build something like this firebomb."

Belissar jumped at that.

"Wait, really?"

Chief Rohsuak slowly nodded.

"I vaguely recall we used to do so back before we became nomads. We lacked the resources to attempt such things on our travels, but that's no longer the case. We'd have to look into suitable fuels, but Juosiutik can probably figure something out with your mana honey. We've confirmed the sigmaka have clay we can trade for, so we can use that to make a shell. And you're already growing flame radish, which we can use to ignite it."

She then made a knowing grin.

"Getting it to explode on command might be more difficult, but we've both experienced Juosiutik's more . . . dramatic experiments, so I suspect we could figure something out."

Belissar crossed his arms while rubbing his own chin.

"Huh. If that's the case, should we try for another mineral?"

Chief Rohsuak smiled at him.

"It's up to you, Sacred Den Master. More resources are always appreciated, and spike traps can be quite deadly to the unaware. Additionally, it will take us time to make a working firebomb, and our first attempts will likely be far shoddier than what the sacred den will make."

Belissar rubbed his chin a bit and then nodded.

"I think that's fine. We have the lava field and the mini-volcano, so . . . I think the mineral is better."

Chief Rohsuak inclined her head while the bees all danced a salute.

"As you say, Sacred Den Master."

*Random Resource Mineral selected.*
*Alum is now available!*

Belissar tilted his head.

"Looks like we got alum. Um, I've heard it's valuable . . . and maybe used for dyes or something? I don't know much beyond that."

Chief Rohsuak shook her head as well.

"I know it as a valuable commodity, but I am personally unaware of its uses. I will ask my people."

Belissar ended up shrugging.

"Maybe the sigmaka will like it. Let's try one more, then?"

Chief Rohsuak inclined her head again while the bees saluted, so Belissar bought one more choice. This time, he was at peace. He had already gotten an uncommon option, so he'd be satisfied even if the next choice was all commons.

*Extra room feature choice purchased. One room feature choice now available.*
*Please select a room feature:*
*- Rare Random Resource Plant (Rarity: Rare, Type: Resource, Variable)*
*- River (Rarity: Common, Type: Water)*
*- Treasure Chest (Rarity: Common, Type: Resource)*

Belissar's jaw dropped. A rare option?! From the DP shop, which had previously given nothing but commons?! And a rare plant at that?! It took all of Belissar's self-control not to select the option then and there. First of all, it was a plant. Plants meant flowers for the bees to gather from. Second of all, it was rare! It was rare for him to receive rare options, especially from the DP store! And a rare plant, with the potential of rare flowers? How could he pass that up? Not to mention, rare flowers might open the door to fulfilling the God of Flowers' mission!

Belissar convinced himself to at least read out the options for the bees and Chief Rohsuak first, if only to see their reactions. He watched the bees intently as he slowly read out the description.

### *Rare Random Resource Plant*

**Type:**      *Resource, Variable*
**Mana Upkeep:**   *Variable*
*Unlocks a random resource plant for use in matching features and rooms.*
*Option unlocked will be of rare rarity or better.*

He smiled as he watched the queens start to fidget and dance around.
"Rare plant?"
"New flower?"
"Rare flower?"
Which was just about his reaction too. He at least forced himself to glance over at Chief Rohsuak. She just made an amused smile and shrugged.
"It seems to me a decision has been made."
Belissar shook his head then turned back to the bees and smiled.
"Rare flower?"
All of them began zipping about at once.
"Rare flower!"
Belissar chuckled as he made the choice.

*Rare Random Resource Plant selected.*
*Soaring Beeblossom is now available!*

Belissar saw all he needed to know he had made the right choice. But, of course, he read out the description, for who wouldn't want to know more about beeblossom?

### <u>Soaring Beeblossom</u>

**Type:** *Air, Nature*

**Mana Upkeep:** *10 per node, 5 to enable in compatible rooms*

*A flowering plant that has taken to the skies. Large, fluttering petals catch and strengthen the wind, enabling this flower to soar upon the breeze and join its pollinators in the air.*

Belissar smiled as the bees burst out into dancing.

"Amazing, incredible!"

And indeed it was. A flower named for bees that could also fly, if he was reading the description right. That sounded very much perfect for his tower. He immediately moved to make a patch . . .

*Current Applications: Flower Meadow, Lava Field, Fairy Grove*

Belissar tilted his head at that. So, he couldn't put this flower in the apiary or the orchard . . . but could put it in the lava field, of all places? That . . . seemed very strange indeed. He shrugged, though, and proceeded to place one in the flower meadow, right where he, Chief Rohsuak, and the queens were gathered.

A small patch of the ground began to glow. The nearby flowers swayed as a gust of wind blew up and out of the patch. A group of white and pink flowers sprouted and bloomed . . . and then the entire patch lifted up out of the ground and soared into the air. The petals fluttered as the flowers soared up and up like a cloud of butterflies. Higher and higher, until the gust cut off. The flowers continued to flutter and occasionally glow, and each time they did a slight breeze blew out and across the ground. The tangle of flowers began to bob up and down in the air as the gust picked up again, the wind of the patch below cutting in and out to keep the flowers aloft.

Belissar and Chief Rohsuak both simply watched with wide eyes as the bees danced about. An amazing and incredible flower indeed.

# A BEE-POSTEROUS PROPOSAL

The King, having filled his domain with new and incredible wonders, called the meeting to an end and retired to his chambers. The karnuq representative left as well. The First of the Fifth considered including her but decided to hold off. She had not yet secured the cooperation of the other queens, so it was not yet time to expand to the outsiders.

The First of the Fifth began to dance before the rest of the queens dispersed. Fortunately, they were all still concentrated together, investigating the King's newest flower.

"Have proposal, can meet now?"

The queens danced the affirmative and returned as one to the memorial. The Conduit remained as well, watching over their meeting. The Firstborn danced first.

"What's First of Fifth's proposal?"

The First of the Fifth didn't hesitate before beginning the dance that could change everything.

"Shortcuts mean all hives close, all flowers close now. All hives can gather from all flowers if want. Queens and gardeners should gather and coordinate foraging. Ensure maximum honey production, cross-pollination for all flowers, and avoid competition."

The First of the Fifth paused. Now was the moment she hesitated, for she knew that she asked a lot. To take additional time out of the queens' and gardeners' busy days to meet was already a sacrifice. To ask them to pool resources, for each individual hive to surrender its claim to its local flowers? That was unthinkable. But the First of the Fifth knew, too, that the King loved all bees to an unthinkable degree. So, she felt that it was acceptable, nay, appropriate even, for the King's bees to take unthinkable measures. That all may grow together as the King desired. So, she prepared herself. She recalled all the arguments and reasoning she had thought up before this moment, and prepared herself to convince all of the other queens, many of which she had held in contempt, that this idea was . . .

"Okay!"

The First of the Fifth froze and stared at the Fourth of the Seventh.

". . . What?"

The Fourth of the Seventh repeated her dance.

"Okay!"

The First of the Fifth stood completely still. The Fourth of the Seventh . . . agreed? Just like that? Well, this *was* the queen that freely gave her honey to the First of the Fifth's daughter, and then joined their hives together, so perhaps she was unusual from the start. Still, having one supporting queen was certainly beneficial. It should hopefully make it easier for her to convince the others. So, she turned to the Firstborn, who surely would be the toughest one to . . .

She found the Firstborn already dancing.

"I agree, is good idea! Hive of hives should forage as one."

Now the First of the Fifth froze, her mind going blank. In all of her predicted outcomes of this talk, not in a single one did she imagine the Firstborn agreeing with her. So, accordingly, she had no idea how to respond to this situation. The Firstborn, the oldest among them, the one who led the King's army, just agreed to give up all her authority over the flower meadow's resources? Agreed to spend her time on meetings which could have been used raising or training more soldiers? All for an idea proposed by the First of the Fifth, the rival who had done all in her power to usurp the Firstborn? The First of the Fifth did not know how to react.

But, well, time spent in shock was time wasted, so the First of the Fifth's mind resumed its activity soon enough. If the Firstborn was convinced, the flower meadow would surely follow. Indeed, the other queens of the flower meadow were already dancing their support. Which meant all she had to do was convince the remaining queens. The bumblebee queens were . . . currently running rapidly in a circle around the gathering of queens. Well, she had expected as much from them. And that just left . . . the Third of the Sixth, newly appointed queen over the lava field, and the rest of the apiary queens.

The Second of the Sixth danced first.

"Yes, am willing. As long as flowers shared fairly."

The rest of the apiary queens followed suit, and the Third of the Sixth had no objections as well. The First of the Fifth was once again stunned into silence.

*All* of the queens . . . agreed? Just like that? Without her giving even a single one of her arguments or reasons? She had known the Firstborn talked about an idea of a hive of hives, but she had not known that all the other queens had committed to the idea to this degree. She found herself at a loss. Had she been . . . the *only* queen to think differently?

But while the First of the Fifth was pondering her entire life's efforts once more, the conversation carried forward. The First of the Second from the flower meadow danced next.

"Need a queen to coordinate. Nominate First of Fifth."

The Firstborn danced the affirmative.

"Is good idea. First of Fifth well organized, good at honey production."

The First of the Fifth snapped out of her haze and spun around, unable to comprehend the proceedings. She, too, knew that it would be best to have an overall coordinator. She also believed herself to be the most suitable queen for the job. One look at the flower meadow queens' honey production methods would convince anyone of that, and the King himself had already ordered her to organize foraging and specialization for the apiary. But even so, she had not planned to take up the task, nor to nominate herself for it. She knew that she had misperceived the King's will early on in her life, and her machinations during that time had surely earned her many enemies. She knew that if she were to take on the task, the others would resist. Therefore, for the sake of convincing the other queens, she had planned to nominate another.

So, the last thing she expected was to be nominated by the flower meadow queens. The Fourth of the Seventh agreed as well, though perhaps that was to be expected, given how closely she worked with the First of the Fifth's own offspring.

The First of the Fifth turned to the apiary queens. The flower meadow queens had lived far away and had authority over flower patches of their own. They, perhaps, would not have understood fully what the First of the Fifth had been like before. But not so with the apiary queens. These were the queens that had been fully suppressed by her in the past. Would they now willingly allow her a position of such authority? They had agreed to her management of the apiary, but that had been a direct order from the King and facilitated by the Conduit. This was a voluntary decision under no such compulsion. The First of the Fifth awaited their objections, which she would accept and step down.

The Second of the Sixth crawled up to her and stood face-to-face, her antennas twitching and her wings buzzing. She then slowly began to dance.

"I . . . agree. Think First of Fifth will do well."

The First of the Fifth buzzed her wings and began spinning about. She frantically brushed the Second of the Sixth, exchanging mana and pheromones directly through her antennas.

"Really? Second of Sixth is sure? I . . . I hoarded flowers, King's attention before! Might do again!"

The Second of the Sixth stood firm under the assault and danced the affirmative.

"First of Fifth did, have not forgotten. But First of Fifth has changed. Helping bees now, gave up flowers. As long as continue, is fine."

She then turned to the Conduit.

"Conduit can watch, ensure flowers shared?"

The Conduit zipped about.

"Okay! Will!"

The Second of the Sixth turned to face the First of the Fifth once more.

"Then is okay. First of Fifth wants all bees to grow now, right?"

The First of the Fifth trembled, but slowly began to dance.

"Yes. Want all of King's bees to grow, will make King happy. Want . . . hive of hives to grow."

The Second of the Sixth danced a confirmation at that and then slowly backed away. One by one, the apiary queens each danced their assent. The Conduit herself then landed nearby.

"Then, decided! Bees gather to discuss foraging! First of Fifth will coordinate! All bees work together for King!"

Every single bee present danced a salute at the Conduit's words. The First of the Fifth then fell still once more, her mind still catching up to this turn of events. The Second of the Sixth still stood before her and danced.

"Keep up changes, okay? Have not forgotten, but will work with as long as First of Fifth helps us grow."

She then flew off. The Firstborn crawled up to her next.

"Great idea, First of Fifth! Will help hive of hives grow! Know you'll help a lot, really good at making honey!"

The First of the Fifth barely managed a thanks dance. At that point, she fell to the ground as a heavy weight collided with her. The bumblebee queens had charged her down and were now crawling over her, grooming her as best they could. The Conduit danced happily about.

"Bees trust First of Fifth now! First of Fifth should work hard to help them!"

The First of the Fifth slowly managed to extract herself from the bumblebee queen pile and stood before the Conduit. Her mind finally began to work again and she danced a salute.

"I will. Will not let bees or King down."

# CHAPTER THIRTY-SEVEN

# AN OVERDUE BEE-VIEW

The next day, Belissar received a special report from Niobee during breakfast.

"Oh, the bees are going to coordinate gathering?"

Niobee danced the affirmative.

"Yes! First of Fifth says with shortcuts, all bees can gather from all flowers now, so going to work together!"

Belissar smiled and nodded.

"That's a good idea."

Indeed, Belissar had some vague ideas about that sort of thing when he set up the shortcut, but to think his bees had already come together and worked it out. They really were the best.

Belissar then crossed his arms and hummed. If the bees were going to be coordinating to that degree, then he should decide how he was going to support them. Previously, he had just gone and made one of every flower type in every room that held bees, so that all bees would have access to all flowers. He had already stopped doing that after speaking with the First of the Fifth about specializing certain hives and then sharing honey, and it seemed that shortcuts would take that idea to the next level. Now, all the bees could share a single patch of flowers no matter where in the tower it was located . . . and the gardeners could help spread those flowers if more of them were necessary.

Belissar nodded and then turned to Niobee.

"Once they've met and figured out their gathering, they should let me know what they think about the flower numbers. Um, specifically, if we need more of a certain flower type, I can make more patches. But if we have too many of certain types, I could also remove some patches and get some mana back to use for others. So, um . . ."

Belissar paused to think for a second.

". . . yeah, let me know once they know how many of each type of flower patch they need."

Niobee danced the salute.

"Okay! Will!"

Belissar nodded at that. While he didn't want to remove any flowers, it would be silly to spend mana on flowers the bees didn't need, now that they were going to share all of them. Reclaiming some of the redundant patches, if there were any, could allow him to afford more of the expensive types, like the new soaring beeblossom.

Speaking of which, Belissar had initially planned to create two more soaring beeblossom patches. One would go in the bumblebee meadow for the bumblebee and apiary queens. The second would go in the lava field . . . mostly because Belissar was curious as to why he could put them in the lava field. But now, he decided to wait until the queens met and reported before making any more. The bumblebees and apiary hives could now reach the battle meadow's flowers as easily as their own. And as for the lava field . . . well, he could always ask the gardeners to spread the soaring beeblossom there and so avoid spending mana just to sate his curiosity. All he needed was a bit of patience.

So, after receiving the rest of the reports for the day, Belissar put aside the beeblossoms and focused on the other two features. He created two alum patches, one for the karnuq and one for the bees. He had no idea if either party could actually use them, but they were fairly cheap at three mana each, so it wasn't a major concern if no one could figure out what to do with them for now.

Following that, he placed a bunch of beeswax candles in two of the three dirt tunnel rooms, the one on the karnuq's floor and the one on the apiary floor. Hopefully, that would make it easier for the bees and the karnuq to gather the materials, plants, and mushrooms within. He did place a few in the first-floor dirt tunnels, which he decided to tentatively call the battle tunnels. He lined them on the final tunnel leading to the battle meadow, so the bees could see any shades about to exit. He also asked Niobee to ask the bees to start providing wax to the candles: normal wax for the apiary floor's tunnels, and then wax from the specialized bee queens for the battle tunnels. Just to see what, if anything, different types of wax would do.

He considered whether or not to ask the bees to provide wax for the karnuq's tunnels . . . but figured he could ask the karnuq to do it themselves now that they had regular access to honeycomb. In fact, he could work that into beekeeping lessons on the various uses of beeswax. He nodded as he made his decision. Maybe one day the bees would take over, if they moved into the karnuq's beehouse, but for now the karnuq should maintain that feature themselves.

With the new features addressed, Belissar set out about the rest of his day, excited to hear what his bees would come up with.

The First of the Fifth was spinning about in circles. She was surrounded on all sides by gardeners and communers, with her own daughters and communers dancing about to try and help out.

In preparation for her task, the First of the Fifth decided first to compile reports from the gardeners. She could not efficiently allocate flowers to foragers unless she knew the status of those flowers, after all. So, she had requested that all the hives with gardeners send reports on the flowers they had visited, so she could compile them all into an overall picture of the King's domain.

As it turned out, the reports were staggering. The King had recreated an entire flower ecosystem for each of the rooms that had been settled by hives, owing to a time when each hive had treated its own resources as separate from the others. There were, therefore, a vast number of flowers to report on . . . and with them, a vast number of issues and opportunities to address.

The mana flowers were, as a rule, overworked, receiving entirely too much attention from the hives. On the other hand, most of the mundane flowers had been neglected to various degrees. Cloudberries and sweetvetch had produced a special honey type especially suited for winter, but then had been neglected as unnecessary since the King's realm maintained a constant climate. The floating flowers the King had planted in the ponds had been written off and ignored after they were found to possess no special compounds. The flowers the King and the Fourth of the Seventh used to weave stems together had not received any cross-pollination since the only visitors were harvesting entire plants rather than nectar and pollen and hadn't been visiting any other flowers on the way there. The mushrooms and plants in the dirt tunnels besides the Ground mana flowers had also gone neglected, as most of the bees had trouble foraging in the darkness and the digging beehive had only recently hit its stride. There was a vine and a mushroom both with noticeable mana density there, neither of which had never ever been foraged, even! Additionally, there was a mushroom the dangerous one had stated possessed a deadly poison; a fact confirmed by the Conduit herself! As for the orchard, the trees there had been receiving some visits, but the gardeners indicated they needed far more cross-pollination before they'd show results. And then there was the question of the flowers in the karnuq hives, which the gardeners pointed out had seen few to no visits by bees whatsoever. Their status as of now was entirely unknown but was assumed to be neglected as a result.

Additionally, only the First of the Fifth's hive had been focused on cross-pollination in the first place. The flower meadow queens had been too focused to spare the effort, while the orchard queens only had mana flowers and the apple trees and so hadn't seen any results. As for the apiary, she herself had actively prevented the other queens from gathering from what she had considered *her* flowers, preventing any sort of cross-pollination efforts by anyone other than her. Even now that she was no longer doing so, the apiary's focus on specializing queens meant she still hadn't introduced cross-pollination methods to the apiary as a whole. As a result of all these things, the gardeners now reported that the rate of cross-pollination was far lower than it could have been.

This was entirely intolerable to the First of the Fifth. The narrow focus of the hive of hives and her own misguided perceptions had combined to produce the worst result she could possibly imagine: staggering inefficiency. Countless opportunities had been overlooked, vast resources had gone unutilized, and favored flowers had been pushed beyond their limits.

The First of the Fifth decided this would change. She decided that this *must* change. If it did not, honey production would drop across the board for all hives while the quality of the honey served at the King's table would diminish. And that could not be allowed, no matter the cost. So, the First of the Fifth received the reports with renewed fervor. The King and the hive of hives both had asked her to manage foraging for maximum efficiency. And this she would do, whatever efforts were required of her to see it done.

But as it turned out, the First of the Fifth's report to the King and optimizations for the hive of hives would have to wait, for something was about to occur that would rock the entire tower.

## OMINOUS BEE-HAVIOR

The Fourth of the Seventh flew across the forest, coming to a rest on top of a large tree branch. Her workers and soldiers gathered around her, along with two communers. One of the communers was her own, but not the other. The other was squat, with thicker carapace, legs, and mandibles, and a brown color to her hair, for she was from the digging hive.

And this was not their first time working together, either. Previously, the King had asked the Fourth of the Seventh to help map out the sigmaka's territory. The digging queen had raised a pair of communers, sending one with the karnuq as the newcomers escorted them through the tunnels below, while the other traveled with the Fourth of the Seventh. As a result, the Fourth of the Seventh and her scouts were able to follow along and figure out where the tunnels below matched up with the surface, at least up to where the sigmaka tunnels went underneath the Hunger. Her hive then marked out those borders. Apparently scouting and foraging for nectar was fine, but building hives was forbidden in that area.

That made sense to her. Her instincts told her that nearby hives could try to rob her own, to which her bees would respond with violence. But apparently the King and the sigmaka didn't want to hurt each other, so it made sense to keep a bit of distance and avoid that sort of thing. Well, the hive of hives also didn't do that to each other, but maybe newcomers living in the Beyond still did. She didn't know, but she believed that the King had it all figured out!

What she did know was that the King had asked her to scout out the surface above the sigmaka's lands, which she was happy to do! So, she and her scout hive flew to the center of the area, then the scouts began to spread out in every direction while the Fourth of the Seventh coordinated via communer. She watched through dozens of eyes as they passed between trees and over bushes, taking note of any flowers or anything out of the ordinary.

So far, it was more of the same. The sigmaka area was on the southwestern side of the King's tower. The ruins where she built her mini-hive, on the other hand, were located to the northwest, with the entrance to the underground tunnels in between them both. From the initial flyover, the Fourth of the Seventh felt the mana concentration in the area was slightly lower than in the north side, and they did not identify any additional ruins. Her scouts sampled the local flowers but found none that they had not seen elsewhere in the Beyond.

The digging communer helped point out where the tunnels below came close to the surface, and so where new entrances between the surface and the underground might be constructed by the denizens below. The scouts marked out these areas as well, flying around them extensively to fix them in their memories. They found at least one additional tunnel that led to the surface, a small hole with signs that some sort of animal had gone in and out.

The Fourth of the Seventh beat her wings as she danced about. She wondered what sort of creature had arrived from underground. The hole seemed too small for a sigmaka or karnuq, and whoever had made it had clearly not stuck around. She assigned one of the scouts to remain nearby and keep an eye out for if they returned.

This discovery meant that the Fourth of the Seventh would need to keep up the scouting patrols, not just here but all across the Beyond. Living things other than the karnuq and the bees were starting to arrive and discover the refuge the King had purified. Soon, the bees would not be alone out here. And the Fourth of the Seventh intended to know when they located new neighbors! Or predators to be stung. That was also possible, perhaps even likely. But that'd be fine, since then the Fourth of the Seventh could try hunting like the karnuq apparently did!

As the day wore on, the scouts continued to make their way through the forest floor. At this point, some of them diverted up toward the canopy, scouting out the view from above, searching for flowers from the trees, and looking out to see if any flying creatures had located the purified area. Some of the scouts approached the border with the Hunger, taking care not to stray too close. The Fourth of the Seventh watched through their eyes, having them stay to observe the enemy for a moment.

It was a writhing mass of black mist with rainbow undertones, so densely packed that it became like a sea, held back only by the invisible power of the King's tower. The border wasn't clearly delineated; the Hunger constantly pushed and flowed into the purified zone, only to fade and disperse the farther inside it got. And this motion was not limited to the border. The Fourth of the Seventh had one of her scouts fly high, even above the trees, to look out across the Hunger. It twisted and writhed, with waves moving across its surface and colliding into one another. Tendrils and wisps and columns all rose and fell from the surface up toward the sky as if reaching for the lights above. Through the constant motion, the Fourth of the Seventh almost thought she could distinguish shapes at times. One wave almost seemed to hold the head of one of the invaders she had seen before it collided into another and dispersed. Sometimes the shifting colors of the Hunger appeared to form into red eyes for but a moment before they melted back into the black. And sometimes the tendrils and wisps rising into the air curled into what looked like wings or legs or other such things.

She instinctively recoiled, even though she couldn't keep her eyes off of it. She felt as if she was being watched by a predator, a monster sniffing about the walls of her hive, ignoring the threatening buzzing of her guards. She could imagine the monsters that invaded her home forming out of the constant motion and charging across the Beyond. She buzzed her wings.

The hive of hives would not allow that to happen, the Fourth of the Seventh included. And to think there was an entire hive of King-like beings living deep underneath it all, without the protection of the King or his tower or the Queen of All Bees, where at any moment the Hunger could pour in and attack. The Fourth of the Seventh couldn't imagine such a thing.

But ultimately, anything she thought she saw melted back into the mist before fully forming. The Hunger was in motion and trying its best, but it couldn't reach her here. For all the fear she felt, the power of the King's tower was stronger. The very mana that flowed within her held the monsters at bay. And so it would, so long as the hive of hives continued to protect their home.

So, even if one of those tendrils formed into something, she wouldn't worry. Even that one that looked like a pair of wings. Even as that pair of wings began to flap. Even as a form broke off from the column of mist it was attached to and began to fly, not dispersing apart as normal.

The Fourth of the Seventh paused, then began to brush her eyes and antennas. She was just about to sound the alarm, her workers and soldiers were already buzzing around her and telling her to return to the King's tower. But . . . the shade didn't approach them. Indeed, it was flying *away* from them, toward other flying shades beginning to form. These, too, flew away from the purified zone, toward a couple more black dots hanging in the sky in the distance.

"Queen . . . need go! Dangerous!"

The Fourth of the Seventh danced her affirmative and took off. But as she started to fly back, she danced out some commands as well.

"Keep an eye on. Hunger . . . doing something different. Need to see, report to King."

Her workers saluted and the communer relayed the order to the scouts. The scouts all began to fly up above the canopy, keeping their eyes on the flying shades as best they could from this distance. The black dots they were headed toward began to grow a bit larger even as the flying shades grew smaller. The Fourth of the Seventh's mind raced as she flew back toward the safety of home. What was the Hunger doing? Why would the shades fly away from the King's realm, which they were so intent on destroying? Were they gathering together for an attack? Was the Hunger about to swarm and escort a new queen somewhere? Did the Hunger even have queens?

Her questions only grew as the dots grew closer and the other shades approached them. Her scouts started to see little flashes of light appear around the dots. That . . . was strange. As far as her workers had seen, the Hunger didn't make lights like that. Even the lightning and fire the invading shades had produced didn't light up the area like normal lightning and fire did.

It was only as she reached the gates of the King's tower that she started getting some answers. The dots flew close enough that they stopped being dots. Her scouts could see some sort of tiny winged creatures flying through the air, sending out flashes of light toward the flying shades that approached them.

She froze right at the entrance, much to the chagrin of her workers.

"Something . . . under attack?"

# CHAPTER THIRTY-EIGHT

# ARRIVAL

Belissar was just walking toward the karnuq for lessons when he felt a frantic pull on his mana. His tower sight shifted to find the Fourth of the Seventh dancing frantically at the tower entrance.

*"King! See something flying over Hunger! Getting attacked by shades!"*

Belissar's eyes narrowed, and he spoke through the tower mana.

*"Niobee, get the army ready! Chief Rohsuak, there's an emergency! We could use you and the hunters!"*

Both of them replied and set about to fulfill his commands. Belissar paused. He closed his eyes and took a deep breath, trying to still his beating heart.

He was reacting before thinking. Chief Rohsuak had pointed out that while responding decisively to an emergency was important, as a leader he should stop and think about the situation as a whole as soon as circumstances allowed. The tower itself was not under attack, nor was anyone he knew. He looked through the eyes of the Fourth of the Seventh's scouts and found the battle was still far away, over the Hunger, so not anywhere they could intervene just yet.

He took another deep breath and opened his eyes. He had time to think. So, some sort of flying creatures were headed this way and currently under attack by the Hunger. Since shades had formed, the army needed to get ready to respond, that much was clear. But . . . what should he do about the flying creatures? They could be wild animals that would turn hostile if they saw him, they could be injured and in need of assistance, or maybe they were even intelligent? There were bear people and skunk people so why not bird people? The point was, he didn't know who they were or how they would react if the bee army joined the battle.

So, he reached out.

*"Chief Rohsuak."*

*"I'm at your command, Sacred Den Master. May I ask what's going on?"*

He nodded even though she couldn't see him.

*"Something is flying over the Hunger. They're currently under attack by shades and headed this way. I'd like to talk about how to address the situation before they arrive."*

Her voice came through, with no hint of amusement or mirth.

*"I understand. Let's quickly consider some possible scenarios then."*

Belissar and Chief Rohsuak started discussing what to do depending on who exactly the newcomers were and how they might act, and how they might best deal with the shades in those scenarios. Belissar could only hope they'd figure it out before the battle arrived.

Niobee landed in the orchard, right before the shortcut to the tower's entrance. The Second First of the First had already arrived and was discussing the situation with the Fourth of the Seventh and the First of the Fifth's First Daughter. All around them, soldier bees were flying in from the shortcuts and assembling into their formations. The three queens all stopped and saluted to Niobee as she arrived.

"Conduit, army gathering. Will be ready to move soon, whenever King commands."

Niobee brushed the antennas of the Second First of the First.

"Good, thanks!"

She then turned to the Fourth of the Seventh.

"Can look through scouts? Want to see."

"Okay!"

Niobee could always get glimpses of what was going on, but for this she would need to look more forcefully, so she thought she'd ask. The Fourth of the Seventh happily agreed, so Niobee gathered up her mana and started to dance. It took a bit more effort since her target was outside of the tower, but Niobee pushed it through until she could fully see everything the Fourth of the Seventh's scouts could.

She watched as the flying creatures approached. She didn't know what they were, but there was something about them that seemed . . . familiar. As they flew closer, she started to see that they weren't alone. There were little figures on their backs.

"More humans, or human-like things. Will probably talk to King."

The Second First of the First danced about.

"Like karnuq, sigmaka? Should help then?"

Niobee danced the affirmative.

"King will probably want to. Will help, but keep eye out. Don't let hurt King if . . ."

But then Niobee froze mid-dance. The three queens glanced at one another before the Second First of the First stepped forward and touched Niobee's antennas.

"Conduit? Is something . . ."

Then Niobee suddenly leapt into the air, buzzing her wings as loud as she could as she extended her stinger. She began to zip about, spreading attack pheromones as she started to dance.

"They're here! Bad humans who hurt King!"

"My lord! Get down!"

Ruckanos threw himself flat against his saddle, clinging on for dear life. Another wyvern flew just above him, its scales catching and tearing the edges of his cloak. Its rider, the captain of his guard, drove a lance right into a shade flying toward Ruckanos's flank, dispersing the monster. Neither Ruckanos nor his captain had any time to comment on the exchange, however, as their wyverns peeled away and spun about to gain distance from one another, just as another pair of bird-shades began to dive toward them. The captain hefted his lance once more while Ruckanos tried to chant a spell through chattering teeth.

Of course the Hunger had decided to strike now, of all times, right when the group was at their most exhausted. The trip from the latest purified zone had been their longest yet, a flight over the largest unbroken sea of the Hunger they had ever encountered. The captain had wanted to turn back, even, for they were forced to pass the point where they would no longer have the supplies or endurance to return. But Ruckanos had pressed on. The gods had laid out this specific path for them, so Ruckanos believed they would find something before their strength was spent.

And now, just when they had spotted a purified zone and his faith had been vindicated, the Hunger struck. It was inevitable, really. People claimed that wyverns flying so high in the sky that the air froze would keep them safe, but there was no such thing as safe when it came to the Hunger. Wyverns flying so high they were barely visible from the ground had been attacked while sparrows flying barely above the Hunger's surface had not, and vice versa. There was no discernable rhyme or reason to when or how the Hunger would attack, only that it eventually would. So, the longer one spent near the Hunger, the more certain it was that they would be attacked, no matter what precautions they took. It had been a miracle they had not been attacked yet on their long journey; Ruckanos had hoped their guiding god would keep it that way.

But now, just before the finish, they would face their greatest challenge yet, when all of them were exhausted and spent. Their fatigue showed nearly immediately. The lancers had been slow to form up and had thus allowed some of the shades to infiltrate their formation and attack the mages. One of the mages fired off a quick lightning bolt at an approaching shade, but it absorbed the attack with no apparent effect and tore the mage to shreds. It then unleashed a wave of black lightning that sent the mage's mount hurtling to the ground . . . along with one of the lancers who had belatedly moved in to assist. Within moments, they had lost two of their number, and now Ruckanos himself was under assault.

The captain glanced around and grabbed a horn tied to his belt, blowing it to grab everyone's attention. He then pointed his lance toward the one clear spot in the distance.

"Break through and make for the tower! And no lightning, they're immune!"

His guards may have been exhausted, but they were well-trained and quickly reacted to the command. The captain took the lead, his lance glowing with mana, and the others formed up around him. They aimed their lances forward and then drove all of their wyverns ahead at full speed. The mages followed along, flinging fireballs and gusts of wind to cover the flanks, while those specialized in lightning began casting support spells instead, boosting the speed of the group. Ruckanos and the augur tried to keep their wyverns in the center.

A group of shades rushed in front of the group and together released a huge surge of black lightning, but Ruckanos's mages countered with a lightning shield of their own. The captain smashed right through the surge, his lance wrapping up the lightning around it as he thrust it forward. The mana coating his lance pushed ahead, piercing through a shade before the tip of his lance even made contact with it. The other lancers followed suit, though they did not fare so well. One was wrapped in lightning by a shade still pierced on his lance. His wyvern stayed aloft but slowed to a crawl and both mount and rider quickly fell out of the formation. Ruckanos resisted the urge to look back as he heard the man scream.

But his sacrifice would not be in vain. The formation had pushed through the flock of shades, and the powerful wings of the wyverns propelled them forward. The shades fell behind, while ahead of them lay the bright green canopy of a purified forest.

Ruckanos's hair tingled as a bolt of black lightning shot past him, but he spurred his wyvern onward. The green grew in his vision even as he saw flickers of black in the corners of his eyes. Below them, the Hunger writhed and more shades joined the fray. A massive tendril of pure Hunger suddenly lashed up from below and the formation scattered. One of the mages made a wrong turn, screaming as the tendril of black mist engulfed him and his mount.

At this point, Ruckanos no longer paid any attention to anything happening around him. His sweat froze as he dug into the sides of his wyvern, channeling as much mana as he could stuff into the reins. Anything he could do to force the beast to move even a little bit faster. His eyes were locked upon the green ahead, the zone of safety just barely out of reach.

And then, finally, his vision turned green and blue. He was surrounded by trees below and clear skies above. He clenched his teeth together as his wyvern all but slammed into the canopy, clutching to the trees as it almost dropped out of the sky. He panted heavily and gulped. He turned around, shivering as he imagined what he might see. His eyes widened.

All around him, men fell into the saddles of wyverns, their exhausted mounts landing right on the trees. The Hunger remained behind . . . and out of reach, held back by the power of the gods. The bird-shades gave up their pursuit, diving down and melting back into the main mass of the Hunger.

Ruckanos took a deep breath.

They had made it.

# CHAPTER THIRTY-NINE

# BELISSAR'S BEE-CISION

Ruckanos was leaning across his saddle, holding his head. Behind him, the augur sat on another wyvern, currently fiddling with some ritual or another. The captain was in the midst of a roll call, checking on the men. He finished up and flew his wyvern over to Ruckanos, a firm and neutral expression on his face.

"My lord, we lost five hands with their wyverns and all supplies. An additional four are wounded, one seriously enough that he will not be able to fight before recovering."

Ruckanos groaned and clutched his head tighter. They had made it, but their force, already pitifully small and lacking in tower guards with full blessings, had been reduced even further. The captain was about the only true tower guard. Ruckanos had not committed to any god prior to gaining a tower of his own, so the rest of his guards had also not been allowed the opportunity until then. If they continued to take losses like this on the journey, Ruckanos might find himself facing his lost tower and its thief all alone.

But then, he heard a voice behind him.

"We're . . . here."

He and the captain both turned to look at the augur.

"What did you say?"

The augur's eyes were open wide.

"I've checked our current position against the charted path. The last flight was longer than expected, so . . . we have arrived at our destination."

Ruckanos stared at him for a moment before he started to grin.

"Captain, prepare the men for an assault."

The captain furrowed his brow.

"My lord, is that wise? We did not have the strength for a tower subjugation even when we started this mission. Now, with our casualties . . ."

Ruckanos shrugged.

"That was the point. You know as well as I that none of us were meant to return. But the situation is different now. We have been led here by one of the gods themselves, to a tower we know is young and led by someone entirely unworthy. It's a miracle the tower still exists, and I wouldn't be surprised if it still lacked a patron. For what other purpose would we have been led here than to cast the unworthy aside and replace them with a proper tower lord?"

The augur frowned.

"I . . . would be cautious about assuming the will of the gods, my lord. But . . . I suppose they were unusually direct with their assistance this time. Still, perhaps I should make another offering?"

The captain nodded.

"That would also give the men a chance to rest, my lord, and allow us to scout the situation. If we are to prepare for an assault, the men will need to be in their best possible condition."

Ruckanos heaved a massive sigh.

"Very well. Let us have a short rest, then, but do not dither about, Captain. We should not keep the gods waiting."


Belissar paused for a moment. He had gathered with Chief Rohsuak and the karnuq hunters now and they were all walking toward the orchard and its shortcuts.

"Okay, looks like there are people on the back of the wyverns . . . so it will probably be a diplomatic situation then? I guess then one of your people should go with the bees?"

Chief Rohsuak nodded.

"Understood. Metsaitti will lead our hunters along with the bee army."

The group passed into the orchard . . . and Belissar's eyes went wide. The air was filled with loud buzzing. The bees were all zipping about, no longer in tight formations but in a swarm flying every which way . . . all with their stingers extended.

"What's got them so agitated . . . ?"

But then, Belissar saw it through the eyes of a scout bee. The face of one of the riders as he landed within the purified area.

The karnuq eyed the swarming bees with concern as Chief Rohsuak turned to Belissar.

"Sacred Den Master, what is the matter?"

But he barely heard her speak. He barely had a thought in his mind at all; he didn't even notice the shades call off their pursuit. Instead, he began to tremble.

It was him. *He* was here. Belissar smelt smoke, saw flickering flames, and felt a sharp pain in his back. His heart pounded and his head felt light. He . . .

Then, he felt a heavy hand on his shoulder. He turned to find Chief Rohsuak looking at him with worry.

"Sacred Den Master, are you alright? What's going on?"

Belissar continued trembling but gulped.

"It's . . . him. H-Humans, the tower lords. I-It's the tower lord's son. The one who burned down my village and nearly killed me."

The bees' buzzing intensified further. Belissar felt more than saw Niobee land on his head. She crawled over him, buzzing her wings and brushing him with her antennas.

"King's enemy! Niobee's enemy! Bees will sting! Protect King!"

Chief Rohsuak patted his shoulder again and he glanced over. He felt heat begin to emanate from her body, while Metsaitti and the other karnuq hefted their spears.

"We are with you as well, Sacred Den Master. If this man is your enemy, just say the word and we will strike him down."

Belissar watched her for a moment as Niobee continued to crawl over him, then closed his eyes and took a deep breath. That's right, he wasn't a helpless peasant living on his own anymore. The bees and the karnuq both stood at his side. So, he tried to turn his thoughts away from fire and smoke and pain and toward the people around him.

He thought of Niobee and all of her efforts to save, guide, and protect him. How she had brought him here, led him to the tower's core, and never hesitated to throw herself in harm's way on his behalf.

He thought of the bees and all the times they had shared together. The flower meadow queens and their resolute courage, facing terrifying shades time after time again without hesitation or complaint. The apiary queens and their restless work, giving him more honey than he knew what to do with. The orchard queens and their joy when he'd built them a home. The worker bees swarming over new mana flowers, the soldier bees training day in and day out to protect the tower, Beero and the others developing magic when their wings failed them, and the bumblebees happily zipping about. He thought of all they had built together.

He thought of all they had lost. The first group of queens who had perished due to his own mistakes. The soldiers who had died facing a wolf-shade for the first time, when the soldier army was still learning how to fight. The soldiers who had sacrificed themselves to keep two shades in a pit long enough for Belissar to burn them. Those who had died trying to hold back the first bird-shade. Beero and the other wounded who had lost their wings, yet still strove to do nothing more but return to the fight. The drones who gave their lives to bring the new hives to life.

He thought of the karnuq, the first people to treat him well since his parents and the old beekeeper. He thought of his lessons with Chief Rohsuak and Juosiutik. He thought of the hunters who had once challenged his tower every day. He thought of Noigakkuq, sneaking in at night to deliver flowers. He thought of

Metsaitti facing down a shade in the forest, of Chief Rohsuak burning the turtle-shade that repelled his bees. He thought of Muuraqi helping him build stone bee-houses, while the soldier bees helped the karnuq build houses of their own. He thought of Juosiutik's passionate conversations with the First of the Fifth. He thought of the karnuq children playing with the bumblebee soldier.

He opened his eyes and glared out into the air, clenching his fists until they shook. A single word came to his mind, pushing past all his swirling thoughts.

No.

The tower lords were not taking another home from him. They would not take all that he and the bees and the karnuq had built, all that they had fought and died for. So, if the tower lords had come here to burn and kill once more, they would not find the quivering peasant from before. Nor would they find a tower lord, but a tower keeper, blessed by two of the gods and accompanied by his count-less friends and allies. One who did not use these divine powers to steal and destroy, but to protect and provide.

Belissar slowly unclenched his hands to reach up and brush Niobee. He glanced at Chief Rohsuak and gave her a nod. Then he turned and looked up at his bees swarming about him. They began to slow down as they noticed his attention.

He felt his heart catch but for a moment at the thought of what was to come, of the bees that would be put in harm's way. But this time, he put the thought aside. The bees were more than ready to defend their home, whatever the cost. It was what they longed to do. Niobee seemed ready to go out and attack even if he didn't give the order. After their last encounter with the man who was approach-ing, he couldn't blame her.

The tower lords would not give him a choice regardless. They thought of peo-ple like the karnuq as subhuman monsters. They thought that the gods hated the sight of a peasant even stepping foot inside a tower, much less taking charge of one. They would not leave him be.

And this time, he could do more than run. He could stop the burning of his home. He could stand up to a tower lord's son. He could fight back.

He narrowed his eyes and opened his mouth.

"Everyone, prepare for battle."

# CHAPTER FORTY

# FACE YOUR DESTI-BEE

**B**elissar looked up at the swarming bee army and frowned.

"Niobee, could you help me calm them down?"

Niobee flew unsteadily in response.

"Calm down? Not going to go sting now?"

Belissar shook his head.

"We will, but let's see what they do first. If they come here . . . no point in wasting all those traps, right?"

Niobee's dance resumed speed.

"Okay!"

With that, she zipped off into the sky, touching antennas with the queens to cool down the attack pheromones. The queens slowly brought the soldier bees back under control, having them cease their swarming and gather into their usual formations instead. Belissar turned his attention back to the incoming humans. They were resting up and passing around some food at the moment. Belissar was a bit tempted to send the army now but decided against it. The wyverns were big and had flown in at quite the speed, reminding Belissar of the big bird-shades. In fact, the wyverns had likely outrun those very bird-shades on their way here, if the shades attacking them were the same type that Belissar had encountered.

That being the case, Belissar didn't want to fight these humans out in the open where their wyverns could outrun the bees and dive through them. He wanted to first see them restricted by the dirt tunnels and the traps within.

He rubbed his chin at that. He thought, and thought, and thought some more.

He made his choice and moved the rooms of the first floor around. He placed the flower meadow just after the dirt tunnels, so that the bee army could wait for them right outside of the tunnels' exit.

The more he thought about it, the more he was concerned about the wyverns' speed in the open air. He did not want to give them a chance to get flying and build up speed. If he forced them to exit the tunnels out into the lava field, the field and its mini volcano *might* stop them before they even reached the bee army . . . but what if it didn't? What if they just flew over the lava and evaded the boulders? If that occurred, then letting them exit the tunnels into a room without the bee army just gave the wyverns a chance to take off and get airborne.

If, on the other hand, they had to exit the tunnels directly into the waiting stingers of the bee army? Then, like the bird-shades before them, they'd be surrounded by bees before they had a chance to move.

Belissar nodded, making his final decision. He went on to let the bees and the karnuq know what the plan was.

He could only hope it would be enough.

Ruckanos sighed as his wyvern finally began to beat its wings and rise into the air. The men were . . . lacking in enthusiasm. They had been silent as they rested and they were silent now as they climbed their mounts, their heads hanging low.

Well, it wasn't as if he didn't understand. His body, too, felt heavy under the sheer fatigue of their previous journey, surely unprepared for the task at hand. But what a task it would be! They had been led here by the gods themselves! Surely the men could show at least a little spirit on behalf of the gods, couldn't they? Sure, the gods remained silent during the augur's offering this time, but surely the lack of news meant their mission hadn't changed?

But there was nothing for it, so Ruckanos remained silent as the group took off and made for the center of the purified zone. They would warm up once the mission got started. And even if they did not, Ruckanos would let nothing stand between him and his destiny.

Soon, they arrived. Ruckanos frowned. They found the tower without issue, and indeed it was young, but it was not as he expected. The tower now rose four stories into the air . . . and had golden banners. The symbol, a bee landing upon a flower, was not one he recognized, but he understood what the symbol itself entailed.

This tower had been blessed by a patron god.

He turned his head as the wyverns landed in the clearing before the tower, glancing back at the old man behind their formation.

"Augur, which god is this?"

The augur furrowed his brow.

"I . . . have no memory of this symbol. It was not one recorded in the archives."

Ruckanos narrowed his eyes.

"That's impossible, isn't it?"

The augur shook his head.

"The gods are beyond the ken of us mortal men, and though it is rare, new ones *have* been discovered over time. Though, if I were to hazard a guess . . . that color is the same as the divinations. I believe the patron of this tower was the one who guided us here."

Ruckanos crossed his arms at that. The god who led them here . . . was the patron of this tower? Why would they do such a thing? Ruckanos had expected the gods to be displeased with whoever was desecrating this tower—but then why would they have given it their blessing? Had the gods changed their minds? Had they given the unworthy would-be lord a chance, only to find them as poor a master as feared?

But how could that be true? Not only had the tower survived, but it had risen to four floors already. It was hardly months old at this stage, so that should not have been possible. It normally took weeks for a tower to gather the mana reserves for a single expansion, much less four of them. If Ruckanos didn't know any better, he'd have said this tower lord was doing impossibly well for himself.

And deep within his heart crept the tiniest of doubts that perhaps he was not intended to take charge of this tower.

But that couldn't be, could it? Whoever was in charge of this place could not have prepared beforehand like he had. They'd have stumbled about, not understanding a thing that they did. It must have been a sheer accident, or perhaps excessive intervention by the gods, that the tower had even survived this long. Perhaps the patron was clearing the way for him, intervening to keep his tower intact, nay, growing even, for the day that he arrived to claim it.

He held tight to that hope as he strode forward.

"Captain, prepare to march."

The captain frowned.

"Commander . . ."

Ruckanos just turned to stare at him, raising an eyebrow. The captain sighed and then saluted.

"It shall be done."

The captain sent a scout inside while arranging the rest of the men into formation, while the augur carved a ritual symbol into the dirt below. He placed a lightly glowing crystal carved with numerous runes in the center, then touched a specific one of the runes. The crystal's light turned green before it melted into the symbol, which itself pulsed with green light.

The signal that they had found a tower. Ruckanos had a brief thought to stop the augur, to let the Conclave remain unaware of his success, but he decided against it. Let the Conclave come; it would take them ages to reach this far into the wild. He'd have long made up for any mistakes he had made by the time they arrived, if they ever did.

He turned his attention back to the tower, just as the scout reported that the initial entrance area was clear. The captain turned to face him and Ruckanos nodded. The captain took one deep breath, and then gave the command.

"Move out."

And with that, Ruckanos marched to his destiny.

In the back of their formation, a wounded rider frowned as he opened up his bag, just before the captain gave the command. He looked down and saw the queen bee exit her hive once again. He bent down to whisper to her.

"Last stop, little one. We're going into that tower and I fear none of us will come out. You need to leave now or you'll die too."

The queen bee stared up at him with those big eyes that felt like they pierced into his soul. Then . . . she began to crawl up out of the bag. She climbed to the top and began to stretch her wings. For a brief moment, the man's heart lifted. Maybe, just maybe, she had understood him?

She paused, though, upon seeing their surroundings, including the tower. She stared at the tower for a minute, and then crawled back down into the bag. The man sighed and his shoulders drooped.

"Move out."

It was too late. The command was given, and they were heading to their doom. He looked up at the tower and its banners. His eyes widened a bit as he looked once again at the pattern there.

A bee landing on a flower.

He glanced back down toward his bag and then up to the banner. Maybe, just maybe, this tower wouldn't be so bad for his little friends? If at least one of them could survive this . . .

He closed his eyes and bowed his head for a moment.

"Please, whichever god is watching over this place . . . take mercy on the little one. She and her children did not choose to come here. They don't deserve to share our fate."

Once he had finished, he looked up and steeled his heart, wrapping his reins around his good arm. With his other arm wounded in the latest fight, it'd be up to his wyvern to do most of the job, but what could he do but attempt his duty as best he could? He doubted he could change his fate or that of his charge at this stage, and after all they had done, he couldn't say they didn't deserve whatever came. He'd hoped to change the fate of his little friends, but he had already done all that he could for them.

All that was left now was to see things through to the end, whatever that might be.

Staring forward as he did, he did not notice the little queen's eyes glow with golden light as one of the banners fluttered.

# CHAPTER FORTY-ONE

# PEER BEE-VIEW

The queen heard the human's voice and crawled out. She understood the voice as some attempt at communication, though how it carried any meaning she couldn't say. It certainly was no dance.

But she did understand when he directed the sounds toward her that they either had arrived at a safe spot or else were about to leave one. Since they had been flying beforehand, it had to be the former, so she crawled out to take stock of their surroundings.

She froze immediately when she saw the world beyond. Before them was a mighty mountain of stone, covered with golden banners. Banners that she had never seen, but still recognized somewhere deep within her.

This place belonged to the Queen of All Bees.

Which meant she had arrived at her destination. She stood still, awaiting instruction. While her preference would be to fly out and sting her enemies immediately, she knew that the Queen of All Bees must have brought her here for a reason. She would not reveal herself until she knew why.

A moment later, she was surrounded by a bright light, and then found herself before the Queen of All Bees once again. She danced her salute dance, to which the Queen of All Bees replied with a single step.

"Wait."

She saluted once again and then found herself back in the world. The Queen of All Bees had spoken. She had arrived, but the time was not ripe yet. So, instead, she crawled back inside her hive at the bottom of the bag and began to quietly awaken her children.

It was not yet time, but she knew that the moment soon approached. She intended to be ready. If all went as she hoped, she would soon have her revenge.

Once the captain gave the all-clear, Ruckanos guided his wyvern to step inside the tower. He found himself inside a subterranean tunnel made entirely of dirt. He scoffed at the sight.

No entrance hall. No guards or servants to receive visitors. No adornments to honor the gods. Look, the shrine of the patron god was left sitting in the dirt, for the gods' sake! The tower was clearly in the hands of some feral barbarian. Even the mindless peasants would know better than this!

He dismounted his wyvern for a moment and strode over to the shrine. It was a strange thing, with a giant bee in place of any sort of man, but it was not Ruckanos's place to judge the gods. Indeed, what greater honor would there be but to introduce a new god to the Conclave? So, instead, he smiled and bowed his head.

"You've suffered much, haven't you? But fear not, your chosen tower lord is here now, and I shall set things right as you have commanded."

The shrine did not respond, but they rarely did. Ruckanos knew the gods would not bother with his words alone, so he intended to prove himself via his deeds. So, he turned to remount his wyvern . . .

Only to find that his men had all dismounted theirs. The captain pointed to the tunnel ahead.

"I'd recommend we proceed on foot, Commander. These tunnels are too cramped for the wyverns. We'll have to lead them through ourselves."

Ruckanos held back a sigh as the men fixed light crystals to their helmets, shining beams of light down the dark tunnels. The frontline soldiers then drew their blades and proceeded ahead of Ruckanos and the mages.

They had hardly begun their march when they came to a stop. The captain stepped forward and poked the ground with his sword. A large section of the ground vanished to reveal a hole. Ruckanos raised an eyebrow.

Pit traps, huh? A waste of a feature choice, and a lazy one at that. Servants and monsters could dig something like that easily enough. Concealing it was another matter but scarcely more difficult in the grand scheme of things. Pit traps were, therefore, something that could be employed en masse with only the barest amount of effort. To waste one of the precious boons of the gods and the tower's limited mana on such a thing . . . well, Ruckanos was once again reassured why he had been brought here.

One of the mages stepped forward, carving a spell circle into the dirt just before the pit. Then, after a quick chant, the ground itself extended in a line across the pit and hardened, forming a bridge. Ruckanos's men strode across easily. The wyverns, on the other hand, were long enough to crawl over the entire pit with little assistance.

If this was all the tower currently had to offer, Ruckanos questioned how it had survived this long in the first place.

They continued onward until once again the captain halted them. He glanced around a bit before taking a step and waving his sword out ahead of him.

A moment later, a stream of golden liquid poured down from the roof. When it hit the ground, it did not spread out in a pool but clung together in a viscous blob. One of the vanguard tilted his head.

"Is that . . . honey? I guess that would explain the bee decorations, but . . . as a trap?"

Ruckanos raised an eyebrow, but the captain narrowed his eyes as he inclined his head so that his light shone across the honey. Ruckanos caught a glimpse of purple in the otherwise golden mass. The captain took a closer look and gave his verdict.

"Stickier than normal and probably poisoned. Easy enough to avoid, but you're in for a bad time if you get drenched. Stay alert."

Ruckanos shook his head as he carefully stepped over the mass. The idea itself wasn't terrible. A sticky spray to restrict mobility combined with a poison, an effective if basic combination. But the execution . . . the execution was atrociously sloppy. The trap had been placed both too close to and too far from the last, so that the group would encounter it after safely passing the first trap but while they were still on high alert. And it had been placed by itself in an otherwise empty tunnel. There were no additional traps or even decorations to distract attention, no follow-up traps to strike if the first was disarmed, not even an ambush prepared to take advantage of the split attention. It was as if the traps had been placed entirely randomly, without any thought as to their use. His tutors would have had aneurysms had he presented such a setup.

More and more, he felt he was dealing with a feral beast rather than an intelligent being.

What followed was an excruciatingly boring journey. The twisting tunnels were filled with nothing but dirt and the occasional, easily avoided trap. No monsters or defenders accosted them, no servants came to greet them. No new traps appeared, nor did the two they had seen appear in any new patterns. They encountered some remnants, as all who challenged a tower did, but these were swiftly dealt with. And, of course, there were no rest zones to manage and contain them.

This tower was strictly amateur in every possible way, it seemed. Even the maze itself featured no particularly novel layout, as if the master had just left it as it first appeared. Which Ruckanos suspected they probably had.

This caused Ruckanos to frown, because something didn't add up. How had such an amateurish tower managed to survive, much less grow as quickly as it had? If the imposter tower lord was this incompetent at basic floor layout, then someone else must be responsible. He, of course, believed that the patron god was preparing the way for his arrival, but he also did not delude himself into believing that the gods would intervene so directly as to defend the tower personally from its own purifications.

That left one answer: the imposter had been exceedingly lucky with their choice of starting monster and had acquired something that could cover for their incompetence.

Which brought up the most important question of all . . . where were all the monsters? They had traveled nearly an entire room and had not encountered a single living thing. If this were a normal tower with a competent lord, Ruckanos would have assumed the tower lord had intentionally placed a cramped, winding maze to buy time, allowing them to observe any incoming threats and prepare accordingly. But he had already established that this imposter was nowhere near that competent . . . so why hadn't they thrown their monsters into the fray from the very start? Unless the patron god had again intervened to clear the way for the rightful tower lord?

"Halt."

Just then, the captain's voice cut through Ruckanos's wandering thoughts. He looked up ahead and saw a dim light coming from around the corner. He smiled. Finally! The way out . . . or at least some civilization. The color of the light and the way it flickered was more indicative of a fire of some sort, maybe a torch?

The captain silently motioned to two of his men and the three of them crept forward together. But then, the captain sniffed and jumped back, pulling the two men along with him. He gave a hushed but frantic whisper.

"Wind!"

The mages pushed forward one of their number, who tried to pull off a chant as he formed a spell circle right in the air with his own mana. The spell was sloppy, his hands shook, and his voice wavered, but he managed to make it work. A gust of wind blew down the tunnel and around the corner, and the light suddenly cut out. The captain spoke to the mages, motioning to the two men nearest him.

"Check them for poison. There was a strange smell on the air."

The captain crept forward quietly and glimpsed around the corner before making his way back.

"Wax candles of some sort, probably the source of the smell. Beyond that is the exit to an open field."

Ruckanos frowned. So, some sort of candle that spread poison via smoke? Again, not a bad concept, but the execution was all off. Letting the light flicker past the tunnel so they'd clearly notice something had changed? Moreover, why hadn't the imposter placed candles throughout the tunnels so they wouldn't suspect anything wrong? He shook his head.

Well, at least it was over. A new room was just ahead, this one wide open. Ruckanos doubted they'd find anything interesting there, but at least they'd pass through it quickly.

# CHAPTER FORTY-TWO

# THE FIELD OF BATTLE

The group rearranged their formation and began their march down the hallway. Ruckanos saw nothing but a sunlit field of flowers beyond the end of the tunnel. Had this been a normal tower, he might have thought it suspicious, or possibly a rest zone. With this tower . . . he guessed the imposter just put a random field of flowers haphazardly, wasting an entire room choice on a useless decoration of a room.

But then, the captain stopped. Ruckanos only heard a light buzzing noise before the captain shouted.

"Brace!"

The lead guards raised their shields just as five bees flew down in front of the entrance, larger than any bee Ruckanos had ever seen, as large as his hand even. They did not make their way inside the tunnels but hovered in place and swung their abdomens forward. A cone of liquid shot from each bee.

Thanks to the captain's quick reaction, most of the liquid splashed against the guards' metal shields. However, some flew past and landed on one of the guards' faces. For a moment, he just dabbed at his face.

And then he started screaming. At the captain's motion, the other guards pulled him off the line to the few mages who knew a bit of healing magic. One of the mages managed to retaliate with a quick fireball, but the bees flew away from the entrance long before it arrived. As soon as the danger had passed, the bees returned and launched another spray. One guard lifted his shield high to protect his face and got his legs drenched. He lasted a moment longer before the poison sank into his clothes, and then he started screaming too.

The captain motioned forward.

"Move out!"

The guards began a brisk march forward while the mages tried to cover them. The bee monsters were too quick and too far away, but the spells at least bought them some time.

"Halt!" the captain suddenly called out, but one guard, focused on the bees ahead, didn't catch the command and stumbled into a pit trap. He fell with a shout . . . and then Ruckanos heard one of those honey traps activate.

Really? The imposter put a honey trap at the bottom of the pit? Why?

The guards could do nothing but wait and endure the toxic sprays as two of the mages formed another bridge across the pit . . . two, because one got caught by the sprays mid-spell.

Once it finally finished, the captain pointed his sword forward.

"Charge!"

The men rushed forward before they lost their nerve. Ruckanos ran with confidence, pushing the mages around him to do the same. They had been surprised, for sure, and had taken shocking casualties from a mere handful of bees. But what was any of that before the will of the gods? A couple of bee monsters would not stop him from grasping his destiny.

Then, Ruckanos and the mages stepped out of the tunnel and into the flower field. Ruckanos was hit with a wall of sound, a cacophony of buzzing noises that nearly drowned out the captain's shouts. His eyes opened wide and his jaw dropped as he saw the sight beyond.

He knew now how this incompetent imposter had survived. He knew now who or what had carried the imposter through. Because all around him, in the skies and on the ground, in every direction, was a countless number of bees.

"Fall back!"

The captain's shout shocked Ruckanos out of his haze. He was about to object when a guard grabbed his shoulders and pulled him back. The captain and the front guards retreated carefully with their shields up, backing up as quickly as they could without disrupting their own formation. They were forced to pause and ward off a group of bees that dove down on them. The captain's sword flashed and three of the monsters fell, but the other guards could not strike quickly enough to counter. Still, they managed to drive their attackers away and pull back into the tunnels.

"Captain, what are you doing?"

The captain didn't even look at him, keeping his eyes on the entrance to the field ahead.

"Commander, retreat is our only option here. The tower lord is already hostile and we do not have the numbers to push through. We will not survive if we push forward. I am not sure we can even safely retreat if they push the issue."

Ruckanos scowled.

"Retreat is not an option, Captain."

The front guards had to lift their shields to block another spray.

"And what would you have us do, Commander? We die if we push forward."

"We die if we leave, too! Do you think help is coming for us, Captain? Do you think the Conclave will simply let us go even if we survive until they arrive? No, Captain, our only options here are victory or death. The gods led us here, so there must be a way!"

The captain grimaced while Ruckanos glanced around.

"Why not the wyverns?"

The captain shook his head.

"The skies are full of bees, they'll never get aloft."

Ruckanos rubbed his chin.

"What about the mages? We could cast a grand fireball to punch a hole through the bees and then fly through."

"That . . ." The captain paused. "They clearly avoid danger, so . . . it might actually work. *If* we can get the wyverns out of these tunnels and airborne."

For a brief moment he turned and looked Ruckanos in the eye.

"We're going to take casualties, though, and we'll have an angry bee army on our tail. If we do this, we will not be able to retreat. There will be no going back."

Ruckanos narrowed his gaze.

"There never was."

The captain nodded and began to bark his orders.

"You four, and you two mages, with me. Everyone else, saddle up and prepare your mounts as best you can. You will not have long."

On the captain's orders, one of the mages on the ground created a powerful gust of wind down the tunnel. The toxic spraying bees showed up once more but were blown off course when they tried to approach the entrance. Ruckanos and the others tried to climb onto their wyverns as best they could. He had to lay flat to avoid bumping his head on the roof of the tunnel, but he managed to strap in as securely as possible.

The captain then nodded and gave the order. He and the frontline guards rushed forward, holding their shields up to ward off another dive attempt by the bees while the two mages followed, quickly casting their spell. A sphere of winds wrapped around the tunnel entrance, warding off the bees. The spraying ones attacked again, but the toxic spray was blown away before it landed.

The wyverns crawled out one by one, digging their claws into the dirt to push through the wind. The wyvern-mounted mages then assembled around Ruckanos. They all lifted their hands and spoke as one.

"God of Fire, hear our plea. Let your fires rage and light our path. Let our enemies burn in the blaze of your inferno. Let nothing remain but ash and smoke."

A magic circle of red light formed in the air above all of them. A massive ball of fire began to form in the air above the circle, flickering in the heavy winds around them. The captain nodded at the two mages with him and they dropped their wind spell. The bees began to dive immediately, but they were too late. A grand fireball had formed, the magic circle flashed one final time and launched the fireball into the sky. Sweat dripped down Ruckanos's face from the heat, even at this distance, but he smiled as the fireball soared.

He grasped the reins and dug into his saddle. In but a moment, the fireball would explode and the sky would turn from black and yellow to red and orange. They would have but a moment to fly while the fire dissipated.

Once they were airborne, Ruckanos doubted bees of this size could keep pace with a wyvern in flight. He would push past this army and move to confront the imposter directly. He knew that whatever the odds, the gods willed his victory. It would work. He knew it would work.

Then, the tower would be his.

At that moment, they heard a growling noise, like that of an angry bear. A blue ball of fire, small but incredibly bright, flew out of nowhere and slammed right into the grand fireball, sinking within it. For a moment, Ruckanos thought he had imagined it.

And then the fireball exploded. A curtain of blue extended out across the sky and engulfed the red flames, redirecting them to the sides of the meadow . . . or back down from whence they came. Ruckanos ducked as tongues of fire fell from the sky. One of the mages was caught in the blaze, screaming as he and his wyvern burst into flames.

Ruckanos's eyes widened. Farther across the field, he saw a group of bestial subhumans approaching, their leader wrapped in bright flames. The bees buzzed angrily above. And there were no longer flames nor winds to stop them.

# CHAPTER FORTY-THREE

# DESTI-BEE FULFILLED

**B**elissar gritted his teeth as he glanced at the three fallen bees, but he tore his eyes away. Deep down, he knew they were unlikely to win without casualties, but he had still hoped to do so. Unfortunately, the tower guard were indeed not to be trifled with.

Worse still was that the humans did not fight like the Hunger. The shades of the Hunger were relentless. Sure, they might try to bypass a fight when they could, but they always continued moving forward at any cost. Not so with humans, apparently. These ones fell back into the tunnels the moment they saw the bee army . . . and between the tower guard captain's sword and the mages' wind and fireballs, Belissar didn't feel safe letting the bees pursue them into the tight corridors.

Luckily, though, the humans had just said their plan out loud where Belissar could hear it, so he knew they planned to press forward. He frowned at that but relayed their intentions to the flower meadow queens and Chief Rohsuak. He then turned to the karnuq. They were all standing in the orchard, right before the wall of shortcuts.

"Could you help us out? It looks like they're going to use some big fire spell to try and push through."

Chief Rohsuak made a predatory grin.

"Oh, are they, now? Worry not, Sacred Den Master. I'll handle it."

She laughed as she began to munch on mana honeycomb. Belissar kept rubbing his chin, though.

"Also, that tower guard captain at the front seems pretty strong, and fast enough to hit my bees midflight. Any ideas on how to deal with him?"

Chief Rohsuak just smiled and turned to Metsaitti. He sighed and began to roll his shoulders. Then he straightened up and struck his spear into the ground.

"I'll handle him, Sacred Den Master. Could you have the bees keep the others occupied?"

Belissar nodded, and then the karnuq ran through one of the shortcuts, emerging right next to the main entrance of the battle meadow. And just in the nick of time, as the humans were in the midst of casting their spell. The fireball was massive . . . though its red colors seemed somewhat dim compared to Chief Rohsuak's spells.

They seemed especially dim as Chief Rohsuak burst into flames and cast a spell of her own. Her fireball was tiny compared to that of the humans, but it burned far brighter. And when it exploded, it wrapped around the other spell and held it down. The bees hovered just over the surface of the flames, but none of them were hurt. Belissar released a sigh of relief.

But the battle had only begun. The tower guard captain began barking out orders immediately, but Metsaitti grabbed a spear from one of the other hunters and lobbed it at the man's head. The captain was forced to block with his shield as Metsaitti rushed forward with his own spear, the other karnuq hunters by his side. The remaining tower guards who hadn't mounted their wyverns yet tried to form up around their captain, but as they pointed their shields down toward the karnuq, squads of soldier bees began diving from above. Some of the humans were stung right in the face and neck and fell to the ground. Others dove to the ground to avoid the bees but fell out of the line as a result. Metsaitti's spear clashed with the captain's sword and the captain was forced to give ground, separating himself from the rest of the humans.

With the spell dealt with and the captain occupied, the bee army began their assault on the remaining humans. Some of the mages formed spells to attack the incoming bees. Smaller fireballs shot into the sky, but the bees evaded them. A gust of wind began blowing the soldier bee squads back . . . until a bumblebee soldier took the lead and powered through it, with the soldier bee squads following in her wake. One of the mages hit the bumblebee with a fireball but she pressed on, not slowing down in the slightest even with her hairs smoking. The bumblebee crashed into one of the mages, knocking him right off his saddle as the soldier bees began attacking his wyvern. The wyvern roared and snapped at them, spinning around to try and knock them away with its tail. Instead, it struck the nearest wyvern, knocking it and its rider over.

A few of the wyverns began to take to the air, but the bees were already upon them. Soldier bees began to sting the wyverns' wings and land on their bodies en masse, pulling them to the ground as they were covered in chitin and angry stingers. Two wyverns managed to break free and begin rising into the sky, only for a shadow to fall over their eyes. Black forms fell across their riders' faces and slammed into the wyverns' heads and bodies, driving them back into the ground with cries of pain. The lancer bees could apparently pierce through wyvern scales without issue.

In the meantime, Metsaitti continued to duel the captain. Metsaitti thrust quickly, pulling back his spear with ease whenever the captain parried him. But the captain's sword and shield were equally quick and Metsaitti didn't manage to land any blows. Indeed, the captain even began to push forward, forcing Metsaitti to step back and keep him at range. Metsaitti grunted and began to stir his mana, coating his spear as he thrust. But the captain did the same with his sword and shield, catching the blow as easily as any other. He knocked the spear away with a swing of his shield and stepped in with his sword. Metsaitti's eyes widened and he was forced to block with the shaft of his spear, having no time to pull the tip back into place. The captain smashed his shield into Metsaitti's side and kicked his abdomen as the karnuq bent forward.

But Metsaitti was not alone.

*"Metsaitti, duck!"*

At Belissar's mental call, Metsaitti let the captain's kick knock him to the ground. As he did, a bright yellow light passed overhead. Beero and the other wounded soldiers had hidden among the flowers as they conducted their dance, and now their lightning sting struck right over the karnuq.

The captain barely had time to bring up his shield, just managing to avoid being impaled by the ephemeral stinger. But the stinger melted away as the lightning composing it jumped to the captain's shield and into his body. He grunted and trembled as the lightning coursed through him.

Metsaitti didn't miss that chance.

He grabbed his spear and scrambled to his feet, pressing the attack. The captain's mana burst as he stopped holding back, forming thick coatings around his sword and shield. He thrust forward before Metsaitti arrived, forcing the karnuq to the side as a spear of mana extended out from his sword. He began to twist to follow up with a slash, but then a squad of sprayers attacked him from above and behind. He barely managed to block the spray, grunting as stray drops showered over him. He had no time to think about it, though, as he had to block Metsaitti's spear once again. He could see another one of those lightning spells forming in the field beyond, but Metsaitti kept him fighting. He tried another shield bash. Metsaitti dodged it this time, but the captain used the opportunity to turn and run in the direction of the magic circle . . . only for a squad of soldier bees to dive him from above. He managed to avoid being stung, but one of them collided with his helmet, knocking him off course.

And right into one of the pit traps strewn around the flower meadow that Beero and the others were using for cover.

He fell with a crash and was coated by the sticky honey trap below. The apiary soldiers, hovering above the battle in wait, began to dive even before he rose to his feet. He raised his shield up as he saw something diving down toward him, but it was only a small sliver of radish that bounced harmlessly off his shield.

At least until it hit the honey all around him.

The wounded guard stood in the tunnels with his wyvern. He turned to the augur next to him, the two of them having been left behind on the death charge. The guard shrugged.

"I guess this is it."

The augur sighed, letting the weight of his age pull his shoulders down.

"I suppose it is."

The guard drew his sword with his one good arm, preparing for the end. But just then, he saw a flash of golden light from his bag. He turned to look.

"Hm? Is that you, little—"

Before he finished, a swarm of bees exploded out of the top of his bag and filled the tunnel.

The queen heard fires roaring and humans shouting and the buzzing of wings. Before she could react, though, she found herself once again before the Queen of All Bees. But this time, the Queen of All Bees did not dance herself. In front of her flew four queens with all their hives. The four queens extended their stingers and sounded the attack, and all four hives flew forward.

The queen needed no encouragement as she returned to the world. She immediately spread as many attack pheromones as she could. Her hive burst out of the bag in a raging swarm and flew down the tunnel. She ignored the two humans behind her, in honor of the one who had carried her here, and instead flew forward.

And there, she saw her target. One of the evil humans, the one who had stood tall above the rest on top of a mighty steed while her home burned. The one who had led the others on that fateful day. She or he must be their queen!

So, this queen knew exactly what to do.

As she flew forward, her vision shifted one more. She felt, rather than saw, the four queens with the Queen of All Bees as if they were flying with her. A surge of mana pulsed out from her and filled her workers, driving them to fly faster than they ever had before.

The visions faded just as her hive burst out of the tunnel.

Ruckanos fell off his wyvern as a truly massive bee collided into him. He rolled along the ground, groaning as he tried to rise to his feet. His eyes widened as he took in the scene before him.

All around him, wyverns roared and men screamed as they drowned in a sea of black and yellow and angry buzzing. A subhuman and the bee monsters worked together to drive the captain into a pit . . . that subsequently burst into flames. Someone, somewhere, was casting magic and flinging bee stingers made of *lightning* at anyone managing to hold their ground. Bees with stingers the size and shape of lances dove from the sky like ballista bolts and pierced right through scales and armor alike.

Ruckanos found himself subconsciously backing up. He began to tremble.

What . . . was going on? What was happening? Were . . . were they *losing*?

"No . . . how is this possible? The gods . . . the gods led me here themselves! They want me to win! I'm supposed to win!"

But then he cried out as a jolt of pain shot through the back of his neck. He turned around to find a swarm of angry bees emerging from the tunnel behind him. He screamed as he vanished beneath angry, buzzing stingers.

# CHAPTER FORTY-FOUR

# FAMILY BEE-UNION

The queen landed on her hated enemy as her hive stung him. She stirred up her mana and stung him with all she had. Then she did it again. And again. And again and again and again until he stirred no longer. Most of her remaining workers were spent on the task but she had no regrets. Her purpose had been achieved.

She danced upon her fallen foe.

"That was for worker! And Hive-Builder!"

Then, and only then, did she take stock of the situation. Unfortunately, she had spent most of her hive on that one enemy, so she wasn't sure what she'd do about the rest . . .

She found herself staring at a swarm of bees. A swarm of bees beyond anything she had seen, save in her visions of the Queen of All Bees. Even the smallest of the bees were larger than her, larger than any bee she had ever seen. The largest of them were comparable in size to hive predators or even the humans.

The humans that were all lying on the ground, dead by the stingers of the giants.

And now she found herself in the territory of these bees. With only a handful of workers of her own. She began to slowly crawl backward, hoping they hadn't noticed her. Her hopes were denied when one of them began flying right toward her. She braced for the worst, but then the big bee stopped right in front of her and began to dance.

"Queen Mother?"

The queen was confused at first . . . until the bee's mana touched hers. The moment it did, she knew, and she began to fly.

"WORKER!"

"Queen Mother!"

She flew to her worker and began to crawl all over her.

"Worker! It's you! Found you! You're alive!"

"Queen Mother! How get here?"

"Queen of All Bees helped! Told come with evil humans, so did!"

Her worker then stopped.

"Right, need to sting the rest. Hang on."

Her worker began to beat her powerful wings. The queen took a moment to look around her. The rest of the evil humans were no more, slain by a hive more powerful than she could have possibly imagined.

The only humans remaining were the two waiting in the tunnels. The queen began to dance on her worker's back.

"Ah . . . that one, not evil. Helped get here, gave water."

Her worker stopped.

"Really?"

The queen confirmed. Her worker hung in the air for a moment. The other bees had begun following her but stopped as she did.

"Hang on, need to ask King."

The queen paused at the unfamiliar dance.

"King, what that?"

Her worker began to zip around in the air.

"King is best king! Leads hive of hives!"

The queen was now thoroughly confused. The dances held meaning, but none she had ever encountered. But as she slowly parsed the meaning . . . her wings began to buzz.

"King . . . is like queen? Worker's . . . queen?"

"Yes!"

Her worker . . . had been taken by a new queen? A new hive?

The queen began extending her stinger.

"Who?! Who took worker?! Show me!"

A short while later, the queen was frozen solid.

"Niobee, who is this?"

He was here. The Hive-Builder lived as well!

Her worker danced as she contemplated the sight before her.

"Queen Mother! Niobee's old queen!"

The Hive-Builder's eyes grew wide, and then he broke out into a wide grin.

"Then that means . . . you were one of my old bees?!"

The queen's mind was barely working at this stage, but she believed the Hive-Builder was asking if she had lived in one of his hives, so she danced the affirmative. The Hive-Builder then held out his hand. Mana stirred and twisted and grew so dense it became visible before turning into glistening honey pooling in his hand.

"Here, come on! I'm so glad to see you!"

Instinct took over where conscious thought failed, and she climbed onto his hand to begin drinking the honey. It was sweeter than anything she had ever tasted. She barely noticed as she was lifted into the air.

The evil humans were dead, both her worker and the Hive-Builder were back, and now she had the sweetest honey before her. For the first time since her home burned, all was right in the world.

Belissar was giddy and nearly skipping. One of his queen bees was here! He had worried they all had died when the village was set on fire, but one had survived! And not only survived but came all the way here! He needed to build her a hive right away and—

"Um, Sacred Den Master?"

He turned to find Chief Rohsuak with a complicated look on her face.

"Yes?"

She pointed toward the dirt tunnel.

"What would you like us to do about them?"

Belissar tilted his head before looking down the tunnel . . . and saw the two pairs of men and wyverns still standing there, staring at the soldier bees hovering in front of them.

"Ah . . . right, them. Um, Niobee, you said the queen told you they aren't evil, or something?"

Niobee danced the affirmative.

"Queen Mother said helped her, gave water on trip here!"

Belissar frowned. On the one hand, these were men who traveled with the tower lord's son. He guessed they would have been part of the group that burned his village, and they had just attacked his tower. His heart twisted in his chest as he thought of the bees that had fallen today.

But . . . apparently at least one of them had helped this queen arrive here. He had saved one of Belissar's bees and helped them reunite. Did that make up for everything else they had done, today and before?

Belissar furrowed his brow before sighing. Honestly, he couldn't decide right now. And he didn't really want to think about humans anymore.

But there was nothing for it, so he stepped forward. The two men's eyes widened. The younger one bowed his head.

Belissar raised an eyebrow.

"What are you doing?"

The man looked up and sighed.

"Awaiting execution, sir."

Belissar turned to the queen in his hand. He pointed toward the young man.

"Is that the one? The one who helped you?"

She danced the affirmative. Belissar nodded.

"In that case . . . I won't kill you."

The man's head shot up.

"Wait, what?"

"I said I won't kill you. You helped the bees survive."

The man's eyes widened and quivered.

"That's . . . are you sure?! I . . . I recognize you. You were one of the villagers, right? The village we burned."

Belissar froze.

"You . . . remember me?"

The man's head and shoulders fell.

"I . . . remember them all. I see you all every night. I don't deserve to live."

Belissar tilted his head. The man . . . felt bad? About burning the village? Belissar had no idea what to make of that. His chest burned and his head spun as he thought of that day . . . so he focused instead on the bee lapping up honey in his hand.

"Look, I don't want to think about that. You saved the bees, so you get to live. Let's leave it at that."

The man frowned.

"You're just going to let us go? We'll have to report to the tower lords, you know?"

Belissar froze.

"That's . . . a good point."

He furrowed his brow and grunted for a moment. Chief Rohsuak stepped forward.

"If you wish to spare him, Sacred Den Master, we could take him into custody for you?"

Belissar's face lightened.

"Ah, thanks. Let's go with that then."

Belissar turned to face the man.

"How about I imprison you, then?"

The young man hung his head.

". . . As you wish."

Chief Rohsuak nodded.

"Of course. And the other?"

Belissar turned to look at the old man. He said nothing, just hung his head low and stared at the dirt with unfocused eyes. Belissar shrugged.

". . . Might as well? Um, unless he causes any trouble."

Chief Rohsuak nodded and motioned to the karnuq. Metsaitti and the others approached the two men. The wyverns growled at them, but the young man turned and calmed them down enough to lead them out of the cave. Belissar asked the bees to assist, so the soldier bee army surrounded the two men and wyverns as the karnuq led them out.

Belissar heaved a sigh. What a day it had been. He glanced down and found a corpse at his feet. If he wasn't mistaken, it was the tower lord's son.

He gulped and found his body had begun to shake. His stomach churned and he began to sweat. Now that he had time to think, he had really done it. By his command, his bees had ended a fellow human life. Several of them.

He took a deep breath and looked up, then shook his head. Fellow humans who had not hesitated to invade his home. Fellow humans who had not hesitated to burn his old home and kill both him and all the other villagers. Belissar hadn't been close to any of the villagers, but that didn't mean he enjoyed watching everyone he had ever known put to the sword. If anyone deserved this fate, it was the men at his feet. He would not grieve their demise.

He just wished he hadn't had to lose bees to do it.

What really got his heart pounding, though, were the implications of this day. The tower lords had found him. They had arrived in force and acted as Belissar feared.

But his bees, with the help of the karnuq, had overcome them. The same group that burned his village had come to kill and destroy once more . . . and instead had met their fate. The bee army defeated them as it had an invading shade. The karnuq had stood by his side and struck down the humans that wanted to kill him.

They could do it. They *had* done it. They had beaten the tower guard. They had defeated a tower lord's own son. They had stopped him from burning their homes.

Belissar gripped his free hand into a fist. Niobee landed on his head and tapped out a dance.

"King okay?"

He slowly nodded.

"We have a lot to do now, but . . . yes. I think I will be. Let's just make sure they can't hurt the bees anymore."

"We will! King is best king! Bees will sting all intruders!"

Niobee began dancing on his head. Belissar felt a smile grow on his face, and his heart untwisted just a tad.

# CHAPTER FORTY-FIVE

# TO BEE REMEMBERED

**B**elissar wanted nothing more than to take Niobee's old queen, show her around, and then build her a nice beehouse, but there was a lot to do to clean up the battle. The most important of which was to address the casualties.

The three soldiers felled by the lead tower guard were only the beginning. With how many opponents they had faced and how coordinated the enemy was, the soldiers hadn't been able to keep up the perfect evasion and rotation they relied on. Soldiers were caught by stray swords and spears, or the wild swings of the wyverns' tails and claws. Fireballs, lightning bolts, and blades of wind cut through their formations when not blocked by the bumblebee soldiers. The bumblebee soldiers themselves had all survived but had taken some nasty hits in the process.

The Second of the Sixth led her medicinal hive as they swarmed across the field, with the Fourth of the Seventh's soldiers helping them carry trays of medicinal mana honey. The injured were assembled and fed honey as the medicinal bees injected healing compound directly into their wounds. Those who had lost wings were already being welcomed by Beero and her team.

And, those who could not be saved were gathered together for Belissar to carry to the memorial.

As for Belissar himself . . .

His face fell as worker bees curled up in his hand. To his horror, he realized that the bees that had stung the tower lord's son were mundane honeybees, likely from the old queen's hive. And that meant they were subject to the normal rules of honeybees, including the loss of their stingers when they attacked larger foes. Belissar did his very best to help them with mana and medicinal honey, but these were normal bees. They possessed no mana of their own, so providing them with more didn't help much. And the medicinal honey was not enough to handle that level of damage.

His shoulders drooped as he let out a sigh, then began to gather the fallen bees to carry with the others. There was nothing else he could do for them . . . save for this. He swore he would give their queen a wonderful home, so that their sacrifice would not have been in vain. The bees died, but the hive endured. Such was the way of things outside of his tower.

But within his tower, he had a say in how things went. And he would do his utmost to make this sort of sacrifice a relic of the past for all bees who dwelt here.

So came his next order of business. Now that the injured had been stabilized and the dead accounted for, Belissar made his way over to Chief Rohsuak and the karnuq. They were currently gathering the dead humans and wyverns and laying them out. They removed the saddles and packs from the wyverns, as well as any packs or weapons from the humans, and laid it all by the respective corpses.

"Hello . . . Sacred Den Master."

Chief Rohsuak was breathing heavily but still managed to give a salute. Belissar nodded at her and then turned to Metsaitti, who was coordinating the karnuq's efforts.

"I'm . . . guessing we have to deal with all this?"

Metsaitti nodded.

"What would you like us to do, Sacred Den Master?"

Belissar wasn't in the mood for his usual questioning. Honestly, he didn't care what he was *supposed* to do with these bodies. He just wanted them dealt with and gone.

"I guess I'll try to absorb them, unless you had plans?"

Metsaitti just gave a salute.

"As you will, Sacred Den Master."

Belissar gave a grunt and stepped forward.

*Absorb lesser wyvern corpse? Samples: 0/3*

Belissar waved a hand to confirm instead of speaking.

*Sufficient samples gathered. Lesser Wyvern Spawner is now available!*

Belissar sighed. Well, he guessed that was something. A spawner for a new monster. A non-bee monster that would likely be prohibitively expensive even if he wanted them around. Right now, he didn't really, even if he could afford it.

*Place Lesser Wyvern Spawner? Upkeep: 150 mana (300 due to Blessing of Bees)*

But he definitely couldn't, so he wasn't even going to waste time thinking about that.

And then . . . he turned to look at the human corpses and frowned. He really didn't want to do this, to be honest. But at this point, he didn't care. These men had burned his home and come to burn another. They had killed his bees. He would do anything he needed to prevent that from ever happening again.

So, he took a step forward and lifted his hand.

And then tilted his head. Nothing happened. No messages appeared, no offers to absorb the corpses. He even bent down and touched one of them, but the tower still didn't respond. Belissar shrugged.

Well, he didn't really want to absorb or summon people, to be honest. So, if the tower didn't want to either, he didn't mind.

"Okay, I got what I needed. You can do . . . whatever you want with the rest."

Metsaitti blinked.

"What of their possessions, Sacred Den Master?"

Belissar shrugged again.

"I guess let me know if you find anything especially useful and share anything that would help the bees. Otherwise, you can have it."

Metsaitti nodded.

"Thank you for your generosity, Sacred Den Master. And . . . what of the bodies? The ones that resemble . . . us."

Belissar sighed.

"How do you normally get rid of bodies? Of . . . enemies, I guess."

Metsaitti's expression softened. He stepped forward and placed a hand on Belissar's shoulder. Belissar looked up at the tall karnuq man, the weight of the hand heavy and warm on his shoulder.

"We did not always have the luxury to decide. But when we did . . . we burned them as we would any other. We always felt that the flames of the God of Fire were preferable to the Hunger's corruption."

Chief Rohsuak stepped forward at that point.

"If I may . . . our rites were developed in our time serving a sacred den of fire. Perhaps it would be best if you came up with something related to the God of Bees?"

Belissar frowned.

". . . I'm not sure what dead bodies have to do with bees, though?"

Chief Rohsuak thought for a second before turning to look down the field, in the direction of the bee barracks.

"Why not bury them beneath the ground, to nourish the flowers?"

Belissar furrowed his brow . . . but then his face loosened. Not only was burial the norm back home, but the idea of nourishing the ground and turning all this death into new flowers to support new bees appealed to him. He nodded.

"That's a good idea. Um . . . if I remember, those flowers by the memorial like death, right? Maybe we should bury them under there."

Chief Rohsuak nodded. Metsaitti stepped back and saluted.

"As you will, Sacred Den Master."

Belissar nodded back.

"Right."

And then he walked off. Now, all that was left to do was to gather the fallen and arrange for the memorial service. Belissar's eyes moistened.

But his heart felt just a little less heavy.

The queen was sitting on her worker's back as her worker hovered around the Hive-Builder. What few of her other workers remained hovered around her, buzzing nervously at all the bees from other hives around them. The much larger bees, all of which held more mana than even her worker used to . . . though her worker had grown dramatically herself since they had been separated. The queen stuck close to her worker, for there was absolutely zero chance she could contend with even one of these mighty hives.

And she stood completely still as she watched those mighty bees, those magical giants she couldn't have imagined existed in this world, as they saluted and deferred to her worker. Her worker would dance commands and then the giants would set off to obey.

The queen was utterly confused. Why would these monstrous hives follow a single worker who lacked a queen, much less a hive? Unless her worker had joined one of their hives . . . but then why wasn't her worker working along with them?

It was confusing, but it seemed for the moment that as long as she stayed close to her worker, she would not be attacked as a robbing intruder. She turned her attention instead to the Hive-Builder. And as she watched him, she could not help but tap a dance on her worker's back.

"Worker, what Hive-Builder doing?"

"Gathering bees! Will carry to memorial!"

The queen was even more confused. None of those words made sense to her. Why would the Hive-Builder carry fallen workers? They had died in an excellent location, far away from any hives where the risk of disease and decay spreading would be minimal. So why would the Hive-Builder move them?

Her confusion only grew as the Hive-Builder carried the fallen bees, from her hive as well as the native ones, to what she recognized as one of his hives, surrounded by stone pillars. And then he put them inside?!

"Worker! What Hive-Builder doing?! Dead bees will cause disease! Should carry away from hive, not back inside!"

Her worker, however, showed no signs of concern.

"No bees live in that hive, is for dead."

That did not answer the queen's questions.

"A hive . . . without bees? For dead?"

Her worker confirmed.

"King honors bees that died for hive of hives."

The queen's dance steps grew ever more unsteady.

"Honor? What that?"

Her worker hovered in place for a moment before beginning her reply.

"King . . . loves bees. Doesn't like when bees die. Likes to thank bees when they do."

The queen . . . didn't understand. But her worker said no more, and she was too confused to figure out what else to ask. So, she simply watched from her worker's back. She watched as the bear-humans carried and buried the evil humans in the ground near the beehouse, while the King gently placed each fallen bee inside the house.

The King then bowed his head, with water running down his face.

"Thank you, for your sacrifice. Thanks to you all, we stopped the tower lords. We did not let them burn our home. I will not forget you."

The queen's mind went blank as she saw the stone pillars begin to move. The images of bees carved into their sides began to move and dance. They told her of bees that had flown into battle. They told her of entire hives that had perished stopping monsters she couldn't comprehend. Of bees who had thrown themselves into pits of fire to ensure their hives' enemies perished. Of bees stuck down by beak and lightning from birds that could wield the very elements.

And then, the most surprising of all.

The carved bee images turned to her. They began a dance of gratitude.

"Outsider queen's hive, three thousand one hundred and twenty-six worker bees. Gave their lives ensuring the enemy leader's demise."

They . . . were thanking . . . her? They counted every one of her workers who had stung the evil human queen?

The queen had no idea how to respond. And while her mind attempted to work, her worker began to dance. A slow, graceful dance, one that the queen had never seen before. All around her, the monstrous giants began to dance as well, following her worker's steps.

She didn't know what was happening. But somehow, she felt something stir within her torso as she contemplated these things. It seemed her worker and the Hive-Builder had changed greatly in their time apart.

# MEET THE HIVE OF HIVES

The Firstborn flew above the memorial, her wings beating strong and steady. This battle had been one of their most costly in absolute losses, yet the Firstborn's mind stayed calm. Nay, she held herself high, having to keep her wings in check lest they carry her higher and away from the proceedings.

Because today, they had won a victory of victories. Today, they had faced King-like beings that the Conduit named "humans," as if the King's glorious form could be expressed with a single word. But apparently he was not the only being to share that form, and the others were nothing like him. According to the Conduit, these humans were enemies. They had destroyed an entire hive of humans the King once dwelt in, burned the King's home, and scattered his hives. They mortally wounded the King himself in the process. He had only survived because the Conduit rushed to his side as the Queen of All Bees pulled her away to create this realm.

In that, they were as bad as the Hunger. Worse, even, for they had apparently caused more devastation and come closer to killing the King than even the disaster that befell the First Dynasty of the First Spawner. The power required to do such a thing to the King . . . was unfathomable. And yet, it had happened. The Firstborn saw herself as the King trembled, brought to great trepidation upon learning these humans approached his lands. He feared them more than the monstrous shades that hounded him so.

But now, the army had laid them low. More and larger enemies than they had ever faced, working together in a manner the Firstborn thought limited to her army. They held claws of cold metal and commanded the very elements through magic on par with the karnuq. They rode on beasts that dwarfed even the largest flying shades and launched fire and lightning and wind as if they had the powers of all the shades put together.

And yet, it was the King's army that emerged victorious in the end. They had triumphed over a foe that eclipsed the disaster of the First Dynasty, that had done worse to the King than any intruder he had faced since. They had brought an end to an evil that plagued the King's very heart and that drove the Conduit to wrath she could not contain.

Today was a day the queens of the flower meadow could truly be proud of. No . . . a day that the hive of hives could truly be proud of, for the flower meadow queens hadn't done it alone. The bumblebee soldiers had taken the blows her soldiers could not. The supplies from the apiary had made the army what it was today. Beero and the wounded soldiers' ceaseless efforts gave the hive of hives magical attacks of their own and defeated a foe faster than any bee.

And she could not forget the karnuq. If the Firstborn had any remaining misgivings about those outsiders, they were now truly resolved. The karnuq had stood by their side, fought their foes, and struck down the King's enemies. The blazing karnuq queen had spared entire formations of soldiers, the mighty fighting one had fought the enemy no soldier bee could, and the rest of their hunters had drawn the enemies' attention so that the bees could aim their dives in peace. The Firstborn could now include the karnuq in the hive of hives without hesitation.

The Firstborn finished her thoughts as the memorial dance came to a close. She gave one final thanks and farewell to her soldiers that had made today possible at the cost of their lives. Just then, she heard a loud clap as the King requested their attention.

For speaking of outsiders, the bee clinging to the Conduit's back had not gone unnoticed. Nor had the Firstborn failed to notice that one of the evil humans had been brought down not by her armies, but by worker bees from a hive she did not recognize. So, she watched with interest as the King called them forward . . .

The queen's mind was still processing all that had occurred when the dance came to a close. She suddenly jumped as the Hive-Builder clapped his hands and all eyes turned to him.

"Hi everyone, could I have your attention? There's someone I need to introduce."

The Hive-Builder held out one of his hands. Her worker flew over and landed on the hand, carrying her along.

"This is one of my queens from before! She's Niobee's mom, too, and she made it all the way here!"

A murmur of buzzing wings sounded throughout the field. The queen was confused one more. The Hive-Builder . . . was presenting her to his new queens? Wouldn't they just attack her as an intruding rival?

A massive queen came flying up to her, one many times her size and as large as her worker. The queen shrunk back, trying to hide within her worker's fuzz. Fortunately, the giant queen stopped before her worker. She then began to dance.

"Hello! I am First Queen of First Spawner's Second Dynasty, first of her line. Honored to meet Conduit's queen mother!"

The queen froze. This giant of a queen who could squash her with a single leg . . . was greeting her? An intruding rival queen? Why would she do that? And who or what was a Conduit?

But before she could voice any of her questions, a second giant flew in, no smaller than the first.

"Hello, I am First Queen of Fifth Spawner's First Dynasty, first of her line. Honored to meet Conduit's queen mother. Hive of hives welcomes."

And then another.

"Hello! Am Fourth Queen of Seventh Spawner's First Dynasty! Is nice to meet you!"

One by one, more giants came to dance before her, giving her greetings she didn't understand instead of impaling her with their massive stingers. Eventually she couldn't help but tap a dance out with a single leg, hoping no one but her worker would notice.

"Worker, what's going on? What are rival queens saying? Why aren't stinging?"

Her worker somehow responded while staying still, her mana shifting about and touching the queen's own in ways reminiscent of a dance. Again she had no idea what was happening, but she could somehow understand her worker's intent.

"Is hive of hives! Instead of fighting, all of King's queens work together! Build one big hive made of many! Queen Mother is Niobee's queen mother and King introduced, so all queens will welcome!"

"I-I see, um, who is Niobee?"

"Niobee is Niobee's name! King gave!"

"N-Name? What that?"

"What King calls!"

Somehow, each answer the queen received only raised more and more questions.

The First of the Fifth's mind went blank as she comprehended the King's words.

The Conduit's . . . queen mother?

She was vaguely aware the Conduit had existed before the King's realm did, in a time before she was the Conduit and before the King was the King. A time where the King was but one of many in a hive of humans, and the least of them. It was a fantastical tale she had trouble believing. How could the King be anything but king? With all his wisdom and grace and power and love? How could anyone treat him as anything but king? The Conduit as well! The Conduit was an existence beyond mere bees. She was connected to the tower and the King and the Queen of All Bees in ways the First of the Fifth couldn't fathom. The rival she couldn't overcome back when she was jealous and scheming, a power she still couldn't comprehend even after acknowledging her position. Sure, the Conduit could *claim* she was a normal bee before, a mere worker even, but the First of the Fifth just couldn't see how that was possible.

And yet, here, today, was conclusive proof of these things. An army of humans had assaulted their home as the Conduit said they had before, requiring sacrifice from the bee army and the intervention of the karnuq to stop. And now a bee stood before them that they were told was the Conduit's queen mother. A tiny runt of a queen with scarcely a hint of mana, who was currently trying to hide from their gaze. The First of the Fifth might even believe it if someone told her this wasn't a monster bee, much less an existence that gave birth to the Conduit!

And yet, the King had stated just that, so it must be true. The Conduit truly was born from . . . a mundane honeybee, of all things. And though the queen before them barely had any mana at all, if the First of the Fifth focused really, *really* hard, she found bits and traces. Bits and traces that matched the Conduit's signature. Not exactly, for the Conduit's mana was fundamentally tied to that of the King's realm itself, but close enough to clearly establish a familial connection.

The First of the Fifth was paralyzed as she considered the implications of all these things . . . until a shadow passed in front of her eyes. The Firstborn moved to greet the new queen that the King himself had introduced to them. With that, the First of the Fifth shook herself out of her haze and flew forward as well, dancing her greeting.

She would decide how she felt about the Conduit's queen mother showing up as a mere honeybee later. For now, the King was introducing a queen he claimed into the hive of hives. It was clear that the King and the Conduit both cared for this queen, and so the First of the Fifth would care for her as well. Such was the way of the King's hive of hives.

As the rest of the queens greeted the Conduit's queen mother one by one, she resolved to take care of this queen and show her the respect and love she deserved.

She just had to figure out how to do so. How exactly should she approach this queen? As the Conduit's queen mother, an existence that would naturally deserve immense respect and deference? As a small queen barely beyond a normal honeybee, who was clearly intimidated by the monster bees all around her? Should she offer her assistance beyond what she would offer of any other queen, or would that be an insult to one who had raised a bee like the Conduit?

But as the First of the Fifth pondered, another queen shot ahead of her with no hesitation at all.

"Wow, you're from the Beyond?! Conduit's queen mother?! Amazing, incredible! Can tell me about the Beyond?! What was Conduit and King like then?! How got here, where came from?! Where Conduit and King came from?!"

Ah, maybe she should start by addressing the Fourth of the Seventh.

# A BEE-UTIFUL DAY IN THE NEIGHBORHOOD?

**E**ventually, the memorial and subsequent celebrations came to a close. Belissar couldn't help but feel a bit better as he watched the bees dance around and slurp up honey. Apparently, they were happier to have won the battle than they were grieved to have lost some of their own. Belissar couldn't remain sad himself in the face of that, if for no other reason than that he didn't want to ruin their celebrations.

Afterward, there was much to do and think about, but Belissar felt drained, so he decided to call it a day and head to bed. He woke up the next morning to find Niobee waiting for him as usual . . . with her queen still clinging to her back. She began her usual salute dance as she saw him.

"Good morning, Niobee. Did your queen stay with you last night?"

"Yes!"

Belissar frowned. He may have been drained by the events of yesterday, but there was no excuse to have left a queen without a place to stay. He needed to rectify that immediately.

He was about to ask Niobee to speak with the queen for him when he paused. He tilted his head and then his eyes widened as he realized . . . he had already spoken to the queen and she had *responded*. He focused more closely on her and found that she now had a bit of mana flowing through her.

It seemed she was not just a normal honeybee anymore. In any case, that was convenient, since it meant he could speak with her directly.

"Hi there, hope you slept well. Sorry I didn't prepare any place for you to stay. I'll show you around and build you a home . . . um, if you want to stay here with us, that is."

The queen stirred on Niobee's back and looked up at him for a moment. She then slowly began to dance.

"Hive-Builder will . . . build new hive? For me?"

Belissar saw a message appear before his eyes but ignored it to focus on the queen. He gave her a warm smile.

"Of course!"

The queen paused for a moment before her wings buzzed and she took off, zipping around in an aerial dance.

"Yes! Please! Will make Hive-Builder lots of honey!"

Belissar laughed and smiled as the queen zipped around him, and then finally took a glance at the messages trying to get his attention.

His jaw dropped once he saw what it was.

*Accept offer of allegiance?*
*New mission received: Accept the Oracle of Bees into your dungeon.*
*You have gained 1,273 sworn defenders.*
*Unnamed bee, the Oracle of Bees, has become your sworn defender,*
*with her hive of 1,272 worker bees!*
*Mission: Accept The Oracle of Bees into your dungeon completed!*
*Reward: One Bee-type Perk Choice*

"Ora . . . cle?"

Belissar stared at the bee zipping around him, his eyes as wide as they could go. *Oracle.* For once, that was a term he knew. Mrs. Imkomos, the old beekeeper, had told them all about them, for it had been her lifelong dream to speak with one.

And that was because oracles could hear directly from the gods. As such, they were afforded a place of great honor by the tower lords . . . and protection. Such people rarely, if ever, interacted with the peasantry, though, so Mrs. Imkomos's dream remained just that to the day of her death. At this point, Belissar wondered if that was the choice of the oracles themselves or if the tower lords had secluded them away.

But now . . . an oracle was here. One of his old bees, even, who herself was descended from the hives Mrs. Imkomos had raised before him. So, not only was he speaking to an oracle now, but he and Mrs. Imkomos had even helped raise one. His eyes moistened but a smile grew on his face.

"I guess I can fulfill your dream now, at least . . ."

He wiped his eyes and took a deep breath.

"So, um, I hear you're an oracle?"

The queen paused her dance and flew before him.

"Oracle? What that?"

Belissar blinked.

"Oh . . . um . . . have you spoken to any gods? The God of Bees in particular."

The queen picked up speed.

"Yes! Queen of All Bees told not to sting evil humans! Told to follow and come here, then sting!"

Belissar blinked several times at that news . . . and then broke out into a massive smile as his heart began to pound in his chest. The God of Bees had appointed an oracle and sent down visions from above so that one of his old queens could reunite with him? He didn't think he could feel even more grateful to her than he already did, but he had just been proven wrong.

"I'm glad you did . . . well, um . . ."

Belissar thought for a moment about what he should do with this news before shrugging. Even Mrs. Imkomos didn't know exactly what oracles did or how the tower lords treated them. Belissar therefore had no idea what, if anything, he should do differently now that he knew the queen was the Oracle of Bees.

So, he decided to treat her first as a bee.

". . . Shall I show you around the tower? You can pick a spot that looks nice to you and I'll build you a home."

"Yes! Please! Hive-Builder is best hive builder!"

Belissar chuckled at that. It seemed the Oracle of Bees was, in fact, a bee first and foremost after all.

The queen zipped around as her worker and the Hive-Builder led her out of the Hive-Builder's nest. The Hive-Builder was not only keeping her, he was going to build a hive for her again! She had not thought he would do so, not after seeing all the mighty and giant queens he had replaced her and her former rivals with. How could she possibly compete with magical giants? How could her hive produce honey on par with one that could sustain bees of that size? How could she drive them from any flower they wished to monopolize? How could she stop bees larger than any hornet from robbing her hive?

Apparently, though, the Hive-Builder did not mind that she was tiny and weak. He was giving her a hive all the same. Once again, he would check her hive and help remove the parasites and the sick. Once again, he'd line her hive with warm furs to keep out the winter chill. Once again, he'd provide them with extra provisions to ensure they could last until spring.

And he was even going to let her decide where the hive should go!

"This is the apiary! The bees here mostly focus on making honey, so there are plenty of flowers!"

The queen spun about, taking in the room before her. As the Hive-Builder said, flowers spread out across the room, including ones she had never seen before. There were entire patches of flowers that were glowing with a soft blue light. The queen's eyes locked onto them; she felt them drawing her in. She subconsciously began drifting toward them . . .

And then she heard the buzzing.

She snapped out of her haze to see one of the giant queens from yesterday fly toward the flower. She quickly retreated to her worker's back, telling what few workers still accompanied her to stand down and avoid confrontation.

The giant queen stopped midair, though, and began saluting to the Hive-Builder.

"You remember the First of the Fifth, right? She's pretty much in charge of the apiary, so she'll help you if we set up here!"

The First of the Fifth danced in confirmation while the queen shrank as much as she could. She looked beyond the First of the Fifth to see gigantic structures in the distance. She would have thought they were human hives, if not for the clouds of bees flying in and out of them, absolutely covering the glowing flowers that had drawn her in.

This room . . . appeared to be occupied.

The Hive-Builder led her to another room. A field of flowers even larger than the apiary spread out before her. There were a handful of beehouses in sight, but no bees came and went from them.

"This is the bumblebee flower meadow. They actually prefer ground nesting, so there are a couple of empty beehouses you could use if you want."

The queen spread her wings and was about to go fly and inspect one when a shadow passed overhead. She began buzzing as something slammed into the Hive-Builder. She nearly activated her attack pheromones but her worker's mana calmed her down.

"Is fine! Look!"

The queen watched with horror as several massive bees crawled all over the Hive-Builder. She thought he was under attack . . . but on closer look she saw the bees were grooming him instead. The Hive-Builder responded by grooming the bees, both parties rubbing their legs all over each other's hair.

"I'm happy to see you all too! This is Niobee's old queen! We're showing her around."

The queen dropped down as flat as she could on her worker's back as one of the giants flew over. She remained as still as she could as an antenna larger than her entire body began to sweep over her.

This room, too, was completely occupied.

The queen looked up at the rows upon rows of flowering trees covering the sky above her . . . but she was not deceived. She knew, at this point, that where there were flowers, there were bees. The only question was what kind of bees she would find here.

"This is where the Fourth of the Seventh lives!"

The queen froze and began to tremble as she remembered the giant queen that had accosted her last night, heedless to her terror as she danced overhead. She dove into her worker's hair and tried to hide as best she could.

"King! And new queen!"

But she was too late.

This room was beyond occupied.

The queen could scarcely move as she clung to her worker's back with all her might. She had seen an army of bees no hornet could contend with. She had seen a wasteland of ash and fire . . . where a magical queen was happily building a hive. She saw tunnels where no light shone, and yet, there too another queen had already claimed territory.

She was beginning to think she'd have no choice but to beg one of the magical queens to take mercy upon her. Clearly, there was no room for a tiny, weak queen like herself to claim a territory of her own.

"Well, that's everything. Any place you liked?"

The queen didn't know how to respond. There were plenty of places she liked, but none that had not been claimed.

"King, not everything? More rooms?"

The Hive-Builder rubbed his chin at her worker's question.

"Well, there's the fairy grove, but we're still checking if it's safe. I guess there's also the karnuq rooms? Um, would you like to see the room the karnuq live?"

The queen just managed to move her legs enough to eke out a question.

"Queen Mother asks what karnuq are! Karnuq are bear humans!"

The queen took a moment to ponder. The bear humans? They frightened her too . . . but they also appeared deferential to the Hive-Builder. So, if she tried to think of them as just a type of human, who were treating the Hive-Builder like their queen, then they didn't seem that bad. She slowly danced her reply, moving her whole body so the Hive-Builder could see.

"Can check."

The Hive-Builder nodded and led her to another room. The queen glanced every which way as the Hive-Builder showed her about. She saw an occasional worker, but only a few foragers and no queens. So, a place the monster hives were scouting, but hadn't claimed just yet?

"I was just adding beehouses here, so I guess you could move into this one if you'd like."

The queen looked at the hive before her, then slowly danced a question.

"No other bees here?"

The Hive-Builder shook his head.

"We just decided to move bees here recently, so none just yet."

The queen immediately beat her wings and soared into the air, landing on the empty hive.

"Here! Will move here! No other queens moving here, right?!"

The Hive-Builder crossed his arms.

"Well, no, not yet. I guess that would work, if you like it here?"

The queen danced the confirmation with all her might.

"Yes! Here!"

The Hive-Builder nodded.

"Got it. Go ahead and check it out, I'll let the karnuq know you're moving in here. Um, try not to sting them, okay?"

The queen saluted with all her might and then dove into the empty hive, taking shelter within its thick and mighty walls.

Safe! She was finally safe! A place she could grow her hive where they wouldn't be immediately squashed by magical giants! She guessed there were the bear humans living nearby, but that was fine, she had lived near humans her entire life, after all. Much better them than rival queens who could crush her at will.

It was only later that she noticed that the beehouse, despite being empty, was already full of honey. As well as the massive currents of mana flowing through its walls . . .

# CHAPTER FORTY-SIX

# GATHER YOUR BEE-SOLVE

Chief Rohsuak's eyes went wider than Belissar had ever seen them. Her jaw even dropped.

"The Oracle of Bees? And you said she's moving into the hive in our village?"

Belissar couldn't hold back a happy chuckle.

"I know, I can barely believe it either. But, well, it makes sense the God of Bees' oracle is a bee, right?"

Chief Rohsuak blinked and then smiled.

"Ah, I guess that is true. In any case, we are truly honored to have her dwell here. I will ensure she is treated with the respect and hospitality she deserves as the representative of our patron."

Belissar returned her smile.

"Thanks. Um, you may want to be careful around her hive for now. She's clearly not just a normal bee anymore, but her workers still seem normal, so they might try to sting you if provoked. You might need to hold off on gathering honey from that beehouse for now."

Chief Rohsuak saluted.

"Understood, I'll let the clan know to give her some space."

Belissar nodded.

"Thank you, sorry for suddenly deciding this without asking."

Chief Rohsuak shook her head.

"It is your right as sacred den master. And we are honored that you would trust us with an oracle's safety."

Belissar smiled for a moment before his face turned grim.

"And that brings us to the other thing. Could you come and meet with me and the queens? Maybe bring Metsaitti or whoever else you think might help."

Chief Rohsuak agreed and then tilted her head.

"Of course . . . but may I ask what the meeting is for? That will inform who I would bring."

Belissar jumped a bit.

"Oh, right."

And then he looked out into the distance, narrowing his eyes.

"The tower lords have found us. We beat back one attack . . . but there could be more in the future. I wanted to discuss what we should do to prepare in case they come again."

Chief Rohsuak narrowed her eyes.

"Understood. I was hoping to speak with you on that as well. We will be there, Sacred Den Master."

Belissar acknowledged her with a nod, then turned to leave. Niobee had already gone off to gather the queens. He took a deep breath before walking toward the nearest shortcut.

Belissar stood by the orchard's Shrine of Bees, watching as queens from all across the tower flew in from the shortcuts. Even Niobee's queen mother was here, clinging to Niobee's back as she seemed to enjoy doing. Chief Rohsuak arrived with Metsaitti and several other karnuq, including Juosiutik. Bees and karnuq both gathered around and saluted to Belissar. He took a deep breath.

"Thank you for coming, everyone. Sorry to interrupt your work, but I'd like to take a break from the purifications today, so let's have the meeting now."

He looked over his bees, smiling as his gaze fell on the Second First of the First and the other battle meadow queens.

"First of all, thank you all for fighting yesterday. Thanks to you, we defeated a tower lord, or his son at the least. I didn't think that was possible, but thanks to you all, we did it."

The Second First of the First and the battle meadow queens began rapid salute dances. The karnuq saluted as well as Belissar thanked them in turn. He then took a deep breath, furrowing his brow.

"However . . . I don't think it's over. The tower lords . . ."

He looked over at the karnuq, his face twisting as he realized what he was about to say. He gulped, but it had to be said. His tower defenders needed to know what was coming.

". . . They think of beastkin as subhumans cursed by the gods. They also think that peasants like myself defile towers with our mere presence. So, I don't think they're just going to leave us alone now that they know where we are. Now that we killed one of their sons."

Some of the karnuq scowled, while the bees began to buzz their wings. Metsaitti narrowed his eyes and gripped his spear. Chief Rohsuak took a deep breath before replying.

"Well, I understand why you were worried about finding people like yourself, then. And you are indeed correct that we should prepare for the worst. Did you have something in mind, Sacred Den Master?"

Belissar began to pace about.

"We'll keep up with the usual methods. More flowers, more bees, and more purifications. We should definitely expand whenever possible. We might need to increase the pace of that . . ."

Belissar frowned as the battle meadow queens saluted. He knew that, ultimately, he was the one holding back the pace. His mana had outpaced the expansion purifications, so he could begin another right away if he wished. The reason he didn't was his desire to ensure they were completely, fully prepared, so that they could keep bee casualties to the absolute minimum.

But if they were willing to accept a few casualties here and there, they could conduct expansions earlier than he normally did. And he knew that the queens and the soldiers themselves were absolutely willing to accept those casualties. He was the only one who wasn't.

It was something he needed to think about, and sooner rather than later now that he knew the tower lords could reach him.

However, he had another idea in mind for right now. He turned to face the karnuq.

"This time I'm also thinking that we should try to work on your blessings. Back when I was just a peasant, I heard stories about the tower guard . . . the personal soldiers of the tower lords. They were said to be invincible. Bandits, witches, or even incursions, it didn't matter. When the tower guard showed up, every situation was handled."

He sighed and shook his head.

"Well, I also know that the tower lords lied about the gods hating peasants and beastkin, so I wasn't sure how much of those stories were true. But after seeing what that captain did, how strong he was . . . I'm worried the tower guard parts might be true after all. So . . . I think we need some tower guards of our own."

Chief Rohsuak nodded along.

"I agree. Our hunters and champions have been static for far too long."

She turned to face the other karnuq.

"The sacred den master has been gracious enough to invite us into his home, with full access to the shrines of the gods. It is high time that we begin to grow once more."

She gave a pointed look to Metsaitti.

"And I don't just mean the young and inexperienced."

He gave a sheepish smile as she turned back to Belissar.

"With that in mind, may I make two requests, Sacred Den Master?"

Belissar agreed right away.

"What do you need?"

Chief Rohsuak held up her hand and created a small wisp of fire that danced around her fingers.

"Would you be willing to share some of the Third of the Sixth's Fire-attribute mana honey with us? I believe that with her help and the God of Fire's presence in your sacred den, it would be possible to raise new champions of fire among our clan."

She made a wry grin.

"Someone to carry the torch whose bones don't ache like mine."

Belissar turned to the Third of the Sixth.

"What do you think . . . oh, she's already dancing yes. You sure you have enough reserves? You need to keep growing, you know."

But the Third of the Sixth just kept up her rapid salute dance. Belissar chuckled.

"We recently evolved a new burning queen as well, so that should be fine. Um . . . you aren't all going to go with fire, right?"

Chief Rohsuak smiled and shook her head.

"No, we will be sure to give the God of Bees her due as well. And that is my second request."

Her face turned serious.

"I would like for our hunters to begin training with your bees, and perhaps learn from them. Additionally, I would like to request that your bees allow us to participate more directly in your purifications. At least to fight along their side, and maybe even to handle the shades on our own from time to time. I believe that the God of Bees will approve of our hunters learning to fight like your bees and directly defending her sacred den."

Belissar turned to the Second First of the First.

"What do you say? Would you be willing to fight with the karnuq, and maybe let them fight on their own some time?"

The Second First of the First gave an immediate salute.

"Brave warriors, helped defend hive of hives. *Part* of hive of hives. Honored to fight with."

Chief Rohsuak glanced at Metsaitti. The hunter blinked, then gave a salute of his own.

"I am honored you think of us so. We would also be honored to train and fight at your side."

Belissar nodded in approval as the bees and karnuq saluted each other.

"Thank you, we'll appreciate the help with the purifications as well. Next, there's something we can do right now to strengthen the tower."

Belissar began to grin as all eyes turned to him.

"The God of Bees gave us a reward. We have another perk to decide."

# CHAPTER FORTY-SEVEN

# DESERVED BEE-INFORCEMENT

**W**ithout delay, Belissar opened the reward.

*Please select a perk:*
*- Bee-Type Speed Boost (Small) (Rarity: Uncommon)*
*- Bee Breeder (Rarity: Uncommon)*
*- Swarming Soldiers (Rarity: Uncommon)*

His eyes widened. All uncommons this time? That was a god's reward, no doubt. After just a second staring at the list without a single common, Belissar started to read out the descriptions.

*Bee-Type Speed Boost (Small)*
*- All Bee-type monsters receive a small boost to speed.*
*- May affect Bee-type rooms and features where relevant.*

"Huh."

Belissar scratched his chin. He hadn't realized that the stat boost perks also affected rooms and features. Though, he wasn't precisely sure how that worked. Would moving faster apply to beehouses or the apiary?

He shrugged. Even putting that factor aside, making all of his bees a bit faster was powerful enough in and of itself. The battle meadow queens certainly agreed, given that they were all fidgeting about. The Fourth of the Seventh had no such hesitation and was zipping around, putting a smile on Belissar's face.

He moved on to the next perk.

*Bee Breeder*
*- Small increase to the rate monster bee queens produce offspring.*

Now this was new. A repeat offering . . . of a perk he had already taken. Well, he knew that was the case for the monster-boosting perks, so he supposed there was no reason why it wouldn't apply to other perks too.

This one, in particular, was simple but powerful. Belissar would never say no to more bees; that would aid in every aspect of his tower. More workers to forage and scout, more soldiers to fight, more gardeners to help his flowers bloom, and more communers to keep track of them all. But, most importantly and unlike the first time he saw this perk, Belissar now knew that the monster bee queens could raise new queens and new hives. A small increase in the number of bees born could become massive when it meant multiplying the number of hives.

Though, the perk did mention monster bee queens specially. Would it also apply to the bumblebee queens? The perk wouldn't reach as far as the speed boost if not, though it was still worth considering. The First of the Fifth appeared to be doing just that as she began cleaning her antennas over and over. The battle meadow queens resumed their fidgeting as well. He guessed they might be torn between the two perks.

Belissar didn't think that the last perk was going to help with that.

*Swarming Soldiers*
*- Monster bee soldiers gain a small boost to speed and strength and a minor boost to all other stats when ten or more gather together. Effects increase with numbers up to a current maximum of thirty.*
*- Slight boost to monster bee soldier coordination.*
*- Applies to soldier variations but not to soldier evolutions.*

All the battle meadow queens froze, and then flew closer as Belissar read the description. He made an amused smile as each word drew them in more and more. He guessed he knew which one they preferred.

Indeed, the perk was powerful. It boosted all of a soldier bee's stats with the biggest boost to their speed and strength, helping them hit hard and fast. And the current size of the soldier bee army was such that it would always remain active, so for Belissar's soldiers it was a straight increase to their power.

It was also useful in that it made soldiers, the most common defenders of Belissar's tower, stronger and more capable. Lancers were powerful but few in number. Sprayers introduced a new element to the army but also couldn't fight well up close. At the end of the day, it was up to the soldiers to hold the line. Boosting their power would help the majority of the army stay relevant against whatever new kinds of shades the Hunger threw at them . . . or whatever new kinds of enemies arrived to assault them.

Additionally, the perk mentioned variations and evolutions. Belissar rubbed his chin at that. If he had to guess . . . it probably wouldn't affect sprayers or lancers, then? What exactly would count as a variation? Did that mean it could affect the bumblebee soldiers, maybe?

If it did, the big bumblebee soldiers getting a boost to their strength could be a sight to see. Though, that would depend on if the perk affected them at all—and if it counted them along with the monster bee soldiers to get to the ten-soldier minimum. There weren't ten bumblebee soldiers yet, as they needed significantly more honey than their smaller counterparts.

So, that was the choice. Faster bees, more bees, or boost soldiers specifically in every way. Before deciding, Belissar turned to his bees and the karnuq.

"What do you think?"

The battle meadow queens conferred and saluted to one another, then the Second First of the First flew forward.

"Think . . . soldier one best. Hive of hives is strongest when working together, good to make soldiers stronger when together."

The First of the Fifth paused and quickly began dancing to the apiary queens. A moment later, she made her dance to Belissar.

"Lots of jobs to do now, lots of flowers to gather. More bees would help, if King decides!"

Meanwhile, the Fourth of the Seventh was still zipping around.

"Any! All of them! Amazing, incredible!"

Belissar chuckled as he turned to the karnuq. Most of them were staring blankly or furrowing their brows. Chief Rohsuak made a wry smile and shrugged while Metsaitti rubbed his chin. He slowly lifted his head to make eye contact with Belissar.

"All of them have their use, but . . . Sacred Den Master, from what I have seen, you prefer to minimize casualties, correct?"

Belissar nodded.

"Yes, that's right."

Metsaitti crossed his arms as he nodded.

"In that case, it may be wiser to strengthen your army than to expand it. Though, I speak only as a warrior, so I cannot tell you which will make your sacred den strongest overall."

Belissar nodded and hummed to himself. Metsaitti had a point. A general speed boost would make it easier for his bees to dodge attacks. A boost to every stat for soldiers would correspondingly help in every way including dodging, surviving hits, and defeating the enemy. The bee breeder perk, on the other hand, would give him more bees, but it wouldn't make the individual bees any more resilient. It could be useful for overwhelming the enemy and absorbing casualties . . . but only if Belissar was willing to take casualties in the first place. More powerful bees also meant he could tackle more purifications and expansions, acquiring more floors and choices in the process.

Though, Metsaitti did say he was thinking as a warrior. If Belissar tried not to think like a warrior . . . that would be thinking more like the First of the Fifth than the battle meadow queens? More bees not only meant more soldiers, but more workers and gardeners as well. More workers and gardeners would mean more honey. More honey would in turn mean even more bees, and not just more soldiers. More honey could allow the army to evolve more sprayers and lancers or let the bumblebee queens raise more of their larger soldiers.

The bee breeder perk would also help regarding new bees and flowers. More workers and gardeners would boost cross-pollination, meaning more flowers, more new kinds of flowers, and faster-spreading flowers. And bee breeder would directly help new queens set up their hives, which would be beneficial when new types of bees arose. For example, the tower guard had marched right through the dirt tunnels unopposed because the regular soldier bee army couldn't fight there. If, however, the digging queen had expanded her hives and accumulated a decent batch of soldiers, Belissar could have attacked the tower guard while the wyverns were unable to fly at all. Or if the burning queen had an army of her own, then he could have considered fighting in the lava field and letting the mini-volcano do some of the work for the bees.

Belissar frowned. This time, he wanted all the options, and so he was having a hard time deciding. Did he want to make the bee army stronger directly? Or did he want to focus on aspects of his tower besides fighting? And how should he pick when one would help the other as well?

He felt Niobee land on his head.

"King okay?"

Belissar glanced up at her and smiled. Indeed, there was one bee who hadn't spoken yet.

"What do you think, Niobee?"

"Whatever King chooses!"

He chuckled at that.

"And if you were choosing?"

Niobee paused and her dancing slowed.

"If . . . Niobee chose?"

Belissar nodded.

"Please, I'd like to know what you think."

Niobee fell still. Then, slowly, she started to tap out unsteady steps.

"If Niobee chose . . . Niobee wants stronger bees. Need to sting enemies without losing bees. Won't let anyone hurt King again."

Belissar's mouth curled up a bit. Niobee . . . had a bit of an aggressive streak, didn't she? He reached up and brushed her back.

"And I won't let anyone hurt the bees."

Belissar made his choice.

*Swarming Soldiers selected.*

He decided that the brave soldier bees deserved the boost. Time after time they risked and gave their lives to protect him and all the other bees behind them. He would not forget them or all that they had done, even if lancers could pierce their foes, sprayers could attack at a distance, or the karnuq could hold the line in their place. He would reward them for their sacrifice, and in the process make them stronger and more capable of handling whatever else came their way.

He closed his eyes and turned his tower sight to all the soldier bees in the dungeon. The battle meadow soldier bee army training for its next battle. The construction squad helping the karnuq build a roof. The apiary soldiers standing guard by the room to the core. Beero and the others demonstrating their dance to their new members.

He stirred up his mana and sent it toward every last one of them.

*"Thank you, for protecting our home."*

Every single soldier bee in the tower paused . . . and then burst out into rapid salute dances.

# CHAPTER FORTY-EIGHT

# WOE BEE TO THE VANQUISHED

Belissar just watched the soldiers throughout the tower with his tower sight, smiling as he did. He didn't know if he had made the best choice, but it certainly felt like the right one. He returned his sight to normal.

"Okay . . . I think that's all for now. Let's get back to work."

Most of the queens saluted, but then the First of the Fifth crawled forward.

"King . . . First of Eighth has question. Can ask?"

Belissar broke out into a wide smile as he nodded.

"Of course. You all can always ask me anything!"

The First of the Fifth did a quick "King is best king!" dance before catching herself and dancing toward another queen, one with purple stripes. The apiary's maddening queen, the First of the Eighth apparently, flew forward and performed a salute dance, then launched into her question.

"King . . . workers found human alive in pit when filling honey trap. What should do? Should sting?"

Belissar froze.

"What?"

He zoomed in with his tower sight to the dirt tunnels and quickly found the problem. There, in the final pit trap in the dirt tunnels' exit corridor, was one of the tower guards, coated in maddening honey with the remnants of a dirt bridge scattered around him. Belissar frowned as he rubbed his chin. There had been a lot going on in the fight, but he vaguely recalled someone falling into a pit trap during the tower guards' initial charge?

Well, he guessed no one else recalled either, since the bees didn't set it on fire. He was about to give the command on reflex, but the words caught in his throat.

The man was groaning. He appeared to be trying to speak, but his face wasn't moving. The rest of his body stayed still, save for the occasional twitch of a finger. His eyes were somewhat unfocused but began to quiver anytime a bee approached.

Belissar crossed his arms. This man, while one of the tower guards, was no longer a threat. He had most likely been, and still was, paralyzed from being drenched in maddening honey. He couldn't even move.

He was one of the tower guards, one of the men who burned Belissar's home and slaughtered his village. He had come along with the tower lord's son to attack Belissar's new home, resulting in the deaths of many bees. And yet . . . now that he was lying completely helpless at the bottom of a pit, Belissar hesitated to give the order to just end the man's life. Not when he had an alternative method of dealing with him.

He heaved a sigh and turned to Chief Rohsuak.

". . . Would you be able to handle a third prisoner?"

Chief Rohsuak saluted.

"Of course, Sacred Den Master."

Belissar nodded at her.

"Thanks."

And then he turned back to the bees.

"Let's get him out of the pit, then, and take him to the karnuq. Oh, um, don't kill him, unless he starts moving and attacks or something."

The bees saluted.

"Sacred Den Master, I do have a question on that topic."

Belissar turned to Chief Rohsuak and nodded for her to continue.

"Do you have any plans regarding these prisoners? In particular, we are not able to speak with them, so we may need your assistance depending on what you wish to do with them."

Belissar tilted his head.

"You . . . can't speak with them? Why? Are they refusing to talk?"

Chief Rohsuak shook her head.

"No, we simply do not understand each other's language."

Belissar furrowed his brow.

"But . . . then how are you speaking with me? I speak the same language as them."

Chief Rohsuak made a light smile as she shook her head.

"That is because you are a sacred den master. As far as I am aware, sacred den masters can speak with anything capable of communicating."

Belissar nodded.

"Oh, that makes sense. Guess it's just another tower power."

Chief Rohsuak smiled.

"Indeed."

Then Belissar crossed his arms once more. What should he do with the prisoners? He honestly had no idea. What did one do with prisoners anyway? He had obviously never had a prisoner of his own. The village hadn't had any either, as far as he was aware. Anyone who did something wrong would normally have to pay a fine to the injured party and the village chief. If they did something exceptionally bad, they'd be exiled or handed over to the tower guard. In either case, they were never heard from again, so Belissar had no idea what became of them.

And even if he had, he did not want to follow the tower lords' example if he could manage it.

"Hm . . . to be honest, I can't really think of anything right now. What do your people do with prisoners?"

Chief Rohsuak shrugged.

"During our sojourn, we didn't take prisoners."

Belissar rubbed his chin.

"I see. In that case, I guess just keep them from causing trouble? Ah, and keep them alive. As for the language thing . . . well, I guess I should talk to them now. I do have some questions regarding the tower lords. Um, if there's anything you need to say to or ask them, I can say that as well while I'm there?"

Chief Rohsuak nodded with a salute.

"Thank you, Sacred Den Master. That should suffice for now."

He let out another sigh.

"Well, I guess we better get to it."

Belissar stood by the pit in the dirt tunnels and relit the beeswax candles, though not the ones made with wax from the maddening bees. He watched as two bumblebee soldiers descended into the pit. Numerous maddening workers crawled over the man, lapping up the maddening honey still stuck to him. The man's eyes were shaking and he was whimpering. The whimpering only grew as the giant bumblebees descended upon him, but he still couldn't move or do anything, so they landed and wrapped their legs around him without issue.

As one, the two bumblebee soldiers lifted the man out of the pit. Belissar smiled and nodded at them.

"Great work, everyone. Let's take him over."

The worker bees saluted. The bumblebees couldn't zip around while holding the man, but they did buzz their wings and wiggle their antennas.

Belissar led the group to the karnuq settlement. Once there, the karnuq dressed up Belissar in the same getup he had worn to meet with the sigmaka, and then Metsaitti directed him to the side of the room. There, a ring of karnuq hunters stood at guard while the karnuq villagers were assembling a large stone structure. The two wyverns were off to the side with ropes lashed all around them while soldier bees buzzed overhead.

Metsaitti led Belissar to a smaller, more normal-sized stone structure to the side of the one under construction. Well, it was only small in comparison. It was still karnuq-sized, so it was large by Belissar's standards. Two karnuq hunters stood at the front of the building along with Juosiutik, another karnuq woman Belissar didn't recognize, and the Second of the Sixth with a group of medicinal workers. The hunters opened up the door as Metsaitti approached. Metsaitti stepped in, then Belissar followed him with the bumblebee pair and his usual soldier bee guards, and then Juosiutik, the karnuq woman, and the Second of the Sixth came last. The room was empty save for three bedrolls, and the other two humans. The bumblebees gently placed the man down on one of the bedrolls, then flew off so Juosiutik, the woman, and the Second of the Sixth could have a look.

Belissar rubbed the two bumblebee soldiers' fuzz, and then turned his attention to the other two men while he waited. The old man was sitting and leaning against the wall, his eyes unfocused. The young man had jumped up as they entered, however, and was watching with wide eyes.

"Is he . . . ?"

Belissar shook his head.

"We found him in one of the pits. He's alive."

The young man nodded. At first, he moved to sit back down, but he paused when Belissar remained. He slowly straightened himself.

"Do you wish to speak with us, Tower Lord, sir?"

Belissar scowled.

"Don't call me that."

Even Belissar was surprised at how he spat the words out. Niobee, who was sitting on his head, and the soldier bees began to buzz their wings in response. The young man took a step back with his hands held up and bowed his head.

"I apologize."

Belissar took a deep breath.

"It's . . . look, I'm not fond of the tower lords. Not anymore. Call me tower keeper, or sacred den master, or any other name for it. Just not tower lord."

The young man's face fell and he nodded.

"I understand, Tower Keeper."

Belissar sighed once more.

"Okay . . . then, I have questions for you."

The young man slowly nodded.

"I figured. What do you wish to know, Tower Keeper?"

Belissar narrowed his eyes.

"I need to know how you got here. How did you find me, how far did you travel, and from what direction? And how soon can we expect more of you?"

The young man turned his gaze down to the ground and let his shoulders droop.

"You shouldn't expect any of us."

Belissar paused at that.

"What? What do you mean?"

The young man took a deep breath.

"We weren't intended to survive. After what happened in your village, the lord of Starami Tower was really upset. I heard the Conclave got involved too. We were sent out as the first wave with an intentionally small force. We were supposed to die. So . . . I don't think any of them care about following us."

Belissar was processing this when Metsaitti suddenly grunted.

"Sacred Den Master, the man in the back flinched. I think he knows something."

Belissar turned his gaze to the old man, who had tried to go back to leaning against the wall. But his eyes were focused now, and he was averting his gaze.

"You there. What do you know?"

# CHAPTER FORTY-NINE

# INTERPRETING THE PROPHE-BEE

The man's eyes twitched and glanced every which way. But then . . . he stopped, looked Belissar in the eye, and then turned his gaze down with a heavy sigh.

". . . It matters not. My life is over, I will not end it with yet another failure. Kill me if you must."

Belissar glared at the man but he refused to raise his head anymore. Belissar turned to the young man.

"Who is he, by the way? Why did you bring an old man like that with you?"

The young man rubbed his chin.

"He's an augur. I don't fully get it, but they're supposed to divine the will of the gods, especially regarding towers? I'm not sure how but he was the one who figured out where to go. Our . . . commander claimed a god spoke to the augur and told us the way here."

Belissar blinked at that.

"A . . . god led you here?"

Belissar frowned. If the gods were getting involved, then the situation could be worse than he thought. He had thought the tower lords had lied about the gods disproving of peasants and beastkin after he was blessed by the God of Bees, but now a god had led the tower lords straight to him? Now that he thought about it, it was true that the gods were not a united monolith. They were unique and separate individuals. They could be different, and they could even be at odds with one another.

So, perhaps the God of Bees and the God of Fire didn't care too much about him and the karnuq controlling a tower . . . but that didn't mean there wasn't a god who did.

Belissar narrowed his eyes at the augur.

"Which god did you speak with? And what did they say?"

But the augur did not respond any further. Belissar continued glaring at him for a while . . . but then he paused. And then Belissar started to laugh. The augur glanced up at him, but Belissar ignored him now.

"Well, that's fine. If you don't want to tell us, we'll just ask the gods ourselves."

Belissar nodded to Niobee and she flew out of the prison. It didn't take her long to reach the karnuq settlement proper, and the beehouse there. Her queen mother stepped out of the hive as she approached.

"Worker!"

"Queen Mother!"

The two crawled over each other a bit before Niobee began to dance.

"King has a question for Queen of All Bees! Evil humans said a god sent them to King, wants to know which one and why!"

The queen paused for a moment before beginning an unsteady dance.

". . . Not sure. Queen of All Bees talks to me, not sure how to ask . . ."

But then she froze and her eyes began to glow with golden light. A moment later the glow faded and she began to dance quickly.

"Queen of All Bees said she did! Wanted to help me find worker and Hive-Builder! Amazing! Incredible! Queen of All Bees best queen of all bees!"

Niobee joined her in the celebratory dance.

Back in the prison, Belissar had a massive grin on his face. He couldn't help but laugh, to the point that everyone in the room was staring at him. He hardly even noticed. He bowed his head on the spot.

"Truly, thank you. I can't thank you enough for this."

He took a deep breath, letting his joy and gratitude wash over him as he exhaled it with a smile. Only then did he notice everyone looking at him. Metsaitti tilted his head.

"Sacred Den Master?"

Belissar turned to him, a smile still on his face.

"We asked the oracle and the God of Bees responded. There's no problem after all, she's the one who sent them. She wanted to help the oracle get here."

The augur froze, his eyes going wide.

"Ora . . . cle? That . . . that must be a lie. There were no oracles with us. Unless . . . no, the three of us are the only ones left and it's not any of us. There's no one else it could be."

Belissar shrugged. Well, the augur didn't seem helpful and he already knew which god he had spoken to, so instead of responding to him, Belissar turned to the young man.

"Okay, you said we shouldn't expect the tower lords to show up again. Are you sure about that?"

The young man jumped at being addressed but began to rub his chin.

"Um, fairly sure. We traveled a long way and skipped over several towers on the way. We barely made the last leg of the journey. It was about as far as the wyverns could fly in one go. If we hadn't found your tower, we wouldn't have been able to turn back. So, even if anyone cared where we went, it would take them a long time to follow us, I think. I'm not sure how they'd make the last leg either, if they weren't traveling as light as we did. Our captain wanted to turn around, but our commander ordered us onward because he believed the gods were leading us . . . which I guess was actually true? It would have been a suicidal decision if he hadn't been right."

Belissar crossed his arms and rubbed his chin.

"So, we should have time. Since you're not reporting back, maybe they'll think you died."

The young man furrowed his brow.

"That's . . . the augur over there did something before we entered the tower. A magic ritual of some sort. I think it's supposed to let the tower lords know we arrived at a tower, or something?"

Belissar turned to glare at the augur again. The augur glared at the young man in turn but said nothing. Belissar instead sent a message to the Fourth of the Seventh.

*"Hi, Fourth of the Seventh? Can you scout the area around the tower? We're looking for some sort of magic ritual or formation or something. It looks like . . ."*

Belissar paused and turned to the young man.

"Um, do you know what it looked like?"

The young man frowned.

"I didn't get a great look . . . but it was carved into the dirt? I think it was glowing green at one point."

Belissar nodded and relayed as much to the Fourth of the Seventh.

*"Okay! Will!"*

He watched as the Fourth of the Seventh began to organize a scouting party and sighed.

So . . . the tower lords might know where his tower was after all. But at the same time, they were apparently quite far away, with several other towers between them and a long, unbroken stretch of the Hunger at the end. In addition, this particular party had not been expected to survive. So, there was no guarantee the tower lords would follow them even if they had passed a message back. Even if the lords did decide to come this way, they would not arrive immediately.

So, they would have some time to prepare. But they would need to prepare, for it was still possible the tower lords would follow this party's path one day. Belissar nodded to himself.

The young man seemed to have shared as much as he knew, and the augur still refused to speak. The most urgent questions were answered, in any case, and Belissar now knew enough to guide his immediate actions.

And that meant it was time to ask what he really wanted to know.

"Thank you. Now, let me ask you something important."

The young man gulped as Belissar focused in on him.

"Tell me about the bees, and how you brought them with you."

The young man froze, and then tilted his head.

"Um, the bees, Tower Keeper, sir?"

Belissar nodded, holding his intense gaze. The young man gulped.

"Um, okay. I found them at the bottom of my pack at one of the rest points. I'm not sure how they got there . . . but they didn't sting me when I found the hive. I . . ." The young man's face fell. ". . . I didn't want to hurt anything else at that point, so I figured I'd let them be. I thought they'd sting me when we took off again or when I needed something from the pack, but they stayed surprisingly docile . . ."

As the young man spoke, the augur slowly turned his gaze to them.

"Bees? What bees . . . ?"

His eyes began to go wide as the young man continued his tale.

"There . . . was a hive of bees traveling with us?"

And then . . . the color of the god who set their path, the banners of the tower, and the defenders that had struck Ruckanos down all flickered in the augur's mind . . . along with the tower lord's claim that there was an oracle . . .

The augur's face began to pale.

But Belissar wasn't paying attention to him. He began to subconsciously smile as the young man described their journey.

"And then I wondered how they were getting water, so I figured I'd share a bit of mine. I tried to get them to leave at that point, since we had found a nice purified zone, but they refused to budge. At first, I thought it was that they considered the pack their home . . . but it sounds like there was something else going on?"

Belissar nodded.

"Yes. The queen is intelligent and can speak with the God of Bees. She was trying to make it here."

The young man blinked, staring blankly into space.

"I . . . see?"

Belissar chuckled and smiled at him.

"She was also one of the queens from my bees in the village."

The young man's eyes went wide and quivered.

". . . The one we burned?"

Belissar nodded.

"So . . . thank you, for taking care of her and helping us reunite. That's why I'm not going to kill you now. So, um, let me know if you need anything. I can't let you go, but . . . I'll take care of you like you took care of her."

The young man didn't respond. Belissar waited for a bit, then shrugged and turned to leave. He turned to Metsaitti.

"Make sure the young man is comfortable. Um, let me know if you need me to speak with him or something. The others . . . well, we'll see when the other guy wakes up. The old guy can just . . . stay here, I guess."

Metsaitti saluted.

"As you command."

And with a nod to Metsaitti, Belissar left, leaving the two humans lost in their thoughts.

# WILL OF THE BEE-VINE

The Fourth of the Seventh zipped about, but one of her scout communers stopped her.

"Queen, over here!"

She spun about and sped at the communer's dance until she saw it. Several of her scouts hovered over a patch of dirt just before the tower. Grooves had been carved in a large, circular pattern. The pattern occasionally pulsed with a soft green light that was easy to miss among the grass and flowers.

The Fourth of the Seventh danced happily about.

"Great work, everyone! Will tell King we found it!"

But just as she was about to relay a message to the King, the pattern shifted. The soft green light turned bright red. The Fourth of the Seventh reacted immediately.

"Get back!"

At her command, her workers immediately flew away from the pattern. The Fourth of the Seventh did likewise, knowing that the workers wouldn't evacuate before her. A moment later, the pattern pulsed with a light too bright to see.

And then it fell silent and glowed no more.

Belissar frowned as he listened to the Fourth of the Seventh's report. They had found the magic formation, but then it did . . . something. Turned red, flashed, and then went dead. Now it was little more than grooves in the dirt, with not even a hint of mana circulating within it.

It had probably completed whatever it had been intended to do.

Belissar sighed. He had a bad feeling about it, but what could he do? Neither he nor the bees had any idea what any of the grooves meant, if anything. He'd have the karnuq look at it too, but even if they knew what the formation was for, it seemed too late to do anything about it. He guessed he should assume that the tower lords knew where he was.

He could only hope that the journey would be as long and difficult for them as the young tower guard said. At the very least, no bees had been hurt by the formation, so it hadn't been dangerous. Belissar wasn't sure what he'd have done if more bees had been hurt by this whole affair.

His mind wandered as he picked up a jar of mead and a tray of every kind of honey he had stored. So, the God of Bees herself had sent the tower lord's son here to help one of his queens find her way back to him . . . as the Oracle of Bees now, no less. He couldn't be happier or more grateful to be reunited with one of his queens, as well as to hear directly from his patron, the God of Bees.

And yet . . . he had to wonder as to her purposes. Because in doing so, the tower lords were now aware of his existence and location. The man she had sent had led an assault on his tower that claimed many bee lives. As many bee lives as some of the worst of the shades, even, excepting the very first purification he hadn't prepared for.

Did the God of Bees want the tower lords to know he was here? Did she think he was ready to face them? Did she have another purpose in mind he couldn't see? And why did she allow the tower lord's son to attack the tower in the first place? Couldn't she have told them to stop?

But Belissar shook his head as he arrived at the Shrine of Bees. He placed everything he was carrying in the wax chest, knelt before the shrine, and looked up at the statue of the God of Bees with a smile on his face.

"Thank you, for everything. Thank you for returning one of my queens to me. Thank you for bringing her safely, and for all your guidance and support."

All of those questions still paled in comparison to the joy he felt at being reunited with Niobee's queen. And if the tower lords came as a result of it, he'd just have to trust in his bees and the karnuq to handle them. He'd face as many tower lords as he had to if it were for the sake of his bees.

As he spoke, the Shrine of Bees began to glow.

A group of monster bee soldiers and honeybee workers hatched out of wax cells on the floor of the Hive of All Bees. They glanced around and buzzed their wings, spinning around in confusion. But as they did, four hives of bees flew toward them, led by four queens. The soldiers prepared to fight at first . . . until they recognized the mana of the queens. In addition to their own, individual mana, the queens each held an identical mana signature within them, a mana that each of the soldiers shared as well.

One of the queens landed and began to dance.

"Hello! Am First Queen of First Bee Dungeon's First Spawner's First Dynasty, first of her line. Welcome to Hive of All Bees, fellow bees of First Bee Dungeon. Thank you for protecting our home."

Elsewhere, the Queen of All Bees watched as the queens greeted the incoming bees. Normally, she let bees who arrived sort out their own place and role, as was normal for bees to do. In this case, though, the newly arriving bees deserved a bit of extra consideration.

That Niobee's former queen had grown enough in mana and awareness to provide the Queen of All Bees a second hook into the world was a pleasant miscalculation. That said queen's new awareness and the loss of Niobee had caused her to lead her hive toward starvation was not. The Queen of All Bees had thus done all that she could to ensure the queen's survival. Fortunately, there had been a group of humans that just so happened to be looking for her dungeon, so it had worked out. She had no doubt her favored dungeon master would welcome her new follower with open arms, even if they hadn't already been acquainted. That her dungeon master and conduit would both be overjoyed to reunite with the queen pleased her as well.

Unfortunately, the humans that carried the queen were hive-burners and enemies of her dungeon master and conduit alike. And establishing her first-ever oracle in order to speak directly to the queen had burned through most of her accumulated authority, not to mention what she had to spend to answer the humans' divination and give them directions. The offering they had made didn't even come close to paying back the authority spent, but she had no other choice.

It was unfortunate as well that the human empire would become aware of her dungeon's location if this plan succeeded, given that she had little influence among them, but they were far enough away that she felt it was worth the risk. With how difficult the journey had been for the group that carried her oracle, she knew that an army had no hope of making the trip anytime soon. Time during which her favored dungeon would only continue to grow, and whom she would support with all the authority she could muster.

Of course, that meant she did not have the authority available to answer the humans when they had actually arrived at her dungeon. And even if she did, she cared little for their fate. They had already burned hives and assaulted her favored dungeon master. They may have carried her new oracle through a long and dangerous path, but if they chose to repeat their crimes against bees, in the dungeon that bore her symbol no less, then they deserved whatever fate befell them. She left it to her favored dungeon master to decide, the strength of his hive more than sufficient to hand them either grace or justice as he deemed appropriate.

Still, she could not help but feel some responsibility for the casualties that resulted. Part of her was amused that her favored dungeon master got so worked up over a handful of workers or soldiers, those whose purpose it was to spend their lives for the hive. But in the end, her dungeon master's grief on behalf of bees struck right at her very core. How could she not resonate with one who cared so deeply for even the least of the bees? How could she not be moved by one who spared no effort to preserve every bee that he could, and who did all that he could to honor those he could not save?

"Belissar best dungeon master!"

She had to calm herself from her spontaneous dance before resuming her train of thought. She would, therefore, not spare any effort to ensure that those bees he had not saved were taken care of as he would have wished.

But in the end, the prize had been worth the cost. She now had an oracle to call her own, safely housed within her favored dungeon master's halls. She could now make known her will directly to the world at a fraction of the cost in authority. Her ability to assign missions and offer blessings would expand dramatically as well and extend beyond her dungeon shrines. And most of all, now that she could interact more directly with the people of the world, her name would grow among them. One day she, too, would be able to act beyond the reach of her direct hooks.

And so, those who had made it happen would be rewarded. The one human who had acted kindly toward bees on their trip would not be forgotten; his key role in carrying her oracle safely would be acknowledged. And then, of course, her favored dungeon master. While she could not reward him directly for the defeat of his fellow humans, she could at least reward him for taking in the oracle. In fact, that oracle only grew because of the worker that became the Queen of All Bees' conduit, and both of those only survived because Belissar took care of both while they were still mundane bees. She intended to see him grow, to ensure his, the conduit's, and the oracle's future safety. And simply because he deserved it.

Now, all she needed was to gather some more authority so she could make it happen . . .

Just then, something pulled her attention. She watched as the offerings and gratitude came pouring in, her favored dungeon master once again filling her coffers . . . and tugging on her heart.

This time, she didn't resist the dance.

"Belissar best dungeon master! Belissar best follower!"

# CHAPTER FIFTY

# AN INSOLENT BEE-QUEST

The Shrine of Bees flashed, leaving a message before Belissar's eyes.

*New mission received: Receive an oracle from the Oracle of Bees.*

Belissar blinked and then smiled. That was one he could do right away! He made his way over to the karnuq settlement and to the beehouse there. He watched as worker bees flew in and out of the hive to the nearby flowers. The hive was relatively small at this point, but with his tower sight he could confirm the queen had started laying more eggs, so it should recover. Well, if all else failed, he'd ask the First of the Fifth to lend a hand. She took good care of her fellow queens.

He slowed down as he got near the hive, wondering how or even if he should approach. The workers were normal honeybees, last he checked, so they might grow defensive of their home. He lacked the thick clothing he'd used before-hand, and he absolutely did not want any of the hive's few remaining workers to sacrifice themselves stinging him. But then he remembered that the queen was his sworn defender now, and he could talk to her whenever he wished.

*"Hello, queen? Is now a good time to talk?"*

Within the hive, the queen stopped what she was doing and crawled toward the entrance of the beehouse, then took off flying. She flew straight toward him and then began to zip around.

"Hive-Builder! New hive is amazing, incredible! Builds comb by itself, makes honey by itself!"

Belissar's face broke out into a wide grin.

"I'm glad you like it!"

Before he could say any more, though, the queen's eyes began to glow with golden light. Once the glow faded, she started a slightly unsteady dance.

"Queen of All Bees says Belissar best dungeon master! What's a Belissar?"

Belissar, however, did not respond. His eyes slowly widened as he processed the message, then his smile spread as large as it could and his entire torso grew warm.

". . . Thank you. I think you're the best god too!"

*Mission: Receive an oracle from the Oracle of Bees completed!*
*Reward: +100 DP*

The God of Bees . . . thought he was the *best* dungeon master? How was that possible? Was he truly doing a better job than all of the tower lords? Or was she just encouraging him?

In either case, he truly was thankful to his patron. He would just have to keep doing his best for her and for the bees they both loved.

The tower occupants mostly rested and reorganized for the rest of the day, with plans made for the karnuq hunters to join the purifications and the bee army training the next day. The next morning, Belissar received a message from Chief Rohsuak.

*"Sacred Den Master, would you be willing to help us speak with the prisoners again? We intend to move the surviving wyverns to the new enclosure and could use the young one's help pacifying them."*

Belissar nodded as he sent his reply.

*"Okay, I'll be there soon."*

Not long after that, Belissar arrived at the prison once more. The augur still sat against the back wall of the room, muttering to himself under his breath, while the young man stood as he entered.

"Tower Keeper, sir. Did you have more questions?"

Belissar shook his head.

"We're going to move the wyverns to a big structure. We should be able to loosen some of their restraints once they're inside, but we can't if they'll be violent. Could you . . . help us keep them calm?"

The young man blinked but then slowly nodded.

"Ah, yes. I'll help with that."

Belissar nodded and left the room. Two karnuq hunters stepped in and escorted the young man out.

A little while after they left, the augur stopped muttering. He looked up and then glanced around. He couldn't see any of the beastkin, either in the room or looking in through any of the openings. He knew that tower lords could, of course, see anything within their tower whenever they pleased . . . but if the tower lord was currently working with the traitor, then maybe he'd be distracted.

This could be his only chance.

He hunched over and began to draw in the dirt floor. He did not notice the bee hidden on the roof, who now began a frantic dance.

Belissar was watching and translating between human and karnuq as the young man rubbed one of the wyvern's heads when Niobee suddenly began buzzing loudly at his side.

"Niobee? What is it?"

She flew before him, extending her stinger.

"King! Evil human doing something!"

His eyes widened. The young man in front of him clearly wasn't doing anything, and the injured one still hadn't fully awakened, so . . .

"You mean the old man?!"

"Yes!"

Belissar's soldier bee escorts were already soaring toward the prison. Metsaitti, who had given Niobee his attention the moment she started to buzz, now barked a command.

"To the prison!"

Belissar stood for a moment before running after the bees and karnuq. He switched to his tower sight and found the old man drawing something in the dirt.

"Careful, I think he's making another formation or something!"

The bees flew in through some windows at the top of the structure, while Metsaitti rushed forward and kicked open the door. He stepped forward and thrust his spear forward as the soldier bees flew in from the sides. The augur gasped and scrambled to his feet, leaning flat against the back wall as Metsaitti's spear stopped just shy of his neck. Belissar signaled to the soldier bees not to attack, so they hovered menacingly around the augur's head, their stingers pointed toward him.

Belissar stepped inside the room a moment later and glared at the man.

"What were you doing?"

The augur gulped . . . and then his face fell. He hung his head and his shoulders as he heaved a long sigh.

"I . . . suppose I should tell you. I . . . was attempting to contact the gods."

Belissar narrowed his eyes at the man.

"The gods? Not the tower lords?"

The augur slowly shook his head.

"I . . . understand you cannot trust me, but . . . we were sent here by a god, only to perish nearly to a man. You now claim an oracle came with us. I . . . I spent my entire life attempting to discern the will and movements of the gods. My entire family has devoted generations to the task, and yet the message I received was the most direct communication anyone in my family's entire history had ever heard of. For it to have ended in complete disaster . . . makes no sense. Escorting an oracle would explain it, but why here? Why to an unknown tower filled with subhumans . . ."

Belissar snarled.

"Don't call them that."

The augur gulped and slowly nodded.

". . . I understand. To an unknown tower filled with beastkin, on a journey fraught with peril that could have easily ended all of us. Why weren't we told of such an important passenger, or of the purpose of our journey? I . . . I must know the truth of the matter. Even if I must perish. My life has little meaning anyway."

The augur took a deep breath and raised his head, looking Belissar in the eye. He then bowed his head.

"Please . . . Tower Lord . . . allow me to visit the shrine of your patron. Please allow me to ask one final question. You may kill me if you must, but I must know the truth."

Belissar frowned and crossed his arms.

"First of all, don't call me that, it's Tower Keeper. And then . . . why? I mean . . . why should I? You're the one who attacked. You won't answer any of my questions either. And now you're trying to do something in secret." Belissar felt a fire grow in his chest and he snarled. "And thanks to you, my bees died, so, you know what? I don't really care what you need. If a *god* sent you here, then why did you attack her tower?! Why did you attack us?!"

The augur's shoulders fell.

"That's . . . we thought the god was helping us correct our failure . . . but then . . . the god who sent us matched the banners of the tower . . . and we still attacked. By the gods, what have we done?"

The augur's knees gave out and he slowly slid down the wall. Tears began to fill his eyes. Belissar continued scowling but then he noticed the bees buzzing. He saw Niobee preparing to charge.

"King's enemy! Bees sting!"

Belissar took a deep breath.

"Hold on, everyone."

He glared at the man on the ground . . . the old man curled up at his feet. Some of the heat drained from his chest. His own eyes began to tear up at the thought of all the bees who had perished. His own shoulders drooped. He turned around.

"Whatever you were doing, don't do it again. Don't you dare do anything more."

As Belissar began to leave, he heard a raspy, stuttering voice.

"Tower . . . Keeper . . . I . . . I will tell you everything. A-Anything you wish to know. Just . . . please tell your patron that . . . I'm sorry."

Belissar froze, a storm raging in his chest once more. He slowly turned around and glared at the augur. The augur lifted his head, tears streaming down his face.

Belissar slowly opened his mouth.

"You are going to tell us *everything*."

# CHAPTER FIFTY-ONE

# THE CONCLAVE'S BEE-HAVIOR

Belissar crossed his arms and glared at the man. Metsaitti pulled his spear back slightly but kept it pointed forward, while the bees continued to buzz around in the air.

"Okay, first question. What exactly was that magic formation outside the tower?"

The augur slowly nodded.

"It was our means of communicating with the Conclave. We activate the signal formation upon discovering a rogue tower."

Then his eyes widened slightly and he sighed.

"I . . . apologize, Tower Keeper, but it is already too late. The formation requires the constant addition of mana to maintain. If it goes twenty-four hours without maintenance, it will send out a final pulse. The Conclave will assume that you are hostile and we are dead . . . they will arrive in force next time."

Belissar narrowed his eyes.

"And how soon will they come?"

The augur's face relaxed ever so slightly.

"Ah . . . in that, the traitor . . . or other prisoner, I suppose, was correct as far as I'm aware. I am no expert on tower conquests, but I agree that our journey was long and fraught with peril. We passed several towers on the way that the Conclave will want to deal with first, and I am not sure how an army would make the final stretch."

Belissar nodded, but before he could relax the augur gulped and continued.

". . . There is another angle you must consider, however. The Conclave is looking for your tower specifically. If yours was but a normal tower, the journey would likely be too far for this Grand Subjugation to attempt. But it is not, so the Conclave will not give up so easily. It may take a while, but they will come for you eventually."

Belissar growled at that.

"Why? What makes my tower so special?"

The augur's face fell and he sighed once more.

". . . That is our fault. We were supposed to bind your tower and ensure it remained where the Conclave could monitor it, but we failed. The very purpose of the Conclave and the augurs alike is to ensure that no tower is misused, and losing your tower from within our own territory was an especially egregious failure. If the tower was born beyond the reach of the Conclave, then we would have had no choice but to accept it as the will of the gods, but in this case it was our own fault. We failed in our duty to the very gods to keep the towers within the right hands. We were thus sent to atone by reclaiming more towers . . . or at least to inform the Conclave of their locations at the cost of our lives."

Belissar glared at him for a moment before scoffing.

"From what I've seen, the tower lords were wrong about the gods in general. The gods don't care at all about peasants or beastkin or any of that. I doubt they cared about your mission at all."

The augur frowned.

". . . You were one of the villagers, correct? I could see why you would think that given the circumstances, but . . . it's a bit more complicated."

Belissar felt heat stir in his chest again. Complicated? This man saw a village put to the sword with his own eyes for a lie and said it was "complicated?" Belissar wanted to shout at him . . . but he also needed to know why the tower lords were after his tower. He contained his fury as best he could and spat out a single word in response.

"Explain."

The augur took a deep breath.

"It . . . is true that the Conclave has exaggerated the gods' views toward the common folk and the beastkin. But, to understand why, you must know the goal of the Conclave. The truth is that . . . the Hunger is no natural disaster."

Belissar raised an eyebrow.

"Yes, yes, the gods sent it to punish the wicked kings of old or something like that. That's one of the first things in the doctrine."

The augur shook his head.

"No, the Hunger was our fault."

Belissar froze solid, his mind coming to a screeching halt.

". . . What?"

The augur's face turned grave.

"I do not know if it was a direct result of an action by the kings of old, or if it truly was a response by the gods. The High Council has specifically restricted the details so that no one may even think of repeating the past. But

I do know that the crisis was ultimately triggered by something that humanity did. Not just a general sense of displeasure with the kings of old, but one single event."

Belissar's eyes widened. No words came out of his mouth as the augur continued.

"The Conclave's primary task, therefore, is to prevent humanity from repeating a blunder of that scale ever again. And in that, towers are a matter of grave concern. As you have no doubt learned by now, towers offer great power to their masters. You have the power to reshape the world within to your liking, to create matter and life out of pure mana, and to escape the very limits of humanity, while those you allow inside your tower have the opportunity to earn blessings and grow beyond mortal men. But power corrupts, and so the Conclave was deeply concerned as the number of towers grew beyond the original members of the High Council and their companions. It was agreed to limit entry to the towers to those with proven faith and loyalty, while the tower lords themselves agreed to restrict their own powers, lest that power corrupt humanity and lead us to defy the gods once again."

The augur paused for another breath before looking up at Belissar.

"That is why it is unacceptable for us to have lost a tower, where the Conclave cannot reach it and where a rogue tower lord might grow arrogant with the powers it offers. That is why the Conclave will come for your tower, now that it has been relocated."

Belissar frowned as he considered this.

"But . . . did the gods actually say any of this to you?"

The augur paused this time. His face began to drain of color.

". . . In truth, I do not know. Only the High Council knows for sure exactly what has been said in the past. Most oracles, divinations, and missions to the tower lords that were recorded and available to me were much more limited in scope. I . . . I never wondered before, but if your patron has sent an oracle from the safety of the Conclave to your tower in the wilderness . . . then your patron, at least, cannot disapprove of your existence."

Belissar thought of his patron, and couldn't help a small smile as a bit of joy broke through the storm raging in his chest. He whispered to himself.

"Well, I don't need you to tell me that."

He took a deep breath and glanced around at the bees hovering above . . . and at Metsaitti, who remained completely focused on the augur. Belissar frowned once more.

"Okay . . . but what about the beastkin? You didn't mention that."

The augur slowly nodded.

"Right. The . . . beastkin were once the soldiers of the kings of old. They remained loyal to those kings even after the Hunger struck. They defied and opposed the High Council, all the way to this day. They, above all others, cannot be trusted with the powers offered by a tower."

The augur then frowned.

"Though . . . if they are loyal to you . . . and dwelling within the tower of an oracle . . . then perhaps the situation has changed."

Belissar's face scrunched up a bit.

"Metsaitti, you hear anything about serving kings of old or fighting tower lords?"

Metsaitti slowly shook his head, though he kept his eyes on the augur.

"Our people's tales don't go past our service to our previous sacred den master. I don't know what is meant by kings of old, but I'm guessing you're referring to more people such as yourself?"

Belissar paused and glanced at the augur.

"The wicked kings of old were supposed to be human, right?"

The augur nodded. Metsaitti shook his head again.

"In that case, we had never met any peoples such as yourself before you, Sacred Den Master, much less served them. If we ever had in the past, then it must have been a long time ago, for we have no memory of it now."

Belissar nodded, and then began to rub his chin. So, the kings of old did something that, one way or another, resulted in the Hunger, and the tower lords were trying to prevent anyone from repeating it by misusing a tower or a god's blessing? And the beastkin apparently helped the kings of old?

He frowned. He didn't see why that meant lying to peasants, letting them die of plagues, and then burning down their villages. That didn't seem like a good use of a tower's powers in Belissar's opinion. And what did it matter what the beastkin once did if the karnuq couldn't even remember such a time?

He was growing angry once more, but he shook his head. It didn't really matter to him why the tower lords did what they did. The gods apparently hadn't specifically commanded it, and Belissar knew he had at least two of their approval at this point. The karnuq, too, weren't serving any wicked king of old that Belissar could see and had been far better people to him than most humans ever were.

In the end, this all changed nothing. Belissar was going to build a tower full of happy bees that the God of Bees could be proud of. If the tower lords thought that was a misuse of the tower's power, then they could take it up with the gods. And if they came here in force once more, Belissar would not let them take all that the bees had built.

Besides, even the augur was now questioning the things he was explaining. Belissar stared at him as the old man curled up and began to mutter to himself once again. Well, the augur had answered his questions . . . and he *had* been sent here by the God of Bees. He took a deep breath.

"Niobee."

Niobee paused, waving her stinger around to dance happily before him.

"Yes, King!"

He looked at her and smiled.

"Could you go ask your queen mother if the God of Bees wants to say anything to this guy?"

"Okay!"

The augur froze and looked up at Belissar, his eyes growing wider by the second. Belissar frowned but shrugged.

"Let's see what the gods have to say about all this. If they want to speak with you, then I won't stop them."

The augur's eyes began to moisten, and he bowed his head low.

"Thank you . . . Tower Keeper."

# CHAPTER FIFTY-TWO

# RECEIVE THE PROPHE-BEE!

A short while later, one of the bee monsters returned, carrying a more normal-sized bee on her back while several more honeybees buzzed around them. The augur watched as they hovered before the tower lord . . . or tower keeper, as he preferred to be called. And a wise man does not defy a tower lord if he can help it.

"Thanks for coming. So, the God of Bees wants to say something after all?"

The bees flew about in seemingly random patterns and circles, as far as the augur was concerned. But the tower keeper derived meaning from them, one of his many gifts from the gods. The tower keeper nodded and stepped to the side.

"He's over here."

The augur watched as the small bee lifted off of her larger counterpart's back and flew toward him, accompanied by the rest of the honeybees. So, this was the oracle that had traveled with them? Part of him wondered how a bee who couldn't speak with any tongue of man could be an oracle, but the augur knew better than to question it. He had been granted the privilege of communicating with oracles in the past, as well as speaking with others who had as well, so he knew that oracles came in all shapes and sizes. A talking tree, a pool of water that imparted visions, even a pile of bones that formed words when dropped. If the God of Bees, as it were, chose a bee as their oracle, then that was their right. So, the augur rose to his feet to greet that oracle.

It did make him curious as to how he would receive the response. The tower keeper *could* translate for the bee, it seemed, but an oracle should be able to pass the will of a god directly. Besides, the augur himself had failed to understand the intentions of this god even after receiving a direct message. He did not wish to hear another message filtered through a third party.

He bowed his head toward the bee.

"I'm honored to speak with you, Oracle of Bees."

The bees buzzed. The augur waited for a bit, then cleared his throat.

"God of Bees, I am sorry. I am sorry that I misread your intentions and allowed my liege to assault one of your towers. And I am sorry I come before you with nothing to offer but my apologies. But . . . if you are willing to consider an unworthy one such as myself . . . please, respond to my plea, and I swear I shall do all in my power to see your will fulfilled."

The bees continued buzzing, so the augur took a deep breath and carried on.

". . . What was your intention in sending us here?"

He looked up and watched the Oracle of Bees. At first, she did not respond, just kept hovering and buzzing about as bees do. But, just as the augur began to furrow his brow, her eyes lit up. The augur's eyes widened as the bee queen glowed with a golden-yellow light, the exact same light he had seen during his divination at the start of their trip.

The Oracle of Bees began to fly in circles and patterns once more. Her workers landed on the ground and began to crawl about. The augur watched them intently . . . and soon his eyes widened once more. The bees were leaving wax on the ground. Wax in the shape of letters.

*"Help tower, help oracle."*

The augur took a deep breath. So, it was true. Ruckanos had gotten it all wrong and led them into disaster with his delusions of grandeur. But the augur had been equally unwise. He knew better, and yet he had not acted to stop the foolish boy. Indeed, if anything, he bore the ultimate responsibility. Was it not the duty of the augurs to guide the tower lords to their destinies? Was it not his duty to divine the will and movements of the gods so that the Conclave could respond? But he had not convinced the boy who was not yet a tower lord, and so the group intended to escort an oracle to her intended home had instead invaded with force.

The augur bowed his head.

"I understand. I will see it done."

The bees left one more word on the ground.

*"Good."*

The augur took another deep breath. He could not help but glance at the beastkin still ready to stab him at a moment's notice. Here was a tower lord without the Conclave's guidance, who had no training or instruction on how to fulfill his task. Who was specifically defying what doctrine he would have known as a simple peasant, seeing as how he had welcomed the beastkin in.

And yet . . . it didn't matter. Oracles were afforded special privileges and protection, the voices of the very gods who granted humanity their towers. None but the High Council could defy them, and most of the High Council never would. If a god, unknown or not, had sent their oracle to this tower specifically, through trial and tribulation, all for the sake of helping it? The augur could not and would not defy them, no matter what the keeper of this tower was doing with his powers.

So he had already sworn. And so he would do.

The augur turned and bowed his head toward Belissar.

"Tower Keeper, the will of the God of Bees was to help your tower. So, I, Sehfitis, swear I will do all that I can to help you."

*Accept offer of allegiance?*

Belissar raised an eyebrow. He had not expected this turn of events. This guy who worked for the tower lords and refused to speak with them . . . now wanted to be his sworn defender? What, really? Just what did the God of Bees say to him?!

Well, Belissar had watched Niobee's queen mother dance instructions to her workers, and he could read the wax messages with his tower sight, so he already knew . . . but that alone had been enough to convince the guy? And now he wanted to join the tower, just like that? After all he had done?

Belissar's eyes narrowed, but then he sighed. So, what was he going to do? If he rejected the guy, would he just keep him here forever? Toss him out of the tower and just hope he didn't contact the tower lords? Execute the old man on the spot? This was a matter of prisoners and gods and oaths, not something Belissar had much experience handling. But handle it he must, for it was the business of a tower lord—which he was, no matter what other name he chose to call himself by.

He didn't know how the tower lords treated prisoners wanting to join them and he didn't want to know. The karnuq, on the other hand, didn't take prisoners. And he wasn't close enough to the sigmaka to ask them. It was up to him to decide what to do.

Or was it? Belissar turned to the one other group in the room.

"Hey Niobee, do bees ever take prisoners?"

Niobee zipped over to him at his address.

"Prisoners? What that?"

Belissar rubbed his chin.

"Um, maybe . . . bees from other hives?"

Niobee flew about unsteadily.

"Intruders?"

Belissar furrowed his brow.

"Um, kind of. They were intruders, but now they aren't fighting."

Niobee buzzed her wings.

"Push intruders out, sting if have to! But . . . other bees but not intruders . . ."

Niobee swayed in the air for a bit before starting to dance.

"Had one worker from other hive try to follow. Lost hive, looking for new one. Worked hard, so bees let into hive. Joined hive."

Belissar's eyes widened and then he smiled.

"I see. Thanks, Niobee."

Niobee zipped about happily as Belissar turned back to the old man.

"Sehfitis, was it?"

Sehfitis nodded.

"Yes, Tower Keeper?"

Belissar took a deep breath.

"I'll let you help, then."

Sehfitis blinked and started to smile, but Belissar narrowed his eyes and glared at the man.

"But hurt my bees, or the karnuq, or try to contact the tower lords, or anything like that, and we're done. Got it?"

Sehfitis nodded.

"Of course, Tower Keeper."

Belissar brought up the sworn defender description one more time.

*Sworn Defender: An outsider who has sworn to defend a dungeon. Bound not to harm the core or the dungeon master, and to defend it from existential threats. Immediately gains a minor blessing from the dungeon's patron and may interact with dungeon mana. Remnants will not spawn around a sworn defender unless they specifically intend to be challenged. Sworn defenders do not cost mana to upkeep, but mana may improve the bond with a given individual.*

He still didn't trust the guy. But the God of Bees had spoken to him and he was making an offer of allegiance. Supposedly, he would not be able to harm the dungeon or Belissar afterward. Belissar could only hope that extended to the bees as well.

If it didn't . . . well, he'd let the bees do what they did to intruders.

"In that case . . . I accept your offer."

*You have gained 1 sworn defender.*

Belissar could only hope this would help him protect his bees.

# CHAPTER FIFTY-THREE

# A BEE-UTIFUL NAME

Okay, so Sehfitis the augur was now his sworn defender. That was nice and all, but now that this affair was handled, there were some wyverns Belissar and the karnuq needed to deal with. So, Belissar just gave Sehfitis as serious a look as he could muster.

"Stay here for now, and don't do anything again. I'll be back when I have time."

Sehfitis bowed his head.

"As you will, Tower Keeper."

Belissar gave one last glance to the man before turning and leaving. Once he left the room, Metsaitti followed.

"It seems it went well, Sacred Den Master? Should we continue guarding him?"

Belissar paused.

"Oh, right, you couldn't understand most of that, right?"

Metsaitti shook his head.

"Not until the end, after he became one of yours."

Belissar blinked.

"Ah, right."

Then he rubbed his chin.

". . . Yeah, I think we should keep an eye on him for now. I'm . . . still not sure about him, even with the oath and all that."

Metsaitti nodded.

"I understand. We'll do as you say."

Metsaitti gave orders to the karnuq hunters at the door, and then he and Belissar made their way over to the larger building next door. There, they found the wyverns now with their mouths and limbs free, though they were still tied to the walls with ropes attached to their harnesses. The young human was calming them down. He turned and bowed his head.

"Ah, Tower Keeper, sir. We were just finishing up here. Thank you for preparing a space for them."

Belissar's eyes widened a bit.

"Ah . . . um, you're welcome? You . . . managed to get them inside all right? I thought you couldn't speak with the karnuq."

The young man and the karnuq hunters with him both shook their heads.

"We couldn't, but . . . we managed to work it out somehow."

Belissar nodded.

"I see. Oh, um, what's your name, by the way?"

"Hirkolos, sir."

Belissar rubbed his chin.

"I'm Belissar. So, Hirkolos . . . do you want to join the tower?"

Hirkolos froze.

"Um, sir?"

Belissar shrugged.

"Your augur friend just swore himself to the tower. Figured if I let him, then I should let you too. You cooperated and helped the bees, after all. It would let you speak with the karnuq, too."

Hirkolos stared out into space.

"The augur did? How did that happen? Please forgive me for saying this, sir, but it's hard to imagine an augur joining a tower with . . . beastkin."

Belissar shrugged again.

"He spoke with the Oracle of Bees. Apparently that convinced him."

Hirkolos blinked at that.

"Huh."

Belissar shook his head before focusing back on Hirkolos.

"So, how about you?"

Hirkolos focused back on him . . . and then began to frown. Eventually, he hung his head.

"I don't know, sir. I'm just . . . confused."

Belissar didn't know how to respond to that, so he didn't. Hirkolos continued.

"You see . . . when I was chosen to train as a future tower guard, we all thought it was a great honor. I was going to be a hero, to fight against the Hunger and the subhumans and witches and anyone else who threatened mankind. I was going to keep my home safe and serve the gods both, right? But then . . . my very first mission was to burn down your village."

Belissar narrowed his eyes as unpleasant memories came back unbidden. Hirkolos looked off to the side.

". . . Is that really what the tower guards are like? How are we supposed to protect villages by burning them down? And if that's what we do, then just what exactly were we fighting for? Was that really the will of the gods?"

Belissar growled and shook his head.

"No. The tower lords lied about a lot of things."

Hirkolos slowly nodded.

"That must be true if even an augur is having second thoughts now."

Then he hung his head again.

". . . I'm sorry, Tower Keeper, sir. But I can't join your tower guard. Not again, not after . . . that."

Belissar narrowed his eyes.

"I'm not going to be another tower lord. My tower guard's going to be different."

Hirkolos slowly nodded.

"I believe you. But . . . I just don't know what I should do, anymore. I'm sorry, Tower Keeper, sir. I can't swear myself to anyone, not right now."

He closed his eyes and bowed his head.

"I'm sorry. Take my life, if you must."

Belissar shook his head.

"I'm not going to do that, I already told you. Look, I'm not going to be like them, alright? So, just . . . do what you want, and let me know if you want to join. I just . . . if that guy wanted to join, I wanted to let you if you wanted to, since you helped the bees. If you don't . . . then that's fine, we'll try to take care of you anyway."

Hirkolos slowly lifted his head and nodded.

"As you will, Tower Keeper, sir."

Belissar heaved a sigh as he turned away. Talking to these humans was proving exhausting, and bringing up a lot of memories Belissar would prefer to forget. But now, it was finally over . . . sort of. Now that the augur had sworn to help, Belissar probably should talk with him and figure out what exactly he could do. He knew vaguely that augurs were supposed to divine the will of the gods . . . but this one had apparently had some trouble with that? Besides, the God of Bees hadn't had any trouble making her will known to Belissar thus far, and he certainly didn't trust someone from the tower lords to take up that job. Which left a big question of what augurs actually did and how this one could help his tower.

Belissar didn't know and couldn't think of anything in particular, so he decided he would handle that later. After all, right now he had thought of something far more important to do. Something in line with the very will of the gods themselves. He turned to Niobee, and the oracle queen on her back, and gave them both a smile.

"Shall we check on your hive?"

The oracle queen paused, and then began to dance rapidly.

"Yes! Hive-builder check hive!"

Belissar chuckled at that and then turned to Metsaitti.

"Could you let Chief Rohsuak know to gather everyone who wanted to learn beekeeping? It's a good opportunity to show them what I do with an occupied hive."

Metsaitti saluted.

"Right away, Sacred Den Master. Or . . . should I call you Tower Keeper?"

Belissar shrugged.

"Either or, as long as you don't call me Tower Lord it's fine."

Metsaitti nodded and set off. Belissar did his best to push tower lords out of his mind and focus on his bees. He made his way to the oracle queen's hive . . . and then looked at her.

"Niobee . . . your mom doesn't have a name, right?"

Niobee danced the negative.

"No name! Not from spawner, either."

Belissar turned his gaze to the queen herself.

"Would you like one, a name?"

The queen danced unsteadily.

"Name is . . . what Hive-Builder calls worker? Worker has one?"

Belissar nodded.

"Yes, I call her Niobee."

The queen's antennas twitched about.

"Why?"

Belissar opened his mouth but then paused.

"Um . . . because she's my friend?"

"Friend, what that?"

Belissar had to rub his chin for a bit at that one.

"Um . . . it's because I like her and want to distinguish her from other bees, so I gave her a name I can call her."

"But can call worker 'worker' already?"

Belissar shook his head.

"There's other workers, though, right? So, I gave her a name that other workers don't have. That way . . . she knows when I'm talking to her and not another worker . . . or something?"

The queen stood still at that for a long while before slowly starting a dance.

"I . . . see. Worker is special, so not just worker. Niobee is name for special worker?"

Belissar nodded. He thought that was right?

"And you're a special queen, since you're Niobee's mom. So, do you want a name, too?"

The queen stood still for a moment before breaking out into a quick dance.

"Okay!"

Belissar let out a sigh and then chuckled.

"Got it. How about we call you . . ."

He paused. He now realized that in his efforts to explain what exactly a name was in the first place, he hadn't given any thought as to what Niobee's mom's name should actually be.

"Um . . . let's see . . ."

The queen danced.

"Um let's see is name?"

Belissar blinked and then quickly shook his head.

"Ah, no, I was still trying to think about what your name should be. It, um, generally is a unique word that doesn't refer to something else . . . sometimes."

The queen looked confused again, so Belissar decided to just think of a name instead of trying to explain. What should he call Niobee's mom, who was also the Oracle of Bees?

"How about . . . Velebee?"

"Velebee?"

The queen danced around once with unsteady steps and then stopped. A moment later, her eyes burst into golden yellow light that flooded the area, forcing Belissar to shield his eyes. When the light died down, he found the queen bee dancing about rapidly.

"Queen of All Bees says she likes!"

Belissar smiled at that. Niobee began dancing around as well.

"Niobee likes too! King is best king! King's names best names!"

Belissar chuckled and was about to respond when . . .

*You have performed a service for the God of Bees: Naming the Oracle of Bees.*
*Reward: +500 DP!*

Oh, it seemed the God of Bees *really* liked it. Belissar broke out into a bright grin. This, this was what mattered.

The tower lords had assaulted his home once more, even claiming some of his bees. Sehfitis had joined the tower, raising all sorts of questions Belissar was loath to consider. And one day, the tower lords would be back, no doubt in greater numbers than this latest assault.

There, too, was the matter of the sigmaka, and whether they would hold to the agreement they had made. Including the karnuq, there were now three different peoples who had come into contact with his tower, all with three very different reactions . . . and the area purified by the tower continued to grow. He had to consider that the people he had come into contact with so far would not be the last. The karnuq aside, the tower lords had attacked and the sigmaka had come close to doing so. He also had to consider what he would do if they met another group that proved to be unfriendly . . .

But Belissar could now put that all aside. The bees continued to grow in numbers, diversity, and might. The karnuq had proved themselves and become stalwart defenders of the tower. Velebee had joined him once more. And he knew now, truly and completely, that the God of Bees was on his side.

So, despite all the potential challenges and dangers looming ahead, Belissar was starting to believe that maybe, just maybe, they might have what it took to weather the storm. The Bee Tower, its tower keeper, and the God of Bees.

# THE HIGH COUNCIL

General Rippotis let out a hum as he rubbed his beard. Before him stood a woven basket, placed upside down with a small hole at the bottom.

"So, the bees like to live in these . . . skeps?"

He looked up at several women in thick clothes standing before him. One of them nodded.

"Yes, High Councilor."

He shook his head.

"It's General."

The woman jumped and immediately bowed her entire body.

"M-My apologies!"

General Rippotis just raised his hand.

"It's fine. You aren't from around here, so I did not expect you to know. But, back to the bees . . . how then do you retrieve the honey?"

The first woman held her tongue after being corrected, so another spoke up instead.

"We use fire, sulfur if possible, to smoke the bees out, then break apart the hive . . . General, sir."

General Rippotis frowned.

"That would kill them, wouldn't it?"

The woman didn't flinch.

"Yes, usually."

General Rippotis crossed his arms and hummed again. The women glanced at one another.

"G-General, is there a problem?"

He grunted the affirmative.

"There is. It is important for my purpose that the bees survive, and that they are happy. Neither of those things will be true if we kill them and break apart their homes."

One of the women titled her head.

"Happy, General?"

He nodded.

"Yes."

Worst came to worst, he could make the skeps and then just not gather from them, but that felt quite passive for a mission from the gods. The women glanced at one another once again. But before any of them could speak, a soldier marched into the room and saluted.

"General, you have a message from the High Council."

General Rippotis waved him to the side.

"Leave it on my desk, I'll get to it."

The soldier shook his head.

"I'm sorry, sir, but it appears to be a priority summon. The entire High Council is gathering."

General Rippotis took a deep breath and sighed.

"Very well, prepare my mount."

The soldier saluted one more.

"Yes, sir!"

General Rippotis took one more look at the skep and hummed. Perhaps a short break would be for the best. He turned to the gathered apiarists.

"I must depart for now. We will resume when I return. If you can think of a way to preserve the hives in that time, I would be most grateful."

With that, he set off, leaving the apiarists exchanging hushed whispers.

General Rippotis flew over the mountains on the back of a red dragon, arriving at the tallest peak. A tower shone there, the light shining at its spire like a second sun during the day and a bright star in the night. White banners adorned with a yellow star draped down the sides. General Rippotis made a small smile. It had been a while since his last visit.

The tower had several platforms opening out to the air on its sides. General Rippotis landed on one of these and dismounted. Before he even climbed down, he saw a woman approach, dressed in simple white robes and a golden tiara. A woman who barely seemed three decades old, though the wisdom in her eyes hinted at a considerably longer life. She gave him a warm smile.

"General Rippotis, thank you for coming."

General Rippotis returned her smile even as he shook his head.

"No thanks are necessary, Oracle Heigiosa. Even were it not my duty, I would always come should you call."

Like Rippotis, Heigiosa also preferred her other title to Tower Lord or High Councilor, though neither of them required the other to use any titles at all. Her smile grew slightly as she shook her head in turn.

"And that is why I shall always thank you."

The two walked along in companionable silence. General Rippotis basked in the oracle's company for as long as he would permit himself before breaking the silence.

"So, what is this about?"

Oracle Heigiosa frowned.

"Apparently, the lost one has been found."

General Rippotis raised an eyebrow.

"The tower we missed?"

Oracle Heigiosa slowly nodded. General Rippotis frowned.

"How? It's impossible to find where they go afterward, isn't it?"

Oracle Heigiosa nodded again.

"That is what we are gathering to find out. But I trust that Starami wouldn't have come before us again if he were not confident."

General Rippotis narrowed his eyes.

"I would assume not. And neither would High Councilor Konilias permit him to do so."

Oracle Heigiosa shook her head.

"I . . . suppose he would not. He's been most cross about this affair. I tried to tell him that in the end the gods will take care of their towers, but he would not hear it."

General Rippotis raised an eyebrow at her.

"And? Did the gods say anything to you?"

She shook her head and her shoulders drooped.

"Nothing as of yet. The God of Light still has not broken her silence and none of the other Oracles have heard anything either."

Then she smiled.

"But . . . I can see that they are at work. It is most fortunate you remained behind this time."

He rubbed the back of his head.

"Yes, well, I suppose you're not wrong. I received a mission right before I set off, from a new god, if I'm not mistaken."

Oracle Heigiosa froze and stopped walking.

"A . . . new . . . god?"

General Rippotis made an amused grin even as he preemptively lifted his hands.

"I was planning to tell you after I completed the mission . . . but since I am here now, I will tell you everything. After the meeting, perhaps?"

Oracle Heigiosa stared intently at him and nodded.

"I will hold you to that."

He gave her a salute.

"As you command."

Shortly thereafter, General Rippotis and Oracle Heigiosa made their way to the chamber of the High Council, no smiles on their faces now. The room was simple, made of rough and common stone. Up on the walls near the roof were carved statues of all the known gods, below which were no further adornments. The room itself held only a single round table with ten seats, seven of which were currently occupied. The pair took their seats, bringing all nine members of the High Council together. Oracle Heigiosa looked to each member and then turned to the door when all were prepared.

"Enter."

At her command, the doors opened up and in marched Lord Starami, the tower lord who had been on everyone's mind lately. He was tense and nearly scowling, but he held his head high as he stepped forward.

"Starami, Tower Lord of Starami Tower and Lord of the Conclave. I thank the High Council for having me today."

Oracle Heigiosa motioned to the last remaining chair.

"Thank you for coming. Please, have a seat."

Oracle Heigiosa gave him a chance to get settled before speaking again.

"Now, I am told that you have news to share?"

Lord Starami nodded.

"I have found the missing tower."

General Rippotis raised an eyebrow.

"I assume you have some evidence for that claim?"

Lord Starami answered by beginning his explanation.

"I sent off my son to atone for his actions as agreed upon by the Conclave. Before he left, however, he returned to the site of the tower's birth and had the augur accompanying him perform a divination. To my surprise, the augur received a response."

Oracle Heigiosa narrowed her eyes.

"You are certain of this?"

Lord Starami nodded.

"I personally observed it through the monster monitoring his departure. I would stake my life on it."

To the left of Oracle Heigiosa, High Councilor Konilias scowled.

"Good, for you do just that if it turns out you are mistaken, Starami."

The High Councilors glanced at one another until Oracle Heigiosa returned her gaze to Lord Starami.

"Please, continue."

Lord Starami did so.

"The augur apparently received a set of directions that would lead them far, far away from the Conclave's territory. I was therefore not surprised that we did not hear from them by the time the rest of the first wave reported in. But then, just the other day, we received word from my son that a tower had been located. Far, far away, in the location the directions would have led him to."

The High Council fell silent at this. High Councilor Konilias frowned.

"The evidence seems quite circumstantial."

Oracle Heigiosa shook her head.

"Normally, I would agree. But . . ."

She turned to glance at General Rippotis.

"It seems clear to me that the gods are at work here."

High Councilor Konilias narrowed his eyes.

"What exactly does she mean?"

General Rippotis shrugged.

"I received a mission from a previously unknown god that delayed my departure for the Grand Subjugation. It seemed unrelated to this matter, but . . . the timing is highly coincidental."

High Councilor Konilias grunted.

"Hm, I wondered why you had not run off again."

Oracle Heigiosa turned to look at the other members of the High Council.

"I have not received any specific instructions myself from the God of Light, however. Has anyone besides General Rippotis heard from any of the other oracles, or received any unusual missions from the gods?"

The High Councilors turned thoughtful, but one by one they shook their heads. Oracle Heigiosa rubbed her chin.

"So, it is up to us to decipher their will. Still, given the circumstances, I feel that something important is going on here. We should not leave this matter be."

One of the other High Councilors, a fashionably dressed woman, tilted her head.

"Could it be that they are helping us locate the lost tower?"

Another High Councilor, a man in simple robes like Oracle Heigiosa's, shook his head.

"Not every tower is placed within our reach. If the gods saw fit to keep one from us, they would not feel the need to help us find it."

The woman councilor frowned.

"But . . . they did not keep it from us? We failed to bind this one, did we not? That's a failure of our entire mandate."

She gave a pointed look to Lord Starami, who managed to keep his face expressionless. Lord Konilias cleared his throat.

"In any case, whether the gods have spoken or not, we have already decided upon a Grand Subjugation. Is there any reason why we should not advance in the direction of this tower?"

A man in armor next to General Rippotis saluted.

"Just say the word and I will lead my army forth."

But Lord Konilias glanced at another High Councilor, as fashionably dressed as the woman before. The man cleared his throat.

"Lord Starami was the one responsible for this affair, and I was the one responsible for him. He shall lead the mission to seek the gods' will, and I shall arrange the campaign necessary for him to do so."

The well-dressed man and the armored man locked eyes. Oracle Heigiosa glanced at General Rippotis, but he just shook his head. She turned to Lord Starami.

"What of your son? He has already arrived at the location. Has he passed back any further messages?"

Lord Starami frowned.

"My son is likely dead. The failsafe broke the signal a day after we received it."

Oracle Heigiosa frowned as well.

"That is most concerning."

She closed her eyes for a moment before letting out a sigh.

"Very well. High Councilor Stadvolous shall arrange for the Grand Subjugation to move in the direction indicated. However, please take care if and when you approach the location in question. The will of the gods is not always obvious, and it would not do for us to move hastily, particularly considering that our first arrival there has not ended well. In that vein, please provide us with regular updates on your progress. In the meantime, we all should pay special attention to the oracles and to any missions we receive from the gods."

Lord Starami bowed his head.

"As the High Council wishes."

After the meeting, General Rippotis and Oracle Heigiosa walked together once more. Oracle Heigiosa's face was scrunched up, causing General Rippotis to frown as well.

"Something troubles you?"

Oracle Heigiosa sighed.

"It is unusual for the gods to get involved this directly. We have never received such a specific location from them, even back when the fate of the world was at stake, so I feel this must be a matter of great importance to them. And yet, the God of Light has not spoken to me on the matter, nor have any other of the gods with their own oracles. I fear we are stumbling in the dark when we need our eyes open most."

General Rippotis's frown grew.

"That's a good point."

The two stood in silence for a moment, lost in their own thoughts. Eventually, Oracle Heigiosa shook her head.

"The only thing I can think of is the mission you received. Please, General, approach it with all the care and determination you always display. I fear it may be more important than we realize."

He saluted to her.

"I would do so were it not important at all. We owe the gods as much."

Oracle Heigiosa nodded.

"We do indeed. If I may ask, and if you are permitted to share . . . what is your current mission? And who is this new god that issued it?"

General Rippotis could not help but make a bemused smile.

"Well . . . it's bees."

Oracle Heigiosa paused and blinked a few times before tilting her head.

"Bees?"

General Rippotis nodded.

"Bees."

# The Glossar-Bee

### Notable Non-Queens

| Name | Other titles/ references | Current Location | Special Notes |
|---|---|---|---|
| Niobee | The Conduit | By Belissar's side! | Belissar's friend from before the Tower! |
| Beero | The wounded soldier | The memorial | The first crippled soldier, personally saved by Belissar. Missing a pair of wings. |
| The Fourth of the Seventh's communer | The Fourth of the Seventh's worker | Orchard | The bee organizing the Fourth of the Seventh's hive . . . instead of her queen. |

### Notable Queens

| Full Title | Common Shorthand | Other Names | Current Location | Special Notes |
|---|---|---|---|---|
| First Queen of the First Spawner's First Dynasty, the first of her line | First of the First | | N/A | Gave her life in the first initial purification |
| Second Queen of the First Spawner's First Dynasty, the first of her line | Second of the First | | N/A | Gave her life in the first initial purification |
| Third Queen of the First Spawner's First Dynasty, the first of her line | Third of the First | | N/A | Gave her life in the first initial purification, prototyped the rotating squad-wave attack |
| Fourth Queen of the First Spawner's First Dynasty, the first of her line | Fourth of the First | | N/A | Gave her life in the first initial purification |

| Full Title | Common Shorthand | Other Names | Current Location | Special Notes |
|---|---|---|---|---|
| First Queen of the First Spawner's Second Dynasty, the first of her line | Second First of the First | The Firstborn | Flower Meadow | Leader of the Flower Meadow queens and the soldier bee army |
| First Queen of the Second Spawner's First Dynasty, the first of her line | First of the Second | | Flower Meadow | Discovered that spreading her own soldiers among the army to pass on her commands improved response time |
| First Queen of the Fourth Spawner's First Dynasty, the first of her line | First of the Fourth | | Flower Meadow | Commanded the army against a bird shade in a minor+ purification |
| First Queen of the Fifth Spawner's First Dynasty, the first of her line | First of the Fifth | | Apiary | Leader of the Apiary queens, top honey producer in both quality and quantity |
| Second Queen of the Sixth Spawner's First Dynasty, the first of her line | Second of the Sixth | | Apiary | Apiary queen who received access to a special flower by the First of the Fifth |
| Third Queen of the Sixth Spawner's First Dynasty, the first of her line | Third of the Sixth | | Apiary | First Apiary queen not to get one of the initial Apiary hives |
| Fourth Queen of the Eighth's Spawner's First Dynasty, the first of her line | Fourth of the Eighth | | Apiary | Last spawned monster bee queen |

| Full Title | Common Shorthand | Other Names | Current Location | Special Notes |
|---|---|---|---|---|
| Fourth Queen of the First Dynasty of the Seventh Spawner | Fourth of the Seventh | | Orchard | . . . what hasn't she done? Let's just say likes exploring and trying new things |
| First Daughter of the First Queen of the Fifth Spawner's First Dynasty, the second of her line | First of the Fifth's First Daughter | | Orchard | The first queen born from a queen rather than a spawner, currently running a joint hive with the Fourth of the Seventh |
| The Conduit's Queen Mother | | | One of the Tower Guard's packs | Niobee's mother and one of Belissar's former queens. Hitched a ride with Ruckanos's group at the behest of the God of Bees |

## Notable Non-Bees

| Name | Description |
|---|---|
| Belissar | The human dungeon master and King of the bees. Considered an honorary bee by the bees despite his lack of a bee-ish form. |
| Ruckanos | The human Tower Lord's son who burned Belissar's village to the ground . . . and failed to acquire a Tower of his own. |
| Chief Rohsuak | The leader of the karnuq, blessed by the God of Fire |
| Metsaitti | The most skilled and experience hunter among the karnuq |
| Tyhgak | A young karnuq hunter in training. Speaks faster than he thinks. |

| Name | Description |
| --- | --- |
| Juosiutik | A young karnuq aspiring to become an expert potion-maker. |
| Leijaliuk | The karnuq quartermaster |
| Rakenliuk | Karnuq architect |
| Noigakkuq | A young karnuq smaller than the others, but with a good nose for mana. |
| Muuraqi | Karnuq miner and mason |
| Second Queen Berbiya | Sigmaka queen, focuses on negotiation |
| Fourth Queen Pezuya | Sigmaka queen, leader of the royal guard |
| King Ratuatapi | King of the Sigmaka, raises giant aphids on the side |
| Sehfitis | Human augur who accompanied Ruckanos |
| Hirkolos | Human soldier and one of Ruckanos's Tower Guard candidates. One of Belissar's former queens hitched a ride in his pack. |

# BEE DUNGEON

Ruins

Sigmaka

Tower

# AUTHOR'S NOTE

Hi, everyone! Author here! Did you know this series was originally a web novel released one chapter at a time? In that version, I included a short commentary at the end of each chapter with my own reactions to its events. In order to preserve the intended experience, I have now gathered all that commentary in one place for you to enjoy.

Please visit Bee Dungeon on Royal Road to learn how the author feels about each chapter of this book!

# ABOUT THE AUTHOR

Icalos is a lifelong fan of sci-fi, fantasy, and video games, and the author of the Terminate the Other World! and Bee Dungeon series, which were originally released on Royal Road. To learn more, visit his website at icalosbooks.com.